Lost in Manchester Found in Vegas

To Helen

Enjoy the Ride!

Viva Las Vegas!

N. Cttk

Spiderwize
Remus House
Coltsfoot Drive
Woodston
Peterborough
PE2 9BF

www.spiderwize.com

A CIP catalogue record for this book is available from the British Library.

The views expressed in this work are solely those of the author and do not necessarily reflect the views of the publisher, and the publisher hereby disclaims any responsibility for them.

ISBN: 978-1-911596-34-9

www.njcartner.com

Lost in Manchester Found in Vegas

N.J. Cartner

Lost in Manchester, Found in Vegas

Copyright © N.J. Cartner 2017 All Rights Reserved

Spiderwize
Remus House
Coltsfoot Drive
Woodston
Peterborough
PE2 9BF

www.spiderwize.com

A CIP catalogue record for this book is available from the British Library.

ISBN: 978-1-911596-34-9

www.njcartner.com

Repaying the faith shown by Rose Cartner – An inspiration, a spiritual beacon, and above all else, always right!

For Sheridana – Reasons for Seasons

'You can fail at what you don't want, so you might as well take a chance on doing what you love.'

JIM CARREY

'No sympathy for the devil; keep that in mind. Buy the ticket, take the ride...and if it occasionally gets a little heavier than what you had in mind, well...maybe chalk it up to forced consciousness expansion: Tune in, freak out, get beaten.'

HUNTER S THOMPSON, FEAR AND LOATHING IN LAS VEGAS

'The most important kind of freedom is to be what you really are. You trade in your reality for a role. You trade in your sense for an act. You give up your ability to feel, and in exchange, put on a mask. There can't be any large-scale revolution until there's a personal revolution, on an individual level. It's got to happen inside first.'

JIM MORRISON

CHAPTER 1

The lyrics of the iconic song, 'Viva Las Vegas', churned over and over in my mind as I sat impatiently in the bar inside a typically busy Terminal 2 at Manchester Airport. After months of build-up, it was only a matter of hours till we'd arrive in the prestigious city of Las Vegas, and then this necessary adventure, that I'd craved for so long, could begin.

The time had just hit 9.45am and I cradled an early morning holiday pint of beer - too early for most occasions in life, but this was no ordinary situation I found myself in as a lifetime's dream neared its culmination. I constantly checked my watch in restless anticipation, but the hands agonisingly appeared to slow down in what felt like a halt in time itself. I could hardly contain my excitement, shuddering again from another wave of spine tingling stimulation that washed over me as images of bright lights and souls set on fire flashed through my mind. I fought hard to resist the urge to let out a bellow of elation, just so I could release a rush of warped adrenaline that had been bubbling deep beneath the surface all morning.

The date was 10th June and a long six months had finally passed since we booked this trip that was, as usual, in my name, Ricky Lever, chief organiser (not by choice) of the group. A trip to Vegas had been discussed annually for the last ten years since the idea's inception, but financial obligations and the everyday obstacles of life had meant the trip had to be constantly postponed. We had always settled for the cheaper Mediterranean option, so to now be on the brink of Vegas meant there was an understandable hype amongst us, in what was to be our first lads holiday outside of Europe, and probably the first in such lavish and electrifying surroundings.

The jewelled city of Vegas was the perfect place to be given a licence for excess...and a licence to live, where we could raise the stakes and experience something diverse and perhaps live a little dissolutely. Bearing in mind this was Vegas, there was also the little prospect of on tap gambling!

Oh, the gambling was something I was particularly looking forward to considering we were going to the gaming capital of the world. I was known amongst my friends as a gambling addict, although that was more a term of endearment than an accurate reflection of my personality. I was far from that slippery slope, but I did like to have a flutter every now and then on football and horses. I joked, with a hint of seriousness, that I would be lucky enough to have that one big win, quietly dreaming that it was my destiny to live the rest of my life in blind luxury by taking millions from the tables and slots. Funnily enough, probably the same foolish game plan every other punter formulates who visits Vegas. Realistically, the best I hoped for was to get the cost of the holiday back, but even that was a stretch. I also jested that my eagerness to gamble would see me head straight to the tables immediately after checking in, baggage in tow, and win or lose big before I'd even entered my room. As the holiday drew closer, I saw the flaw in this plan, so it was best to remain level-headed and wait until the time was right to hit the tables hard, envisaging that it wouldn't be too long after dumping my bags anyway.

In my far-fetched imagination and blind wisdom, I saw the gambling as the key to starting a new life, but it was a bitter pill to swallow knowing the odds of that coming true were stacked against me. The same old job in the same old office, surrounded by the same old miserable people would still be lurking upon my return, bringing me back down to earth with an almighty crash.

I worked in customer services for an insurance company, which was just as mundane as it sounds. The nine to five rat race routine, having to put up with the everyday bullshit, petty rules and power trips of corporate office life was draining to say the least. Still, given the dark cloud of the economic climate we were under at the time, I was thankful just to be employed so I could fund this journey, but it still didn't stop me being frustrated and daydreaming of pursuing a better way of life.

My fantasy induced trance broke when my three friends - Johnny, Turner and Ian - returned one by one from Burger King. We'd known each other for nearly seventeen years, meeting during our high school days. Looking back, it was strange that these individuals were the ones I would be travelling to Las Vegas with.

It's funny how life can turn out as none of them were considered a good friend of mine for the five years of school. It was in Sixth Form and in approaching adulthood where opinions and attitudes changed and friendship groups altered. As life transpired, it was in these three guys, and others who were missing out on the trip, that I found a close set of mates where we challenged life's difficulties and experienced life's highs together.

Turner took it upon himself to say a few words, not exactly out of character for someone who was full of charisma and confidence. He raised his glass and began, 'Lads! It's taken a while for us to get here, but we've finally made it and this is going to be *the* holiday of our lives. There can be no excuses! This is Vegas for fucks sake. Forget our lives and situations back home, the past is the past.' Turner's eyes glanced purposely over to mine before continuing, 'Let's have a massive blow out never to be forgotten. It's finally here boys. Vegas Baby, Vegas!'

'To Vegas!' we all shouted, clinking glasses before taking a huge swig of our beers as the buzz etched up a notch. The conversation moved swiftly between what we were planning to do in Vegas and reliving the last night out we had together, which was quite fittingly in Stalybridge, known widely amongst Northerners as 'StalyVegas', although there was quite a large contrast in what was on offer. The laughter and light-hearted piss taking continued freely as we each bore the brunt of a ribbing, forced to relive past demeanours we'd committed when stories were regurgitated, such as:

who got naked at a friend's wedding and ran through a field in search of a scarecrow, only to return to find his clothes had been robbed by a group of girls who had watched the whole ordeal unfold? Or who fell off the bar trying to break dance in a last ditch failed attempt to impress a girl? Or who dyed their hair bleach blonde trying to be trendy, only to be ridiculed beyond reckoning? And who fell off a moped and landed in a ditch by the side of the road in Ibiza? The excitement simmered, and we knew more tales of hilarity would be added during our time in Vegas.

I emphasised Turner's enthusiasm by reading out several text messages he'd sent to me in the run up. He constantly sent me messages on the same theme that dramatized our trip. One read,

'Hollywood would learn of our exploits and make a film about the trip, *which would have me slamming several Las Vegas beauties after winning big in the casino on the craps table (even though I have no idea how to play it). I will be sat on the throne in a penthouse suite surrounded by these beauties, and they'll be fulfilling every sordid whim while rinsing me of all my winnings. The flagship scene would end up in me being stood on the roof of Planet Hollywood with tear filled eyes, not a penny to my name, cuffed to the stanchions refusing to return home at all costs.'*

That was Turner all over, coming up with random statements that made us laugh. He was a character to say the least, providing entertainment in any situation at any time, carrying the gift of being able to change a bad mood into a positive one in a flashing instant. His first name was Ben, but he'd been known as Turner from the first day I met him. He was quite a cool looking guy with bright blue eyes, and light brown hair, styled messy and choppy, purposely a bit scruffy. He was tall and slim, quite a gangly figure, and his thin face matched his frame, which gave definition to his cheekbones. He had an attractive aura that drew people in to laugh with him, a quality that acted like a magnet to women, carrying the sort of confidence that came with the 'gift of the gab', which he had in abundance.

Turner was an entertaining personality to say the least, easily going into character mode to make you laugh by taking off famous people, characters from films and TV shows, or creating his own characters given certain situations. It was impossible to escape a slating from him if you embarrassed yourself, never fully growing out of that teenage attitude where you couldn't put a foot wrong for risk of social suicide. Underneath his jokey exterior he was an ace friend, the sort you go to when you need a shot of livening up to take your mind off things. He was unquestionably someone I loved going on holiday with and all my lad holidays had involved him.

The first pint went down far too well, as did the burgers, and we still had time for another drink before the flight would be announced. We didn't want to consume too much alcohol too early as we had an inclination into how a night in Sin City could possibly pan out, and we were desperate not to fall under the category of 'people who can't handle Vegas'.

As expected for this time of year, the youth culture was well represented in the airport. Several groups of girls and lads ranging between late teens and early twenties swarmed the walkways. Most were obviously venturing to some Mediterranean 18-30s style holiday judging from their brightly coloured t-shirts that labelled their destination and reasons for going. 'Boys on Tour: Ibiza' declared one group, 'Kat's Kittens' declared another, all having nicknames and numbers showing on the back. It suddenly dawned on me the age gap between them and us. How did we become so much older? When did that happen? But there was something different about this crop of teenagers compared to our era and eras gone by. I considered my own generation the last in a certain way of thinking that had similar values and ways of approaching life. Of course, every generation differs and detaches itself from its predecessors, history tells us that, but this generation was growing up and perceiving life in a very different way in this new world of reliance on modern technology, social media, reality TV, and the increased emphasis and influence of a false celebrity culture. It was quite frightening in comparison to our own upbringing.

Now at the grand old age of twenty-eight, it didn't seem that long ago when I was of a similar age and about to experience the first holiday away with mates, completely unaware of what was going to happen. I brought that up with the rest of the lads and we reminisced about ten years earlier, back to our scary jaunt to Benidorm of all places.

It felt poetic that this year marked the tenth

anniversary of that first holiday together, where we were the naive youngsters playing the game of, 'how many girls you could pull'. Our drinking strategies were very different back then, choosing to follow the unwritten rule of, 'as much as you can, and as quick as you can', which ultimately led to most of it being thrown back up in the can. Eight of us went that year, and Turner, Johnny and Ian were all part of that experience. We remembered that time vividly as I almost saw myself in a past light eagerly trotting the same hallways ten years earlier, but a little thinner, with shorter hair and non-existent stubble. It brought back some amazing memories, thinking we knew everything because we'd just finished Sixth Form, when really, we knew fuck all.

Not many of us had much sexual experience in those late teenage years, and we perceived that being away on holiday for the first time in such a youthful environment would give us a platform to fulfil those adolescent desires. Those desires that seemed so far out of reach with the girls we came into regular contact with on Friday and Saturday nights in Oldham, Rochdale or Manchester or wherever.

In our haste and over excited state at this first taste of freedom, we all bought condoms from the machines in the toilets at Manchester Airport, being far too embarrassed to purchase them directly from a supermarket or chemist. It turned out to be a pointless exercise as we failed miserably to accomplish what we set out to do, despite having a memorable time together. How times changed in the holidays that followed in Ibiza, Bulgaria, twice to Zante, twice to Malia and Kos, where confidence and knowledge of the opposite sex came naturally with time, age and experience, and we could eventually put right the mistakes from Benidorm.

The past holidays had all been special and monumental in their own right, but they all revolved around the purpose-built towns and strips that suited rowdy Brits in a booze fuelled environment, and quite frankly I felt that I was getting a little too old for that, certainly for two weeks of it. The year before we found ourselves in Sunny Beach, Bulgaria, and I was certain we were in the oldest age bracket then. Perhaps the end of the usual 18-30s type destination signified that a specific circle of life neared its completion, and a new one was being conceived, like two waves entwining: as one dips, the other is in ascendency, a kind of crossroads where Las Vegas was the pivotal point. It was symbolic of a new age and a new approach to life.

Maybe the others weren't really thinking this deeply but, for me, the painful and personal events of the past few months had brought a lot of issues into focus, and with being the wrong side of my mid-twenties, I felt that something drastic needed to be done in life, and Vegas was strangely a place that I'd earmarked to shape my future in ways that were unknown to me yet.

Turner urged me to bring out the 'Vegas bucket list' for a quick recap. In the months leading up to the holiday, Johnny and I had done some extensive research, jotting down all the options that might interest us. Although I was all for taking each minute as it came, usually the plan adopted for any holiday, we wanted to be prepared and cram as many activities in as possible during the day and make sure we hit the right places at night. The list had become extensive and varied. As I began to read it out loud, it seemed unrealistic that all this was available in one resort - and this was just the tip of the iceberg! Roller coasters, stage shows, pool parties, gun shooting, museums, mafia tours, scores of casinos and an abundance of bars and clubs were just a few things to mention. It was silly of us to think we would have the time or money to get through everything, but there were a couple of attractions on the list that really stood out.

After discussing the Vegas bucket list, Turner took a pen to add a point at the end. He turned the page back to me and I leaned forward to see that he'd scribbled the words, 'Sort Ricky's head out!' Guilty as charged. My heart sank heavily into my stomach as the past flooded back with Turner's untimely reminder.

He was referring to my recent traumatic break up with Mandy. This was the situation I found myself in prior to us setting off that had caused so much heartache and confusion. It had been a whirlwind past couple of months to say the least. The break up didn't just throw up issues directly related to my relationship status, but it also brought my own position in life under scrutiny.

Two months or so before take-off and my world had flipped upside down because of the separation. I'd tried to mentally prepare myself for the chaotic and uneasy ride that comes with the end of a five-year relationship. I knew I'd have to go through similar torment and hardship as felt eight years earlier with the loss of my first love, something that took me a while to get over as first loves usually do. If the parting had been straightforward then maybe I could've relied on that experience and wisdom to haul me into the necessary frame of mind compulsory for such a journey. It wouldn't have been easy, but certainly manageable with time. However, the circumstances were very different now, and the shit from the separation just kept coming back to haunt me over and over.

It wasn't just my relationship woes that troubled me. The knock-on effect meant I finally realised the unhappiness that surrounded my general working life. I was stagnated, solely existing as a worthless cog in the capitalistic cultural machine that was set up to control our minds and lives. There was more life in a zombie when it came to functioning in office hours, but I'd lost the willpower to do anything about it, accepting that this was life – I'd let the bastards grind me down. But, the silver lining of my relationship ending was that it acted as a rude awakening and realisation that I finally had to do something about it. The thought of working in my office, or any other office for that matter, trapped in a tornado of tediousness for the rest of my life, left me feeling strangled. I had dreams of doing something a bit cooler and more daring, keeping in line with my (now suppressed) rebellious attitude and love of rock 'n' roll music and the religion that came with it. Somewhere in the last two or three years I'd lost the edge and drive I once had, falling into a trap of playing it safe with no risk whatsoever. It was essential to get that back so I could do justice to my own expectations of life, and pacify my soul rather than hurt it any more than I already had.

This was why Vegas had become so important! I needed to come to decisions about my life and head in a direction that was more aligned with who I was. I'd wasted too many years rotting away in an office, and I was at the end of my fuckin' tether with it! I also had to work out and get over what happened with regards to my relationship, because at this point in Manchester Airport, I was still struggling. I hoped that by having a timeout away from everything with my friends and in such an enticing place, I would be able to see things from a different angle, and maybe have the revelations needed that would enable me to move on from this whole mess.

Perhaps the notion of self-exploration whilst in the middle of Sin City wasn't the best plan in the world, but it was all I had to cling onto since the booking and payment came before the actual break up. People usually get away for a period in a peaceful atmosphere to rediscover themselves, or go travelling around Europe or South America. Unfortunately, limited funds were against such a long, self-discovering adventure. All I had was six nights in Las Vegas, in some ways one of the most dangerous places on earth, where a man can lose himself so easily and become his own worst enemy, seduced by all that is considered holy in the middle of the unique desert civilisation, especially when you're in a bit of a 'don't give a fuck' mood. I was a man still reeling from a turbulent break up, who also found himself at a very puzzling crossroads in life generally, but I was also a man about to land in Las Vegas, which wasn't a bad silver lining at all!

I had to push all these conflicting thoughts out of my head and refuse to wallow on such a big day with the impending arrival in Vegas. In the midst of being so philosophical about life, possibly placing too much emphasis on the impact this was to have, it nearly escaped my attention that our flight was being called. The first leg of our excursion was nearing the beginning.

CHAPTER 2

We were due to fly at 11.15am and arrive locally in Philadelphia at 14.20. Then we had an hour and a half wait until a further five-hour flight to Las Vegas, arriving at a perfect time in the early evening. Including transfer times, the whole journey would take an agonising fourteen hours. What the hell would I do for fourteen hours? I'd never gone beyond a four-and-a-half-hour flight before so this was going to be painful.

Eventually the gate opened and we boarded the vast Airbus A330-300 aircraft. This was the biggest I'd ever been on, and was separated into three sections, split by two walkways. I was relieved to find I was in an aisle seat of the middle block, giving me the much-needed leg-room for such a long journey. I was sat next to Ian, and unluckily for him and Johnny they were sandwiched between me and Turner.

I wasn't the best flyer in the world, and being paired with Ian didn't hold much relief as he was equally as panicky. Ian Edge was quite tall, probably about 6ft 2in and had thick, dark brown hair that had an indie rocker look about it. He had light stubble that matched his mysterious, hazelnut eyes. He was a huge fan of the origins of blues and rock music and, much like myself, that influenced most of his attitudes to life. Ian and I came from very similar backgrounds and had comparable upbringings, both having parents that were very much into their music that inspired our own tastes, and dads that were tradesmen too. Because of that we'd become alike in many ways, which is why he was the one out of the three that could most closely relate to my situation.

Ian was very knowledgeable and philosophical, a true trait of a Sagittarius, full of wisdom and great advice. He possessed a calmness and quiet demeanour that sometimes made him look like he lacked interest, which couldn't be further from the truth. Now and then he could be frustrating with his perceived lack of confidence, but really, he was a good-looking guy with bags of personality, seeming to spark curiosity wherever he went. Sometimes I thought it was just an act and quietly he was full of it, but he did hold back – baffling considering his profession as an assistant regional manager of a large retail outlet where he dealt with people every day. It was a job that I wouldn't necessarily associate with him, but we were in a time when we had to take what we could get to some extent. People could be forgiven for thinking Ian was ignorant or rude because of his stillness, but rarely was this accusation thrown at him. Maybe they intuitively knew that there was a lot more to him than met the eye, and you just had to get to know him on a deeper level to see that side of him. Still waters certainly ran deep, but he did have a wild side when the mood took him, and that side always shone on holidays or trips away.

After a half hour or so wait we steamed down the

runway and were finally in the air. My mind and spirit were already in Las Vegas, and my body was now playing catch up for an imagined reunion of epic proportions.

Thankfully, the journey was passing rather quickly, helped by the range of entertainment on offer from the personal TV screens on the seat in front, which boasted a variety of shows and films. On approach to Philadelphia I had to listen to, 'Streets of Philadelphia', by Bruce Springsteen, for obvious reasons. It never dawned on me beforehand, but as the Boss sang about being bruised, battered, and unrecognisable, I became aware of how the words described my situation and recent mood. Unrecognisable indeed!

Stage one completed and we landed in what I liked to call purgatory. Manchester was my hell that I needed to escape from for a short while, and Vegas was my heavenly utopia, but in between was the purgatory of Philadelphia, even if it was only for an hour and a half of waiting around.

After leaving the aircraft we had to suffer the rigmarole of an excruciatingly long wait at Passport Control. When I finally reached the desk, I was surprised to learn that I had to have my fingerprints scanned. They really were on the cautious side over here. The Passport Control Officer warned me not to get married in Las Vegas, which was apparently quite a common and regrettable thing to happen, emphasising that Vegas can be 'pretty wild and crazy' as she put it. I wasn't sure if she was joking or not, but her stony poker face suggested that she may have been serious. While I took heed of her marriage warning, it did make me think how funny (or disastrous) it would be if I ended up getting married to some random stripper. Maybe that was my destiny, to live in squalor in a dire Las Vegas condo, with a stripper as my wife who worked for tips to feed my out of control gambling habit. My demise would be horrible. She'd return home one day to find me flaked out, face down in a pool of my own vomit, still clutching the bottle of JD that'd done me in. Better than an office job, I suppose. Certainly more interesting!

Turner suffered a nightmare at customs, being called into an office to be security checked further, which involved them asking all sorts of questions from his place of work, to where he lives, to the colour of his underwear! They even ordered him to open his suitcase and relentlessly rummaged through all his possessions. Luckily, he hadn't brought anything too embarrassing with him like a collection of pervy sex toys or a Fuckmaster Pro 5000 blow-up latex doll, but he did have a selection of facial creams and moisturisers, which was embarrassing enough. As we waited, the rest of us pictured him getting an absolute grilling, not discounting the possibility of a full body cavity search. Thankfully for him, he appeared in the distance *not* walking like John Wayne, so we scurried through the airport to check in our luggage for the second flight.

Now we'd finished with the dull side of landing, it was time to find ourselves a drink. We marched into a departure lounge that more resembled a mall than an airport as we were greeted by a tirade of shops and restaurants. Rather than look around this vast complex, we chose to have a drink in a typical American sports bar to relax our nerves for the second leg. It became clear that we were in, 'The Land of the Free, Home of the Brave', as there were no signs of the sports we loved being shown on the TV screens: well pretty much a lack of football, or 'soccer' as it was now to be referred to as. Baseball and Basketball were all that dominated the numerous screens. All we had time for was a quick 'glass' of beer, only realising that the term 'pint' was a lost phrase in the American dictionary after Johnny had caused the barmaid considerable confusion when he barked, 'four pints of lager please.'

We were called to board the next flight and we had to endure the second take off of the day, which wasn't exactly my idea of fun. We boarded the plane again and this time I found myself sat next to Johnny in a window seat. Johnny Holt was a lively character, possessing a very cheeky persona that allowed him to get away with murder. He was the smallest out of the four of us and his head was shaved by choice, despite us constantly winding him up about going bald. He had light brown stubble, very faint, that blended in with his rugged, roguish complexion. He was a bit out there and could be eccentric, coming up with random ideas about life that flirted between the ridiculous and the ingenious, but he generated great intrigue as he explored the possibilities. He was a laid-back character most of the time, but he occasionally exhibited a needless panic and worry over insignificant mishaps, which were always exaggerated. Perhaps his forwardness served to cover-up this fact. Along with Turner, he liked to be the centre of attention, and when it came to women it was priceless to observe them battling for the same one. The girl would have no idea what was going on, but for those that knew them both it was like watching a comedy sketch show. Johnny used to be subdued, having had a childhood sweetheart type girlfriend for a few years in his late teens and early twenties. It was after that split when he came into his own, being much more outgoing and unconventional. He didn't go to university, choosing to follow in his elder brother's footsteps in plumbing instead, but that didn't stop him visiting us at Sheffield Hallam University every chance he got, and a part of him regretted not attending full time. He'd done very well for himself though and, unlike the three of us, he had no student loan to repay. Five years ago, Johnny would've shunned a trip of this magnitude, but the change in him meant he was one of the first to sign up.

Stage two of the journey, despite being a couple of hours shorter, was far worse than stage one. There was no in-flight entertainment so I watched, 'The Hangover', and, 'Fear and Loathing in Las Vegas', on my excruciatingly small iPod screen to get in the mood for Vegas. Though two very different films, both encompassed the madness a period of time in Las Vegas could lead to. I secretly hoped that our holiday would have some resemblance to what I was watching, despite the element of despair throughout both films. If you could live to tell the tale afterwards, look back with fondness and see it as a crazy experience, then whatever happened in Vegas would be worth the mental collapse or freedom. As Dr Hunter S. Thompson iterated in

'Fear and Loathing in Las Vegas', *'Buy the Ticket, Take the Ride'.*

As we drew closer to our destination, the captain announced that if we looked to the right of the plane we could see the beginnings of the Grand Canyon, one of nature's most overwhelming landmarks. From the air, it was difficult to see anything of it without invading the personal spaces of fellow flyers on that side of the plane. I did manage to steal a glimpse, but from this height and angle it was too far away to inspire any sort of reaction. I'm certain that if we were stood next to it then the impact would've been greater and I would've appreciated its enormity and significance to natural history. It was something that had been added to the bucket list, but because of costs and time it was unlikely to happen on this trip.

As my head was turning to catch a last glimpse before it faded out of view, I realised that we'd descended way below 30,000ft, and the end of our fourteen-hour journey was about to come to a deserved end.

Much like the descent to Philadelphia, I felt the urge to listen to a song to dramatize my arrival in Vegas. This was a carefully thought out process and there were so many songs to choose from that would capture the situation at hand. Keeping in line with the 'Fear and Loathing in Las Vegas' theme, the decision was simplified, choosing the song that's played with high impact in the opening scene. The two main characters speed along the desert highway towards Vegas listening to, 'Combination of the Two', by Big Brother & the Holding Company. This energetic, hypnotic and psychedelic tune not only captures the atmosphere of the opening scene, but also the 60s in general with specific reference to San Francisco. Listening to this song as we approached shook the tiredness out of me, and my energy levels began to soar as excitement flooded through me. It felt like we were not only entering another part of the world so far from home, but also a different period in time altogether.

CHAPTER 3

A few minutes later we landed. The tedious and exhausting haul was over, made all the better because we didn't have to suffer the same chaos we had at Passport Control in Philadelphia.

When we arrived inside the airport we instantly knew we were in Vegas. Talk about an airport to match its city's reputation! It looked like it had more slot machines than in all of Manchester's very own gaming establishments put together. The place was alive, dominated by huge billboards advertising an array of hotels and shows, accompanied by pictures of idols to help the sell. If the airport was this extravagant then what would our hotel and the others along the Strip be like?

Once Turner picked up the last bag we eagerly headed for the exit where the heat assaulted us like multiple hot pokers prodding our bodies. Coming from the unpredictable, but usually cold weather of Manchester, the moment the intense, dry heat strikes down on your skin in a foreign country is one of those feelings that makes working worthwhile.

Turner and I welcomed a much-deserved cigarette, which after several hours felt like a gift from the gods. The others could never understand, but they didn't dare to argue when we demanded holding off jumping in a taxi until we had satisfied our cravings. After having a couple of fast ones each we hopped into a token yellow cab and proudly requested, 'Planet Hollywood, please.' The engine revved and we careered onto the open highway. All I could think of was the amount of times I'd seen characters in films enter Las Vegas, and that built up my anticipation as the adrenaline started to pump through my veins.

· Within minutes we could see the buildings in the near distance suddenly becoming larger than life, like we were being thrust into a different world to anything we'd ever seen before. How long I'd waited for this moment! I became delirious at the vivid imagery as we approached. All the famous hotels we'd seen on TV and in pictures hundreds of times suddenly became an overwhelming reality. Dusk was setting in, providing the perfect backdrop against a dimming orange sky that accentuated the lights on the Strip as we began to drive down it for the first time. First up was Mandalay Bay, standing gloriously to welcome visitors to Vegas. Next to that was the pyramid landmark shooting from the ground that was Luxor, also marked with a replica of the Great Sphinx of Giza. We couldn't help but shout out the other names of the famous hotels as we passed them, reminding me of when I was a kid travelling to Blackpool, competing against each other as to who would spot the tower first. This was the grown-up version of that game! We eyed MGM's Emerald City colours; the Hard Rock's guitar embedded into the roof; the re-creations of New York outside…well…New York New York of course; Caesars Palace's columns; and the Bellagio Fountains. The assortment of glamorous landmarks swept by us one by one, and it felt like we were starring in our very own film, hoping that what we were about to experience would be worthy of a movie itself. All that was missing was some music to go with the mood. Perhaps some Frank Sinatra or Dean Martin would've been apt considering their status in Vegas, but I found myself in a spirited, rock 'n' roll mood so chose to stick 'She Sells Sanctuary' on by The Cult. The one earphone I had slotted into my ear kept the soundtrack loitering in the background for this most memorable entrance to our adult playground.

I was starry eyed not knowing where to turn, and I couldn't believe I was experiencing one of the most famous drives ever, the drive into Las Vegas! I felt like I was following in the footsteps of so many of my heroes, past and present, real and fictitious. They've all experienced the Vegas dream with the same impulsive attitude, but now it was our time to shine! This was the platform to become whatever we were meant to be. Sin City was now at our disposal, the grandest of stages. Opening night nerves slowly stirred deep within, but those nerves were interpreted as a sign that something very special was about to transpire.

The taxi entered the underground lobby of Planet Hollywood. The vastness of the drop off point was enough to emphasise that we weren't in England, let alone Manchester, anymore. The place was gargantuan with Limos and stretched Hummers parked along the side of the road. Staff members worked efficiently to ensure people waiting for taxis were serviced quickly. Reps handed out flyers and wristbands for the abundance of entertainment within the hotel, but in a much smoother and more gentlemanly manner than the reps on an 18-30s type holiday (the reps here wore suits, not vests and swimming shorts for a start).

We got out of the taxi, and Turner paid the fare as the rest of us retrieved the luggage from the 'trunk'. We were immediately made to feel important as we walked towards the entrance and the suave reps greeted us with, 'Good day, Sir. I hope you enjoy your stay with us,' whilst simultaneously opening the dark tinted doors for us.

The hotel lobby blasted a river of coolness over us as we entered, relieving us after our brief stint in the relentless heat. There was a mysterious ambience to the reception area as blue squares danced on the walls from the eclectic lights that swayed feverishly from the walls and pillars.

After queuing for a torturous fifteen minutes, we were eventually called to the front desk by the young, well dressed oriental receptionist, who welcomed us to Planet Hollywood and Las Vegas with a fake, robotic smile, clearly well trained in the art of hospitality. We handed over our accommodation documents on her request. After much deliberation and computer checks we were finally given key cards for two rooms and instructed to take the lift to the soaring heights of the fourteenth floor.

Ian and I used our key card to open the door and my first impression was that the room was awesome; very spacious, classy and great for our needs. I headed straight for the window where there was a breathtaking view of the Bellagio Hotel and the Eiffel Tower, which was part of the Paris Hotel next door. The room was chilly from the air con that had already been left on in anticipation of our arrival, and the remnants of lemony cleaning products filled the fresh smelling air. There was one double and one single bed, which pretty much meant that a fight for the double would occur every night depending on who returned first, but I suspected after a heavy night drinking we wouldn't be too bothered about which bed we slept in, just as long as we made it back to the room in one piece. Of course, all these rules were null and void if one of us brought a woman back, in which case the other had to vacate and not even have the consolation of the single bed to sleep in. The choices were either get on the floor in Turner and Johnny's room or sleep in the lobby…or the bath, which actually looked quite comfy in such a luxurious room.

One of the unique features of Planet Hollywood was that each room had a piece of Hollywood memorabilia contained within it, but I was disappointed to realise that our room theme was, 'Getting Even with Dad', a cheesy film starring Macaulay Culkin and Ted Danson. Hardly the dizzy heights of Hollywood memorabilia I was expecting. Culkin's t-shirt was the main attraction locked in a clear sealed box that doubled up as a convenient table to throw clothes on at the end of a drunken night. Turner and Johnny's room theme was, 'City Slickers', starring Chuck Norris, and was only marginally more impressive.

We freshened up and got changed, eager to get out and about for our first night. We acted like a couple of giddy schoolgirls who were trying out their fake IDs for the first time, debating about what to wear for the big occasion.

I set up my iPod speakers to enhance the mood, already having my playlist ready, consisting of Elvis', 'Viva Las Vegas' and 'Ace of Spades' by Motorhead, for obvious reasons. Dean Martin's, 'Drink to me Only', recorded live at the Sands was essential, regarded by many as one of the best live performances and shows on record in the history of Vegas, before the iconic hotel was knocked down and replaced by The Venetian Hotel. Also, no gambling trip would be complete without the mellow, chilled musings of Kenny Rogers', 'The Gambler'. The words of this song would, in theory, form my gambling mantra at the tables over the next six nights. I had to try my best to remain prudent enough to know when to hold and fold the cards, and know when to walk (or run) away. That was easier said than done when the Vegas devil was hanging around your neck like a vulture.

After endless posing in the mirror, perfecting hair, spraying deodorant and splashing aftershave, we were finally ready just as Turner and Johnny arrived. We were all smartly dressed in shirt, jeans and shoes, suitably attired for the occasion and ready to make an impression on Vegas. Game faces were now portrayed as we left our room and the river of hysteria started to spill over the banks.

We scrambled into the lifts and Johnny pressed the

'Casino Floor' button. The lift door closed and it shot down, and we exchanged glances knowing that the rapacious night was seconds away. Telepathically I felt like I was picking up on everyone's restlessness as the anticipation reached its optimum level. The silence was deafening between us. It felt like we were in the tunnel getting ready to play in a cup final, hard work now a whisker away from the experience, exhilaration and the unknown of how the game would play out.

The lift pinged and the doors opened. We turned down the small marble floored corridor, following where the sound of music blasted from as something special simmered. One more turn to the right and it would all open up in front of us. I briefly closed my eyes knowing that the next time I opened them it would be there in all its unadulterated glory, the dream finally becoming an instant, heart filling reality. I took a few more steps and the time then became right. I slowly lifted my eyelids just as Turner remarked, 'Wow!' and in a blinding flash, the marvel of a grand Vegas casino lay before me!

CHAPTER 4

Within seconds of opening my eyes I felt transported to some sort of delirious periphery of heaven, mesmerised by what lay in front of us. The casino floor was a gargantuan area full of life and energy, circled by purple, pink and blue iridescent lights that illuminated the room with colours never seen in any Manchester establishment. We were surrounded by hundreds of slot machines that flashed effervescently to an unknown orchestra being conducted by a great power hovering over Vegas. There were so many it was impossible to see any further than just the few in the immediate vicinity. The music was awesome as AC/DC's, 'Highway to Hell', hollered from every orifice at a pitch perfect volume, a legendary rock tune that inspired confidence and swagger - well worthy of walking into any venue around the world given its lyrical connotations. I was half tempted to pout my lips and break into a full-on air guitar solo, which wasn't beyond the realms of possibility after a few beers, but I resisted the urge to make a tit out of myself after only a few minutes of being in the public eye.

We wandered languidly within the labyrinth of 'fruities' until we could find a place that served alcohol. Gorgeous women strutted their stuff and seemed to cross our paths from every direction, very much aware of the gifts and attributes they possessed. We weren't talking a collection of Manchester's finest – this looked like a gathering of the world's finest. It was almost as if you weren't allowed to be in Vegas unless you matched up to the unrealistic expectation of any fantasy driven motive in the minds of its sinners. None of us could help but follow the women with drifting eyes, instinctively regressing back to teenage adolescence, acting like we'd never seen semi naked women before…shades of Benidorm ten years earlier began to creep to mind. There were mixtures of every desire and origin: Whites, Orientals, Latinos and African Americans, all sporting different hair styles and colour, but all exposing flawless, photoshopped like complexions and figures. The female staff were just as stunning as they suggestively presented themselves in red basques, black stockings and suspenders, displaying their large fake breasts with perfect cleavage in full view for all to see and admire. Dancers wearing next to nothing swayed seductively on raised platforms behind the dealers, serving as a combination of entertainment and distraction for the players. Sex was everywhere, and in this part of the world the lines of seediness and normality were somewhat blurred. It felt like we'd received a personal invite from Hugh Heffner himself and were unleashed around the Playboy Mansion surrounded by all the Playmates.

Our exploration eventually took us to the central reservation where we eyeballed the Heart Bar. It was open plan and slightly darker than the casino floor, full of comfortable brown leather sofas located around the edge. I noticed that there were screens built into the tops of the bar itself, allowing you to have a bet whilst ordering a drink, which was such a cool feature, but also part of the overall ploy to surround you with the temptation to spend (lose) money.

It was Budweiser's all round as we toasted our first night in Vegas with a certain glint in our eyes that reflected an energy that bounced around us like a ping-pong ball. Without feeling the need to get comfortable, our attentions turned to more business-like matters, and to put 'operation life changing win' into action.

I'd made a promise once Vegas was booked that my first gamble would be big (well…bigger than normal for the UK but miniscule for Vegas). My so-called 'lucky numbers' were 0, 10, 26, 29, 32, and I'd planned on betting $20 on each which would net me $700 if one came in. All I wanted was that first big win to set me up for an excellent night, just a little bit of luck was all I wished for.

Entering the 'Pleasure Pit', as it was known, was an experience in itself. Hordes of people congregated around scores of tables, eyes fixated below them at the cards, dice or roulette wheels, all of them desperate for fortune to be favouring the brave. The music was still top quality, staying on the classic rock theme as Creedence Clearwater Revival's, 'Run Through the Jungle', smoked out of the speakers, keeping the swagger and lip puckering in full flow. As I strolled through the area grooving to the music and keeping a watchful eye for an opening, I could hear a mixture of groans and cheers from various tables. Most of the cheers seemed to be coming from the edge of the Pleasure Pit where the craps tables were. Having no clue on how to play the game, I avoided peeking for the time being as there were more pressing matters at hand.

I found an opening with ample room at a roulette table, so I quickly darted over. I perched on a stool and without caution threw over $100 to be converted into chips, as if this was all in a day's work for me. I felt a flutter of nerves as the croupier nodded at me, then he handed me a stack of chips that I distributed evenly across the table in accordance with my pre-determined numbers: $20 on each one!

There were four other players and they were throwing far more chips in than my initial bet, making my misplaced 'Billy Big Bollocks' attitude droop like the final waves of a Viagra pill. It looked like the other players were trying to cover every option possible just to have a winning feeling regardless of the overall profit. The music momentarily became swallowed up by the loud chatter of other gamers in the vicinity, typifying the 'loud American' stereotype with their cheesy chants and over the top animated statements at the end of every hand.

The dealer spun the ball around the wheel, which made the players work faster placing their bets. Moments later he called, 'No more bets please,' and I became lost in a tirade of foolish visions of what a few big wins could bring. I saw myself swagger from the table with an abundance of chips in both hands as women flocked towards me to take a piece of my good fortune. Pit Bosses and Floor Managers would surround me and offer me all sorts of luxurious hospitality treats: penthouse suites, champagne, VIP accesses, the whole shebang. Are these the kind of desperate hopes and dreams Vegas imposed? I needed a reality check as I waited optimistically, focusing on where the ball would land as it continued to make a hypnotic rolling sound that eventually slowed down, bouncing in and out of numbers like a hot potato. It seemed to take an age to finish while my head circled in sync with the ball movement. I sustained hope and prayer, pleading under my breath to some higher power above. I took a nervy gulp! The ball stopped! I froze! My stomach plunged! My arse fell out! Red 12! I slumped! Un-fucking-believable! I really thought the win was going to happen, but I guess that's what sucks you in. A fit of madness struck me, and I temporarily lost all sense, quickly opening my wallet and pulling out another $100, slamming it down on the table with force in exchange for more chips. 'Ricky, what the fuck are you doing?' I thought. The chasing game was now in effect, but this was Vegas, and an element of stupidity is what made gambling so much fun. I continued with the same numbers as the dealer spun again. A couple of Americans shouted loudly directly behind my ear, 'C'mon baby! One More Time!' which made me jump out of my skin. I froze again as the ball fizzed and time slowed. My wild imagination pictured the ball landing on my number, where everything would suddenly slow down as 'Chariots of Fire' played in the distance. I could see myself dancing and jigging about with a typical Manc cockiness to show my delight. Reality swiftly ensued when the ball finally landed, and the anticipation on my face was quickly wiped and replaced with despair. Red 34! My arse sank much quicker than it took for the dealer to brush my lost chips into his pot. Oh well, $200 down in Vegas and I'd only been on the floor for five minutes. I now understood how the hotels managed to build these outrageous modern-day resorts. It's because of the stupidity of people like me. It seemed like a good idea to throw so much money in right away, but now I was struck by devastation at the inevitable outcome. Perhaps on some psychological level I bet so much money to try and deflect from the anguish I was feeling with regards to my personal life, but all it achieved was adding something else to the list of things that were currently fuckin' me off. I had to quickly get over the loss and not let it play on my mind. I was dealing with too much shit as it was, and, after all, this was opening night in Vegas, so it was time to get a grip and move on...until the next bet came along.

Ian came to the table and threw down $10.

'Still maintaining a cautious gambling attitude, I see.' I sneered sarcastically.

'Well, it's only the start. I'm not going crazy. How much have you done in?' Ian replied.

'Two hundred fuckin' dollars!'

'You're joking! You've got a problem.'

'Bollocks, I'm in Vegas. I've waited all my life for this and I have money to lose.' Who was I trying to justify that to?

'You'll be hitting a cash machine by the end of the night.'

'I'm way off that slippery slope yet. You wanna double up on bets?'

'Yeah go on then.'

'I'll throw another $10 in then to match your pitiful limit,' I retorted with a smirk.

We threw on small amounts, covering most of the table, and managed to pick up a few insignificant wins that kept us playing for a further twenty minutes or so. I walked away recuperating $15 of the $200 initially lost. It was hardly the high rolling start expected, barely taking note of the wise words of Kenny Rogers himself, although it wasn't the appropriate game for such wisdom. Johnny and Turner suffered small losses too, but they, like Ian, didn't go in high, instead choosing to part with $20 each. Maybe Ian had the right idea, bet small and take small winnings and accrue increments over the course of the night. It made sense, but with the giddiness and elation of finally being in Vegas, it wasn't going to be in my nature for the next few days. My extremist thrill-seeking ways wanted to feel the jubilations of a huge win, perhaps to mask over the pain that was nestled deep within me.

Gambling had been done quickly, and only Ian was slightly up. It would've been so easy to carry on playing and attempt to redeem our misfortunes, but this was our first night in Las Vegas, and there was a lot to see and do. It was time to move on and explore the outside world so many die-hard gamblers in Vegas rarely appreciated. We would've liked to have been out of the hotel earlier, but finding the exit seemed to be a longer journey than the actual flight itself. I could see why the place was designed to be so difficult to leave. It probably forced punters to stop and gamble in their frustration, consequently pumping more money into the huge bank accounts of the casinos.

CHAPTER 5

When we finally made it outside it was astounding! It was as if the night had lit up the Strip brighter than the sun could ever manage. The heat hit us instantly, especially after spending time inside the air-conditioned casino. The insatiable night was unblemished, made even more atmospheric by the huge, perfectly round, glowing moon that looked like it was acting as a peephole for the eyes of the universe to observe the world's most surreal place. Swarms of people roamed the 'sidewalk' and the Bellagio Hotel loomed large directly opposite. Caesars Palace was visible a little further down, as two of the world's grandest and well-known resorts stood side by side. We hovered on the steps outside Planet Hollywood for a moment just to soak it all in and bask in its glory.

It was difficult to decide what to do first, but we decided to cross something off the bucket list and spend the night in one of the hotspots of Vegas nightlife: the club, Pure at Caesars Palace.

The walk there was an obstacle course of street reps advertising women through business cards and photos. It was strange because by law prostitution was illegal, but in Sin City it was obvious that sex was part of the foundation of the underworld - our brief walk through Planet Hollywood, seeing the attire of the staff and the dancers, alluded to that. The reps weren't allowed to advertise this guilty pleasure by spoken word, so what they did was bang the cards together in front of you to make a clicking sound in an attempt to grab your attention. As we walked further down the Strip, I could see the floor littered with these cards and pictures of the naked women available. It was like the Vegas version of Top Trumps. Judging by the thick binders the reps carried, there must've been an incredible number of hookers that were on offer to cater for everyone's erotic desires, no matter how depraved. I was also astonished at the ease with which you could have a woman sent to your room. I only knew this because the reps wore fluorescent t-shirts stating, *'Women to your room in twenty minutes'*. Only in America, or only in Vegas? Or was this readily available anywhere in the world and it was just that Vegas advertised it more openly?

Caesars Palace was a remarkable and vastly impressive resort. The colossal marble columns, arches and eye catching ancient looking architecture paid homage to the feel of Rome, and within an instant we'd crossed continents into another dimension, into another holiday entirely so it seemed. Just outside the main entrance was a remodelling of the Coliseum, a replica of the original in terms of its shape. This imposter to the real landmark has played host to many of the biggest events in the world, mainly boxing title bouts. For some reason, I remembered from my youth that Wrestlemania 9 took place here, back when I thought the fighting was real and would persecute anyone who refuted its legitimacy.

Having been limited to a couple of bottles of Budweiser in Planet Hollywood whilst gambling, we aimed to get into the bar and be free from the distraction of roulette to prepare ourselves for Pure later on. After a walk through a hallway built up of restaurants, which didn't fill us with enthusiasm, Shadow Bar appeared before us, tucked away in the corner of the casino floor. It wasn't that busy in there, just a few regulars occupying seats at the bar. As we settled down we noticed *why* they were sat quietly with eyes dead ahead, and why it was named Shadow Bar. A huge screen ran the full length of the back wall with three strippers dancing provocatively behind it, but all we could see was their shapely silhouettes, resembling something of the forbidden channels on Sky TV. The noticeable use of sex as an advertising tool was becoming more and more evident, and we'd only been here a couple of hours. It wasn't necessarily a bad thing for those that looked to fulfil sordid desires.

We were finding it hard to get drunk with no beer on draught and being forced to drink bottles. Of course, it was possible to take the quicker route by downing shots and doubles, but financially it wasn't very viable to maintain that level throughout the night due to the extortionate prices. The annual 'first night blues' may not occur this time around. 'First night blues' was a statement coined by ourselves from past holiday experiences, and consisted of getting absolutely blind drunk on the first night. Underestimating the heat, combined with the strength and quantity of the alcohol, topped off with the adrenaline rush and excitement the first night of a holiday brings, usually resulted in extreme drunkenness, severe memory loss and crazy random antics. I've had the misfortune of suffering many times. However, we were in Vegas and *was it really* that important to be plastered to the point of memory loss? I wanted to remember the experience and for it *not* to be a drunken haze having to retrace footsteps like the film, 'The Hangover'. Not that we'd remain teetotal, far from it, but when you've waited as long as we had to experience Vegas, not exactly a regular jaunt, then it had to be remembered for all its worth.

Time crept upon us, and the point had landed to take the night to the unpredictable next level in this new world. We marched through the casino, impressed by its grandness, and just like in Planet Hollywood, we couldn't help but watch the gorgeous women that seemed to sprout up from every inch of the floor. Where were the women of this calibre back home?

Once again, we had to navigate the web of hallways and corridors to find the club. The hotel was immense, and although extremely absorbing, I envisaged that this constant searching for our destination would eventually become frustrating. I made a quick pit stop to the toilet to find the size, cleanliness and design made for better living conditions than my whole house. How can a public toilet look classy enough to live in?

We arrived at the entrance to Pure, an enticing opening in the wall next to the casino and sportsbook area. There were only a few people in front of us so queuing didn't take long at all, but it was in those few seconds where an Anglo-American cultural issue arose. We'd heard a rumour that no matter your age, carrying and presenting ID regularly in Vegas was a necessity. Luckily, we all had a form of ID with us, but others in front were not so fortunate, resulting in them being painfully turned away regardless of being over the age of twenty-one. The admission fee was $20: expensive for England, but this was a whole new ball game and the expectancy was it would be well worth the money.

We were let through the rope and continued through the archway into a wide corridor that separated the calm, sophisticated exterior from the energetic, heart thumping interior. The colours instantly transformed, ploughing us into a shade of darkness that emulated the tone inside. Half way in and groups of people amassed at the end of the corridor where the bar and dance floor opened into a ferocious nightclub. The floor was tiled and the walls were lit with a dark fluorescent blue and purple that enhanced the atmosphere. R&B music thumped louder with every waking step, sending shivers throughout my body as it seemed to recoil off the walls and melt in the air. The thrill and eagerness inside of me rushed to new peaks, and I couldn't wait to get inside.

The vibe hit us like a ruthless tidal wave when the club emerged. I quickly scanned the area to see the masses congregated on the dance floor and by the bar, leaving many areas sparsely populated so I could see how the place was laid out. The dance floor was separated by seating areas that were contemporary and eclectically designed to enhance the chic and cosmopolitan character of the club. VIP areas segregated the floor even further, and within these confines were beds and long sofas with drapes hanging from the ceilings to create an area of sultry privacy. It was extraordinary how far people would go to make their club the best in town, but I wondered if this was due to the excessive demands of the clientele, or was it just the owners showing off? A bar, a dance floor and great music were all we required back in Manchester, and in most cases, the dirtier and grimier the better, but there was a completely different expectation in this part of the world. What was one to do apart from milk it to its very core? In that moment, there was no need for alcohol. We were high on the atmosphere, northern cockiness overriding a more normal British reserve, culminating in us doing the 'walk to the dance floor dance'. No matter where you are in the world, some things just never change from back home.

We hit the epicentre, unfazed by the scores of people already jostling for position on the so-called battlefield, fighting to be near all the gorgeous women that appeared out of thin air. Life at home was a distant memory and the spirit of Las Vegas was a cleansing change.

The past had eroded a chunk of self-belief from my personality. I'd not even had the urge to go trawling for women back in Manchester as I tried to come to terms with my current single status. Considering the artificial feeling of invincibility I was feeling, so rarely felt in these moments, confidence seemed to come naturally. It was as if I'd held off on meeting women solely in preparation for this moment. I don't know what it was, but that primal urge to meet girls was now overpowering me in a thrashing storm of headstrong crazed lust, and suddenly it became a necessity once more. I was ready to get back in the game, throw my money down and roll the dice to take an overdue risk. Whether it was because of the freedom of being on holiday, the expectancy of Vegas, or the petty need for vengeance, remained unclear, but it was a sensation not felt for a while.

Whilst transfixed in my own little world, Ian and Johnny had wasted no time whatsoever. I was unsure how as I hadn't been paying attention, but they somehow got chatting to two girls, who I shortly found out were from Bolton of all places. It was fine work in such a short space of time, but we'd come all this way to escape our routine lives in Manchester and the first two girls we met were from Bolton! They entertained them stood around a high table next to the dance floor, but I wasn't particularly interested. I'd not come all this way to get involved with girls who lived about five miles away from home. I wanted to explore *some* sort of cultural difference, and take advantage of the fact that I was an Englishman in America, and find out whether the theory that American women loved English men was true. I reminded Turner of that presumption, and his eyes lit up, gesturing for us to get back in the mix on the dance floor to test the waters.

JD and cokes started to surge despite the inflated price. Bollocks to taking it easy and to saving pennies now, this was our first night in Vegas and we were being consumed by its irresistible power! Numerous visits to the dance floor had passed, and the pace of drinking quickened, which meant that the initial burst of burning lust I felt on arrival was slowly dwindling, but there was still plenty of flame left yet.

On further observation through slightly misty eyes, I was starting to become aware of the contrasts between English and American male attitudes towards women within a club. In America, or perhaps just in Vegas, every time a girl braved the dance floor she was surrounded in a matter of seconds by hordes of horny Americans. Now that wasn't really the difference because that happens everywhere. The distinction came in that the men always made their way behind the girl and attempted to illicitly grind her to a pulp, but always from behind, never having the courage to approach them face-to-face. It was somewhat different to the politer English attitude, where in general we adopt a more standoffish approach, biding our time, and the approach usually comes from the side or head on. Never surprise a British girl from behind if she doesn't know who you are. A dry slap received when I was eighteen from some boisterous lunatic will hold testimony to that. Because of that incident I'd learnt from an early age that *that* wasn't the way to go about 'pulling'. It may work in some quarters, but rarely do we go straight in all guns blazing and start grinding away from behind like some rabid dog with fleas, not if you wanted the desired result with a girl of class and style. These guys ripped the heart and soul out of what should be considered an art form, but maybe it was all part of the changing face of the world today. Did I mention that the perceptions of this new generation were frightening? There was certainly an element of teasing from the girls' point of view as they seemed to entertain the idea to score free drinks. Being in Sin City with this amount of money flying about, why not take advantage of a man's lecherous thinking, however fickle and deceptive the icebreaker may be? I noticed the same girls grinding with several guys all night and I couldn't quite work out why the men bothered. These girls portrayed interest, playing the 'buy me a drink card', even though they clearly weren't. Did the men accept this knowingly, or were they just naive frat boys?

My own tactics weren't exactly a shining example so far as I realised just how rusty and lacking in belief I was. It was becoming tough to interpret whether any girls were interested due to them being incapable of cracking a smile or holding any eye contact, only bowing down to communication through the barrier breakdown of grinding. I couldn't get my head around what the dynamics were. It wasn't big headed of me to think that I had more to offer than this characterless strategy, plus I had the big advantage of being an Englishman in America. Would the myth be proved correct that American girls love the English? At this point we wouldn't know because the only girls who had given us the time of day were the two girls from Bolton.

By this time, we had heavily surpassed the twenty-four-hour mark of being awake, but I felt that I could go on much longer, like I'd been on some speed fuelled drug binge all night that was keeping me alert. I was on my fourth JD and had just received my pitiful change from a twenty when out of nowhere it happened, completely unplanned and out of left field as is usually the case in these circumstances. I locked into a momentary stare with a stunning woman, who made my heart skip a beat and my skin flush like I'd been spiked with several acupuncture needles. Our eyes met when I faintly brushed shoulders with her on my way back from the bar, which sent a tingling sensation vibrating down my arm. I reached Turner, who was hunched over our table by the edge of the dance floor, before turning to face her from a distance. She hadn't looked back, yet I sensed something in that moment when her eyes sparkled at mine that made me lose all reservations and self-defence, powerless to her beauty. She looked bleary from this distance as the darkness and smoke shrouded her presence, but from what I could tell she looked perfect.

I stood with Turner, not really listening to what he was saying, choosing to remain fixated on this girl, taking heed that her and her friend rejected a few lads when they staggered over chancing their luck. It didn't fill me with confidence seeing this, but then again, their tactics were that of pissed-up college fledglings, blundering over spouting all types of bollocks. It seemed it wasn't just on the dance floor where they were having trouble.

She looked over in my direction once or twice, but didn't emit any clear sign of a green light, so I couldn't be sure if it was deliberate. I told myself that the glance was too quick to be intentional and could be a miscalculation on my part. I had to interrupt Turner and bring him up to speed as to what was going on so I could be sure of not making an arse of myself by going over. He was useless and couldn't offer any words or pearls of wisdom, but he probably wasn't looking as intently as I was. I wanted to be sure before making any attempt. An outright rejection was *not* what I needed with my self-confidence already being on the frail side.

Eventually, the pussy footing around subsided, and I momentarily lost all fear of rejection. I turned to Turner and snapped, 'Right, that's it! I need to stop being a soft arse about this.'

'About time!' Turner agreed. 'Just like riding a bike mate.'

'You reckon? I don't even know what to do anymore it's been that long.'

'Don't worry, you'll be fine! Be like me,' he grinned.

'Fuck that, I'd rather stick my genitals in a bees nest than be anything like you,' I replied, borrowing a line from an episode of 'Bottom' for a well-timed insult.

Turner laughed, keeping the scene's dialogue alive, 'Kinky!' he said in his best Eddie Hitler voice.

I couldn't help myself and had to carry on the scene, adopting Rik Mayall's role. 'What do you mean, kinky? How am I kinky?'

'You want to stick your genitals in a bees nest,' he replied in the same voice.

'No I don't, that's the whole point, it's sarcasm...' We burst into laughter before I could finish.

'Fuck off now!' I was still laughing. 'Let's get back to the task at hand. You're supposed to be sorting my head out remember.'

He composed himself before we got locked into a full

rendition of the whole 'Bottom' episode. 'Just go over and say something like, "Hello Big Tits, fancy a snog?"'

'Sod off! Be serious, you clown.'

'Ok, what about, "Will you go with me?"'

I pissed myself laughing yet again, 'What? I'm not twelve years old at a roller rink you know.'

Turner then stopped clowning around. 'Ok, ok. Just be confident and don't look like the nervous wreck you do now.'

'Oh, thanks mate! Do I look that bad?'

'Meh!' I'm sure he was enjoying my struggles.

'Fuck me Ricky, pull yourself together,' I muttered to myself in a last-ditch attempt to psyche myself up.

'You look adorable. Like a million bucks, skipper.' His sarcasm was not welcomed, but he continued, 'If you don't go over then I will.' That was enough motivation for me. I wasn't prepared to let Turner go over and ruin this moment, so I took a deep breath and nervously soldiered forward, switching my posture to an optimistic frame, hoping that my body language and expressions would outshine the unease I was feeling deep down. The confidence felt on arrival had well and truly been erased.

'Time to roll that dice, Ricky,' I mumbled, as several thoughts raced through my mind: a combination of hope and fear. I carried on into the unknown, appearing through the smoke like a tense 'Stars in Your Eyes' contestant. The smoke that had shielded her face was no longer a barrier, and despite my inner protests, I boldly made my way towards her.

She was side on as I neared. Her friend sharply shifted her eyes as I drew closer, revealing a look that suggested she knew what was coming. Her eyes flicked back and forth between me and my goal. I couldn't judge whether it was a good or bad expression. Perhaps she was thinking, 'Here we go again, another idiot trying it on, just leave us alone.' Everything happened in slow motion. The object of my desire spun gracefully to face me as I came into sight, seeming to recognise me as the guy who'd been treading around and trying to eye her up for the past twenty minutes. She looked completely radiant, almost making time stand still as her long autumn brown hair swished around her shoulders as she turned. All knowledge of words became temporarily lost as I stared in awe.

I quickly gathered composure and buoyantly asked, 'Hey, how's it going?' I was encouraged by a smile from both girls, which I hadn't seen when the other guys had tried it on.

'Hi! I'm good! How about you?' she answered. Immediately from her accent I could tell she wasn't English, maybe not even American.

'I can't complain.' I kept it cool, before asking, 'Where are you girls from?' Using the 'get out of jail free' line all lads play in a foreign country to spark a conversation.

The one I liked replied, 'We're both from Puerto Rico, but I live in San Diego now.' She nodded towards her friend. 'Annalise still lives there.'

Annalise then said something that I didn't expect, 'She has wanted you to come over and talk to her all night by the way.'

I was stunned at the bluntness, but it made me smirk. The girl I liked looked embarrassed and flashed Annalise an evil stare. Just those few words alone were enough to convince me that the looks I'd been trying to decipher were indeed positive and I could now relax into the conversation, especially having seen her reject so many others beforehand, except little old me from Manchester who was shattering all odds given by Ladbrokes, a 20/1 outsider making a late dart to the finish to upset the apple cart.

I didn't take advantage of the revelation, deciding that it was best to keep playing it cool and quietly dismiss it rather than push it. I changed the subject. 'So, you're Annalise? I'm Ricky.'

I turned to the other girl. 'And your name is...?'

'Eva!' There was a look of shyness as she was still reeling from Annalise's revelation.

Just as I was about to offer to buy them both a drink, Turner came ambling over having seen I'd not been shunned. I introduced him and he immediately started talking to Annalise. He highlighted his wingman credentials by taking her out of the conversation to leave me alone with Eva, or perhaps he was using me as a decoy to do his own dirty work, seeing a predatory opportunity to try it on with Annalise.

Annalise was attractive and an obvious Latino with her dark, olive skin tone and features. She had a hugely animated face, exposing a wide, infectious smile that showed her perfectly straight white teeth. She had faultless skin texture and large, round eyes. Her hair was black, shoulder length and wavy around the sides, and initially she seemed the bubblier of the two, but that probably had more to do with her embarrassing revelation about Eva. She wore an all-black long dress that came down towards her ankles and had patterns of summery flowers embedded in the side.

Eva, on the other hand, was slimmer and slightly taller than Annalise with a tight slender figure. She had thick, undulating autumn brown hair that reached down the full length of her back. She too had an untarnished complexion, and her lips were somewhat full, divulging an irresistible pout that had the subtlest of light pink lip gloss coated on, which sparkled when the light caught her mouth. A twinkling silver cross pendant hung from her neck, and I detected similar glints in both her ears. I caught the slightest scent of fruit and patchouli from her fragrance, an encapsulating smell that seemed to wrap itself around me like poison ivy. She was wearing a knee length black dress with shades of strong pink across the top and down the sides. She had a mystifying air to her expression that carried deep into her eyes whenever she smiled, which intrigued and gripped me greatly as soon as my eyes fixed on hers.

I leaned in towards Eva. 'How come you now live in San Diego?'

'My family moved there when I was little. We moved from Puerto Rico when I was about ten.' Her accent had a tinge of being Americanised but was still very Spanish in tone.

'So, what brings you to Vegas then?' I asked.

'Annalise has never been so we thought we'd go on a road trip when she came over to stay with me. This is our first day because she only arrived this morning, but we're only here for one night.'

'What road trip is that? Route 66?'

'No, no. We're going to L.A. tomorrow, then San Francisco, then back home to San Diego. Not quite as long as Route 66.'

Again, another of those dreams and fantasies I've always wanted to do which is so easy for those that live on the West Coast. A drive down the M6 back home didn't quite have the same appeal.

'That sounds amazing. I've always wanted to do something similar. It's a bit of an ambition of mine,' I revealed.

'You should, it's a beautiful drive. Why don't you?'

'Well, money mainly, but I've never really had the opportunity because I live so far away.'

'I've done a similar drive before through Napa Valley, but not as long as this. Where are you from to live so far away?'

'Manchester, in England,' I said, proud of my roots.

'Oh cool. I've never been to England but I'd like to one day.'

'I think I'd rather live where you do. It's strange, isn't it? No matter whereabouts in the world you're from, you always perceive somewhere else to be better, but the locals of that area would rather be in your position. I guess we're all guilty of thinking that the grass is always greener.' My insightfulness was down to Tennessee whiskey.

'I guess you're right. Maybe you could show me Manchester and I'll show you San Diego and we can decide for ourselves,' she smiled.

'I wish life could be as easy as that sometimes,' I replied, thinking about how weird and wonderful that scenario would be, before adding, 'So, how long are you on a road trip for?'

'Hmm, about ten days or so.'

'Have you planned it or are you just booking hotels along the way?'

'Unplanned. We figured that we'd be able to get in somewhere along the way and not have the pressure of time.'

'Why Vegas for one night only? I'd have thought it deserved a longer stay?'

'Annalise wants to spend more time in L.A. and San Francisco.'

'I think I'd like to spend ten days in each of Vegas, L.A. and San Francisco.'

'True. That'd be some trip. How long are you staying in Vegas for?'

'Six nights, and just like you, this is our first.'

'That's cool. We'll be looking to get on the road at about three tomorrow, so we'll not even have been here twenty-four-hours.' She took a seconds pause before saying, 'You should come, it'll be so much fun. You could be our token hitch-hiker we picked up in Vegas. You seem okay, I trust you're not a freak or some wack job,' she giggled.

I was taken aback and flattered by the quickness of her invite after such a short time of chatting, even if it was probably a joke anyway. Part of me went into complete madness, dreaming of what the consequences would be for venturing off into the unknown with two Puerto Ricans and going AWOL from work. I was tempted but knew I couldn't - could I? The angel and demon within my subconscious started to wrestle, and I had to remind myself to see who won that fight a bit later in the night.

'You know what? I'd love to, but this is our first night and we don't have that freedom I'm afraid to just do one up the West Coast.'

'Do one?' She looked puzzled.

'Sorry, it means "to go". My drunken Manc slang obviously didn't translate well.

She giggled again, and playfully repeated me, '"Do one!" I like that. It's cute.' Our eyes knowingly caught each other's in the split-second silence.

She asked, 'So how come you're here? Is it just you and your buddy for a bachelor party or something?'

'No nothing like that. There's two others sat at the other end of the bar. We've just come because it's always been a dream to go to Vegas together.'

'That's so cool. There are usually a lot of bachelor parties here, but you just came for the hell of it? That's pretty cool dude!'

'Well I think in life you've got to do the things you've always wanted to do,' I replied.

'You're right. I guess that's what brings us here. I

suppose it was Annalise who got me motivated to do it because I've not seen her for so long. I'm not that great at impulse really.'

'I used to be, but I think that part of me has been lost for a while. I suppose I'm trying to get it back, which is why I'm here in many ways.'

'Oh yeah? How come?' She looked at me inquisitively.

'I guess I've been blind to aspects of my life over the past few years and should've stayed on the path I was on five years ago rather than the mistake I took. But you live and learn don't you, and what doesn't kill you makes you stronger, right?'

Eva looked on intently before I added, 'I guess at the moment I'm in the middle of a soul-searching mission, looking more for spiritual inspiration rather than what my head and heart have always told me.'

I think being in Vegas, coupled with JD, was sending my head on a bit of a tangent as I was voicing statements that were usually left to the confines of my mind. I wasn't usually so open, especially with complete strangers, but Eva seemed fascinated as if she understood exactly what I was talking about.

'Very interesting.' She was coy in her delivery, smiling curiously like a detective trying to extract a confession.

'Interesting in what way?'

'I don't know… but I'll find out by the end of the night.' She brought a finger up across her lips, as if deep in thought.

'Oh yeah, does that mean you're sticking around?'

'Sure, why not?'

'Well I better get you another drink then.'

'You better had. Rum and coke with ice please, easy on the coke.' She winked, taking the last sips of her drink through a straw, raising her eyes over the glass as she reached the end to flash the subtlest glance in my direction. On seeing the last of her drink disappear, I turned to the bar to catch the bartender's attention to order another round. Luckily the bar wasn't too busy so he was over in an instant, pouring the drinks and serving them in just as timely a fashion, which deserved a tip, so I signalled for him to keep the change out of the bastard $40 I handed over. That's a full night's cash in the local pub, and here it only paid for two drinks!

I turned back again to Eva and asked her what Puerto Rico was like. She told me in stimulating detail as we remained leant against the corner of the bar engrossed in conversation. Her father still lived there and she'd go and visit him a few times a year, staying in the hotel that he part owned through a consortium. She had moved around a lot in her teens due to her father being in the military, but San Diego was where they had set up a base with other family already living there. She described the tropical climate of Puerto Rico and the beaches, telling me that the sand was crisp and golden, and the sunsets were heavenly. It was all quite mesmerising listening about her life, and how very different it was to my own back home. The contrast of our worlds, from the paradise setting of Puerto Rico and West Coast America to the grim and grey hurried life in Manchester was crazy, making the fact that we were getting on so well quite bizarre.

Eva had remained in San Diego for career opportunities, working with war veterans in a variety of places, which I found admirable. I sensed her upbringing and family ties had a lot of influence on her working in such a profession, but I could tell she was someone who naturally liked to help others because of the caring manner in the way she spoke. She had a maturity way beyond her years, that I suspected came from the wisdom imparted by the older generations she had worked with. She loved what she did for a living, telling me how rewarding it was to help people who had served their country. I didn't have the same enthusiasm when she asked about what I did for a living. She didn't find it boring though, and she continued to probe to find out more about me, with particular reference to my earlier comment about soul-searching, but I was reluctant to reveal anything other than the basics for now. I was far more interested in her and how her life was so different from my own.

Due to her being from Puerto Rico, I had to ask whether she'd read Hunter S. Thompson's book, 'The Rum Diary', set in San Juan, one of my personal favourite reads. I was impressed that she had, even more so when she claimed he was one of her favourite writers too. She carried on about Thompson, delving into theories about him and why he was so brilliant. I was beginning to think that *she* was brilliant. I'd never encountered such a woman with this knowledge that was parallel to my own interests. Why is it that the older you get, physical appearance seems nothing compared to mental stimulation? It was more of a turn on that she'd read and understood Hunter S. Thompson's work than her obvious striking good looks.

The conversation flowed and there weren't any awkward silences whatsoever. The shyness she portrayed upon our initial greeting had long since departed. We occasionally flirted, but in such a classy, imperceptible way that it was barely noticeable to any onlooker. We both knew what was going on, sharing the greatest kind of connection when words are no longer needed, and communication is unspoken, but rather through indefinable looks, shimmering smiles, and engaging body language. I could've easily taken her back home with me, but a girl like Eva wouldn't look the same in the grotty little local pub on a cold, bitter English night. She was someone who flourished and shone in the glorious setting of warmer climates, like a blooming flower... or a Puerto Rican rose!

The music had shifted from R&B to a more general mix of rock, pop and dance from across the ages. The sizzling and strutting innuendo ridden track, 'Cream', by Prince started, and Eva's face lit up. She grabbed my arm, 'Oh I love this song. Come on, you can show me your English moves on the dance floor.'

Now I don't profess to be the best dancer, but when someone as beautiful as Eva asks you to dance then you call upon every bit of experience and knowledge you've attained over the years just to get by and not look a slouch, or do anything stupid like a David Brent routine.

She led me by the hand to a fairly spacious area where the once vast crowd had slowly dispersed. She turned to face me, her eyes glistening in the strobe lighting. I automatically placed my hands on her sides, feeling her slender body through her silky dress. My hand meandered around her hips and to the top of her firm backside, and we moved to this blistering track. She pushed me away to give herself space to roam, moving in a much more cultured manner than me, displaying a Flamenco/pole dancing salsa style with elusive eroticism that mirrored the song's funky beat. I caught her stare and flirtatious smile a couple of times as I attentively watched her. She subtly mouthed the evocative lyrics to me, continuing to bewitchingly gaze at me throughout the song, making me feel a little powerless. She had the sort of sexy bombshell look on her face that was necessary for a track ridden with such promiscuousness. She continued to move eloquently back towards me, solidly grabbing my waist as soon as she was within range, moving her own hips in a snake like manner, perfectly in tune to the rhythm. I felt my own tempo slow to a grinding halt, and before I knew it I was just stood motionless on the dance floor watching her in front of me. The urge to grab and kiss her filled my mind, but I showed restraint – more from fear than self-control. I remained rooted to the spot, completely eclipsed by Eva's own moves, but I didn't care. Just watching her was mesmerising, like having a front row seat to a theatrical performer.

Luckily, I wasn't stood still for very long as the song ended, which broke my reverie. Massive Attack's, 'Unfinished Sympathy', began and she shifted towards me, slowly leaning into my chest and clasping her hands on my hips. She moved delicately this time, a rhythm more to my speed, all the while looking up at me and grinning in such a licentious way. It was like she knew deep down that she'd just completely seduced me – a filthy trick if you ask me when one can move so well, and when a song of such lyrical suggestion was playing. Not that I was complaining. She must've read my mind or felt how jittery I'd become after watching her, taking pity on me, leading me by the hand to the bar for a much-needed drink to calm my palpitations.

It must've been about four in the morning. The lads wanted to call it a night and head back to our hotel for a nightcap with the two girls from Bolton (Vicky and Julie). I had no idea if any of them were hoping to get off with either of the girls. I'd not been paying attention since I first saw Eva. Even Turner had succumbed to getting involved in their foursome since finding out Annalise was engaged to be married, so god knows where the night was heading for them. The moment of truth had now arrived as to how my night would end, so I asked both Eva and Annalise if they also wanted to come back to our hotel and carry on the night in the bar within the casino.

Eva replied, 'Of course. Remember, I still need to find out the meaning of that comment.'

'Well I guess you'll *have* to come back to find out.'

'We have a rental car parked here so come with us if you like. Annalise doesn't drink you see.'

'Chauffeur driven back to the hotel? How could I say no to that?'

I told Turner that I'd be going back in the car with the girls. He winked, shook my hand and departed with the others.

I was now on my own in Vegas with two strangers from another world and culture, separated from my peers, blissfully unaware of how the night was going to turn out. It was all exciting stuff, living life in the fast lane, getting myself into the chance situations I secretly craved to be in out here. Having only been here a matter of hours, the madness was beginning to unfurl, and the movie inside my mind was beginning to take shape as the plot began to thicken.

CHAPTER 6

I swaggered proudly like a rock star through the opulence of Caesars Palace with a Puerto Rican girl on each arm. I couldn't believe the surrealism and unpredictability of how the night was unfolding. I got the feeling this was all part of my personal destiny for the trip, separate from my friends' who had their own paths to follow – and that, so far, seemed to be safe gambling and re-experiencing Bolton in Las Vegas!

We reached the exit doors and with true English gentlemanly politeness I held them open, causing the girls to comment and laugh as if this innocent act of courtesy was beyond their own world, making me feel kind of suave like James Bond. Yeah right, more like Johnny Bloody English!

Despite it being early morning, the air was warm, and there wasn't a breeze to be felt amongst the picturesque and green outside foyer. Annalise pulled a ticket out of her purse and gestured to the valet outside, who was smartly dressed in a satin red waistcoat, a crisp white shirt, bow tie and black trousers. I'd never been in a party where we had to use a parking valet before, but this was probably where our modest Mancunian culture differed from the flamboyance of the mega resorts.

Inside the black Toyota Yaris, the conversation and

laughter continued. I revealed my insights into how England was different to the States, making specific reference to the attitudes of men and women that I'd noticed earlier in the night. They said they were used to most men behaving similarly - it was common practice apparently. They added that the men they encountered were usually clueless with an immature attitude, but flatteringly they both said I wasn't in that bracket. I think that's just the English way really. We're stereotypically seen as being overly polite and it's never noticeable to us, but I understood that in some ways our conduct was more refined than other cultures, despite a few idiots giving us a bad name.

It was nearly five in the morning when we arrived at Planet Hollywood. As I shifted to exit from the back seat, Annalise turned to me and said, 'You two have a good time. Look after her, Ricky!'

'What do you mean?' I asked, confused.

'I'm beat and need my beauty sleep.'

'Are you sure? You're more than welcome to join us.'

'Yeah I'm sure. I think I can trust Eva with you.'

'Don't worry. I'll look after her and make sure she gets back safely.'

'I know you will. You're good people Ricky. Maybe I'll see you again in the future. Take care of yourself.'

'Yeah you too! It's been great meeting you, Annalise.' I leant over to give her a half hug and kiss on the cheek before saying goodbye and leaving the car.

Eva sat in the front seat and began speaking Spanish. Annalise tittered at whatever was said before they embraced. I held the door open for Eva as she elegantly stood from the car, noting the polite gesture again as I shut the door. We waved to Annalise, and the Toyota sped up the ramp onto the vibrant Strip. Once the car was out of sight I was suddenly plagued by paralysing fear. I was now acutely aware that I was alone with Eva, and given the recent rarity of such circumstances, this made me apprehensive as I recognised the possibility of what could be the next chapter on this mystifying night. I turned to her sheepishly and let out a deep sigh to calm myself, gesturing towards the hotel entrance. Eva held her hand out to me and I took it gently. She squeezed it tightly as if she was reassuring me in some way. It worked instantly as this small comforting token made me more at ease and wiped all reservations from my troubled mind. She loosened her grip from my fingers and we strolled into the ever-alive Planet Hollywood where ZZ Top's, 'Gimme All Your Lovin', ripped off the walls to greet our arrival.

The others were gathered around a roulette table near the central Heart Bar with the Bolton girls. I caught a glimpse of all five of them downing a shot before they eyed me making my way through the crowd. After briefly acknowledging them, Eva and I sat down on a table inside to be alone in quieter surroundings. The gaming seekers of the Vegas night hadn't let up from earlier, still probing for the hit that would invoke so much financial reward. It was incredible to see such dedication and buzz at this time in the morning, but it was that commitment that made the atmosphere what it was, truly living up to the reputation of being a real twenty-four-hour party city.

It was incredible how well Eva and I continued to connect, despite our cultural differences. We began talking about music, and I was enthralled to learn that our tastes were in perfect alignment, both loving the older classics in the wider rock genres from down the years. I couldn't recall a time where I was so engrossed in such a depth of conversation about music with someone I wanted so much. Mandy, past girlfriends, and one-off dates, never carried the same passion and knowledge as Eva was showing. This quick and sudden bond we'd forged was a bit overwhelming, but inside I was beaming from the experience. It made me realise there were people out there who thought on the same level, who without knowing, encouraged you to express the deepest introspections of your soul because they also want to express themselves in a similar way.

With the night being what it was, there was an inevitability about Eva's next question. 'So how come you don't have a girlfriend Ricky?' She caught me off guard, before adding, 'Well I assume you don't anyway.'

'What do you mean?'

'You're a handsome guy. You're definitely not a wack job. I thought you'd have a girlfriend.'

I didn't really know how to respond so put the emphasis back on her.

'Well, why don't *you*? How come you're not seeing anyone?'

That's right, divert all attention from myself, I thought.

'Most of the boys I meet are immature like I said earlier, so I'm not interested.'

I laughed. 'So what makes me so different?'

'I don't know.... something! There's something different about you. I kinda like it. You seem wiser than most boys I meet. Like what you said earlier about being lost and striving to get it back, and the soul-searching stuff. It intrigued me. I've never really spoke to anyone who grabs my attention so quickly and appears to be so shrouded in mystery.'

'Maybe it's because we're from different backgrounds and opposite sides of the world so it's more intriguing for you.'

'No it's not that! Yes, it's cool that you're not from here, but that's not it.'

'Maybe it's because I'm four years older than you?'

'I've been on dates with boys who are older than that and they still need to grow up.'

It got me thinking. Were English men in general more mature than Americans? If that was true was it to do with our younger drinking laws? Having a beer at the age of twenty was common practice, whereas in America, that was deemed to be rebellious.

She spoke again. 'I take it you are single? I sense some sort of sadness in your eyes and I take it the two are related, and that's the reason for the soul searching?'

Was I really that transparent? Despite my best attempts to forget the past and portray confidence, could she really look into my eyes and see the unhealed and gaping wound that nestled deep within me?

'Is it that obvious?' I asked.

'It is to me. Who is she?'

'Somebody that I used to know. Or thought I knew.'

'You can tell me. But only if you want?'

I was reluctant, unwilling to pour my heart out to someone I barely knew.

'I wouldn't want to bore you with it Eva. We're in Vegas so we shouldn't be talking about the past.'

'Ricky, it's honestly ok. Maybe I can help?'

Without going into too much detail I told her of my recent relationship split and how I'd been shell-shocked given the manner of it. I wasn't ready to face it in great detail myself, let alone talk to a stranger about it and potentially ruin the night. The very mention of it did bring about discomfort in my stomach, which clearly meant I'd have to confront it properly soon enough. Maybe tomorrow, definitely not tonight! Eva was here for one night only and there was no way I was going to use that time waffling on about my demons, despite her interest.

Johnny and Ian had left the casino floor and gone for something to eat with the Bolton girls. Turner was busy talking to a good-looking blonde American girl he had just met at the bar, and he appeared to be pulling out all the stops judging by his body language.

I remained with Eva and felt firmly under the spell of Mr Jack Daniels, becoming more daring with what I was saying to her, leading the conversation more and more down a suggestive road beyond flirtation.

She responded in an equally teasing manner by complimenting my dress sense and hair, also having a fascination with how cool my dark blue jeans were. River Island's finest, I might add!

I knew what I wanted to do, and what I *had* to do, but nerves were getting the better of me. It was one thing talking and getting on well with someone, but a whole new level moving in for that first kiss. It'd been so long since I attempted such a manoeuvre and I doubted whether it would be reciprocated. I hesitated, waiting for the optimum moment, whilst in the meantime wrestling with myself as I tried to build up the courage to stake another wager in this gambling haven.

I drifted off into a world of my own, losing track of what Eva was saying as I psyched myself up. She stopped talking, sensing the distance in my expression. A moment's pause ensued before she looked at me with affectionate eyes. In that instant my valour overcame fear, and before I knew it I was going in for the risky lean. As my lips connected with hers, a magical, unexplainable sensation consumed me. She draped one arm around me, bringing the other up towards my neck, gently stroking my stubble and cheek with the palm of her tender hand. Her lips were deliciously soft, and she moved her mouth at such a slow but passionate pace that I became totally at her mercy. We kissed for what seemed like hours, but I think I'd become lost somewhere amongst the seconds of reality. I was unsure about who pulled away first, but on retreat, Eva's eyes were gently closed, as if she too was lost somewhere. She slowly opened them and again I became entranced by her tingling stare and melting smile. The flavour from her lips had now transferred onto mine, a sweet taste of strawberry. Being so close to her and touching her skin meant I was now wrapped in her aromatic perfume.

As I leant back against the sofa, she did the same. Our body language became much more intimate now as we sat back holding hands, leant against each other. Flirting escalated to a lot more playful touching between us, and we spoke to each other much closer together, breaking down personal space and boundaries, inches away from each other's lips.

The kissing must have boosted my self-assurance as I thought it sacrilege not to take this further.

'So…do you wanna…come and see my room?' I said unsubtly and a bit sheepishly.

Her face turned into a half laugh, half smirk. She threw her hair back behind her shoulders and began to answer me in a playful, flirty tone. 'Oh I don't know about that. I'm a good girl you see.'

I looked her dead in the eye, refusing to break away from this hypnotic stare. 'Yeah right! You can't fool me. Good girls don't dance like that. You knew what you were doing on that dance floor.'

'Ha. As if! I was just dancing to one of my favourite songs. I don't know what you mean, Mr Englishman.' She needed to work on her poker face.

She planted another kiss on my lips, remaining a mere couple of centimetres from me as she pulled away, still looking deep inside me and searching for something.

I asked again, this time in a quieter and more

confident manner given the profound moment we were sharing. 'I think you should come upstairs with me!'

She paused, still searching my eyes. 'I think you might be right,' she whispered without breaking her gaze. We held that moment for several seconds as some sort of electricity roiled between us, and it was petrifying me as I uncontrollably fell into a pool of vulnerability, despite the cockiness I initially portrayed after kissing her.

We both stood up together and headed for the elevator. Once we were in, that electricity we both felt reached overload and we started kissing much more passionately and intensely, almost falling back against the side of the lift like a scene from 'Fatal Attraction' or something of similar debauchery. The opening of the lift doors was timely because if it'd gone up an extra floor there was the slightly perverse possibility that an item of clothing may have been removed.

We streamed down the corridor, almost running as I led her by the hand. Once we reached my room, I told her to wait outside for a second as I thought it best to make sure it was empty. I cautiously entered to find Johnny and Ian stood by the beds by themselves, no girls in tow. Bastards!

I couldn't even greet them with the usual acknowledgement of 'Hello!' I just forcefully blurted, 'Eva's outside, what are you two fuckers up to?'

Johnny answered, 'Calm down Captain Panic. Don't worry yourself. We're off upstairs, probably for the night so fill your boots, you dirty dog.'

Ian butted in, 'You've brought that Puerto Rican chick back here?' I sensed he was impressed.

When I nodded, he shook my hand.

'Dude! Nice work! You need this, please don't fuck it up!'

He then went on to explain their situation, 'Those girls are staying in our hotel so we're taking the party back up to their room. We've only come back to get my iPod.'

'Hope you have a splendid evening. Now get the fuck out!' I urged.

They laughed before opening the door to leave, smirking like juveniles when they passed Eva. I imagined it must've been embarrassing for her waiting outside having to watch them leave the room, understandable really, but this was Vegas, known as Sin City, and nobody should have to apologise for anything they do out here!

She stepped inside the room and the door thudded behind her. I grabbed the remote for the iPod speakers and clicked play, confident that whatever I had on my playlist at that point would be suitable. The unforgettable opening riff of the Rolling Stones, 'It's Only Rock 'n' Roll', filled the room. I turned to Eva for some sort of approval. She looked up and raised her eyebrows, 'Apt choice!' I darted towards her and we immediately resumed our passionate kiss. No words were necessary anymore as we made our intentions crystal clear. Playful flirting had now manifested into flaunting the raw attraction we were both pulled by. Our hands explored each other's bodies, and our breath became heavier. She led me towards the bed, still kissing as we both stumbled onto it in a surge of overpowering lust. I looked down at her. She appeared so vulnerable lay on her back awaiting my next move. I shuffled over onto my side and carried on kissing her, working my way towards the nape of her neck whilst guiding my hand up and down her body, feeling her firm breasts for the first time. She encouraged me to go further, showing no sign of awkwardness or restraint. My hand moved underneath her where I felt the zip of her dress. I began to slowly unzip it. She arched her back to help me pull it down, whilst simultaneously kicking her fashionable heels off. Once the zip reached the bottom I began helping her out of the dress, and then I threw it helplessly to the floor once she was free.

I stood up at the end of the bed, taking a necessary moment to admire and appreciate her perfectly toned half-naked frame, made sexier by the salacious, fiery red lingerie she'd been concealing. The sparkle from her necklace hypnotised me as it caught the light. She moved down towards me and sat on the end of the bed, and the cross pendant fell centrally between her breasts. I bent down to kiss her again as she slowly began to unbutton my black shirt, helping me out of it as the last button pinged loose. I began to move my hands around her back to undo her bra, which fortunately unfastened with minimal effort. I slowly pulled down the straps from her shoulders, causing the bra to drop to the floor, allowing her pert breasts to be free.

She looked up at me innocently, her hands finding the belt of my jeans. She calmly unbuckled it and pulled the buttons open one by one just as the music changed to

The Doors, 'Break on Through'. She looked salaciously at me, 'Another good choice,' she remarked, before carrying on unfastening the last button. I stepped out of the jeans and she shimmied her way back towards the top of the bed. I climbed back on and shuffled up towards her, touching and caressing the soft, smooth skin on her chest and flat tummy.

My hand moved across her thighs and meandered to her backside, gradually moving back again towards the inside of her legs. As soon as my fingers touched her through her soft panties she let out a gasp that brought about a flood of self-satisfaction, so I carried on teasing and pressing more firmly. I could feel her body quiver as she let out a series of moans and Spanish words that I didn't understand, but words that I didn't need to know the meaning of – the language itself was enough of a turn on! I never expected such a reaction from a gorgeous young woman, and her hypnotic accent just made me even more insatiable. I moved my hand away and knelt by the side of the bed, beginning to softly kiss and lick her inner thighs. I put both hands on either side of her panties and began to roll them down till she was completely stripped. I hesitated for a minute or so, letting her excitement build up as I reached her moist labia, flicking my tongue subtly so that only the tip touched her, before fully sinking my whole mouth around her. She arched her back sharply, letting out a groan that made me shudder. I had an inkling that I was good at oral sex (on a woman that is!) but this reaction was wild even for my vivid imagination. The fact she was enjoying it so much spurred me on to be more avid and daring, and with the strutting rock tunes still blazing through the speakers, it added an extra layer of confidence and coolness to what I was doing.

A wave of desire overcame my whole body, forcing me to stop and reach for a condom tucked inside the 'secret' compartment of my wallet, that may or may not have been close to its expiry date. Whilst I fumbled to rip the packet, she demonstrated her flexibility by opening her legs as wide as possible, leaving me in complete wonderment. I could only imagine how this was going to enhance the experience, and that image caused me to fumble further as my hands turned to jelly.

I eventually succeeded in my personal grapple and vendetta with Durex packaging. I yanked down my boxers and rolled the condom on before hovering over her. The build-up of all the hurt, frustration and passion that was stored inside of me rushed to the conscious surface, and before I knew it I was inside her. The moaning continued as she whispered, 'Oh my God!' Her voice struggled to let the words out. Her eyes were gently closed, and her mouth pursed open, which only served to heighten my own sensation. I began to move my hips slowly, but steadily, not wanting to rush the experience as our bodies locked sensually together.

The slow rhythm continued for a few minutes before the pace subtly quickened. It reached a point where my adventurous, animalistic side was overpowering, and she sensed that, gesturing for me to flip her over and start from behind, which I did with vigour. I became much more zealous, exerting slight aggression with my hands grabbing onto her clenching body. Watching her bounce up and down after hearing her repeatedly gasp was becoming too much. I turned her onto her back again to prolong the experience. Once inside her I penetrated harder and faster, and the pleasure now reached its extremity as we both moaned louder. I couldn't hold on any longer, despite my desire to keep the sensation going for as long as humanly possible. Before I knew it I uncontrollably released the tension, as did she, both climaxing together as her finger nails dug deep into my shoulder blades as I collapsed on top of her.

My head span in a whirlwind of rapture, and our breathing was heavy for the few seconds I remained on top of her. Her sweet taste and smell was heavenly, and the strong scent of her perfume was almost overpowering as my lips were planted deep into her neck. A range of emotions steamrollered me: relief, calmness, content, and a connection. Eva was still panting, and in the midst of her breathing, looking up at the ceiling, she could only verbalise the words, 'Fucking Vegas!' in that deliciously spellbinding tone of voice. I couldn't help but laugh as I lay immobile. Fucking Vegas indeed! I'd been here for about ten hours now and I could already get on board a statement like that.

We were both still breathing deeply, trying to comprehend what had just happened. I started to play with her again as my sexual instincts were now at a heightened point. I was making up for lost time and seizing the opportunity. It wasn't taking her long to reach climax again, seemingly unable to prevent herself from having orgasms. I lay nonchalantly beside her as she confessed that she didn't know what was happening to her as these multiple spurts of ecstatic joy seemed to attack her at my will, which had me bordering on cockiness.

She changed position to reciprocate the favour and told me to lie on my back and relax. Her head went down and as her mouth touched the tip of me it sent me into a world of ecstasy, causing me to mime inexplicable words. She was using the whole of her mouth and tongue, and the thought and feeling of those luscious, full lips around me was driving me wild and insane. The tension built up inside, but I didn't want to finish this way, I was too ravenous and wanted to see her pleasured. I reached for another condom, luckily having two in my wallet – wild man! I gestured for her to stop and pulled her up by her hips. I moved to sit on the end of the bed, beckoning Eva to position herself on top with her legs wrapped around me. We sat cradling each other, and she began to move up and down, grinding slowly but forcefully. She was still heavily moist, making me slide in and out with ease as the experience became just as perfect as the first time. She moved a little faster and I couldn't help but pick her up into a more adventurous position. I was standing up with her legs still wrapped around me, finding strength from somewhere, thrusting harder and deeper inside of her. The sensation was unbelievable! I fell onto the opposing bed with her, penetrating faster as I positioned her leg up high and outstretched, holding her close to me with my other arm gripped underneath her shoulders. Both her legs were now lingering helplessly in the air, flailing with every thrust. She brought her hand up to bite her finger, keeping her eyes closed as the encounter neared its end. I drove more powerfully, and my head was tucked into my chest as I inevitably reached the point of no return. The pace quickened, again the moaning grew louder, and visions became blurry as this euphoric feeling ran through us when we both climaxed together again. My head was spinning as I dropped on top of her, and I couldn't help but kiss her lips and neck as she lay writhing with a satisfied glow plastered all over her smiling face.

Her eyes slowly opened, but remained narrow, watery and blurred. She stared deep into mine with a look of beautiful innocence that made my heart dissolve. It felt like we were momentarily acting out a fantasy. Reality was clouded in those seconds, and my thoughts drifted. The image of us in that hotel room at that time looked like we'd been together for years, living in the middle of some old quaint village in the middle of nowhere in a deep rural part of Italy or somewhere similar, with a man playing 'Concierto de Aranjuez' on a mandolin outside our rustic apartment. This was an utterly crazy and forbidding feeling to have on this first night in Las Vegas! A hurricane of emotions engulfed me at the thought of how unthinkable and highly intimate this first night had turned out to be. I never expected this whatsoever! What had Vegas done to me already?

She began to speak, softly telling me that her mind had gone elsewhere, and she was powerless to stop herself from shaking, sensitive to the slightest of touches on her flush skin after what she'd just experienced. I played on that revelation and had her completely at my mercy. How the tide had turned after she had me at her mercy on the dance floor.

We lay on the bed completely naked and intimately toyed with each other, like all that mattered was within the confines of this Vegas room. She pulled herself up to lie on her side, using her hand to support her head before breaking the mood.

'Well Mr Englishman. That was unexpected,' she proclaimed.

'You're telling me.'

'I've got a confession.' She paused, before admitting, 'That's the first time I've had sex in two years.'

My eyes widened, startled. 'Seriously? How is that possible? Have you looked in a mirror lately and seen how gorgeous you are?'

'I guess I'm kind of fussy and don't just go with anyone. Don't get me wrong I've been on dates, but I've never really been attracted to anyone like this before.'

I moved my arm across her to stroke the silky base of her back, sensing the compliment that had just been thrown my way.

'You don't have to say anything similar. I know you're not in a place to say the same. I just think you're great Ricky, that's all.' I detected sorrow in her tone.

The thing was, in those intimate moments I did feel something similar. Was it because this was the first girl I'd been with since Mandy? Or was it because we were in Vegas? Maybe it was real, maybe not, but it certainly felt strong. It was an intense connection that I'd never felt before, but under such unrealistic circumstances

I couldn't be entirely sure what it was I was feeling. My vulnerable state could've been playing a part, and I was fully aware that the situation of being in Vegas was possibly deceiving me. I was not naive enough to confuse the issue like some loved up teenager. However, I was pretty sure there was something more profound at work here, and I shared those sentiments with her.

Eva agreed, 'I understand totally. It's just a shame we live on opposite sides of the world.'

'You're telling me. Life isn't fair sometimes. You'll forget all about me once you leave tomorrow...or in a few hours I should say,' I joked.

'Yeah, I probably will,' she sarcastically returned, adding, 'Don't be silly!'

She playfully hit me over the head with a pillow before nuzzling up on my chest, letting out a lethargic sigh.

We carried on talking about music, commenting on each quality song that ran one after another on this most potent of playlists. The rambunctiousness of heavier rock waivered and gave in to a calmer series of tracks from artists such as Neil Young, Bread and America - songs more fitting to the chilled mood.

Despite Eva's age she wasn't some airhead who was only into what was popular at the time. She appreciated the 60s and 70s music of the West Coast as well as the 'British Invasion'. She went on to talk about Mama Cass and the influence she had on her life, also saying that Genesis were probably her favourite band, especially the Peter Gabriel years. That was a strange choice from someone of her background, but maybe her travels around America as a kid had influenced her in some way, perhaps picking up the different music of diverse backgrounds and cultures. She even revealed that 'Solsbury Hill' was her favourite song of all time. I was impressed, but it made it even more intolerable to think that I had to let her go soon, and this gorgeous, intelligent young woman was about to be taken away from me as quickly as destiny had thrown her into my path.

Just being with her and talking in such depth throughout the night was like I finally understood the lyrics to Oasis', 'Talk Tonight'. Being with a girl so far away from home, who could possibly be saving my life on some level, was comparable to the song's profound meaning. I searched for it on my iPod and immersed us in this Mancunian love ballad. She had never heard the song before, but when she listened intently to the lyrics, she was moved by the similarities and how it related to us. From there we were practically commenting on every song being played that followed. Some she'd heard before and already loved, and some she hadn't but thought were cool. She even educated me on some bands that were more local to West Coast America, based on bands that she already knew I liked. I made a mental note to check them out when I returned home.

Time dragged on and eventually she lifted her head from my chest and turned to face me, giving me several repetitive kisses on my lips before quietly whispering, 'I have to go Ricky, but I've got another secret to tell you.'

'What's that then?'

'I don't want to leave.'

'I don't want you to either, but you know you have to.'

'You could come with me.'

I pondered on that fantasy again for a moment, but I knew I couldn't.

'Any other time in life then I'd be packing my bags right now, but I have to stay here. Apart from this only being my first night and wanting to see this place for all its worth, I know I'm meant to stay here for a reason. I hope you realise how much it pains me to say that.'

She nodded in acknowledgement, indolently lifting herself from the bed to get back into her clothes that were scattered around the room. I have to admit that I was saddened at the thought that very soon I would probably never see her again. Not that I yearned for a holiday romance or anything like that, especially in Vegas of all places, but I didn't expect this to happen. If she lived closer to home I'd certainly meet her again in a heartbeat, but I had to be realistic. She lived on the other side of the world and we both came from entirely different cultures. The temptation to take her up on her offer to go with her on the trip up the West Coast was hard to resist, but I was in Vegas for the long haul. I wasn't prepared to abandon it after one night of passion and a possibility of letting vulnerability cloud my judgement. My place was here and something inside told me that whatever I was searching for was right here.

There was a slight lull in the conversation, not out of awkwardness, but more out of melancholy emotions. I opened the door to our room and followed her out, putting my arm around her shoulders as we unhurriedly walked towards the lift. As the lift doors opened she turned to fling her arms around me and hug me tightly, whispering in my ear that she'd had a fabulous time. I flashed a wry smile back to show her I couldn't have agreed more.

Once we were outside Planet Hollywood she requested a taxi from the valet and there we waited quietly for a few minutes, not wanting to add more sentiment to the conversation to make parting more difficult than it already was. She turned to me again, piercing me with those seductive Hispanic eyes, lightly grabbing the front of my shirt to pull me towards her for another alluring kiss.

She then broke away and began to speak, 'Listen you! Make sure you enjoy the rest of your vacation. It will get easier. I know it will. By the time Vegas ends you'll see the bigger picture, I promise you that.'

I nodded before changing the subject. 'Some night eh?'

'You've got that right. Amazing really! Fucking Vegas!' We both laughed at our own newly found private joke.

The taxi pulled up and she spoke softly in my ear, 'If I don't go now I never will. You take care of yourself.'

'You too. Enjoy your road trip and be good,' I responded mournfully, before giving her one final affectionate goodbye hug and kiss.

She got into the cab and kept her eyes fixed on mine, blowing a kiss at me through the window before the taxi pulled away and disappeared around the corner, creating an uncared for sorrow in the pit of my stomach.

It was now ten in the morning, meaning I'd been up for thirty-three hours straight, a personal record that was fitting to smash in Vegas under such inconceivable circumstances. I made my way back up to the room as I reflected on the last twenty-four hours or so, focusing more on Eva and how mind blowing the experience had been.

Once I got in bed my mind wandered again, but the smile that had dominated the whole night slowly eroded when the harsh reality of the ex flooded back. Before I knew it, all the great thoughts of Eva were washed away as the anger, hurt and puzzlement rushed at me again. It was like the evening had only papered over the cracks. I knew there had to be a point where I would have to face this head on and find answers that felt right for me to move on. It was as if the past still had a hold over me, and I was bound by some weird connection that I couldn't understand and certainly didn't want to be tied to. I had to keep faith that Vegas would provide answers in the form of something that hadn't made itself known to me yet.

I had been in Las Vegas a matter of hours, left in awe at its greatness, and had a fantastic first night, but that wasn't enough to find peace. What was this hold over me? Why couldn't I move on and live this adventure free from grief. I know you have to go through trauma to get over something, but I felt I'd done that. It was clear that I hadn't gone through enough!

Dominated by troubled thoughts, I fell asleep...for

three hours before I was wide awake again, hoping that answers might come on this first full day in Las Vegas.

CHAPTER 7

I was wakened by Ian entering the room shortly after 1pm. Initially I felt awful - unsurprising after only having a few hours sleep. I began to come around quickly due to the amount of oxygen being pumped into the room from the air ducts. My mind was a little hazy, and it took me a few seconds to recollect the events of the previous night with Eva. I checked my phone to see I had a new message from her. All it read was, *'Fucking Vegas! X'*. But my smile was promptly wiped when the past came flooding back, yet again shadowing any goodness going on in life. I longed for the day when it wouldn't be the last thing I thought of when I went to bed, and the first thing I thought of when I woke up.

I lay back against the headboard, arms clasped behind the back of my head, remembering that Ian and Johnny had had their own night to contend with.

'Hey! How was last night? I almost forgot you stayed with those Bolton girls.'

'It was all a bit mad! I ended up sleeping in Johnny and Turner's room with Julie,' Ian explained.

'Refresh my memory? Which one was Julie?'

'The smaller one with dark hair. The least attractive one.'

'Ah right. Go on!'

'Nothing happened in *that* respect, so don't start! I could've done if I wanted to but I wasn't into her at all. I was fuckin' knackered and just wanted to go to bed, but she kept yapping at me all night. Gob bigger than the kitchen sink, that one! I just wanted to find the off switch on her.'

I smirked before he continued.

'I can't say the same for Johnny. He ended up in Vicky's room so I presume he got lucky considering he was hanging around her like flies around shit all night. You should've seen him smooching her before they left. Sloppy tongues and all sorts of horrible sounds. Embarrassing!' Ian shuddered on recollecting the image.

'I've already spoke to him this morning though. We're gonna get some food if you fancy it?' Ian suggested.

'Definitely, I'm starving! What about Turner? Did he not come back?'

'Not seen Turner since we left the casino last night. He was talking to some blonde, wasn't he?'

'Yeah, but I left before he did. He must've got lucky himself then.'

'I'm sure he'll tell us all about it later once he surfaces. Anyway, what about you? What happened with that Latino bird? She was smokin'!'

'She was! Amazing is all I can say.'

'See, that's all you needed mate. I bet you're feeling better already about that bitch from home?'

'You'd think so wouldn't you? I think it's only papered over the cracks.'

'You're odd! You've probably just been with the fittest girl of your life, you're in Vegas, and you still can't get over her, can you?' His voice had taken on a sterner tone.

'It's not that I *want* to be like this. By rights last night should've been the key to moving on, but it's not. There's still some shit there I need to deal with. Don't worry, I guarantee it'll be gone by the time we go back home. I won't be moping or being a miserable bastard. How can I be? I'm in Vegas, like you said.'

'I know you won't pal. Just deal with this quickly and forget about her. She's a dick! You know it, I know it, everyone knows it.'

'I wish you would've told me that a few years ago.'

'Well she had us all fooled. Anyway, bollocks to this morbid conversation! Let's get some food. I said we'd meet at Johnny's room.'

I threw on my newly purchased Superdry shorts and Manchester United vest to illustrate where my allegiances lay, and to also be a token Brit abroad, but I didn't quite plummet to the ridiculousness of socks and sandals.

We met Johnny outside his room. I couldn't help but give him a cheeky grin implying that I knew what he'd been up to.

Before giving me a chance to say anything he began, 'I don't know what you're grinning at! What happened with you and that Puerto Rican chick?'

'A gentleman never tells.'

'Well it's a good job you're not one then isn't it,' he snapped.

The heat was blistering out in the open, causing us to throw our sunglasses on. The sun was high in the sky with only a few clouds scattered about to offer a moments shade and comfort from the sun's piercing rays. We walked down the Strip, heading further into Las Vegas Boulevard where hordes of people roamed the streets. Surprisingly, the guys who could deliver, 'women to your room in twenty minutes', were still working at this time of the day. You had to love Vegas!

We came to a casino about ten minutes down the road called, Bill's Gambling Hall & Saloon, and we stopped to get something to eat as the heat was already beginning to tire us out.

The place had a dated, but cool vibe, awash with the weirdly addictive stench of cigars, bourbon and gambling. It wasn't like the grandeur of Caesars Palace or Planet Hollywood that we'd already experienced, but there was a history and unpretentious essence that was captivating in nature. 60s and 70s rock 'n' roll music echoed through the hall, paying tribute to greats such as Lynyrd Skynyrd and Pink Floyd, perfectly in keeping with this rough and tumblin' venue. The clientele looked like the original pioneers of a glorious age in music. Faces looked weathered and full of character, mirroring the spirit of the Wild West saloon theme. I presumed that amongst the punters there must've been some wild stories to tell.

I felt the need for a strong coffee and a fresh orange

to cure the dry mouth and slight hangover. Johnny coaxed me into telling him what happened with Eva, so I began to tell bits of the tale, but not in any great detail whatsoever. Some things had to remain private. I returned the question, and his night seemed a little less meaningful than mine as he bluntly told us that he, 'just ended up shagging her, nowt special.' He added that, 'it wasn't exactly a performance I was proud of,' blaming his own drunkenness, tiredness and 'first night blues' for the anti-climax and awkwardness. He went on to say that the girls were leaving later that day so there would be no danger of running into them again. I was quick to point out that because they lived in Bolton, one day he might run into them again. His face dropped at that thought.

The food arrived, and the truth behind the legend of American portion sizes became apparent. The omelette I ordered was ginormous, Johnny's burger was gargantuan, and Ian's club sandwich came in four triple-deckers covering the whole plate. At least we knew we were getting our money's worth, despite all of us struggling to finish them.

We slowly staggered back to the hotel, letting the food digest properly before heading down to the pool for a relaxing afternoon. The swimming pool area at Planet Hollywood was very different from what we were used to in the Mediterranean. Pools on our previous holidays had been relatively small with beds surrounding the area. The pools themselves were standard in terms of a shallow end at one side, which gradually got deeper at the other end. Pool areas are usually a place to chill and laugh, with frequent games of 'Donkey', which was in essence just volleyball 'keepy uppy' in the pool: a game that was highly entertaining and broke down barriers with fellow pool users, usually of the female variety. Unfortunately, the game was impossible to play in Vegas because the pool had no deep end, and it seemed like it was a place for posers to stand and show off their ripped and waxed bodies. As no such bodies existed amongst us, there would be no requirement to pose in a similar fashion, so we found some beds out of the way, quietly proud of our hairy chests and untoned bellies.

Of course, the bonus of this environment was that the posers weren't just men, as the women were guilty of the perfect body too. So much time was spent constantly turning our heads and commenting on pretty much every girl that walked passed us. They all wore bikinis or sarongs, not an ounce of fat on any of them. You could bounce a penny off any of their arse cheeks at ten paces. Once again, I felt like I was in the middle of Playboy City, forget Playboy Mansion.

Down the steps from the pool was a sunbathing haven, where the air was greased with the odour of Ambre Solaire. We spent the afternoon recapping on the night, and I found myself badgering on about Eva like some kid who'd just lost his virginity. I was still receiving text messages from her that brought the odd sarcastic remark from the others, about being 'loved up' and 'smitten' already. I declined to comment. Johnny thought it'd be funny to wind me up further, and on top note sing, 'It Must Have Been Love', by Roxette, which brought about peculiar stares from our fellow sunbathers.

The laughs continued when Turner eventually surfaced to join us. He looked a complete wreck, having made no attempt to clean himself up. His hair was completely dishevelled like he'd been dragged through a hedge backwards. The night clearly had an adverse effect on him as he slumped onto the sunbed with his towel wrapped around his head for comfort. The same questions were put to him as they were to me and Johnny, and he confirmed our presumptions, telling us that he had spent the night in the room of the American he was talking to. She was a friend of one of the cocktail waitresses working behind Heart Bar, and due to this connection, she managed to score a free room for the night on the sly. I asked whether he was going to see her again. He brushed off the question as being ridiculous. Perhaps it was just me who found sentimental value on the first night...or was I just the soft arse of the group? Probably the latter.

Nonetheless, the holiday had got off to a flyer and we were riding high indeed, not just from our first night, but being by the pool was a great laugh in general. Ian had inexplicably, and in error, brought some glittered Hawaiian Topic sun cream. Priceless! We stifled our sniggers as we watched him smear it all over himself before he noticed. He looked a prized prick, taking an almighty and deserved ripping for such a blunder, but I suppose if you're going to wear glittered sun cream anywhere, then Vegas would be the place to get away with it. He washed it off in a nearby shower and borrowed some of my more appropriate cream before anyone other than us noticed.

Johnny and Turner were in fine humorous form, recreating scenes and lines from comedy TV shows. 'Bottom', along with 'Alan Partridge', was the main source of amusement yet again. The laughs moved on as we brought up classic stories and incidents from our past, like: who got so drunk that they fell asleep in a stranger's front garden? Who suffered complete embarrassment by being caught having sex in the bathroom by their own mother? Who shaved too much of their beard off and coloured it in with a black biro? Who lost his shoe when trying to jump a taxi? Who went to the toilet in a club only to find there was no toilet roll so had to use their socks as a bog roll? And who spent the night in cells for public urination down the most secluded alley way imaginable? It's such an important factor on holiday! There's a need to laugh constantly at jokes that are born from the current trip or the revisiting of classic ones from the past that have shaped our friendship.

Johnny and Ian eventually went venturing into the pool to ogle at the women, whilst Turner and I caught some rays, although grabbing some shut-eye was a necessity for him. I slipped my iPod on and listened to a medley of Fleetwood Mac hits to provide a soundtrack to the relaxed atmosphere. An opportunity arose now I was chilled in calming surroundings. I knew at some point I had to be brave and submerge myself completely into the events of the past few months. The time had come to revisit the whole story of why, and how, I was in such a mess over my ex, Mandy. 'Dreams' by Fleetwood Mac started playing and encouraged the recollection process.

CHAPTER 8

It was by complete chance that I met Mandy. Call it a twist of fate if you will, but it really did boil down to some kind of calling of destiny, making me believe that I was going to spend the rest of my life with this woman.

It was just over five years ago, and I was on Turner's birthday night out in Manchester with lots of friends. We were in a club that was a bit of a dive, and despite it being late into the night and most of the others wanting to stay put, me and Ian wanted to move on. There was only an hour or so left of the night, and the restrictions on licences weren't as relaxed as they are today, but I remembered saying that we needed to go because, 'something unexpected can still happen tonight that isn't happening in here.' Ian agreed with me, but probably more out of desperation to leave the club we were currently in rather than any kind of epiphany.

We left and walked down Peter Street till we came to a bar called Life, a place I'd seen on several occasions, but never actually ventured into. From outside, we could hear a soulful Motown-esque band playing that sounded fantastic, and on looking inside we could see the dance floor was busy.

'What do you reckon to here?' I asked Ian.

'I dunno. I was thinking of going Mojos.'

'It can be a bit hit and miss in there. This place looks a good laugh though. We should check it out. Who knows? It could be a future haunt.'

'It's up to you. I'm just glad to be out of that shithole. Fuckin' terrible music! At least it sounds decent in here, but Mojos might be better. It's your call.'

'Let's leave it up to fate. Heads we go in Life, tails we go Mojos.'

And just like that, left to the gods of chance, where I assigned 'heads' to Life, my whole life direction would completely change. I fell under the spell of an excitable feeling, as if there was a reason why I was meant to be there that night, and I was just waiting for that reason to make itself known to me.

The resident band rocked the venue to create a great atmosphere by playing a series of old classics, which appeased the punters. The clientele looked a little older and more sophisticated than the people who frequented the usual places we visited. That appealed on several levels, almost like being with more like-minded people.

After buying a bottle of Budweiser each, me and Ian hit the dance floor to get our groove on amongst everybody else and attempt to soak in the good vibes.

We must've only been on there five minutes or so when I felt someone grab my hand from behind and slip it into a second person's hand. At first, I was startled and jolted, having no clue what was going on, but upon turning around I was hit by the proverbial thunderbolt as Mandy stood in front of me. She looked gorgeous, body to die for and long blonde hair that complemented her tanned skin tone. Her eyes were striking, dazzlingly sultry with the way her dark make-up had been brushed on, and I knew the moment we locked eyes with each other that she was the girl I'd been looking for, and why I'd felt this weird premonition and pull to come into this bar in the first place.

As it turned out, it was her friend who had grabbed my hand and planted it into Mandy's. Her friend, Wendy, had taken it upon herself to find a bloke for Mandy that night and had chosen me. Apparently, they had been watching me as soon as I hit the bar.

The rest you could say was history up until recent events. We began casually seeing each other every couple of weeks, and then the length of time without meeting became shorter and shorter, until after three years we eventually moved in together. I couldn't have been happier in those early years of the relationship, and I genuinely thought I'd found the person I was meant to be with for the rest of my life. We went on many relaxing beach type holidays together, ate out often, enjoyed many private jokes, and were very comfortable and very close to each other in those days. Yeah, I suppose you could say that I was very much in love with Mandy. She was a bit of a high flyer and was a highly regarded solicitor within the law firm she worked at, which was very different to who I was. Our beliefs were different, but we still seemed to work perfectly together, and we kept work life separate from everyday life. Maybe the notion of opposites attracting really held some weight.

I wouldn't say I was intimidated or belittled by her

success at all. I embraced it and felt proud of her for what she was accomplishing, and I never expected anything from her despite her earning much more than I did. As far as I was concerned we were on a level playing field, and how much money she earned or how highly regarded she was in her profession meant nothing when it came to the idea of love and having a real connection with someone – at least that's how I saw it.

However, despite us enjoying a great time together, the last six months of our relationship had become a little disjointed. Admittedly, I was getting more aggravated with my working life, but I never brought that misery home with me. Mandy, on the other hand, appeared a little distant, becoming more and more short tempered as arguments began to creep into our life, something that had never happened in the past. She blamed it on the stress of work in many cases, but sometimes I felt like there was a dig in there aimed at me, almost like I wasn't good enough anymore, or I wasn't matching up to her status of working in law. Her remarks about money were sometimes unnerving. She earned at least double what I did, but we still contributed equal shares to the rent and bills and were still comfortable after that first of the month expenditure. Nonetheless, I started to sense she wanted more, despite her lofty salary. Greed breeds greed, so I was slightly concerned that Mandy may have been slipping down that slope, but I ignored it thinking it was just a moment she was having and it'd pass.

There weren't really many humdinger arguments where I thought that's it, we're over. I just put it down to a rocky patch and we would eventually come through it. I was even half thinking of making the grandest gesture of all in the weeks leading up to our split. I thought that the possibility of proposing could get us back on track, but I hadn't made my mind up yet on that front. The idea remained lodged in my mind somewhere to be used in the future when the time felt right. But that time would never come!

One Friday evening I found myself stuck in work later than usual. Considering Mandy was extremely distant the night before and refused to tell me what was wrong, I didn't mind staying late on this occasion to avoid going home.

I parked up outside the house to see that her car wasn't there and I assumed she'd worked late too, making me aggrieved that my reason for staying late was pointless. I got out of the car and made my way up the short driveway to the front door of our rented town house. Once I'd let myself in I headed straight for the stairs to where the kitchen and living room were on the first floor. Rather than slump straight away on the couch, I headed for the kitchen to begin dinner to get the chore out of the way. I reached the doorway and stopped short as I was about to head to the fridge. An envelope caught my eye, stood upright resting against an empty pint glass on the kitchen counter with the word 'Ricky' scrawled across it. I wondered what the hell it was. It obviously hadn't been sent in the post having just my name on, and the handwriting was instantly recognisable as being Mandy's. The curve on the 'y' gave it away.

I didn't know what to make of it as I stared intensely at the envelope. In all the years we'd been together she'd never left a note. This was the twenty first century, all communication was by text messaging, phone call or social media. A note didn't feel right. I began to feel apprehensive, sensing something bad was nestling in the words written inside. My stomach was doing somersaults, and all sorts of random ideas of what lay within ran through my mind. I should've just opened it immediately, but I froze with fear. I turned away and bypassed the fridge and ended up at the drinks cabinet, pulling a nearly full bottle of Jack Daniels from the front. I took a clean, small breakfast glass from the neighbouring cupboard, poured myself a shot and sat down on the stool within arm's reach of the letter. I continued to stare, shitting myself, knowing that my life could turn on its head as soon as I opened it. I downed the bourbon to try and calm myself, not even flinching as the burn ran down my throat and into my belly. I poured another and reached over, taking the envelope cautiously by its edges, spinning it in my hand as I contemplated my next move. It wasn't even sealed properly so it opened easily. I pulled out the note that was folded and written on plain white paper, and faced reality as I unfolded the letter and began to read its earth-shattering content.

Ricky,

This is the hardest thing I've ever had to do and

I just didn't have the heart or strength to say this face to face and end up having an argument. I think we've hit a wall in our relationship and I can't see us coming back from it. I've realised in the last few weeks that we're becoming two very different people, and I think we'll drag each other down if we stay together. I think I'm better off not being with you anymore and I need to start afresh somewhere else.

Please don't try and contact me. I won't answer the phone. It's probably best to be done this way to avoid us going through hours of discussing and arguing and making it worse.

A part of me will always love you.

Take care of yourself.

Mandy

The note fell helplessly to the floor as I lost all feeling in my hands. My head began to spin. Anger and hurt boiled up inside me as I released a roar of emotion that echoed through the kitchen. The cursing and shouting started too, and my head fell into my hands against the table. The tears flowed as the hurt and confusion poured out of me. Refusing to take heed of Mandy's advice, I reached for my phone and called her several times, but every time it went straight to voicemail. On the fifth attempt, I left a message along the lines of,

'What the fuck is going on Mandy? How can you do this to me? Please contact me so we can talk it out!' It wasn't exactly the calmest of messages I ever left, but given what had just been thrown at me, it was well justified.

The JD became a source of comfort, and before I knew it I was pouring myself another shot, then another, then dispensing with the glass all together as I began to swig straight from the bottle, slumped on the couch now with tear filled puffy eyes, trying to contain my grief. When the bottle ran out I went straight for the remaining half bottle of Brandy. It didn't take too long to polish that off too, and inevitably I passed out, only to wake up with the mother of all hangovers, made worse as I recollected the previous day's news.

Every attempt to contact Mandy in the days that followed was unsuccessful. Her phone was constantly off, and she wasn't on social media, so I couldn't even contact her that way. I didn't have any numbers for her friends, and she didn't have much family about, certainly no one close enough who might know where she was. I even went to her work one day and was told that she had booked some time off without giving any specific reason for it. The mystery escalated when I learnt this had been booked a couple of weeks before she left me. It did seem that they were just as much in the dark as me about why she was absent. It was as if she'd fallen off the edge of the earth and really had run away with no explanation. The more I thought about how she could do such a thing, the more puzzled I became. It was extremely difficult to take and I felt something more was going on that I couldn't get to the bottom of. I constantly churned over the situation, conjuring up all sorts of illusions surrounding our relationship, trying to find any one reason that may have resulted in her leaving in the manner she had, but I always drew a blank. I even felt guilty about booking the trip to Vegas months before she left, as if that somehow contributed to her leaving, however silly that sounded. She didn't appear pissed off about it though. After all, I'd been away with my mates every year we'd been together and it'd never been an issue.

The emotional pain became a constant irritant I couldn't shake off. I knew I still loved Mandy and I didn't want to split up, and it didn't seem like we were in any real danger of splitting beforehand, so it became extremely hard to take on the chin. I still harboured hopes for reconciliation at some point, half expecting her to waltz back through the door, putting her exit down to a moment of madness. I suppose I was in denial, but the thought of us being over was too unbearable.

A week had passed and I'd given up trying to contact her as it was proving a futile activity. The psychology of emotion kicked in and impacted hard when the lonely nights drew in. I began to blame myself for everything in my ominous grief, thinking about where I could've done things differently. A split under these circumstances, with not one direct incident big enough to justify it, can cause more psychological fuck ups than anything else, leaving me to battle with my own conscience, and that was driving me insane.

I turned to music, which can be a dangerous road to turn down. On one hand, I could temporarily mask over the pain by listening to some heavy rock like Led Zeppelin, but then be caught unexpectedly off guard when a song came on that reminded me of her, instantly having the capability and power to take me down again. It's amazing how many songs you can associate with your ex, even ones that had no bearing on the relationship whatsoever. There are ones that do mean something, and probably always will, but then any cheesy love song about heartache is instantaneously associated to the situation, as if the songwriter had you in mind when writing the lyrics. Artists like Sinead O'Connor, Barry White and Al Green, despite their obvious talents, immediately become the work of the devil. I even did my Rocky Balboa moment, revisiting the past whilst driving at full pelt down the motorway at midnight to Robert Tepper's, 'No Easy Way Out', without a care for speed limits or any dangers to myself. It's staggering the shit you can come up with when you're feeling vulnerable.

Three weeks passed and still no word from Mandy. I couldn't carry on living under this cloud and being so miserable all the time. I had to attempt to move on, however hard it felt. Of course, it still caused a torturous pain inside whenever I thought about what had happened, but I couldn't wallow in self-pity like I had been doing so far. I had to try and move forward for my own sanity. The Vegas trip was nearing, which I'd half forgotten about in my grief. The trip threw a spanner in the works of moving on straight away because of the money I'd need to make sure Vegas was to live up to expectation. A break up of this magnitude usually required being out all the time, getting pissed and meeting women, trying everything and anything to take my mind off what was happening. Of course, I could still go out and enjoy myself, but to the extent of being out three or four times a week, as I'd done after a past break up while at university? That was a definite no, no. This time I would have to go through the split properly, and not mask over it with a drink and sex fuelled binge that only succeeded in papering over the cracks. Given the circumstances, I wasn't sure if I could survive it this time around without breaking down due to my over analytical nature.

It proved more difficult than I imagined. The reality of the change in relationship status and hardship of loss hit me like a knockout blow! All the emotional sorrow came out! Tears, head trauma, constant stomach churning, and panic crept up my spine. I yearned for her return. All those negative feelings made an unpleasant and unwelcome appearance and I slowly slipped into free-fall within an emotional abyss.

There seemed nowhere for me to go at that point and all thoughts of Vegas were lost. I was completely washed away in a whirlpool of my own sadistic world, surrounded by chaos in an over imaginative and over analytical tornado with no way out. I was locked in a cell of emotion, unable to see beyond my own imprisonment, failing to grasp the opportunities that could lie ahead as a single man.

Although I was failing to find the motivation to go out drinking and trying to pull, I did try another way to move on, and that was keeping me occupied. I was rekindling old interests that began to take up much of my focus and attention, keeping me busy during this difficult period. I was actively attending gigs on the underground scene in and around Manchester, which required very little cash and, because I drove, I didn't have to drink.

It was a breath of fresh air to be subjected to hearing all the great new music that would probably never be commercialised despite its creative ingenuity. It gave me hope that rock 'n' roll wasn't dead. It lived on in these hidden pockets of city life. Knowing this provided a suitable distraction from Mandy, and I was thoroughly enjoying the different bands I'd see most nights, being blown away by several. I had an old university friend, Matt, who flitted in and out of the music industry in a volunteer/working capacity. He was a photographer by trade and did the odd shoot with bands. When he heard about me and Mandy splitting up he invited me to a gig. 'Just like the old days' is how he put it. He was right. It was good to feel like I had done years earlier, but this time I felt more of a connection with the sound, more attuned and experienced in the ways of music. Matt encouraged me to get more involved. 'At uni you always said about working in music. I always thought you would've done and should've done. Why not try again? I have a few contacts to get you started.'

I was tempted and considered it. In what capacity? I had no idea, but just attending gigs, getting a feel for the scene and speaking to people was enough of a distraction at that moment.

The Las Vegas trip was looming, and I was finally starting to build a buzz about that. It started entering my dreams: what was going to happen and how would it all look. I could feel myself slowly moving on now, and I even managed to successfully go on a night out without any emotional repercussions, but lingering in the depths of my soul was always that question – why had she left? One day I was sure the truth would come out, but until that day I had to focus on getting myself in the right frame of mind to continue with life.

There were two weeks to go until Vegas and I allowed a little giddiness and anticipation to seep into everyday thinking. Whilst still feeling a little vulnerable and emotional, I was more accepting about moving on, and it was so important that I kept my focus by attending gigs to divert the attention away from my emotions.

Then at lunchtime on a Tuesday afternoon, I ventured to the supermarket near work like I usually did. After parking up some distance from the entrance, I saw a figure get out of her car at the same time and approach me.

'Hello Ricky!'

My nerves unravelled, completely unprepared to see Wendy, a familiar friend of Mandy's and the instigator of our relationship some five years earlier. Initially I was stunned into silence, but then I thought this was my chance to finally get the answers that had evaded me for so long. I suspected that was why Wendy happened to find herself in the same supermarket I go to at lunchtimes from work.

Her face looked awkward upon seeing me. 'You're looking well. How're you doing?'

'How do you think I'm doing?'

'Look, I know it must be hard, but I wanted you to know that I completely disagree with how Mandy has handled this.'

'Well that's comforting to know.' I hadn't lost my ability to be sarcastic. 'You spoke to her then I take it.'

'Yes. I've spoke to her.'

'Well I'm glad some fucker has.'

'She just didn't want to tell you the truth to your face, Ricky!'

That jolted me, a real bolt from the blue now that I knew there was more to this than met the eye. For better or worse did I want to know the truth at this point? I'd worked too hard to get my head straight without knowing. The truth at this stage could set me back, but it seemed that Wendy was going to tell me whether I liked it or not.

'You deserve the truth,' she continued.

'Do I want to hear this?'

'You have to. Mandy wants you too.'

'Well why the FUCK won't she tell me herself?'

'She's afraid to tell you.'

'Fuckin' coward…what could be so bad that she couldn't tell me to my face?'

'She's engaged to someone else!'

Wendy's words were like poison. The sheer weight of them made me feel light-headed and dizzy. A sickness grew in the pit of my stomach to the point where I thought I was about to throw up there and then. I suppose deep down I knew, on some level, that someone else must be involved, but to hear the words confirming that, stung like a fucker. At least it started to make sense.

'What...?' My voice tailed off.

'She's engaged.' Wendy repeated.

'Who to?'

'Is it important?'

'Who the fuck to Wendy?'

'Some guy she met at a law conference.'

'Another solicitor then?'

'Yeah.'

'Have you met him?'

'Look….'

'HAVE YOU MET HIM?'

'Yes.'

'What's he like?'

'Older.'

'Thought so. How much older?'

'Fifteen years.'

'Fifteen years older!? Are you fuckin' kidding me?'

'He's a partner in a firm I believe.'

'Well that figures doesn't it...older and richer, and can do wonders for her career. Probably an arrogant fuck too.' The anger began to boil. Wendy smiled in a way that suggested I'd hit the nail on the head.

'Yeah...I thought as much. So, what do you expect me to do with this information?' I asked.

'I just thought you should know.'

'Whilst she was with me I take it?' I dared to ask the question.

Wendy looked down and paused before answering, 'Yes.'

'Fucking great! How long?'

'I don't know Ricky.'

'How fucking long Wendy?'

'About three months.'

'Three months?? And engaged after three months?? What kind of…?? Never mind! Is she happy…or is that a stupid question?' I asked.

'I don't know what's going on Ricky. Honestly, I liked you both together and I'm disappointed this has happened, but something isn't right about it. It just doesn't seem like her to do something so dramatic.'

'Well the signs have been there Wendy. I didn't know it would extend to this, but she's talked about money and status for the last few months now and it's been unsettling.'

'She has acted a little differently lately, but I don't know what's going on in her head. I'm not convinced how real this is.'

'Well…it doesn't matter now does it. That's where she's at. Thanks for delivering the good news. Tell the happy couple to expect my gift in the post…that's if I knew where the fuck she was. Where the fuck is she now anyway?'

'Alderley Edge.'

'Haha. Really? Well the plot comes together. Well I never expected Mandy would go for the quick fix of selling her soul to the devil. I guess you never really know someone until the carrot is dangled. Tell Mandy and Lord Fuckin' Whatshisface to fuck the fuck off, and when they get there, fuck off again.'

I left without getting lunch and went straight home, phoning work on the way to say that I'd been struck down by sickness and wouldn't be back that day. I went straight for the JD again and spent the rest of the day wrapped in a glass case of emotion, drinking myself into oblivion, and like a dickhead I got my phone out and committed the cardinal sin of drunk texting Mandy.

'Just seen Wendy! Why Mandy? Why? How the fuck did it come to this?'

And then, by magic, my phone beeped and I had a reply, and one that completely gutted and demolished me in one foul, uncalled for swoop.

'I'm sorry, but I've met an amazing man and I'm really happy, and we're looking to the future together. I wish you well. Mandy.'

She should've remained quiet and neglected to reply, which is what I did after she sent that. Anger, disbelief and shock were all emotions that rushed to the surface as I felt like dropping to my knees, completely robbed of all strength. What was the point in sending a text saying that, and in such detail? The words 'amazing man', 'really happy' and 'looking to the future' stung me. It was so cruel, calculated, bitchy, callous, ill mannered, childish, and unprovoked. Five years together burnt to the ground as if it meant nothing at all. It felt like she was trying to rub it in, but what had I done to deserve to be treated so badly? There was no need! She had broken up with *me*, not the other way around!

I hadn't even contemplated the idea of her running off with someone else whilst we were together. There was never any indication of that. Yes, she used to go on about money and status in the latter months, but I had no idea this was related to someone she'd been seeing behind my back. But I guess you can never see what's right under your nose.

I didn't know what to believe as several possibilities raced through my mind. Was it the whole truth or some sort of delusion on her part? Three months of being with someone, sneaking around behind my back and then getting married just seemed farcical. An older man too! 'Mr Amazing' as she referred to him! A proper twat I reckon. What part did he play in all this? Did he know about me and yet still pursued her? I felt an anger and rage like nothing before, and there was fuck all I could do about it. I struggled to see how I could come back from this. With Vegas only two weeks away, all thoughts and excitement had been lost.

The days flittered away and with only two days till the trip, I had to concentrate on getting my head a little straighter, but it was difficult. My mission statement and mantra had changed. I clung onto the prospect of Vegas being an opportunity to step away from everything, where it would hopefully act as the catalyst to rid me of the pain caused by Mandy, and to discover what was next in my own life chapter.

There was still time for Mandy to drive the knife in further with only two days to go till Vegas. Whilst at work I received a phone call off her on my mobile. I ignored it. She had nothing to say that could interest me anymore and with two days to go I wasn't prepared to risk another emotional battering beforehand. Five minutes later it rang again and I instantly rejected it. On the third call, fifteen minutes later I answered angrily, shouting, 'What?' down the phone. All I could hear was background noise, no answer, no voices. It was as if the phone had gone off in her pocket, which I felt was just too much of a coincidence to be the absolute truth. Accidental calls had never happened before, so why did they happen now after all that'd gone on. The phone didn't ring again all night.

The day before Vegas was dampened by a further call from Mandy. I answered the first one and the same background noise happened for five seconds before the line went dead. What the hell was going on? She knew I was going to Vegas the next day, so was this just some cunning ploy to get in my head beforehand and stop me enjoying it? It added to the confusion in my mind, and a further three calls I rejected that day only added to the mystery.

● ● ●

As I lay baking in the Vegas sun, recapping on the past couple of months, now soundtracked by Fleetwood Mac's, 'Go Your Own Way', Mandy remained in my thoughts, yet I still wrestled with finding the answers as to how things got so messed up. I had to put these thoughts to bed for the day because it just confused and hurt me even more, but one thing was for certain, I still couldn't let go and I was still feeling the pain!

Early evening was approaching, and the night would soon be upon us. We left the pool area to get ready after it'd been decided we'd visit one of Vegas' many strip clubs. Turner had been talking to a bloke called Tony the previous night whilst I was with Eva and the others were with the Bolton girls. He was a guy who arranged Limo rides and free entry to the strip clubs for $20. I wasn't a huge fan of strip clubs. I'd lost all interest when I was a bit younger, having been tied up onstage and subjected to a strip tease from two strippers in front of everyone on my 20th birthday, which ended with my shirt coming off and ice being thrown down my jeans. No dance could better that, or be more humiliating, so I hadn't bothered since. Also, with age, I'd seen through the whole charade - how the strippers manipulate you to part with your money. However, the lads were up for it and let's face it, it would've been a cataclysmic sin not to visit and experience a Vegas strip club…and, ahem, maybe have a dance too!

CHAPTER 9

The unquenchable splendour of New York New York Hotel and Resort was to be our first destination on the second night. The plan was to have something to eat, have a little gamble, a few drinks, and then head back to Planet Hollywood to meet the rep, Tony, who would organise the transport to Olympic Gardens Strip Club. Turner was a vision of eagerness beforehand, first to be ready so he could meet Tony on the casino floor to book the outing.

We decided to soak in the scenery and atmosphere and walk down Las Vegas Boulevard to New York New York, which was in the opposite direction to Caesars Palace. As we reached the resort, the landmarks that made it instantly recognisable loomed upon us: The Chrysler Building, The Empire State Building, Brooklyn Bridge and the Statue of Liberty all formed the architecture to distinguish it from the other super resorts.

Inside was just as impressive! The casino was grand and packed, full of life. It was designed in a way that replicated a court fit for a King, with bars and restaurants surrounding the outskirts. Tucked away in the corner was a re-imagining of a small New York block. The golden grandeur that glossed the casino was replaced with the dark orange and brown brickwork that imitated the building work of 1950s New York. Little restaurants and shops weaved through the artificial streets, not too dissimilar from a block in Manchester's Northern Quarter.

After eating in a fine Italian restaurant, we did a lap of the main floor to immerse ourselves into Vegas life, and observe all the weird and wonderful elements that make it what it is. It wasn't long before we found ourselves gravitating towards the pulsating action of the gaming tables. I was ready to change my fortune from the opening day's swift gambling loss, moving from roulette to blackjack, a game I'd never played inside a casino before.

The Eagles', 'Life in the Fast Lane', came blasting through the speakers just as I approached the table. I sat in the middle of three Americans, only throwing $50 down to be converted to chips at first to see where that took me, hoping that I wouldn't need more. I placed a meagre $10 down on the first game and watched on as the deal commenced. An eight was initially laid in front of me and the dealer had a four. Early signs were good and were bettered when I was dealt a King to take me to eighteen and give me a great chance of victory. The two players to my right both stuck on nineteen and twenty respectively. Seeing that they waved their hands in front of their cards when prompted for their next move by the dealer, signalling they were sticking, I repeated the action to indicate my own intent. The player to my left was on seven and prodded his finger on the table to signal another card. He was given a four so he hit again in the hope of securing his grip on victory. The ten he coveted was slapped down and he'd reached twenty-one. We were all in a strong position to win and I waited with hope for the dealer's fate. He dealt himself a ten that took him to fourteen. He had no choice but to hit again, and a Queen gleamed in front of us meaning he had bust so we had all won. Little cheers murmured from the two to my right and I turned and smiled at them in relief at having got off to a winning start.

The next game started and straight away I was dealt an Ace after betting $15. Nods of approval from my fellow gamers were seen at my possible good fortune. I held my emotion, praying for a ten of some sorts to give me blackjack. When it came around to my card being overturned a King was planted down. I was an instant winner because the dealer had no chance of equalling me, having been dealt a two initially. The improved odds on the blackjack win of 3:2 meant that I won $22.50 plus my stake. I tipped the dealer the 50 cents and added the rest to my pile, pleased that my first two wins had given me a healthy cushion to play with. I had to be cautious as I knew how quickly fortunes could turn in Vegas - quicker than the Manchester weather can turn really. I remained composed and bet sensibly in the early stages, learning to enjoy the whole experience for all it was worth.

Wins were outweighing losses, then the victories began to happen more frequently, and the chips stacked higher, forcing me to split them into two piles to stop them looking like the Leaning Tower of Pisa. I became more adventurous in my stakes, and I was fortunate enough to win on 'double downs' when the opportunity arose. This was when you doubled your bet when initially dealt eleven or lower from the two cards, in the hope that you could be dealt a solitary strong card to take you closer to twenty-one. But you only risked it when the dealer had low cards and your chances of winning were better than theirs. It was the best way to increase your money quickly, and when it pays off it's a truly exhilarating feeling. It's those intense and nervy moments that suck you into the addictive world of gambling, and I was quickly discovering that euphoric side of it, but it's easy to say that when you're winning. I already knew how it felt to be a loser after the previous night's shambles.

What struck me the most was the camaraderie and musketeer spirit across the table. There was a real sense that everyone wanted each other to win, and I bought into the solidarity with my fellow 'American Dream' chasers. It was great entertainment, especially when someone got blackjack, which was always greeted with a series of high fives, fist bumping and shouts of congratulatory messages around the table. What had been an annoyance the previous night, when I was playing roulette, had now turned into part of the fun. I felt like a hypocrite. What enhanced the experience more was being able to claim free drinks whilst playing. However, I quickly sussed the ploy within this. The drink wouldn't arrive for five or ten minutes after being ordered, which meant I needed to remain hot at the table or else I'd be forced to dip further into my pocket, or sacrifice the drink completely if I was beaten into submission. Fortunately, I got through two bottles of

Corona whilst playing. The adrenaline from winning made me get through them in quick succession.

The more I played, the bigger my balls got as I searched for the big win that would lift me to levels rarely experienced from gambling. Addictive stimulation clouded my usually cautious rationale, and because of that fearless approach, the number of chips I staked began to steadily increase.

The others had been playing roulette and it obviously hadn't gone well because they were all stood watching me play from over my shoulder. I was up $160, but I perceived the good run wouldn't last forever, so I had one last big bet. I put my $40 down and was dealt a six, which wasn't the best card at all given the dealer was also dealt a six. The second card dealt for me was a King. I had reached sixteen, which was risky, but could still potentially win by relying on the dealer to falter. I decided not to risk a further card, so stuck on sixteen. The dealer's second card was an eight, meaning he had fourteen and would be forced to hit again. The hope was for an eight or higher, but something told me it'd be lower just to piss me off. The rest of the players had decided their own fate before the dealer turned over his final card. Sure enough it was a seven that took him to twenty-one! That was my cue to walk away from blackjack and enjoy the winning feeling for the first time in Vegas.

I was up $120, which put a dent into the previous day's losses, but this was Vegas, and it was hard to just walk away without prolonging the fun and risk. With another rush of blood to the head, I decided to put the full amount on red or black on roulette. I found a relatively empty table and saw that the last seven spins had been red. Dilemma! Would it continue to be red or would the inevitable change in luck occur? Decisions had to be made quickly. Turner and Ian encouraged me to go red; Johnny went the other way and opted for black. It was only a 50/50 chance but I decided to go against the trend and back Johnny with black, certain that the run was due a change. $120 on black was laid down, the biggest personal bet of my life, but in Vegas, a miniscule amount. The dealer span as the intensity of my eyes focused on the wheel turning. My nerves jangled like a jailor's set of keys. The ball started to settle and bounced between the numbers, eventually landing on… red 36. 'Fuckin' typical!' I shouted. 'Just fuckin' typical!' My friends laughed, winding me up as we so often did to each other when one of us suffered misfortune.

I couldn't believe I'd not learnt my lesson from the agony of the previous night. I cursed profusely, and then stormed out of New York New York, flicking the middle finger at the others for their relentless piss-taking, which carried on pretty much all the way back to Planet Hollywood.

We returned to meet Tony, who was providing us with a Limo to the strip club. He was already waiting when we arrived, leaning against the railings near the entrance, watching a folk band playing to the people sat facing them in the bar. We signalled to him and he raised his hand. He was a tall guy, quite bulky and wore a New

York Yankees blue cap. His brown hair curled out from underneath, hiding just how bushy it was. He seemed a little pale, odd for someone living in the desert, but with the evidence of ties to New York, he was probably from the East Coast. He wore a scruffy, dark blue hoody and jeans. In any other environment he probably looked a bit untrustworthy, but the way he roamed freely within the casino, advertising his services in front of security, suggested he was legit. We had to break down the stereotypes and trust in Vegas, however insane that felt knowing we were staying in a city of sinners, schemers and hustlers.

Tony informed us that the Limo would be arriving in fifteen minutes, so we grabbed another bottle of ice cold beer and sat in the bar on the comfy, red leather sofas, chilling to the folk band that wasn't exactly inspiring us in preparation for the devil's experience of a seductive and sinister strip club.

Turner struggled to contain his excitement. He always had a boyish attitude towards strip clubs, never seeming to tire of them or realise the deceit behind the whole idea. Our inexperienced younger days had us believing that these hot women fancied us, but in reality, everyone is looked upon with a big £ sign hovering above their head. For me, the appeal and attraction eventually wore off with age, and had been dead for the last six or seven years. I must admit though, I was intrigued about visiting one in Vegas. It had a very different appeal somehow to the ones back home, especially given the standard of women we'd seen walking about day in day out, and that was just the barmaids and croupiers. Imagine what the strippers would look like?

Turner turned to Tony in his giddiness. 'So, what are these women like in here then? Big tits and dirty I bet?'

I nearly spat my drink out at his outright frankness.

'Yeah man, the girls are awesome. You won't be disappointed. Just be wary of the working girl.'

'What do you mean?' Ian interrupted.

'This is Vegas man. Yer got yer strippers, yer escorts and yer hookers all working the same game. If you're not careful, BOOM, you could get hit for a lot of dough. But what you do with yer money ain't my business.'

I didn't feel too comfortable about this. It could get annoying in England with the strippers hounding you for money, but an attack on three fronts could be unbearable. It was the perfect plan thinking about it. All these women would be prowling the walkways keeping a keen eye out to pick up an easy trick from drunken college kids in frat parties, who were unable to restrain their enthusiasm. The strippers would prep you with a seductive dance to stir your arousal, and then the hooker could seal your fate by influencing the decisions of men who can't control their own lustful animal instincts, resulting in uncontrolled expenditure and a frenzy of Vegas debauchery. I would like to think I wouldn't suffer a similar fate. I'd never been with or intended on being with a hooker for fear of who was there five minutes earlier. It had to be consensual with no money exchanging hands for me to be interested. I preferred the chase and achievement to the cheating short cut. I sensed that the others thought the same, but this was Vegas, anything could happen out here and maybe one of us had a secret obsession to go this one step further, but which one of us?

Tony got the call from the driver, who had now arrived, so we swiftly moved down the escalator to the lobby. As we walked outside a car drove slowly by, and the driver signalled to Tony. I think we were a little dumbstruck as this ludicrous stretched yellow Hummer pulled up alongside us. None of us had ever experienced anything like this before. Such antics had become tacky in Manchester, but in Vegas it had a very different meaning.

We entered the Hummer one by one, and the thunderous sound system rumbled the whole interior. It looked like it was something from the future with its strange silver and black cube shaped speakers and gadgets circling around us. Ideally, the music could've been better, tarnished by the shit gangsta rap track that was playing. Did the driver not know we were kids brought up on rock 'n' roll? A Led Zeppelin track, possibly, 'When the Levee Breaks', with Jimmy Page's guitar wailing out and Robert Plant's screams would've been a much cooler entrance song. Still, the pulsating bass line making the seats vibrate was quite an experience, having a very similar effect to a vibrating bus stood stationary, which wasn't good considering we were about to be thrust into a strip club. We didn't need a jump-start on unnecessary stimulations.

Tony told us that Olympic Gardens Strip Club was situated down the bottom of the Strip, but we turned off heading away towards the airport. There was a certain degree of uneasiness now and questions were asked about whether this was kosher or not. We felt we could trust him back at Planet Hollywood, but this detour seemed to reduce that faith. It crossed my mind that we might end up in the middle of nowhere and get 'clipped' by a crew waiting for us. I think I'd watched the film 'Casino' too many times. Surely we wouldn't, but we did seem to be getting further and further away from the heart of the Strip. Tony justified the route by saying the police were out in force at the end of Las Vegas Boulevard after a road accident, and this was a quicker way despite its detour. How were we to know? We'd only been in Vegas for a little over twenty-four hours and none of us knew the traffic or police situation, so we had no option but to trust, but to also be prepared.

CHAPTER 10

It turned out we had nothing to be concerned about as we pulled up outside the strip club. We'd definitely seen one too many American mafia movies to think something ill-fated would take place.

We followed each other out of the Hummer, and a few people in the queue eyed us up to see if we were anyone famous because of the vehicle we'd arrived in. We stood outside, marvelling at the deluxe building and surrounding gardens that appeared in front of us. This didn't look like a strip club at all. It was very different to the back-alley establishments highlighted by a burnt-out neon sign in the shape of a pole dancer that we saw back home. This resembled more of a Country Club if anything. But I suppose on some perverse level, strip clubs in Vegas are the equivalent of Country Clubs in a so-called respectable society. I'm sure a similar amount of underhandedness and corruption happened in both.

Tony was true to his word and we piled in ahead of the queue having already paid. Turner was like an uncaged wild tiger that hadn't been fed for weeks, making a break for it as soon as he was let loose inside. 'Welcome to the Jungle', by Guns N' Roses, belted out of the PA and I chuckled at its suitability. I scouted out my surroundings once we'd been pushed through the barrier. It was quite impressive in more ways than one. The place was huge and the number of strippers I could see on the prowl clearly outnumbered any that I'd seen in strip joints back home, very much like a jungle where we were at the mercy of these predators. Predictably, staying true to the Vegas standard, they all looked ridiculously stunning. The lights were severely dimmed apart from tinges of false red light plastered against the walls and corners, making the ambience dark, sultry and gothic, like it was the seductive lair of a wealthy vampire. The air was laden with a variety of fruity scents and sweat, emanating from the exposed flesh of the semi-naked women who prowled the walkways.

The stage was towards the edge of the room near the entrance rather than in the middle of the main floor. It was shaped more like a catwalk with a circular platform at the end, from which two poles rose to the ceiling. Two strippers, one blonde, the other brunette, were already dancing, teasing each other and the punters with their erotic moves. They were both already fully stripped, big fake breasts on show, and they displayed their flexibility and acrobatics by swinging violently, yet smoothly, around the pole.

We were shown to our table, which was located towards the side of the main floor near the walkway, about ten metres from the stage. Straight away I felt anxious. I sensed from this unprotected position, with a walkway directly next to us, that a lot of the time would be spent knocking back the advances of ladies of the night attempting to lure us into parting with money in exchange for a few minutes thrill. I was right! As soon as we were seated I was approached by a stunning, busty blonde who sat on the arm of my chair, asking me how I was doing. I couldn't say I was surprised at the speed of the approach due to past experiences in strip clubs, but I just couldn't be arsed with the hassle of having to resist the advances of strippers every ten seconds. One dance was all I was prepared to have, and not within seconds of arriving. I respectfully declined her offer, much to her disappointment.

Within the next five minutes I was approached by a further two girls, and again, I had to reiterate that I didn't want entertaining just yet. One looked angry, the other took it with a pinch of salt, but it was already starting to get on my nerves as the vultures circled in. By rights I should've indulged and gone on a crazed rampage, blowing a shit load of cash on numerous, meaningless strippers, but I didn't need an epiphany to work out that strippers weren't the answer to my problems. It would more than likely lead to a river of financial regret in the morning.

On closer inspection of what was happening around me, I noticed that this strip club, probably much like all the others in Vegas, adopted very different rules to the ones in England. I was expecting a room at the back where we'd receive a private dance. No such luxury existed here as we found out when Ian succumbed to the charms of one of the dancers - a dark haired, typically large breasted vixen dressed in purple and black attire. The service was given to you there and then, in the chair you were currently sat in, in front of everyone. Worst of all, it was in front of your friends too, who got to see your face whilst the dance was happening. It's one of those faces that should never be seen in public, along the same lines as a 'cum face', which no one should ever have to see! Another shock was soon to reveal itself. It seemed customary and expected to touch the dancers pretty much anywhere you wanted, apart from 'downstairs'. I thought this kind of balanced out the awkwardness of having an audience. At least you could cop a feel, or did this just add to the seediness and embarrassment by putting on show how you usually acted in the privacy of the bedroom for all to see?

Johnny yielded to an African American girl and it wasn't long before Turner followed suit, surrendering to the charms of an Eastern European looking blonde, but I showed no signs of breaking...for the time being!

I was constantly being 'chatted up', and like before, some girls were fine with rejection, while others showed their bitter side, making snide remarks as they trawled off. It made me feel like I'd done something wrong, despite a warped sense of sadistic empowerment at snubbing the advances of gorgeous women.

I'd previously mentioned to Ian that if a stripper danced on stage to AC/DC's, 'You Shook Me All Night Long', then she would be the chosen one. There was something about a girl who had the ability to knock someone out with her American thighs that I found appetising, and far too tempting to resist. Unfortunately, none of them used this song, which didn't matter because before I even had a chance to choose, or was even ready, a stunning, petite, oriental woman plonked herself on my lap, purposely resting her left butt cheek on the sensitive region of my crotch. She flung her arms around my shoulders and basically told me she was going to dance for me rather than waiting to be asked. I thought, 'What the hell!' Well, I didn't really get a choice in the matter so I just sat back to let her do her business. I was quite uncomfortable at first, especially as touching was permitted, but I was reluctant to indulge given the audience that was surrounding me. However, I knew that in the privacy of a booth, my hands would've been exploring everywhere, free from the shackles of the rules of, 'sit on them' or 'keep them by your side', which was common practice back home.

She started off on the floor in a cobra like position, giving me the sexiest of glances, rolling her tongue across her luscious red lips whilst maintaining eye contact. It all happened so fast from the moment she spoke to me that I didn't really see what she looked like. But now I had the perfect view, absolutely stunning and sexy as hell. Her long, straight black hair fell right down the length of her back. Her body was immense, not a crease to be found. Her eyes were ravenous, but somehow hid a troubled past that had led her to this career path, concealed behind this forceful, provocative exterior. Her lips were a sizzling shade of red that complemented her attire of the same colour, which was seconds away from being on the floor. Her breasts were high, huge, perfectly round, and obvious implants - a necessity to make it in this game in Vegas. She flipped over to face away from me, showing just how pert her arse was, and in my mind, I was being lured into a place that I didn't want to be, submissive and surrendering control. Alice Cooper's, 'Poison', belting out should've served as a warning, but it only succeeded in making the steamy situation a little more perilous. Clearly, filthy rock music was being played mid-striptease to cloud the judgement of innocent beings like myself, and level-headedness was in serious danger of being smothered by the cravings of erotic desires. At least that's what I'm blaming it on. I cannot be held responsible for my own actions. It's the fault of rock 'n' roll!

She stood up, strutting over to me with purpose, falling to her knees and moving her head tentatively from my chest down towards my crotch. Her hands firmly clasped my knees, yanking my legs wide open, almost causing a groin injury from the force, which would've been awkward to explain to my football manager back home. She thrust her body towards me again, never failing to take her sultry eyes off me. Her legs somehow ended up above my shoulders, displaying the flexibility of a champion gymnast. She pressed her breasts tightly up against me, making them look even bigger from my bird's eye view, not that they needed any more enhancement. I was being battered from pillar to post before she slowed right down and looked deeper into my eyes, inches from my face. I always hated this situation with strippers. What kind of look are you supposed to have on your face? Do you look at every inch of her body? Although slightly lecherous, it's probably what they want. Do you maintain eye contact throughout? That might end up looking a bit creepy. Do you try and look a bit cool with a vaguely cocky smile? Or do you have a normal facial expression showing no emotion, inadvertently looking more like a mug shot? All critical questions! I usually mix it up between all poses, but mainly focusing on the attempt to look a bit cool, despite the stripper probably thinking I was anything but a perverted, horny dickhead. If this was in a bar and a girl looked at me in this seductive way, then I'd be tempted to plant a kiss on her, succumbing to the natural laws of instinct. She was lucky that I didn't stand up with her still attached to me like a limpet, and take her in the back (pardon the pun), for a quick two-pump bang, which would without doubt be the best three seconds of her life. Should I go for the fateful lunge and attempt to plant a kiss on her? 'She's asking for it, begging for it,' my ego told me. Sensibility stepped in though, 'Remain calm, and suppress the urge at all costs to avoid a beat down by the bouncers, you fool!'

She was now straddling me, grinding me ever so delicately, teasing me to the point of self-detonation. It was a good job, or maybe not, that I had tight jeans on, so the stirrings in my boxers wouldn't be able to fully bloom. I wondered what strippers thought of that? Although the guy might be quite embarrassed, the stripper had to expect it. Did they like it? Did it feed their own ego knowing they'd done something right? Maybe they would be disappointed if they danced for a lad (or girl, this was Vegas after all) who didn't get aroused. Something told me that in Vegas the girls probably saw the erection as a sign that they could offer more deviant services, thinking that you were more likely to surrender with the brain transferring to the trousers.

She continued to be centimetres away from my face. Her lips and body were enticing me do something, but I was fearful to cross the line. I remained frozen with terror. My hands were like magnets that had to be forced down so I wouldn't grasp her perfect body. I had been disciplined and schooled in the English way of strip clubs, displaying that stereotypical, polite attitude. I couldn't bring myself to break the cycle now, not unless I was told directly that I could. Just give me the sign, baby!

She finished dancing as the song drew to a close, but she told me that she was going to dance through another, just as stripper's favourite, 'Pour Some Sugar on Me', by Def Leppard, began with its heavy and blistering opening. Like a sucker I fell for it and didn't object. 'This time, don't be so shy,' she said. I had to laugh considering what I'd just been thinking, but I surrendered to her request, taking heed of the invitation as my hands shot up faster than a virgin's dick. I began to fondle and grab a bit of flesh, and even though I knew this was a ploy, my wicked mind started to wander into unlikely fantasy, convincing myself that she wanted me. Funny, after all these years of experience and knowing how the game was played, my judgement could still be clouded and illusion could be so blinding, especially when a pair of tits were squashed against my face that were just begging to be sucked, bitten, chewed or licked, or even to do the 'wibble' (motor boat) between. I couldn't do anything, it felt too seedy in front of everyone, but perhaps I stuck my tongue out a little, more out of instinct from the circumstance rather than a genuine filthy desire to get stuck in. She tasted salty from the sweat, that flavour I'd tasted so often in the secrecy of a bedroom, the sweet taste of sex.

She seized my hands, moving them up and around every bit of her body, fully navigating them around her soft skin. Those tight jeans that were a godsend earlier were now becoming a nuisance. Control was crumbling away. My strength and guard broke down like the Walls of Jericho. I became fully seduced by the power of the stripper. The second song finished and she carried on through the next, Mötley Crüe's, 'Girls Girls Girls'. She didn't even break to ask if I wanted her to carry on. Three rocking tracks in a row suggested that there was some sort of mind reader knocking about that knew exactly what to play to seduce me into the depravity of 80s Sunset Strip rock. How could one say no to a dance when this type of music was being played? I felt bamboozled and swindled. I thought she was enjoying this more than me, but her acting was Oscar nominee standard. I fell hook, line and sinker to her devious motives. The grinding on my crotch continued, having a knock-on effect of encouraging me to grope her with more vigour. She knew full well that I was semi-hard, and she didn't seem to care as she continued to powerfully thrust her pelvis into me. She carried on rubbing her breasts across my face and moved my hands to touch them. God knows how this looked to outsiders, but I was like a man possessed now and didn't give a shit. I managed to come up for air, noticing that Johnny and Ian were having another dance, and Turner had gone. Where? I did not know, and in that moment, I did not care!

The third song finished and horniness gripped me as I became entranced by her seductive power. She remained straddled, kissing me gently on the cheek before whispering in my ear, 'So, you wanna take this party into the back room?'

'Oh fuck,' I thought. I knew exactly what she meant. She was the hooker, the escort, and the stripper I had been wary of all rolled into one. I had been deceived by the sinful devil herself, and that tactic I thought of earlier, about what better way than to get you all horny for the hooker to finish you off, was now being applied to me. I was struggling to regain control. Was there any way of turning back? Or had I come so far that I was about to be a victim of my own rule? Rules were there to be broken, but then I'd be a hypocrite with no principles.

I couldn't help but flirt back and say, 'What have you got in mind?' Why would I ask such a question? It's not like she's going to say, 'Come around the back of the curtain into a secluded booth for tea and ginger nut biscuits,' is she now? She's going to tell me all the dirty deeds she can offer in X-rated detail to stimulate my own warped desires, hence making the idea of saying no a distinct impossibility.

She leant back, looking more appealing and gorgeous than ever, running her tongue all the way around her top lip, slowly and suggestively. I knew exactly what she was inferring, causing me to feel quite faint and distant. My mind wandered through possibilities of how this endeavour would end. She flicked her hair back out of her eyes and leant forward, saying, 'And that would just be the start. I know you wanna fuck me, that much is obvious.' She glanced downwards referring to the straining bulge in my jeans, before adding, 'I'll let you do anything you want.'

So, there it was! I could do anything I wanted to with a stripper/escort/hooker. How could a man resist? Just the small matter of how much this was going to cost might have some influence, and like a complete tool, I had brought my credit card with me to a strip club of all places. If this was to go any further I needed to know how much it was going to cost.

I turned into her ear. 'How much to do anything I wanted to then?' I think I had some saliva lodged in my throat as my voice seemed to go up an octave. She held up four fingers and I presumed she meant hundreds, not thousands for one full corrupt hour.

$400 of my hard-earned cash, a quarter of what I hoped to spend in six nights in Vegas. Could I do it? Had I been driven so far by my past that my principles were shattered too, taking shape into the new *me* that was emerging? I was on a quest of experience as it was, and this would just be another story to tell, or maybe not. I could go down the road of keeping it a secret. What happens in Vegas stays in Vegas, right? But what would be the point of that? It's only money, I argued. How much would I really miss $400 in the long run anyway? Would my friends understand? Or would this be the start of a ridiculing to last a lifetime that would be brought up at every opportunity. But still, a night with an oriental stripper/escort/hooker could be a monumental experience, although possibly not one to tell the grandkids about.

I was seriously wrestling with my conscience! She

waited for an answer. If I did it, would she enjoy it? Being a professional who had probably shamed my own personal total, she'd surely had some to remember. Would I match up? Given her experience too, would it be like waving a stick in the Grand Canyon? I might not match up to the physical expectation! I might even fail to get it up once there, overcome by waves of self-manifested panic. Who had been there beforehand? *That* was the key question. Would I be the first that day, night or even hour? The thought of being there immediately after some ugly, fat, rich, balding fuckwit, who had ruined her by sweating all over that exceptional body was enough to put me off. I couldn't exactly ask her if that was the case. I'd expect a lie in return anyway, but it was that thought, the one that had served me so well in the past that brought the control back, and as she pressed for an answer, I had to refuse her. She pleaded with me a little more, but I stuck to my guns. Eventually she accepted and transformed into accountancy mode, enlightening me of the bill I'd racked up so far. $60! Unbelievable! I had budgeted $20 for one dance and ended up paying $60 for a three-song dance. Then I also got stung for a tip too. In parts of England you could probably buy into an orgy for that, not with the same calibre of woman as in Vegas, but still, value for money. Also, I was now forced to spend the rest of my night with blue balls. No wonder strippers make so much money and women love to work in this circuit. It's because of idiots like me...and Turner, Johnny and Ian, who had all succumbed to three or more dances each. In fact, I think Turner had bought a season ticket complete with a customer loyalty card, and was feeling that shameful about having numerous dances in front of us that he found a seat elsewhere on his own, or was currently conkers deep in the back somewhere. God knows what deviance he was getting himself into that he didn't want us to witness, and to be honest, I didn't want to know.

To make matters worse, the oriental stripper who nearly got me to abandon my principles came back over a few minutes later, deciding it was appropriate to tell me about the business that she ran on the side, which involved providing girls to functions and private parties. Obviously, she had been misinformed, as it sounded like she thought I'd just won the lottery. Considering that I'd just refused to pay $400 for extras, why would I pay about $3000 to hire a load of women to come to my hotel room for a private party? I'm not saying the idea didn't appeal to me, I wouldn't be human if it didn't, but only a gambling win of substantial proportions would enable such a 'Sopranos' style of living.

The strip club showed no signs of calming down, and scores of people poured in from the heaving queues at the door. I'd never seen a queue to get into a strip club before, so this was quite a sad eye opener. The music was apt though, very much carrying connotations of the art of seduction. It looked as if more and more girls were creeping out of the walls as the crowd grew. What started out as being two dancers on the stage had swiftly turned to four, including the oriental princess who had danced for me earlier.

I was becoming more agitated and restless being in

the strip club because of constantly being hounded by women looking to perform open wallet surgery. Boredom began to set in. There were only so many unattainable pairs of tits and arses that I could look at, and the whole scenario became mundane and lost its appeal, venturing towards seediness now I'd been here a while. I didn't want to chance another dance for fear of explosion, and having already waxed $60, I'd decided the money would be better spent elsewhere... like gambling...a much more productive means of expenditure.

However, it was worth hanging around to witness what happened next. Ian was on what must have been his fourth dance, evidently loving the hands-on rule, undeterred that he was fumbling about in full view of me and Johnny. All I could see was the stripper jockeying Ian, with only his legs sticking out, not his hands or face though, they were firmly buried elsewhere. Over his shoulder was another group of lads sat a few metres away from us. One of them was sat with his back to Ian but slightly to the left as I looked. I'd noticed a few minutes earlier that a dark-haired stripper dressed in a black negligée was dancing for this guy, but I didn't think anything of it at first. I only started taking note when she grinded this desperate chump so hard that his chair started shifting back a couple of centimetres after every continued push and thrust, dangerously encroaching onto Ian's dance. You could see what was going to happen without intervention. Firstly, we had to move our table of drinks when the back of the guy's chair collided with it and knocked all the empty bottles over like skittles across the table. Cries of, 'Whoa whoa

whoa' rang out amongst us in comical fashion, but they were oblivious to our shouts. We pulled the table back, which was a mistake for Ian as this created a vacant space next to him that the chair of the other guy could now be pushed back into, so they would end up being parallel. The chair inched further back as predicted, and Ian and this other guy were pretty much side by side, shoulder to shoulder, half looking at each other mid-erotic dance, wondering how the hell they'd ended up in this position. They could have had a conversation they were that close.

Ian's dance abruptly finished, but the other guy carried on, entering what must have been his seventh or eighth song. He was either incredibly stupid or had a bit of money to throw about. I'd like to think it was the former. The dance must've totalled at least $140 or so by now, but you'd think he would've gone for extras if he was able to splash that amount of cash just for one dance. Ian attempted to swivel his chair to get away from him, but it was hopeless. The chair had no room for manoeuvre. He was trapped. Sensing that the poor punter was going to pump more money into her stockings, the stripper showed no remorse or signs of stopping, continuing to heavily grind him to the point that, from where I was sitting, they could've been screwing. The chair began to shift again, but instead of hitting the table of drinks, they barged into and wedged on Ian's leg. Ian tried to lean over, but couldn't release his leg from where it had been lodged. The stripper even began to use it for leverage at one point, causing Ian to bob up and down in perfect rhythm to the stripper's moves. The tears streamed down our faces as we burst into fits of laughter, even more so when the stripper looked up at Ian without a care in the world, winked and casually greeted him saying, 'Hey Sugar! You wanna get in on this?' as if this was the most natural thing in the world. The guy in question looked like he'd been in a battle by the time he finally yielded. I wondered how much that dance cost. It wasn't worth it in my eyes, whatever the amount! The horror on his face when the mention of payment came was priceless. It was an obvious schoolboy error.

Turner returned and we told him we were ready for leaving. He was reluctant as I think he was ready to pull an all-nighter. We quizzed him on where he'd been for the last forty minutes or so, but he refused to answer us. For Turner not to tell us meant he must've been somewhere that he was too ashamed to admit. We persisted, but he kept schtum, trying to palm us off by saying he was just having a dance where it was less crowded. We didn't believe him.

Just before we stood from our seats, we looked up on the stage to see a poor young man on all fours dressed in bondage gear. He had a dog collar on which had a lead coming from it, held by one of the feistier looking dancers, who was then given a whip by a fellow stripper. The bad memories of my dance onstage in front of everyone all those years ago on my 20th birthday came rushing to the surface. With the night obviously about to take another twist into the depraved, we thought it best to get the fuck out of the strip club before one of us was called onstage too.

CHAPTER 11

We had to take a taxi back to Planet Hollywood because Tony said the Hummer was going to be at least another hour, and we weren't prepared to wait that long and waste any more time with it already passing 1.30am. The plan was to get back to our hotel and check out the club within Planet Hollywood, Koi Bar.

The place was a lot smaller than I imagined, not as busy as Pure the night before, but the drinks were just as expensive. It was a modish, intimate venue, but there weren't enough people present to give the atmosphere tenacity. As Ian pointed out to me later that night, this wasn't really the main club of Planet Hollywood. The main one had closed for refurbishment over the summer, much to our disappointment.

Ian and I sat on the stools, casually people watching at the bar. Turner and Johnny had resumed their comedy sketch show of trying to chat up women, but it seemed like they were struggling as no one was paying them any attention whatsoever. The magic shrouding us the previous night, where it seemed we carried an aura of attraction, had diminished, but they still provided a comical outlet for me and Ian to observe.

Ian leant over to me. 'Look at those two idiots. Nothing ever changes, does it?'

'Ha. No matter where we are in the world, they'll always compete for women,' I replied.

'How you doing with everything? Has the strip club exorcised those demons?'

'Are you kidding? I've still got a semi-on so I'm edgier now than before. I know what I'll be dreaming about tonight.'

He creased over laughing, and when he composed himself he asked, 'You know what I mean. Mandy? How're you doing with that?'

'Well the very mention of you saying her name made my arse drop so still not great.'

'It does get easier mate. I know it's a cliché but it does. You've been there before and so have I, and when you look back on it you wonder what all the fuss was about.'

'I know, you're right, but neither of us have experienced anything this harsh. It's on a whole new level. It's like I'm still in some sort of shock with it all. It's probably all egotistical in many ways,' I answered.

'Possibly, but you're allowed to feel like that. What she did was unforgivable, but you're starting to see her for who she really is now aren't you?'

'My head knows that but I still can't seem to get past it. It's fucked up!'

'You'll be alright. Look at what happened last night with the Puerto Rican. She was stunning. If you can pull off something like that then you have nothing to worry about.'

A cheery stroke to my ego, I thought.

'But that's a holiday thing where people from different worlds are more attracted to each other.'

'You think? Well why isn't it working for them two pricks then? Jesus, they're a right embarrassment sometimes.'

I looked up to see both Turner and Johnny talking to two stunning girls, but judging from the girls' body language, it didn't look promising. The northern wit seemed lost in translation, but still they persisted.

'Haha. They are entertaining though,' I said.

'So, is your little Puerto Rican girl still texting you then?' Ian quizzed.

'She is indeed.'

'You know what mate, we were giving you shit before about getting involved in holiday romances and that, but given your current situation I'd be tempted to meet up with her again at some point. You obviously hit it off from what you were telling me.'

'In theory that's a great plan, but when did I come into a shit load of money?'

'Okay. Fair enough. But let's look at this objectively. You're now free from Mandy, and you hate your job. You always said you only live once and should have no regrets in life.'

'Is that what I used to say? Sounds like I had it all figured out back then.'

'You still can! Take a chance and start living. Start afresh. See what happens.'

'What you getting at? Move to San Diego?'

'Maybe not that drastic but at least look at seeing her again. What's waiting for you back home? That's all I'm saying.'

It was an interesting proposition, but there were too many barriers and obstacles to overcome for that to happen. Money was the main thing as a prolonged trip to San Diego would be expensive, and if I quit my job, how would I earn? I quietly dismissed the idea as impossible.

We got another drink, still laughing at the feeble pulling attempts of Johnny and Turner. After twenty minutes or so they both returned like they'd been doing a hard day's graft, huffing and puffing having put in an unsuccessful shift.

'No shot then Turner?' Ian began winding him up.

'Got to be lesbians!' He refused to admit that he was just having an off night.

He downed the rest of his drink. 'Come on. I've had enough of it in here. Let's go to the casino.'

We sniggered at this sulky attitude arising from his unproductive attempts, and continued to poke the bear on the walk down to the Pleasure Pit.

We should've really stayed in Koi Bar to see out the night because the casino only served to strip my wallet further as another $80 was liquidated quickly on blackjack. I blamed the loss on being distracted by the dancer on the platform behind the dealer. She was possibly one of the sexiest women I'd seen in my life – a proper blonde bombshell, tanned from head to toe, wearing a silky white negligee. How could I concentrate when someone of that calibre was dancing suggestively directly in my eye line? I'd get her back later on in my dreams, I thought.

It may have only been a tiny amount I was losing compared to what others lost, but it was starting to pile up. I didn't earn enough to keep throwing all this money about and I'd done in about $400 already in the collective gambling sessions. Add to that being seduced and pillaged in the strip club and the inflated drink prices, then I had to hope that my fortunes were going to change at some point, or else this holiday was about to get a lot more expensive than first envisaged.

Ian had decided to turn in for the night, feeling the effects of a heavy drinking session where he'd hammered a lot of Vodka. The rest of us decided to get some food from the twenty-four-hour bistro within our hotel.

The menu was costly, and it was too early to order breakfast (or too late in the night). Me and Turner ordered cheeseburgers and Johnny decided to try out a very typical English dish, in America of all places, which could never work. He ordered a 'corned beef hash'. There were so many things wrong with this! First of all, that's probably the last thing on my mind in terms of food after a night out. Secondly, did Americans know what 'hash' was in terms of food? Thirdly, did they know what 'corned beef' was? Fourthly, even if they did, would it in any way resemble a typical English 'corned beef hash' like your mother can rustle up? The answers to all these things were clearly no! For starters it came with an egg and pineapple resting on top??

There was no gravy/sauce or mashed potato, and the American definition of corned beef looked more like chopped up, cubed, processed ham. It was a total food disaster, providing the first 'food biffle' of the holiday.

'Biffle' is a term coined by our group of friends several years earlier. It's used to highlight any unfortunate incident or mishap any of us became the victim of. For example: falling over, tripping up, knocking something over, errors in judgement or misreading signals with a girl that results in rejection etc. Ian's purchase of glittered sun cream was a *definite* biffle. A food biffle was the same principle, but involved receiving something you didn't order, something that reacts on you the morning after, or as in Johnny's case, something that doesn't resemble what you thought it would, hence a food biffle. By all accounts after the first few mouthfuls, the taste of it also constituted a food biffle.

It must've been getting on for 6am when we finally left the bistro, and we made our way upstairs to bed knowing we had a big day in front of us. The USA had a football match going on, which we were intrigued to watch and see the reactions of Americans when it came to 'soccer'. Me and Johnny were in a very giddy mood as alcohol heightened our usual tolerance levels of humour.

Johnny turned to me, 'Let's see if Ian's still up?'

'Why?'

'We can do shit to him if he's sleeping.' He was bursting with excitement.

In my own giddy state, I agreed. Turner decided

to turn in, choosing not to participate in our youthful antics.

Johnny and I scampered down the corridor full of drunken, galvanic enthusiasm, hoping Ian was in the land of nod.

We opened the door quietly, trying not to snigger too loudly, and saw that he was completely out of it lay on his front, head slumped to the side, mouth gaping and one eye slightly open, but totally unaware of anything happening around him.

'Opportunity knocks mate!' Johnny said.

'What do you want to do?'

'I know, grab that alarm clock.'

I tip-toed over to the clock between the beds and handed it to Johnny. He placed it perfectly on top of Ian's head. That one object sparked a stream of innovative ideas to add stuff to him until he woke, or until the room was bare. I got my phone out and took a picture of Ian with the alarm clock on his head that displayed 6.22 am. A box of cigarettes resting on his shoulder and a couple of empty bottles of Budweiser were placed in his hand. I continued to take a picture after every new object was added. He didn't stir so we continued to add more and more items, taking pictures every time we did from the same place so it looked like a work of art when we scrolled through the photos quickly. We added my shoes, the iPod speakers, a lamp, Ian's suitcase, the iron, the bin, stood the ironing board up on the bed, and covered him in magazines. Every time we added something different, Johnny and I collapsed on the floor in hysterics.

It came to a point where we struggled to add any more appliances, but we weren't done yet, not by a long shot. Johnny reached into his pocket and pulled out a shiny red square packet.

'What's that?' I asked, trying to contain my laughter. He ripped open the top and pulled out a condom, waving it in front of me.

'I'm raising the stakes,' he blurted.

Johnny went into the bathroom and emerged with a complementary sachet of shampoo. He opened the top and poured half the contents into the condom, forming a nice little build-up of what could've been mistaken as semen at the bottom. He then went over to the table and retrieved a straw from an empty milkshake cup. With Ian still well away and a cluster of objects all over him, Johnny pulled down the back of his boxer shorts, and using the straw for leverage, cautiously nestled the condom in between his arse cheeks before sharply yanking the straw out with nothing attached, like a magician waving a wand after completing a trick. I disintegrated onto the bed, using the pillow to muffle the howls of laughter I struggled to restrain. The thought of Ian waking up and wondering what the hell this weird uncomfortable prop lodged in his arse was, only to find a condom filled with some unusual white substance, left me breathless with amusement. The panic that would run through his mind would be devastating. The ultimate prank! Johnny and I agreed on a story we had to play along with to keep the joke running, which meant we had to remove all the items that surrounded and covered Ian. It took ages for the hysterics to calm, but once they did, Johnny went back to his own room and I got into bed, just as another text message came through from Eva.

> *'U need to realise you have everything going for you. You are free! No one should ever dampen your spirits, only lift them. You are special, and I'm so happy I met you. You taught me something last night, in a quiet way. Keep your head up. X'*

I didn't know if she was drunk or not, but it was a heart-warming text to receive just before giving in to a surge of sleep, and it made Ian's earlier suggestion of perhaps meeting up with her again a little more tenable.

CHAPTER 12

'WHAT THE FUCK??!!' A voice cried from behind me. I was still in a drowsy, disorientated daze. The scream woke me from a typically vivid nightmare about the past. My eyes sluggishly opened as the air con had left them sticky and difficult to fully widen. I was facing the wall, and I slowly rolled over to view the room in the open. Ian was stood wearing only his Boxer shorts, fumbling in the back of them with a very concerned look on his face as he pulled out a crumpled up ribbed condom. It all came flooding back, and slowly I pulled the duvet over my head to cover my sniggers until I could compose myself to face him.

Ian repeated himself, 'What the fuck is this?' He was holding the condom by the tips of his fingers with a look of disgust on his face.

I loosened my own expression and rolled the duvet back from over my head, looking just as bemused as him. 'Where's that come from?'

'My fuckin' arse!!' Ian exclaimed. I was dying to break into hysterics, but knew I had to keep this going.

'Well what's it doing there?'

'How the fuck should I know!'

'Well you should. If a man pulls a condom from his arse, I think he should know where it came from.'

Ian's face was a picture of bewilderment, stunned into anxiety.

'Well I fuckin' don't right. It's got fuckin' jizz in it too.'

I fought unbelievably hard not to break.

'What did you do last night? You left us in the restaurant. Where did you go afterwards you pervert?'

'Fuck off, I came straight here.'

'Well where's that come from? Did you do anything to appease some deep dark fetish you've been too ashamed to tell us all these years?'

'Did I fuck! I was sat with you the whole time.'

'Well it must have happened on your way back to the room. You were pretty pissed mate, hammered in fact. Do you remember getting back?'

'No, but I would've remembered if I pulled…wouldn't I?' he asked with uncertainty.

'You might not have pulled a girl.'

'What do you mean?

'Well…we are in Vegas. Anything can happen.'

'Fuck off!'

'Eh, it's not uncommon, especially here. You might have been date raped...by a bloke,' I mocked.

'WHAT??? Bollocks, I would've remembered.' He was getting more and more agitated now and his face reddened.

'No you wouldn't, that's the whole point.' The pain

of not breaking was killing me, like *I* was the one under torture.

'Bollocks, you put it there!' he accused.

'Me??? Believe me I don't want to go anywhere near your arsehole. Come to think of it, you weren't here last night when I got in, and we came up ten minutes after you did.'

If I had a camera to capture Ian's face at that precise moment, it would've been fit to hang in the Louvre as a real work of art.

'Aw fuck me, this ain't right. Where did Turner and Johnny go, they must've done it.'

'They came up with me and went straight to their room. I'm not being funny but you better report it to the front desk and then get yourself to hospital.'

He looked at me distressed. Just then we heard a knock on the door.

'Eh up, this might be lover boy now.'

Ian just scowled at me before shouting apprehensively, 'Who is it?'

'Room Service!' A fake woman's voice replied back, sounding very similar to Johnny's.

He carried on in the same accent, 'Would you like me to come in and fluff your pillow, Mr Edge... and maybe more?' Ian opened the door to let them in.

'What's going on?' Johnny's voice went back to normal seeing the worried look on Ian's face.

'Ian's been bummed,' I shouted.

'What?' Turner appeared shocked.

'Fuck you,' Ian snarled, before asking, 'Did you two pricks do anything to me last night?'

Johnny and Turner denied the accusations.

'Well, is your arse sore?' Johnny asked.

Ian said nothing, but we couldn't help but chuckle. This just sparked a barrage of questions and statements to wind him up.

'Was he a big guy?'

'Did you pay for it? We all have our little perversions Ian, and don't forget...this is Vegas.'

'It's not gay if you don't back into it.'

'Were you pitching or catching?'

'Were Wham playing?' Johnny said

'Wham? He was walloped,' Turner added.

We creased over uncontrollably and had to cave in because it was just too unbearable to keep going.

Johnny finally surrendered. 'Of course it was us, you tit.'

'Fuck me, I don't know whether to twat you or hug you.' The relief in Ian's tone was clear.

Johnny confessed to Ian what really happened the previous night, showing him the montage of pictures we'd taken when adding objects to him.

'You're both a set of tossers,' he responded. He then threw the condom at Johnny's head, striking him square on his forehead, causing a bit of shampoo to eject and leave a print above his brow. Fits of laughter echoed around the room yet again.

We were quite fortunate that the USA were playing Germany in a friendly whilst we were in Vegas, so we could watch a 'soccer' game while we were there. The sports bar in Planet Hollywood was rammed with fans, and even for a friendly it appeared to capture the imaginations of many people. Most were American, but there was still a contingency of Germans watching too, highlighting just how far the lure of Vegas went.

The game started and the place was awash with pulsating energy even at this early time in the morning. Most people would've had minimal sleep, possibly even going right through the night straight to the game. That was the power Vegas wielded. It bullied the usually sensible into abandoning their principles on their way in, and if they chose to collect them on the way out, then Vegas hadn't done its job properly.

Germany took an early goal lead, but just before half time the USA equalised, bringing about monstrous roars and over the top celebrations. I was glad half time came when it did to stop the excessive cheering from some of the more passionate fans.

In true American fashion, we were given a treat like what I imagined happened at intervals in the more popular American sports. A group of stunning looking cheerleaders duly arrived on the stage in front of the big screen, performing a short dance routine to keep the atmosphere buzzing. They disappeared into the crowd once they finished and were making their way through everyone for some reason. By the time they reached us it was apparent they were promoting something, but what I didn't expect was that it was free shots of tequila, and when I say 'shot', I mean closer to half a pint! Being a group of lads, they naturally assumed we'd be up for one, which really wasn't the case the way I was feeling. A dilemma struck as they expected us to down it whilst they were watching. Did we look a bit manly and hardcore and all do it together in front of six cheerleaders, or shit out due to pounding heads after yet another heavy night? We all looked at each other, searching for direction from one another. I didn't think it was possible for me to down it for risk of ruining the day. Without hesitation Turner slammed the full lot down, coughing his guts up after he'd swallowed it. The cheerleaders applauded, and that prompted the rest of us to hammer ours down if it meant a round of applause from six hot cheerleaders. It burnt the back of my throat as I gulped it down and I immediately regretted the decision. This could be a potential biffle. It was a heavy price to pay just to gain some sort of kudos from unattainable women. It made the second half interesting anyway as I felt like I was floating about.

If the equalising goal wasn't enough of an over the top celebration, then the winning goal near the end was the catalyst for pandemonium. The crowd went mental having beaten the World Champions in a friendly. It was quite unbelievable to see this sort of reaction over a non-event. The final whistle blew to screams of delight and chants of 'U S A, U S A, U S A!!' It was painfully overdramatic!

CHAPTER 13

We decided to make the most of the day and take in some of the attractions that were on the bucket list, aiming to visit as many hotels as possible in the time we had available.

Surprisingly, cloud had settled heavily over the Strip. I was wearing a vest when, shockingly, the rain came showering down and the wind blew with great force despite the warmth circulating the air. We noted that this could only happen to us. Only Northerners could bring our typically grim weather with us to a desert of all places.

We entered the casino within The Mirage, greeted by a plethora of advertising for, 'The Beatles: Love', a show exclusive to the hotel, performed by Cirque de Soleil. On any other occasion we may have booked tickets, but with the way the nights were panning out there was slim chance of us attending. Sat watching a show for a couple of hours was a distraction from full scale drinking and we didn't want to miss a minute of that.

We had to fight our own impulses and resist the temptation of gambling that was everywhere you looked within the casino. We couldn't maintain an all-day gambling session... we'd be skint in no time. The urge passed when we reached the indoor Tropical

Rainforest, which is why we visited The Mirage in the first place having heard about the rainforest attraction. As we entered the 100-foot-high dome, countless palm trees and tropical flora swarmed the place, and the landscape switched from the rabble of gaming to a more peaceful and tranquil setting, complete with the trickling sound of a waterfall and lagoons weaving through the forest. Even though it was stunning, I was slightly disappointed given my high expectations. I had built it up in my own mind to resemble a mini jaunt through a re-creation of the Amazon Rainforest or something similar. Considering the theatrical forward thinking that Vegas presented, it wasn't so far-fetched to assume this was possible. It was in fact quite a small area with a short path that ran through it, and within seconds we pretty much saw everything we needed to.

A short walk away was The Venetian Hotel, a theme derived from Venice, Italy, which had a replica tower of St. Paul's Campanile as one of the main distinguishing features, along with man-made canals. There was a wedding taking place outside that had just finished, and photographs were being taken by the canal that ran as a moat around the hotel. A Gondola could be seen in the distance, highlighting the lengths the owners went to in order to replicate absolutely everything. It was as if they were trying to make you forget you were in Vegas, but had somehow stepped into some parallel dimension of various cultures from around the world. Maybe that's what Vegas was – a weird sort of fantasy driven time machine.

The hotel was majestic and pristine. The shopping

area was made to look like you had just stepped outside into a typical part of Venice itself, with the emphasis on archways and stony walls to create a period effect. It was made more believable by the ceiling being painted in such a way as to look like the skyline, with its bright blue skies and white clouds hovering above. The design created an illusion suggestive of dusk settling in, giving off a very relaxed, artistic, and authentic European ambience. On closer observation, the canal ran through the mall down below, which added to the effect that we'd been transported across the continent. A gondola carrying a woman and two children appeared from the dark tunnel. As they drifted into full view of the watchful crowd, the gondolier started singing, Dean Martin's, 'Volare', in a beautiful operatic voice, and everyone joined in until the final note was sung. Applause and whistling rang through the crowd, leaving the woman riding the gondola red faced. She remained seated, head bowed down trying to hide her blushes.

We carried on walking slowly through the mall, popping our heads into various shops to see whether there was anything of interest. One shop that did strike me was offering highly professional digital photographs of natural beauty set against a moody, black ambience that shrouded the shop's interior. The photos were enlarged and showed rainforests, beautiful coastlines, sunsets, sunrises, snowy mountaintops and deserts, all put into elegant artistic frames. But it was one photograph in particular that really grabbed my attention. It was one that displayed a glistening aerial vision of Puerto Rico, showing the blissful coastline bordered by the deep, tranquil blue sea with crisp golden sands running parallel. I thought of Eva, imagining her residing in such a state of paradise. The more I stared, the more I became lost and entranced. I began to conjure up images of an unrealistic future with Eva and I walking hand in hand along the calm beach in a picture of peace and happiness. I remembered her saying about us swapping lives for a time to show how the other one lives. Although I loved being from the North of England with all it stood for and how the culture is an entity of its own, something was very appealing about exploring a fantasy existence in this utopia setting with such a beautiful woman. But that's all it was, pure fantasy and highly improbable, just as we sometimes imagine ourselves acting out a Hollywood film type scenario. With that grounding thought I broke from the hypnotic stare and we left The Venetian.

Thankfully the rain had finally stopped and the clouds had evaporated. The sun's appearance had made the temperature rise, which finally justified my vest attire and helped me escape a biffle by the skin of my balls.

We swiftly moved down the Strip on our expedition towards another super luxury resort and casino, described as 'Life imitating Art' and 'Imperfect Dreams'. Towering above us in the near distance was the Wynn Hotel, regarded as one of the best hotels in the world. It's the flagship resort of Wynn Properties, pioneered and named by Steve Wynn, who is a sort of father figure to Las Vegas. There's usually a distinguishing feature to draw the punters into all the mega resorts along the Strip, but the Wynn carries no such pull, preferring to appeal to the curiosity of people's imaginations, knowing that the regular Vegas tourist in search of grandeur will have to make the hotel a must visit.

We walked through the shopping mall within the Wynn where all the top labels in the world were under one roof within a few yards of each other: Gucci, Louis Vuitton, and Christian Dior! It was obvious that the hotel was one of the more exclusive establishments in Vegas. Even in mid-afternoon the minimum bets on the tables were higher than prime time at other hotels. Considering my bad luck so far, I decided to spend my money elsewhere on the slot machines. I ordered my free drink, a coffee, which brought a look of bemusement and an icy stare from the waitress, who obviously expected me to be drinking beer – Sin City indeed! But what was wrong with a brew and a cig in the late afternoon, I thought?

I got quite into the slot machines. They weren't like normal fruities in the typical working man's pub, where you had to have some sort of knowledge and a strategy. On these machines there were several different possibilities that could zig-zag in various lines, rather than the usual three in a row straight line we were used to back home. To win big the highest stakes needed to be placed, but by playing with pocket change it hardly affected the bank balance. Gone were the days of hammering quarters into machines and expecting the wishful 'Cha Ching Cha Ching' sound of coins crashing to the ground in a blazing frenzy. You could only play with notes in this modern era, and depending on what machine you were on, $10 could give you half an hour of fun whilst taking free drinks, and even have the very slim prospect of a cash windfall. Any winnings received once cashed out were printed on a ticket to collect from the cage. Any major win we might have been hoping for was only ever going to happen on the slots. I think on blackjack and roulette we would agree that once any of us were up a significant amount, our bottle would've gone and we would've preferred to happily cash in.

We spent an hour or so in the Wynn, and regrettably we didn't explore any further than the slots. Time was dragging on to early evening so we thought it best to head back to the hotel and prepare for the night. We were flagging a bit from all the walking so we took a taxi back. The idea of traipsing back up the Strip that took us so long to get down was a daunting proposition we didn't relish.

CHAPTER 14

I was first to be ready, tactically showering before the others so I could have a bit of alone time downstairs. It was that time again, recapping and attempting to come a bit further in my quest for answers.

I sat in the Heart Bar in Planet Hollywood, supping a bottle of Budweiser in a secluded corner away from distraction, and by distraction, I meant the super-hot busty barmaid who'd served me. I lit a cigarette and took a couple of quick, deep puffs, feeling the rush as the baccy went straight to my head. My eyes became distant and I slowly became unaware of my surroundings and lost inside myself. Tom Petty's, 'Free Fallin', was aptly playing, and faded into the background of the elusive trance I'd dropped into.

I drifted back into the past, churning over events, trying to decipher the actions of Mandy and my own personal feelings of where I was with it. I was still a bit rocked by it all and couldn't quite work out how I felt. Being too close to the situation clouded my judgement. How did things get to this point? We used to be like best friends, so why suddenly turn on me and get engaged so quickly, even if it was already going on behind my back? Why send the brutal text too, using such shattering and cruel descriptions? Unless it was purposely done for some inexplicable reason. All it achieved was to bruise my own self-worth and wipe away all meaning of five years in one foul swoop. It didn't add up.

I didn't know what had upset me the most, the way she left, the fact she was with someone else, or the way she reaffirmed that fact in a text. I hated her for what she'd done, but there's a fine line between love and hate, and that was part of the confusion. Maybe it hurt more because I'd been blinded for five years and I was now seeing her for what she really was - money orientated, manipulative, controlling, and selfish!

It was dawning on me that the latter part of our relationship was more on her terms. When I thought more about our time together there were lots of elements of control I'd failed to recognise at the time. Perhaps she felt like she'd lost some sort of control over me and in some sadistic way tried to get it back by terrorising me with images of her happy new life. If she was truly happy though, then why bother? And why the constant missed calls?

My train of thought continued away from Mandy, focusing on my own personal journey now I wasn't with her. I knew that when I returned home I needed to think about my career position. I was going through so many changes as it was, and it underlined my unhappiness in what I was doing day in day out. I had to take my life in the direction that it should've been going in years ago. I had very little interest in aspects of business, despite my whole career revolving around office work. An element of me was disgusted that I'd succumbed to the pressures and manipulations of

21st Century living, simply settling for a job that was the complete opposite to the viewpoints and teachings from those that inspired me. The thought of working in offices for the next forty years left me nauseous.

Despite all this troubled emotion, I was nearing my third night in Las Vegas and I really was having an absolute blast. I turned to the happier, more recent times of the past two days that gave me a sense of worth. I recollected on Eva and envisaged that prominent Hollywood fantasy with her as I had done earlier in The Venetian. Thinking of Eva was slowly becoming a remedy to the poison inside of me. My mind could see it, my heart recognised it, but I just couldn't feel it yet. Texting her and reading the philosophical poetry she spouted in reply was inspiring. Her last text sent over an hour ago read:

'Always give without needing to receive. Ask and it will be granted. You are so worth much more than you think, and I know you don't see it yet. You will, that much I do promise. Eva. X'

Who was this girl? How did she come up with such inspiring words? Was she in fact real or had the desert thrown up the ultimate mirage in Vegas. Twisted thoughts entered my mind, searching for whether I could recall Johnny, Turner or Ian actually speaking to Eva at any point. It was like I'd conjured her up out of some schizophrenic necessity, and what she was texting me was all from my subconscious. Surely not! I wasn't that fucked up - yet!

Strip clubs weren't on the agenda this evening so there was no danger of wrestling with my principles again. Tonight was about a good old-fashioned booze up and if whoever we met decided to come along for the ride, they would be privileged to have bought the ticket.

It was still relatively early so we decided to have an hour or so in the casino in Planet Hollywood. I was convinced my luck was about to change. It simply had to! I made my way to the low minimum blackjack table, taking up a pew amongst the few Americans already sat there. Again, I was greeted in a friendly manner, shaking hands with the two suave gents either side of me, feeling the same spirited camaraderie experienced the previous night. I laid out three creased $20 notes on the table and waited for the dealer to take my money and pass over my chips. I started on the minimum bet of $10, but felt a little out of my depth upon seeing the amount of chips the guys either side of me were throwing in. My measly $10 chip was embarrassing compared to the piles of $50 chips these guys were haphazardly throwing in. This was an insight into the real Vegas and an example of just how much money can be laid out on the table at any one time. I don't think I could ever see myself playing to the same level. Where would the fun be if you were loaded anyway? Although seeing the amount of money in this one game alone was fascinating, I had a sneaky suspicion that this was still relatively low in terms of just how high the stakes can be in a game of blackjack elsewhere in this city.

The game commenced and I eagerly anticipated the outcome, but was mindful to not get too excited at a $10 win in front of these high rollers. A very risky twelve was dealt to me and I didn't take the chance of busting considering the dealer had been dealt a five, meaning I had a good chance of beating her. Her second card was a nine! She had no alternative but to hit again, and as she turned her third card there it was, a King that beamed, she had bust! It was a great feeling to get off to winning ways, and the games played out like that for the following hands. The high rollers who were flanking me were winning too, but they rarely showed emotion when they won. It was incredible. They must've won several hundred dollars per hand and it didn't seem to matter. They must've been after some serious money.

I, on the other hand, was quite content taking enough money to keep me in beer for the night, and a couple of double down wins and a blackjack win later ensured accomplishing that mission as I walked away with a further $100 to my name. This time I wasn't going to blow it on a 50/50 chance despite the enticing Vegas urge. I cashed my chips in, pleased that I'd put a dent into the losses I'd suffered so far, wished the gentlemen either side of me good luck and bolted from the table before temptation reared its ugly head.

After watching the others finish up their own gambling exploits, where the biggest winner was Turner with $30, we decided to move on to see our next super luxury resort, unanimously selecting the famous MGM Grand Hotel. The premier club there was fittingly named Studio 54, so it couldn't exactly be a let-down considering its tribute to the infamous club in New

York. Strange that New York New York Resort didn't hold the rights to this famed name.

As we entered we were greeted by the legendary bronze statue of the MGM Lion! Apparently, the real lions are kept elsewhere, which would've been cool to see, but once the sun had hidden behind the desert canyons and our collective thrill-seeking natures kicked in, there was little chance of that type of visit happening.

The casino itself was incredible and unsurprisingly huge with a vast hallway fit for royalty. Although the awe factor wasn't wearing off as such, nothing appeared astonishing anymore. The expectation was always to see greatness and splendour everywhere we went, and we were rarely disappointed.

To make the gambling a little more interesting we managed to find a completely empty blackjack table, where all four of us could play at the same time. Finding an empty table at prime time in the MGM was nothing short of a minor miracle really, so I took it as a good sign. I sat third in line from the dealer: Turner first, then Johnny, with Ian to my left. I looked with satisfaction at the four of us huddled around the blackjack table in one of the world's most famous hotels. This was a moment to savour on the trip, and in that instant, we were anyone we wanted to be at the tables, all acting a little cooler than our average esteem allowed... that was until we each pulled out a meagre $50 to begin with, bringing our perceived towering status crashing back down to earth.

The dealer gave us our chips and we threw a whopping

$5 in each to begin with. Something snapped inside of me at the sight of this. Perhaps it was seeing the amount of money the guys back in Planet Hollywood were betting that influenced me.

'Hold on a minute. We're in Vegas and we're all betting $5 each? That's ridiculous. Come on, we're all on the blackjack table together. Let's live a little dangerously and go all in from the off.'

Ian took a big gulp and Johnny and Turner eyed each other.

'Alright, "Big Balls". I'll go with that for the crack.' Johnny was first to respond.

'You know what? Fuck that. Let's go $100!' I raised the stakes in a display of blind courage.

'Are you nuts?' Turner countered. His voice was filled with reluctance.

'Well I'm still in a pretty dark place, I have a shit job, my ex-girlfriend was having an affair, and I'd like to forget those facts and bet big, because that's what people do. Are you with me or are you gonna stick to your low minimum limit?' I goaded.

Johnny gave me a look. 'You want to go $100 I'll go in with you. Fuck it, you're right. It's only money and this is Vegas.' He dug out another $50.

'Knew I could count on you, Johnny. Turner?'

'You set of bastards. Go on then,' he replied, reaching into his pocket to dig out another $50 to throw to the dealer.

'Ha. You're so easily led,' I said.

I turned to Ian who was wafting his shirt collar to get some air.

'Got a bit of a sweat on there Ian? Are you in?'

Ian paused and bobbed his head up and down in thought. 'You guys are fuckers. I actually hate you.'

'Vegas baby, Vegas!' I reminded him.

'Christ...fuck it! I'm gonna kill you if this doesn't work.'

'You're gonna double your money boys... at least. Trust me. This will set up our night.'

The tension mounted within me at the sudden thought of possibly screwing over my mates. God, I hoped for the sake of the night that this move would pay off.

'I don't know how you're affording this Ricky,' Ian commented.

'One life, live it! I'll worry about that when I get home. We're not gonna lose anyway. Positive thoughts only.'

The first card was planted down in front of Turner, and I noticed the change in music from Bob Dylan's, 'Like a Rolling Stone', to 'Vertigo', by U2, just as we saw that he'd been dealt a ten. Good start. The dealer was swift in his motion and before we knew it Johnny had been dealt a nine, me a four and Ian the lucky fuck was dealt an Ace. The dealer gave himself a five before the second wave of cards followed. Turner was given a King that caused him to give a little cheer. Johnny followed suit at his Queen, both having twenty and nineteen respectively, giving them a great chance of winning. I was dealt a nervy eight. Shit! I was on twelve - possibly the worst hand to be dealt, but with the dealer being on five I was still in with a shout. Then came Ian's next card. His hand grabbed the top of my arm as he saw the picture card coming his way, which was another King. 'Blackjack!' he shrieked, before fist punching and screaming, 'Ahhhh-Ha-Ha!' impersonating Ray Liotta in Goodfellas when he wins a card game. We all laughed as we recognised the famous scene he was re-enacting. The smug grin could not be wiped off his face knowing that he'd just won $150...all from my suggestion mind you.

The rest of us couldn't get too excited for the time being as there was still something to play for. Turner and Johnny stuck, so they were close to sealing a win, but it was nervy times for me as I looked at the dealer's five and my twelve. Was it worth hitting? I just knew that the next card would be a ten or a face card as so often is the case in these situations. I grimaced and bit my lip ponderously, then waved my hand to signal to stick. The dealer overturned the next card - a Jack – fifteen! His eyes locked onto mine and widened slightly as he saw what card he was about to turn over from his forced hit - another Jack - meaning he had bust. I couldn't contain my joy, roaring a muffled 'Fuckin' get in!' through gritted teeth and a mini fist punch to myself. All four of us had won and Ian had got blackjack. What a ballsy and spawny move that was. Never again would I suggest something like that without anything behind us from a big win first. However, now we had that win, I tempted the others.

'We going again?'

'Hell yeah!' Johnny said whilst leaving his $100 in

and taking the other $100 for safe-keeping. Turner followed suit without saying a word. This time Ian took $50 away from his initial $100 and left $50 to bet with, pocketing the other $150. 'Only half this time. I'm not you. I want to enjoy some of this win.'

'Fair point,' I agreed.

The dealer set out to deal the cards again. Turner was dealt a six, Johnny an eight, me a seven, and Ian was dealt another Ace.

'You gotta be fuckin' kidding me?' Turner said when he saw Ian's card.

The smugness in Ian's face grew more evident.

The dealer dealt himself an eight. Alarm bells initially rang. This game was going to be tight. Back to Turner and he was dealt a five taking him to eleven. Johnny was dealt a ten to make eighteen, and I was dealt a six. 'For fuck's sake!' I uncontrollably blurted. I had thirteen which was a shit number to have in this situation – again! But before I got to make my decision I had to suffer Ian's goading ways when a Queen was slammed down in front of him to give him blackjack again. The Ray Liotta impression made another appearance and just like the first time we all laughed despite the pressure that was unfolding.

Time for Turner's decision and he risked a double down. He was on eleven and hoped for a ten or face card to take him to twenty-one. He put a further $100 worth of chips next to his initial bet and waited for his solitary card to be dealt. Nine! Good effort indeed. He had twenty but he wasn't over the line yet. Johnny stuck on eighteen and it was now my turn. I had no choice really but to go for it. It was likely the dealer would beat thirteen with whatever cards were dealt next so I had to hit. I pointed downwards to the table to signal another card and he slowly laid it out in front of me...a two! Shit! Fifteen! Not good enough. The others ooh'd as the pressure mounted. 'Go for it', I thought! I prodded again for another card and closed my eyes, opening them when I heard Turner exclaim, 'You lucky bastard!' I opened my eyes to see a three shining in front of me. Jesus! Eighteen! That was too damn lucky. I signalled for no more cards. We collectively hoped and prayed that the luck just ran on into this game. The dealer's next card was overturned and it was a five. Thirteen! Agonising, but that was good. Surely the next card would be a nine or above. Time stood still as the next card came into view. The Queen that we all prayed for seemed to wink at us as it was overturned, and we all won again as the dealer bust! We embraced each other and together we cheered - in relief more than anything else. Turner was especially happy given that he'd just won $200 on that one hand alone. This was what Vegas gambling was all about. Ok it may not have been the lofty amounts most gamble with, but this was what we could afford, and to take winnings at this level meant a great deal to us. For me, it had put a severe dent into the first couple of nights' stupidity, but for the other three, they pretty much had money to play with for a few days.

I think the nerves started to get the better of us, so we took the risk factor down a bit. We were happy with what we'd won on two rounds of big bets so there was a decision to reduce the stakes to a more reasonable amount to make sure we left with a hefty win. The stakes lowered to $10-$20 for the next twenty hands or so that followed. Losses did occur, but so did a few wins too, including wins on blackjack and double downs, meaning we all cashed out with a strong profit.

I counted my chips when they were returned to me and they tallied $350! This was my biggest ever win in a casino and it happened *in* Las Vegas and *in* the MGM Grand. Surely that was written in the stars? But more importantly, I had clawed back more of the money lost to gambling in the past two days. Ian had taken $300, Turner was the big winner at $450, and Johnny, despite getting a little carried away with his stakes at times, still walked away $250 up. None of us could complain whatsoever.

We sauntered through the casino enjoying our free beer from that game, soaking up the vibe with no need to gamble further. As we neared the bottom of our Budweiser bottles, I gestured to drink up quickly. The scores of people that walked past us heading in the direction of Studio 54 hadn't escaped my notice. Judging from the vast numbers, it seemed that the club was possibly going to throw up one hell of a night. Feeling blessed with the abundance of money we now carried, we joined the queue in anticipation of the night fully shifting into a higher gear.

CHAPTER 15

After waiting in the queue for what seemed like an eternity, we entered something resembling a dark cauldron of the vivacious underworld of Vegas flamboyance. The music was absolutely hammering. The vibrations shuddered through my bones, and the ground and walls effervescently rocked, pulsing to the deafening bass firing from inside. The lights flashed vigorously, and streams of lasers dashed around, resembling a Pink Floyd gig. On first look it was staggeringly awash with those who took pleasure in sinning to the early dawn. The perceptible energy fuelled their existence and created an electric atmosphere.

The dance floor was to the right-hand side about half way in as you entered. It was somewhat narrow and raised up by a step that had a barrier running around it. A further stage was mounted on top and set against the wall - obviously designed for live performances. Considering the size of the place and the number of people flocking in, it seemed like it was going to be a privilege just to obtain a foothold on there, yet that didn't stop Turner and Johnny wanting to get straight in amongst the crowd and make their presence known.

Ian went with them, but judging by how much of an effort it was for the three of them to get a position on the floor, I knew it'd be too cramped and awkward for me to even try. I couldn't be arsed being packed in like a sardine and being so close to the annoying actions of some of the American men. Their fascinating attempts at pulling were again on show. Some had no shame, or knowledge of the dynamics of meeting women, seeming incapable of initial conversation or even scraping the barrel of a corny chat up line. They just bounced their way over, slipped in front of, or behind, any woman and grinded like an oversexed reptile with hands wandering everywhere, eager to feel the warm, sweaty flesh of a woman's skin. It began to irritate me, but why should I care? It made no difference to me. Something else was bugging me evidently, enough for me to break away from my friends and hang alone by the bar instead.

Despite the club being packed, the queue for the bar was empty, and I could quickly get served. Perhaps the queue was non-existent in the same way the queue for the bar at the infamous Hacienda used to be non-existent, in that people didn't need drink, but relied on other forms of recreational stimulation. Judging by the current energy, it was a distinct possibility.

I sat against the bar at the far end, looking like an alcoholic alone with his thoughts. A cigarette pursed my lips adding to the effect as the club continued to thump along. My troubled mind had not been eased by the huge win earlier, and it drifted aimlessly from thoughts of the Hacienda onto the current music scene. I wondered how a Hacienda type club would be received in Las Vegas. Now that's a scary thought!

The venue began to play an array of songs from

today's era in a mash up medley. Watching people on the dance floor get off on this new tripe was deflating, and I slumped further into the bar with disappointment, especially because the venue was perfect for great rock 'n' roll music. Considering what I'd been seeing and hearing at gigs in Manchester, I couldn't believe that this was what was now popular in today's world. Fair enough, I didn't expect underground Manchester band music to be played in a Vegas club, but what about the classic rock genre that helped shaped American culture? How had the quality of music diminished so rapidly? I always saw today's 'pop' scene as music to appease others, as if people only liked it to impress those around them because it was the latest thing out that day. There was no soul or depth to the songs produced nowadays in commercial music. Rock 'n' Roll band music, and guitar orientated solo artists, on the other hand, were a completely different kettle of fish. It was about yourself and how it made *you* feel, having to impress no one because it's all about your own state of mind and emotions. You could gain knowledge from the lyrical and musical content that showed you something about the world and yourself, something that can't be taught in any school.

There was a time when all these fantastic bands dominated the airwaves in bars and clubs around the world. It was born out of a youth culture that had something to say and they fuckin' said it, but it doesn't appear to exist anymore on any substantial level. There's too much interest in the latest iPhone, who's said what on social media, who's wearing the latest designer outfit, or what the plastic celebs are up to these days for anyone to be concerned with the profoundness of musicians. This shallow mindset has contributed to the crushing of proper band music, preventing its return to its rightful place, and all we're left with is uninspiring and soulless talent competitions on TV.

The past was an era that was regarded as the best time for music, so why pollute that memory with the lacklustre shite of today. And why were these people dancing to the likes of this apparent 'phenomenon', Justin fuckin' what's his name? In terms of music, more than most things, the world has gone mad.

I could feel myself delving deeper into this theory, as always happened after a few beers when the music being played was shite, where lyrics are either cheesy or more about affirming egos. No wonder the music industry is on its arse today. Characters and legends are never born anymore. The business and money side of it has seen to it that the Jim Morrisons, Keith Moons and Keith Richards of this world will never make it again because they wield too much power that poses a threat to the status quo. Music moguls would much rather manipulate a set of pretty boys or sexy looking women than back anything or anyone of any substance, and that's a sad state of affairs. Part of me doesn't blame them though. Targeting music (if you could call it that) at teenage girls is a real money-spinner. But, what if you began targeting a real band at them? Do teenage girls dictate how music is evolving, or is it imposed on them by the industry? It's a chicken and egg question, but I suspect it has been forced on them...along with many other contributing factors within the media that has helped shaped this new age of society.

All in all, we will never again experience the quality of music or the crazy antics of band members that the golden decades of the 50s, 60s, 70s, 80s and 90s produced. Maybe I'll fix that on my return and create my own record label called, 'Fuck the Gentry', and wage my own personal war and crusade, leading a revolution of armed musicians into battle against the establishment. Our anthem would be The Who's, 'Won't Get Fooled Again'. History tells us we'll lose but at least we'll have glory in defeat and have at least fought for something worth fighting for, our freedom and love of music. But before we do, we will burn down every office that embodies a nine till five regime where shirts and ties are compulsory. Burn them all down I say, let their petty rules and regulations die with the bricks and mortar that come tumbling down.

Jesus! My anger was bubbling and nearly exploded into something tangible as these crazy thoughts dominated any calmness left inside. I think my anger was shifting from recent life events and manifesting itself in my thoughts about music. I thought it would be wise to get a JD, light up another cig, and calm the fuck down before I ended up launching a bottle into the crowd for no other reason than to incite a riot, just for the hell of it. What the fuck was happening to me? The adrenaline was causing my hands to shake and the blood rushed to my head. It was necessary to clear my mind before I did something ridiculous and got myself arrested. Was the initial fear and danger of being in

Vegas with a troubled and precarious mind now toying with my vulnerability? Beforehand I'd perceived that Vegas could be a dangerous adventure or an ingenious recipe to rid me of past pain and cleanse my mind. Was the former slowly trickling through the vessels in my brain so that eventually I'd be lost in a whirlwind of depraved anger with no way back to normality - whatever normality was out here?

I closed my eyes and began taking deep breaths to try and calm down. Thoughts of Mandy were still swirling about in the background and I had to try and wipe them from my mind, as well as the anger around music too. My heart rate was slowing after a period of thumping. After a minute or so I opened my eyes and felt much calmer, and in the meantime, someone had taken up a stool next to me at the bar, which momentarily broke my train of thought from these extreme musings.

I could see in my peripheral vision that a girl was looking at me, but I was in no mood for entertaining the idea. It seemed I didn't have a choice though when she tapped my shoulder and smiled as I turned to face her. She was small with a slim figure and shoulder length black hair. She appeared quite young looking and had a very cute face that amplified her look of innocence. Her eyes were unbelievable: large, dark and mysteriously brooding, standing out as her most noteworthy feature, suggesting that this cute portrayal led you into a false sense of security. Her smile was melting and meaningful with dimples forming on both cheeks. She wore a fashionably strapless, silky, turquoise dress that came down to below her knees, fitting her slender body perfectly.

She began to speak, 'Hey, are you Ricky?'

'Yeah!' I looked bemused. 'How do you know my name?'

'Is it Turner, your friend over there? He asked me to come over and talk to you because you look sad.'

It turned out the others had been watching me in my trance, taking the piss out of me before chatting to a group of four girls, sending the prettiest one over in a rescue attempt. Little did they know the anger that I was feeling, instead misinterpreting it for sadness. But I must admit, their plan worked, and all twisted thoughts faded further, and a sense of regularity resumed.

'What are you doing over here all alone?' she asked.

'Nothing. It's not important really. Just having a little time out,' I lied.

'Where are you guys from anyway? You have beautiful accents.'

'Beautiful?' No one has ever said our strong Mancunian accents were beautiful before, but this was America, a place known for a love of us English, so I suppose any accent from another country is deemed a bit sexy when it deviates from the normal dialect… unless it's Scouse!

'I'm from Manchester, in *England*. Where are you from?' I asked, emphasising England so as not to be confused with the one in New Hampshire.

'Phoenix. I'm Lucy by the way.'

'As in, "In the Sky with Diamonds"?'

'What?'

'Never mind.' She looked too young to understand, but I felt a need to justify myself so I didn't look like some mentalist sprouting out random jargon.

'You know, like The Beatles song, "Lucy in the Sky with Diamonds".'

'Ah right!' she exclaimed, 'Yes, I love The Beatles.' Nice save I thought, but I shouldn't have tried to be funny in the first place.

'What brings you to Las Vegas then?' I asked.

'What?'

'What brings you to Las Vegas?' I raised my voice.

'I'm sorry?' She leaned in closer, close enough for me to catch the scent of some type of Jasmine based perfume that had me tingling, almost making me forget my initial question and my earlier qualms about music.

'Why are you in Las Vegas!?' I nearly shouted in broken English.

'Oh, sorry! It's my friends 21st birthday. What about you?'

'Random Holiday!' Under my breath I muttered, 'Good Question!'

What was I doing here? What was the meaning of this trip? Given how much I'd built up the life changing aspect beforehand, I refused to believe it would end up being just another holiday. Don't get me wrong, I was having a fabulous time in fabulous Las Vegas, but the deeper meaning and the change in mindset that I yearned for hadn't yet come to fruition. I perceived my reason to be here was to search for the answers I needed so much. Where was my revelation and my release from Mandy and the past? Where was the epiphany that would change the course of my career and life? I guess I just had to keep rolling the dice and go with the flow until that moment arrived…if at all.

It was too loud to get into a proper conversation with Lucy. The walls and floor continued to vibrate and explode to the dance anthems ringing out, so I signalled to her to join the others on the dance floor now that a little more space had been created. We made our way over, squeezing past people until we hit our group, but Lucy stayed just outside the circle of her friends and began to move coolly to the thumping beats.

I could hardly say I was surprised when she turned her back on me, retreating half a yard or so till our bodies touched, eventually adopting the position and move of a slow grind as she backed right up against my groin. I had become the very thing I'd ridiculed for the last few days, but with Jack Daniels circulating through my body, who was I to give a fuck? She moved seductively, grinding against my crotch whilst interlocking her fingers in mine, placing my hands firmly on her hips. I couldn't remember the last time a girl who was so much younger than me last showed an interest, barring Eva of course, but Lucy was a few years younger than her. It always seemed to be the older women who wanted to take me home and adopt me, but I wasn't arguing with the change that Vegas brought.

I lifted my head and couldn't believe my eyes as

my friends were all in the same position, each stood behind one of Lucy's friends whilst they grinded away, and to top it all off we were in a perfectly formed circle now. I bet there was a group of English lads stood on the other side of the venue taking the piss out of us in the same way we'd been doing at the very same image. How ridiculous we must've looked, but we blended in perfectly with our American friends.

It began to get too crowded again on the dance floor, so I asked Lucy if she wanted to come and get a drink with me - I was more in the mood for drinking than dancing. She accepted and followed me off towards the bar where we chatted and I learnt a little more about her. She was twenty-one years old and was experiencing Vegas for the first time, seven years before I'd got around to it. Of course, she lived a lot closer than me but it still made me think. She was still in college studying American History and wanted to get into teaching once she'd finished.

Tongue in cheek I said, 'American History must be very easy because it's only about two hundred years old. You want to go to Europe where there's proper history.'

She put me in my place, revealing, 'I've been to Europe actually. Rome, Paris and Barcelona a couple of years ago.'

I was impressed, yet I envied her. She'd travelled further and more often than me, experiencing a fair deal of life already. It made me realise just how much I'd missed out on by being in a dead-end relationship, and highlighted a void in my life. I'd been to Barcelona and Paris, but not till I was twenty-four, and they were only a couple of hours away on a plane. Lucy had travelled half way across the world already and probably knew more about those places from a historical point of view than I did. Perhaps she had parents who gave her a shit load of money so she could experience these types of things, but that didn't matter. Life had been moving fast and was still moving on all around me whilst I settled into a brainwashed, insignificant and uneventful lifestyle. To see someone so young embarking on such adventures just made me resent my past relationship that little bit more. My true adventure seeking self that was brimming at University had slowly been eroded, all because of a woman who clearly didn't give too much of a shit about me. Anger rose again as I thought this. I really needed to suppress this rage that kept rushing to the surface. It wasn't a good sign that thoughts of my relationship with Mandy could lead to this reaction. I lit up another cigarette to calm me down, necked the remainder of my JD, and ordered another to throw down whilst Lucy was still only a third of the way through hers.

The JD continued to flow and to some extent curbed the anger. It was not the ideal way to stifle the rage, but it'd have to do for now. Lucy was drinking Vodka, Lime and Soda, and I was only too happy to be buying them for her, probably because of my blackjack win earlier, but if this situation was in Manchester, at these prices, then I would've been a tight bastard and only bought her one, and a single at that.

I noticed that the others had separated from Lucy's friends. They still stood close by, occasionally chatting to them, but I could tell they were looking elsewhere for the next group of girls to prey on. I was just happy that Lucy seemed to be enjoying my company, and it was cool being with her without feeling like I needed to instigate a move of any sorts. She was a great girl, but she didn't invoke the same thunderbolt I'd felt with Eva. Despite her being a beautiful young woman and getting on well with her, something just didn't seem right about everything. It was nothing to do with her at all, but there was just something within me that couldn't be bothered taking it any further. I was content to enjoy the rest of the night and carry on the excellent Vegas-style time with the drinking, laughing and the never-ending grinding.

It must have concerned Lucy that I hadn't made a move because she hit me with a question out of nowhere.

'Hey, I'm pretty sure I know the answer to this, but do you have a girlfriend?' Her directness took me by surprise.

'No, but once upon a time I did. It's a long story that I'm not getting into.' Why did people keep asking me that question, forcing me to remember?

I decided to turn the tables. 'What about you? Do you have a boyfriend?'

Her devious smile and lack of answer was evidence enough.

'You have, haven't you?' I was surprised.

She nonchalantly shrugged her shoulders, slipped off the stool, brushed her hand across my shoulder, and returned to her friends leaving me with my own thoughts on the matter.

It was about four in the morning and it was only at this point as I began to stagger out of Studio 54 that I realised just how drunk I was after numerous Jack Daniels and bottles of Budweiser! Once the bouncers had ushered us outside, the four girls invited us back to their hotel at New York New York for more drinks. None of the others had pulled any of the girls, never going further than dancing, or 'grinding' as we now referred to it as. There was a temptation to go back to their hotel and carry on the night even if nothing happened with any of them. Sometimes the night doesn't necessarily become about trying to pull, sometimes it's just about experiencing something a little different with no strings attached, and having a laugh with people from a culture that differs from your own. From my point of view this was one of those nights, which is why I hadn't bothered probing any further as to whether Lucy had a boyfriend or not. I realised that it didn't matter as I wasn't really interested, and it felt good not to put myself under any pressure to do anything more. New York New York was only over the road from MGM so we were there in no time.

CHAPTER 16

New York New York was a blast! We were sat amongst a cluster of slot machines and whittled away time by playing drinking games. It could've been more extreme but the girls were clearly not seasoned pros in excessive drinking. The conversation inevitably steered towards a more boyish, suggestible, and cheeky North England humour level...well, pub talk! Over the years, holidays and nights out tended to go down this route when we met a group of girls for the first time, especially when we were all outside our comfort zones.

Turner, who was the first to divert the conversation down this road, suggested we played, 'Never Have I Ever'. I had to laugh! It was vintage Turner, always intrigued to find the deepest and darkest secrets the girls had in their closet, whilst simultaneously eyeing an opportunity to tell his own story and cause shock with some of his own filthy antics from down the years. Perhaps the truth about where he disappeared to in the strip club would come into play at some point. 'Never Have I Ever' is a drinking game where you all take it in turns to make a questing statement about something that you may or may not have done. If any of the group had done said activity, then they drink. Depending on the question it could cause potential embarrassment or, on the flip side, raise your 'kudos' levels.

Turner showed no restraint, asking several leading questions from the start, like, '"Never Have I Ever" had a one-night stand', or '"Never Have I Ever" slept with someone not from my country'. I think he was trying to find out which of the girls was the more likely to sleep with him, but he found it tough to detect. These were 'nice' girls who obviously hadn't been corrupted in the same way we had. Initially, the questions they asked were very tame and completely unrelated to sex, much to Turner's disappointment. After his encouragement, they revealed more, but Turner seemed frustrated that the answers they were giving showed no sign of helping his lustful cause. Adding to his frustration was that Lucy looked the most adventurous of the four and it appeared she was more into me than him, having moved from her chair to sit on my knee. It quickly became apparent that the four girls had been quite reserved in their sexual exploits, making the four of us guys look like deviants in comparison. Once Turner sussed this out he stopped the game and went to get more drinks.

Another couple of rounds later and I was done, slowly slipping into a chasm of extreme tiredness compounded by the amount of alcohol I'd consumed. I struggled to lift my eyes and I felt bleary and drained of life, completely smashed on the mix of drinks devoured throughout the night. Everything was cloudy and my thoughts were all over the show, but I clung onto an ounce of control where I just about knew what I was doing. It was only my legs and eyes that had a mind of their own.

Amid my drunken stupor, I'd noticed that one of the girls, Sally, had made a move to sit on Ian's lap. She was a plain looking girl on first glance, but she carried a subtle attractiveness the more you looked. She didn't dress specifically sexily, but behind her plainness was a lot of laughter and an infectious giggle. Her smiley eyes made her look kind of cute too. Ian had done well and that quiet confidence that I knew he'd been hiding was shining through.

Turner and Johnny continued to fight for the other girls, Kayleigh and Ashley. They pulled out all the stops with their typical quick-witted banter as a source of ammunition. The girls were amused by it, but judging from their tame answers in 'Never Have I Ever', it seemed a wasted exercise. They were just happy to have a good time and enjoy the night for what it was, without being led astray by two Mancunian horn dogs – but I don't think Turner and Johnny could complain with how the night had gone. It'd been hysterical and certainly one to remember for a while.

Ian and Sally sloped off towards the lifts and chatted alone for a few minutes. It acted as the catalyst for us all to propose calling it a night. I'd reached my limit with alcohol and couldn't take any more. Ian signalled for five more minutes when we shouted our intentions to him. We said goodbye to the other girls, but Lucy stayed behind, looking like she wanted to be alone with me. In my drunken state I couldn't really garner what to make of it. Ian returned and I said I'd catch up with them to give Lucy her wish. Once we were alone and her friends had got into a lift, she asked me to walk her back to her room. I was reluctant because I knew how big this place was and I was desperately tired. Being a gent though, I led the way. Lucy caught up after a few steps and linked her arm in mine as we walked slowly - and unsteadily - to the lifts.

We weaved our way around several corners on god knows what floor, until we came upon the corridor that led to her room. We stopped short on the corner, ten yards or so away. She held back so she could continue talking to me. This time she steered the conversation directly to our personal lives and I asked, 'So come on then, you've avoided the subject all night. Tell me the truth, do you have a boyfriend?'

She looked deep into me and gave me the answer I suspected, 'I do, yes.' My suspicions were confirmed. I divulged what was going on in my life in only a few slurred words. My voice tailed off as I bared a few thoughts from my damaged soul to her. Her face transformed to a look of empathic concern.

She started to speak again, 'Look, we're in Vegas and yes I do have a boyfriend, but not serious. I like you Ricky, but if you don't want to go any further that's ok.' I suspected the answers given in 'Never Have I Ever' were a smokescreen given what she was implying. Or was this simply what Vegas does to people's minds and inhibitions?

Her words did show a maturity beyond her tender age. She was very understanding for a twenty-one-year-old and that frightened me. I shouldn't be all that surprised if going by certain American TV shows was any indication. Shows like, 'Dawson's Creek', and, 'One Tree Hill', were full of dialogue from teenagers that seemed way beyond their years, something that wasn't part of British youth culture. We always considered it to be quite dramatic and cheesy, but I was rapidly finding myself in the middle of a fuckin' episode of one of these 'T4' type shows.

Lucy remained quiet as I thought hard about what was right. She was leaving with her friends the following day so this would be the last time I saw her on this trip. She bit her bottom lip indicating an awkward vulnerability, an innocence that eventually won me over and I couldn't help but give her what she wanted. I pushed her back against the wall in a fit of passion, momentarily losing all inhibitions. She let her guard down, throwing her arms around my neck and shoulders in a display of amorous affection. We must've been kissing for only a few seconds when it hit me like a knockout left hook. I pulled away sharply. She took a quick, deep breath. Her kaleidoscope eyes were unfocused and watery.

'What's wrong?' she cried.

'I can't carry on Lucy.'

'Why not? Is it me?'

'No, not at all,' I said sincerely. I couldn't look at her…my gaze turned downwards towards the floor. Images of Mandy and everything that happened rushed to the surface like an 80s movie montage that battered me senseless. It was enough to make me abruptly pull away and lose all motivation to go any further with her.

I suddenly realised that in my quest, the answers didn't lie with women, and to some extent they made it worse. It served to be a massive cover up for what was really bothering me. I never thought I'd see myself break up a kissing frenzy that was on the cusp of escalating to the bedroom, but I couldn't explain this Mandy rage that overwhelmed me. She continued to have this hold over me and it was getting beyond the absurd now. Uncovering the reason as to why she popped into my head now, and why she made an appearance just after Eva left, was bordering on a psychologist's wet dream!

'I'm sorry, I just can't do it. It's not you. I just know this isn't right, for me or for you.'

Her shoulders sank but she still managed to flash that cute smile.

'I understand Ricky. It's ok. Come here.' She reached out to put her arms around me.

I felt like crying, overcome with frustrated and drunken emotion...and I hadn't even had any Stella! Why couldn't I want Lucy and be normal doing what most men in my position would've done without a second thought? Why did this shit with Mandy keep attacking me? Why couldn't I swerve passed it? Why did this ruthless woman from my past have such an effect and hold over me? If the answer wasn't in women, then what the fuck was it in? The old adage of the 'the best way to get over someone is to get on top of someone else' wasn't working.

We stood in the corridor holding each other. She reiterated her understanding after I finally revealed the full weight on my mind. I grasped her disappointment, but I made her aware that mine was greater.

She loosened her arms from around me and slowly side stepped away. We looked at each other with grave sadness and a regretful smile, thinking it best that we say our goodbyes there and then. I watched as she reluctantly opened the door to her room, giving me one final look and a reassuring grin before disappearing, officially sealing our night together. The door closed and I remained motionless in the corridor, shoulders wilting under the weight of angst. A solitary tear formed in the corner of my eye and I fought hard to hold it back. I cursed myself as my mind shaped thoughts that could lead to madness. Fear that I couldn't get out of this mindset gripped me. Loathing myself for letting it get the better of me. 'Fear and Loathing in Las Vegas' one might say…that sounded like a good title for a book.

After a few wrong turns in this labyrinth, I found my way to the lifts, and despite seeing two of every button, I managed to prod the correct one that brought me to the ground floor.

I was physically, emotionally and mentally drained, as well as completely stinking drunk. I passed a Starbucks on my way out and decided a strong coffee was well needed at this moment, especially as the free coffee served in the casinos was dour. I ordered a regular Americano and stumbled towards the exit, stopping short with the realisation that I really needed the toilet before tackling the dreary and lonely twenty-five-minute walk back to Planet Hollywood …perhaps longer given my state.

I made my way into the toilets near the exit, filled with relief at the number of unspoiled cubicles available so I could take a dump in peace and not be disturbed. I plonked myself down in the furthest 'trap' and did what I had to do. I got a little too relaxed, and in my distortion from reality, I slowly drifted off into a snooze, jeans nestled around my ankles with my body hanging over to the left against the frame of the cubicle.

As my body sagged further, I keeled over off the seat and woke myself up when my head crashed against the door, scaring the shit out of me (pardon the pun). How long was I asleep for? I don't know, but I was mortified to realise that for some reason I'd slipped into the surrealist of dreams starring Buffalo Bill from, 'Silence of the Lambs', and his basket full of lotions that he wanted me to rub on my skin, or else I'd get the hose again. Creepy shit, I tell you! I could've been there seconds, a minute, a few more maybe, but surely no longer than ten? Imagine if I'd slept there all night? God knows what Buffalo Bill would've got up to then! With that realisation, I knew that I needed to get back to Planet Hollywood pronto. I sorted myself out and picked up my coffee, which was lukewarm, providing evidence that I had perhaps been sat there a bit longer than I first thought, and proceeded to get the fuck out of New York New York before any other embarrassing biffles occurred.

Upon exiting the large doors, I realised that time really had no meaning in Vegas. The sun was shining brightly overhead, and for the third night in a row I was still up and about at an ungodly hour and seeing daylight before sleep. This was how I had wanted Vegas to be and I wasn't disappointing myself in that respect.

Any normal person, even myself back in Manchester, would've plodded straight up the stairs and got some much-needed rest once they reached their hotel. However, this was Vegas and things are done differently here, just like in Manchester as Anthony H. Wilson once proclaimed. I began to develop a second wind, probably from the fresh desert air that had reinvigorated my battered body. I wasn't ready to let the night/morning go to waste for a petty thing like sleep.

The casino was still relatively busy, certainly busier than I'd expected for that time in the morning. It was still full of all the die-hard gamblers in search of a big win. I wondered how much money most of them were down? It may have been thousands of dollars in some cases. The fact that I was willing to join them made me wonder whether I was just as bad in terms of addiction?

I made my way through the Pleasure Pit where all the roulette, blackjack and variations of poker tables were situated. I looked for a low minimum table and found one that was empty. The croupier was a stunning oriental woman who looked at me enticingly as I glanced over. She beckoned me to the table with a bubbly smile and a warm wave, so I plodded over to take up a stool, and put $80 on the table.

She spoke in an American accent, 'Alright! Let's win you some money, man.'

I began to ooze confidence, feeling the good fortune at the table. She asked me about my night.

'I'm still here now so it's all good.' My response was

unnaturally enthusiastic given what had just happened with Lucy and what time it was. Maybe it was in gambling that redemption lay, which was a terrible saving grace to rely on.

She said, 'This is Vegas, man. You're supposed to be up all hours.' I chuckled and sprang to life encouraged by her motivational words as I continued to live the unrealistic dream. The first cards were dealt and I immediately hit the ascendancy. A couple more hands followed and I was beginning to get on a roll. Every time I won she would high five me looking more pleased with the win than me. She apologised for the occasional loss, but redeemed herself by dealing me blackjack or successful double downs. She was the best croupier I'd ever met, not only in terms of her good luck charm, but her manner, energy and attitude made me feel like a high roller. I showed my appreciation for this by tipping her $5 every time she dealt me blackjack or a win on a double down, which was probably why she was so receptive, playing me like the drunken fool I was. The frequency these wins came out was surreal and I must have tipped her about $70 in total, but what did I care, the wins kept on rolling. At one point, I hit being about $300 up, but like all card games and gambling, that luck eventually ran out and slowly it diminished. I should've walked away with the big winnings, but I was enjoying myself too much by pushing my usual boundaries. However, I did end up being surprisingly sensible, choosing to walk away with a further $200 win to add to this very impressive night of gambling.

At least the night had ended on a positive note, but

in reality, it didn't mask over the issues I still faced, and the pitiable situation of the whole Lucy ordeal that I would regret one day. Any normal person would still be involved in a frantic sex session with her right now. Not me though, I'd become far too pathetic to enjoy myself that much. Maybe this was all just a sign of the times and part of growing up. Perhaps sex with strangers was becoming less of a priority and all that was left was to quietly wallow with a few beers and complain about how shit life and music has become. Surely life couldn't get that depressing? I wasn't ready for that! I thought it best to leave the philosophy in the lift before I entered my room, and hope that a new day would bring a better mood as I would again roll the dice in this everlasting quest for answers.

CHAPTER 17

The sleep that my body craved was defeated by sheer resistance in my mind. The overindulgence was beginning to take its toll, but I saw that as a minor sacrifice for the greater good. I was developing a mental strength that demanded to experience everything possible in Vegas, and that was overcoming normal practices.

After only a few hours' sleep I was sat up in bed. Of course, the fact that the past constantly nagged at me also contributed to this lack of slumber.

The plan for the day was to begin with a visit to the Stratosphere Hotel, home to the famous, yet daunting three roller coaster rides that lurched precariously on the roof of the hotel. There was also an option to take the Sky Jump, which was a bungee style dive from the top of the hotel at 800ft, straight to the bottom, feet first like a leap of faith, or a leap of death as I saw it!

The journey to Stratosphere was littered with abuse thrown my way by the others for not taking advantage of the situation with Lucy. I tried to block it out, but I fully deserved my slating, no matter what my excuses were. I was heading to the right place if I wanted to momentarily forget – adrenaline fuelled, thrill-seeking roller coaster rides seemed a good idea to create a respite from reflection.

We arrived at Stratosphere just in time to see some lunatic plummet from the top of the skyscraper down to the ground in this controlled fall.

'I guess that's the Sky Jump then?' Turner said as we all looked up.

'Fuck that! Lunacy!' Ian stared aghast.

'Too right! That looks scary as fuck!' I agreed. 'You get me on that thing and I'll end up being bandied about the internet in a photo titled with the word, "PRICELESS!" under my shit stained shorts.'

'It does look a bit high! The three rides are on top of that thing?' Ian looked up nervously, before pointing up. 'I can see one of them from here! It dangles you over the bastard side!'

'I bet its mint! Stop being a pussy, Ian,' Johnny goaded.

'Sensible! Not a pussy!'

'Since when did sensible ever stop us anyway?' Turner countered.

I must admit, looking up and straining my neck just to get the whole view of the hotel left me feeling a little nauseous, but there was no way I, or any of us, could back out. It wouldn't be worth the ribbing for the rest of the holiday, which would predictably extend to when we returned home when our other friends would also undoubtedly hear about it.

If I felt a little nauseous standing outside at the bottom of this gargantuan tower, then what I was feeling stood on the roof must've been close to a full-blown panic attack! Jesus, we were high! My thrill-seeking nature had been quite content with the 'Big One' at Blackpool, or 'Oblivion' at Alton Towers, but this was psychotic! Which pillock had the idea to put three rides on top of a skyscraper? Surely it wasn't safe!

A breeze whispered through the air that wasn't felt hundreds of feet below. There weren't many people knocking around, meaning we'd quickly be on whichever ride we decided to go on first, which was probably a good thing, giving us little time to think too much about it. We knew it wouldn't be a long wait before the feeling of complete terror would drench us!

'Right, which one first lads?' Turner asked eagerly.

'You can fuck right off!' Ian snapped.

'Bollocks, you're coming on all of them.'

'I ain't getting on any of them. You must be fuckin' mental the lot of you!'

'Don't be a ponce Ian. You know you'll never hear the end of it if us three go on and you don't. Once you're on you'll be fine, and at least you can say you've done it.'

'He's right you know. Remember back in the airport? It's about experiencing this together so if you don't then you're letting the side down,' I almost pleaded.

Ian caved, 'I'll tell you what! I'll do one to start with, but the least scary looking one.'

'I don't think that's going to help. Have you seen them? They all look shit scary,' I retorted.

'Well I reckon we should go on the Big Shot. It's just like that ride at Blackpool.'

'Except 1000ft higher!' Johnny laughed at that fact.

'Who gives a shit? We're going on all of them,' Turner chipped in.

'Come on, let's get this done with! Ricky?? Please hold me!' Ian clutched his arms around me in a jesting manner, but I sensed he was only *half* joking.

The Big Shot was a ride where you sat in rows of four around a cubed tower that eventually launched vertically to the very top at a whopping 1081ft above ground level. Out of the three rides, this was probably the least scary because, unlike the other two, it didn't dangle you over the sides, and I felt I needed to build up to that!

We were just in time to see the end of the current ride, with most of the riders being teenage girls who screamed loudly, not exactly filling Ian with a lot of confidence. Funnily enough, The Killers', 'Mr Brightside' was playing, which I hoped wouldn't end up being an ironic story. I could see the headline:

'Ride Kills Passengers as The Killers Play'

The ride finished and everyone unbuckled their seat belts and left the area. They were all ecstatic, yet terrified with excitement, talking hurriedly to each other about how petrified they were.

The barrier lifted and the steward ushered a few people on before he reached us. He escorted us to the other side so we could sit as a four. Ian made a point of sitting at the end next to me so he could be away from the clutches of Turner and Johnny, who would surely make the ride even worse by constantly barracking him. Johnny was the other side of me, and Turner sat at the other end. The ledges and the angle we were sat at blocked the scenery from this height, but it would only be a matter of seconds before we would see the full panorama and could marvel at the whole of Las Vegas whilst simultaneously crapping our pants.

The rest of the riders were locked into place and the steward made his way out of the immediate vicinity. This was when strong guts were needed, as terrible, unrelenting thoughts paralysed me. A few annoying daredevils shouted in excitable anticipation, far too over the top and giddy for my liking. It was made worse by Johnny and Turner emulating them, not seeming to care one bit about what was about to happen.

We suddenly shuddered up a couple of inches, which startled me, but we hadn't risen to the heights we were about to hit just yet. This just seemed like a signal! The ride started to settle back to the ground before slowly moving up again, and then, in a moment of madness, we bolted like a missile at high velocity straight to the top. A barrage of screams could be heard all around the ride, but none as loud as Ian's, who bellowed like a child, causing me to wince from the sharp sound that deafened my ear. I'd been too busy trying to come to terms with the sudden jerk that shifted us up and down at tremendous pace to notice, but once I settled down I managed to take a prolonged look ahead at what lay beyond the ledges of the rooftop. It was an absolute spectacle! What a magnificent sight to behold! The whole of Vegas glistened in front of us, going on for miles upon miles, and from this height I could see beyond the city limits and into the crisp, orange desert regions that held so much mystery. It was quite an electrifying feeling to be perched at one of Vegas' highest points and be able to look around the whole city. In some ways, it was a peaceful moment - if you could block out the screams from everyone else.

The ride ended and Johnny, Turner and I were fuelled on adrenaline, talking of how unbelievable the ride was, eager to pursue the next thrill. Even Ian admitted that it was quite something despite the initial terror he felt, but he wasn't sure he would go on the next one until he saw what it was like. Onto Insanity we marched!

We joined the back of a queue that was longer than the one for the Big Shot. People were being let on but we wouldn't make the next ride. We just had to watch and take in what it entailed and contemplate the reasons why we were embarking on the insane. We watched as people loaded up, sat in pairs facing each other in a broad circle, but only ten people could fit on at a time. Once everyone was seated, the mechanics of the ride shifted everyone to the edge of the building, leaving them to dangle in what surely must've been a completely terrifying ordeal. The ride began to slowly spin around and around, but then the cradled seats that everyone sat in began to open up, leaving them estranged from safety, staring at the floor from this suicidal height and disturbing angle. It looked horrible and Ian couldn't contain himself, shouting, 'Oh no! You won't get me on that thing!' in his best Peter Kay voice. The ride began spinning to a force of 3 G's and even the adrenaline junkies, Johnny and Turner, looked apprehensive. No backing out now though! The seats grew wider and wider, almost making the riders horizontal, and the screams and sickly moans could be heard bustling through the wind!

The ride eventually slowed and everyone filtered off, looking a little dizzy.

I turned to Ian, 'You gonna be alright on this?'

'Fuck it, might as well now we're here.'

'Good lad. I knew you'd come through,' Johnny said.

We tentatively made our way onto the seats where we were securely strapped in. I was sat next to Ian again. I made sure my shorts pockets were buttoned up before clinging onto the handle in front of me. The handle didn't look very secure at all, but that still didn't stop me gripping onto it for dear life. There was only this handle to grip, a seat belt around the waist holding me in, and a small platform for my feet. I started to feel a little off, but it was too late to back out as we began to move towards the edge, having Vegas literally beneath our feet. Once we were over the edge, the feeling was horrific, despite the view once again proving to be outstanding. I felt conflicting emotions, but I quickly forgot about the view when we began to spin and tilt up at an angle, making the whole experience unnaturally alarming. Ian and I both shouted through gritted teeth, 'Fuckin' Hell!' as we were forced to look down at the ground that appeared so far away. The wind shrieked violently, colliding with the force our bodies were moving at, making our hair stick up like some dodgy 80s do. It felt like one of those dreams you have when you fall off a building. Well this was that nightmare becoming a teasing reality. I lifted my head up to see Turner and Johnny adjacent and could see that Turner was gripping on and squealing too. Johnny had his arms off the bar and outstretched as if he was pretending to fly. The crazy bastard! Not that the fact I was hanging on to a flimsy bar was the difference between safety and death, it was just that this feeling was too abnormal to comprehend. It was another step up in entertainment that we weren't used to, and very different to the feelings experienced in Blackpool or at Alton Towers.

Gradually, the ride slowed and we returned to a level position before being brought back to the roof. Ian and I breathed a heavy sigh of relief, nervously snickering to each other now it was over. We wrestled our seat belts off and got out as quickly as possible.

Ian staggered out uneasily saying, 'Bollocks to that! I've had enough. I ain't doing the other one.'

Turner surprisingly agreed, 'I must admit, that was pretty fuckin' scary.'

'Woo! That was awesome! Where to next? X-Scream?' Johnny piped up.

'You're a lunatic Johnny! How could you enjoy that, you sicko?' Ian asked.

'Because I'm not a pussy. Come on now Ian lad, stop messing about. I wanna do the last one, chop chop.' Johnny continued to taunt.

'Just give me a minute for fuck's sake. I feel shit after that!' Ian shouted.

We hung around on the rooftop for a few minutes while Ian and I regained our composure.

Eventually we calmed down and began to walk towards X-Scream, a giant teeter-totter that propelled you 27ft from the edge of the tower and back again.

We watched the next set of riders. The carriage careered down a ramp at pace towards the edge of the roof before abruptly stopping, and fuckin' dangled off the edge of the roof! Then it reversed and continued to repeat the madness over and over again. It looked like the worst of the three to endure.

Ian recognised this. 'I can't do it. Fuck that! I can't do that. That's just insane!'

He wasn't wrong! It looked like hell to have to go through the feeling of being on a runaway carriage that was about to dive 900 feet or so from the top of a skyscraper. Even I had my reservations, but Johnny terrorised us into going on. Although Turner wouldn't admit it in that moment, I think Insanity had got to him. There wasn't as much conviction in his persuasions now.

I tried to motivate Ian. 'One more ride, mate. You know "Ant" and "Dec" will never let you live it down if you don't.'

He snorted at my adopted names for Johnny and Turner. It seemed to work as he nodded and reluctantly followed me into the kamikaze pit.

So here we were again, strapped into a carriage attached to runners on a ride that was about to provide probably one of the most distressing feelings ever, the feeling of being in an out of control car about to fly off the top of the building in a true near-death like experience! Johnny wasn't helping matters by clowning around. 'Imagine if the carriage comes off, Ian? It doesn't feel too safe this ride.'

Ian tried to block out his bullshit, but it was all in vain. Johnny had put the seed of doubt in both our minds and it all got a little creepier.

Suddenly the ramp tipped and the carriage thrust forward at full throttle. The bottomless pit of Las Vegas Boulevard abruptly came into a worryingly full view. We carried on rolling down, looking like we were about to plunge off the edge. My stomach hopped, my heart pounded, and all four of us shouted, 'SHHHHIIIITTT!!' I uncontrollably let out a fart from the sudden force, and I was close to following through. How could you not nearly shit yourself on this thing? Ian had his eyes closed next to me, and I was peering through one eye for all the good it was doing. Turner held on tightly, and this time even Johnny couldn't bring himself to wave his arms in the air like he had before. That first thrust forwards that tipped us over the edge was enough for me, but I wasn't prepared for the moment we jerked downwards as if we were falling, causing me to emit the campest of squeals. Turner heard it and gave me a look that asked, 'What the fuck was that, Ricky?' We then tilted upright as if we were about to be launched like a rocket, before reverting to the original starting position. I just wanted to get off, but we had another minute or so of this toing and froing. Every time we dangled off the edge and dropped, I couldn't help but retch. I turned to see that Ian had gone very pale, and I feared he might pass out or throw up all over me at any moment. He looked like a baby that needed burping, and I couldn't help but belly laugh at seeing him this way. He caught me and bellowed, 'what the fuck are you laughing at, you dick,' said with all the distress of a man at the end of his tether.

This was certainly the worst ride I'd ever been on and the most I'd contemplated death on. I could handle most roller coasters, but this was one that really scared the shit out of me. It was a huge relief to eventually slow down, reverse and halt so I could get the fuck off and never return.

All four of us agreed that the feeling we'd just endured was horrific. Ian remained very pale and cursed us for putting him through it, but at least we'd done it. We'd conquered the three rides at the top of the Stratosphere. Granted, I may not do it again, I may not want to, but at least I had! It was all part of the Vegas experience, pushing things to the limits with no regrets, stepping outside the comfort zone and living life to its full potential. Say yes to new experiences, and never say no was an instinctive mantra we were living by out here. In that hour or so of shitting myself on three hell-raising rides, I'd momentarily forgotten about the past and the previous night with Lucy.

CHAPTER 18

We departed the Stratosphere Resort after the petrifying torment of the roller coaster rides. The breeze that was felt hundreds of feet in the air had now weakened, and the clammy heat perforated our attire.

We were all quite hungry since we hadn't eaten in preparation for the stomach-turning rides, so we looked for a place to get some food. We scanned up and down Las Vegas Boulevard, noticing that the Stratosphere was situated at the bottom of the Strip and was the final mega resort amongst this wealth of riches. The change in scenery looking further down the road was bizarre. The whole landscape altered about twenty yards or so away from the super resorts. The area beyond the Stratosphere signalled the end of the Strip, and the buildings suddenly looked older, dated and far less glamorous, showing Vegas' less dazzling side. It was more noticeable that we were in the desert in this part of the city as the sand became visible in the less developed land. I could tell that this side of the Strip was becoming a bit dodgier and rougher. Within minutes we were passed by a desperate homeless guy, who looked as though he'd suffered severe facial burns from the sun. No sooner had he passed than we were approached by an ugly and unsavoury hooker.

'Hey y'all! Let me use one of your cells?' she demanded.

'Cells?' Johnny sarcastically repeated.

'Yeah boy. Yer know! Cellular phone!'

'You mean mobiles?' He continued to provoke her.

'Pfft! Mobile? Am not talking about no mobile you ass! Am talking about a cell phone. Give me one! I need to make a quick call!' She spoke with the dramatic attitude associated with a Jerry Springer guest, and dressed like one too.

'Sorry love. None of us have one,' Johnny lied. As if we were going to let this loose cannon use one of our phones.

She changed her tune. 'You boys looking for some action?' She stood with one hand on her hip in a failed attempt to look sexy.

Johnny played along. 'You mean all four of us?'

'If you boys want. I can do you a special tourist deal. You ain't from round here ain't ya? Where you from? Australia or something?'

We collectively sniggered.

'England actually,' Johnny corrected.

'En-ger-land? Is that near London?' Her knowledge was astounding.

'Erm...not quite,' Johnny answered.

'Well I don't give a damn where it is. Are you boys gonna purchase the goods or you just wasting my time?'

'I think we'll give it a miss this time love, but thanks for asking.'

We turned away to cross the road, hearing her

mumble profanities at us. Apparently, we were all, 'Bitch Ass Mutha Fuckas!'

The reason we entered further into this more unnerving area was because there was a Denny's Diner located over the road, perfect for what we were looking for and something that I'd always wanted to do. It may sound silly, but I'd always wanted to eat in a typical American diner in the States, preferably one that looked into the middle of nowhere as seen on several TV shows and films. This Denny's faced away from the Strip, not looking out into complete isolation, but it was enough to appease my wishes, and the view wasn't obstructed by our hooker friend either.

We entered the diner, and Turner and I joked that we felt like Jules and Vincent in 'Pulp Fiction', dressed in casual beach attire of vests and shorts, but not like *a couple of dorks*. The smell of grease and lard filled the air, an odour to savour. We were seated in a booth pushed against the window and we all ordered the same, classic American burgers and chips. We devoured the lot in no time having not had breakfast, and it really was delicious.

Johnny and Turner nipped over the road to buy a couple of bottles of spirits from a supermarket for later, and that's when Ian brought up the past again, reiterating what I already knew. He pointed out a couple of home truths, saying everyone had noticed Mandy change in the past few months and that she had become more money orientated and agitated whenever she was out, as if things simply weren't good enough for her anymore. He implored me to listen to him when he said, 'You shouldn't blame yourself for any of this as it isn't your fault. You're just a victim of circumstance.'

The problem was that guilt was part of the grieving process, so I did blame myself to some extent. Once again, I realised that I had been too close to notice, but having stepped away from everything I could see he was right. My head knew that, but the pit of my stomach and heart just couldn't fathom the suffering. He then brought up Eva again, and the very mention of her name filled me with joy.

'Has that experience with her taught you nothing Ricky? She was gorgeous and from what you said, perfect. Don't you see that you're better off without Mandy and you're more than capable of being happy with someone who deserves you? Not some two-faced fuck up who's only concern is about how much money circulates around her.'

'I know mate,' I whispered, head bowed.

'You need to push through this shit and move on. I know it hurts, I know its shit, we've all been there before and so have you, but you got to get past it.'

I took a moment's pause before answering, 'I know I've been here before but not like this…none of us have ever had this shit happen to them in that way… just leaving without a word and running off with some jumped up prick. I just can't shake that off. I don't know what I did to deserve it. I'm not feeling sorry for myself, but I just can't get my head around it. It's that thought about basically being dumped for money, and being cheated on for that reason. Was she always on the lookout for money and I was just a stopgap for five years? I just feel used by it all. I should be happy to be rid, but it's not that simple, is it? Probably just my ego talking. Typical pathetic male ego bullshit.'

Ian was direct, 'No, you have to go through it to get over it. Just do it sooner rather than later. Fuck her!'

I agreed, before moving on to other topics of conversation. Too much time had been spent on her and there was a bagful of entertainment remaining to fill the rest of the day.

The others returned and we discussed what to do next. I wasn't really bothered as long as we did something that was interesting and different, so we turned to the Vegas bucket list. Ian, being a huge fan of Elvis, suggested we go to the Elvis Museum at Imperial Palace, located half way down the Strip. After all, it'd be sacrilege to come to Vegas and not visit a museum in honour of 'The King' himself.

Imperial Palace, although huge and fascinating, wasn't as extravagant as the other mega resorts we'd already visited. It was more down to earth and more our style. It was hard to judge how things looked in Vegas because the expectation was always something magical. If it didn't appear like that at first sight it was hard to gauge where it would rank in normal circumstances. Maybe I was being a bit harsh on the older, less modernised casinos, but having experienced and partied in some of the top hotels/casinos in the world up to now, it was hard to get excited about anything less than perfection. If it was situated in Manchester it probably would've made more of a startling impression, but out in the desert, in this surreal, supernatural world surrounded by brilliance, only excess and something sensational impressed.

We spent about thirty minutes inside Imperial Palace trying to find where the Elvis Museum actually was. The lack of information to direct us had struck again. Before we found it we'd already taken the wrong lift to the residents' floor and had to ask two separate people where the museum was. It was all very confusing! I bet Lord Lucan was holed up in a Vegas hotel room, that's why no one can find the fucker!

After navigating our way through the Crystal Maze, we eventually found the museum. It started with a gift shop of Elvis memorabilia and souvenirs with his music providing the soundtrack to the journey. The music merged with interludes of him talking in interviews on the various screens dotted about. The tour started with his early teenage life, chronologically journeying through his life story, displaying countless, priceless artefacts from that time. It was interesting and a privilege to see personal possessions, such as his bed, judo suit, jewellery, belt, and the last car he owned. Ian found it far more fascinating than the rest of us, the same way that a Jim Morrison museum would've held more appeal to me than the others. It was still a thrill to be able to say that we'd been to an Elvis museum, a man who was one of Vegas' and the world's biggest legends, who brought so much entertainment and had such an influence on the generation of his time and beyond. We spent about forty-five minutes in the museum before embarking on the short walk back to Planet Hollywood.

A white Cadillac Escalade ESV was parked outside the main door of Planet Hollywood that wasn't there when we left. It turned out to be part of an auction that was taking place in the future, with the goods being displayed now. The car turned out to be Tony Soprano's car from 'The Sopranos', and given his legendary status in TV history, we all had our picture taken next to it, adopting gangster like poses with hands clasped in front of us, feet shoulder width apart and head bobbed a bit to the side.

We then learnt that an auction for some of Michael Jackson's possessions was being prepared on the Mezzanine and was open to the public. It wasn't only his possessions being auctioned. There was a collection of outstanding memorabilia on show from various films and TV programmes, including the clothing worn by different characters in the 'Sopranos'. Indiana Jones' famous attire was perhaps the pick of the bunch amongst many other famous blockbuster movie artefacts.

Lots of musical memorabilia was situated in the room where Michael Jackson's assets were gathered. Johnny Cash's guitar signed with the lyric, *'I shot a man in Reno, just to watch him die,'* (a famous line from his song, 'Folsom Prison Blues') was one such item of great musical importance being auctioned. More fascinating were the guitars of Jimi Hendrix and Prince! What an honour to see some of the instruments that helped shape rock history. If only I had the money to own such a priceless piece of history.

Michael Jackson's assets were unreal. He had a wall painting of himself portrayed as an angel, and a sofa that was extraordinary, emblazoned in red and gold, resembling something fit for a king to rest on. Other possessions included his diamond glove, many hats and expensive clothing, recognisable from various concerts he'd performed at over the years.

It turned out to be quite a star struck day in the end. It was something I hadn't envisaged happening in Vegas, but as ever, this place continued to throw up the unpredictable and the spectacular.

CHAPTER 19

The consensus for the evening was to start in the Hard Rock Café then hit XS at Encore, which was located next to the Wynn, and was built by the same consortium. It was the same shape and colour, faced the same angle, but looked like its little brother because it was marginally smaller.

We left it later than usual to go out as we all grabbed an hour of much needed sleep. It was essential if we were to party to the early hours of dawn again. Maybe we were all feeling the pace a little because the giddiness and excitement of the first three nights had quietly dipped. However, we were all united by a common desire to push through the pain and exhaustion barriers. We knew that once we got a few beers down us we would get livelier.

Before we jumped a taxi to Hard Rock, we decided on a quick beer and gamble in Planet Hollywood in an attempt to raise energy levels. Unfortunately, my unenthusiastic flutter on blackjack resulted in an $80 loss. My luck seemed to take the same turn as my vitality. Worse news followed when I realised that in the thirty-minute period between entering the casino and getting out of the taxi at Hard Rock Café, I'd lost a further $100. It had somehow disappeared from my pocket. I couldn't rule out pick pocketing, but I couldn't recall an occasion where I'd left myself open to such an act. I sensed that the exhaustion, coupled with the loss of money from gambling and misplacement, was a sign that tonight might not be my night.

We entered the Hard Rock, a destination that we really wanted to visit given its great association with rock 'n' roll. Iggy Pop's, 'Lust For Life', was pulverising the speakers. Plus, it was the scene of the 'Entourage' episode where they visit Vegas, adding more sentimental spice to the visit. The casino was a bit different to the rest. Of course, they had hundreds of slot machines piled one after the other like an out of control game of dominoes on steroids, but the main gambling arena, where the blackjack and roulette took place, was right at the end, separated in a bulbous shaped extension to the main, long hall. The token circular bar was directly in the centre just like the other hotels.

The Hard Rock boasted a ridiculous number of the most gorgeous women in Vegas. The croupiers wearing their purple and black gothic style basques were especially awesome. Who were the men that ended up with these women? The super rich or the famous I suspected. Unfortunately, we were neither!

I was determined to win back the $100 inexplicably lost, so I marched my way to the blackjack table on my own. The table I inadvertently found myself at was slightly different to the others I'd gambled on. It was played with a single deck of cards rather than several decks in one box. Not that the rules of the game were any different, but the code of conduct was. I made two biffles on my first hand, highlighting my inexperience. Firstly, the two cards were dealt face down and I reached to pick them up with both hands. The dealer explained that I can't use both hands, and even picking them up with one hand was considered naive. I was supposed to use the one hand to carefully lift the cards and secretly note what they were. When I tried this I again got a ticking off because of bending the cards too much. The issue with this was that if I had a clue what I was doing I could've bent that card and waited for it to appear again if the dealer acquired it, thus knowing beforehand what their card was. Not that I was capable of such a slick move to enhance my winning chances, this was completely down to naivety. A hustler, I was not! Once I got my head around the manner of the game, I started playing with the same confidence built up over the last couple of days, taking more wins than losses, finally cutting off when I reached $80, putting a huge dent into the $100 misplaced earlier and salvaging some sort of redemption and satisfaction.

I bragged of my performance to the others, who remained on the roulette table, not willing to take a similar high-stake chance on blackjack like we had done in MGM. It seemed that they were going to be there for a while having just got drinks in. After a few minutes I became bored, and that only added to the desire to gamble again as I was itching to take another win. I was becoming a victim of the gambling phenomenon imposed by the fiendish spirit of Vegas, and all coolness was lost as my head gave in to sinful need in this sinful city. Despite my best efforts to stop the craving, I couldn't resist the sensationalist urges that overwhelmed me. After all, this *was* Vegas, but could I produce another fortuitous run, or would I suffer a further downfall? Fuck it! I went to find another blackjack table to put down the $80 won earlier and try to satisfy this greedy impulse burning inside of me. This time, knowing the language of playing with a single deck, I sat down more at ease.

The subsequent game was a complete biffle! The dealer diddled me every time and, in my wired state, I was convinced the game was a fix. I lost all reason, refusing to believe my own stupidity was part of my plight. When I had nineteen or twenty, the croupier would deal herself fifteen and end up pulling a five or a six out of the bag, thus drawing with, or beating me. Needless to say, with the cards falling in that manner, my $80 was lost very quickly. What should've made me learn a valuable lesson didn't in any way!

I had to gather my thoughts away from the casino and resist temptation. I ventured into the Hard Rock shop hoping to see some memorabilia or a great rock 'n' roll t-shirt, but I was disappointed with what was on offer and exited just as quickly as entering. I became more irritable thinking about the loss only minutes earlier. My judgement slowly slithered off into an unknown paradox somewhere between the shop and the casino floor.

I trotted like a man possessed back to the blackjack table for one last gamble, meeting Turner on the way, who came with me to witness the same scenario as I got completely hustled out of the game again. I was down to my last $60 on the table so whacked the whole lot on. Surprise, surprise, a six and a five came into play, totalling eleven. I had the option to double down. What would I do? The dealer was dealt a six so I had a good chance of winning the game. Was it worth throwing a further $60 down to risk it? The Vegas euphoria passed judgement for me and I delved into my pockets to fish out further cash. I prayed hellishly for one of the face cards and Turner was anxious for me. The dealer turned my final card and it was a five, giving me sixteen. Although all was not completely lost, I knew the winning chances had been reduced. The dealer turned over her card to reveal a seven. She had thirteen and was forced to play another card. The face card I'd desired for myself, I now desired for her. She slammed the final card down, hammering the nail in my coffin as a plucky six lay in front of me, totalling nineteen. Now I was seriously pissed off and I frustratingly pulled myself off the stool, letting it crash to the ground such was the force of my movement. I stomped away like a petulant school kid, refusing to pick it up!

Not only had I lost $200 on gambling, but with a further $100 mysteriously disappearing, I was now facing a loss of $300. I could feel fatigue setting in too, which made me agitated, and the whole situation was becoming unbearable. With my bad mood came a rekindling of anger towards Mandy, which was bubbling over to levels that should've been kept suppressed. I had to talk myself down and keep cool or else something bad could happen tonight. On checking my remaining money, I only had $50 left on me, so I borrowed $100 from Johnny to see me through. I knew that XS at Encore was not going to be cheap at all, so it was a much-needed cash injection.

Although we'd all lost money in the Hard Rock, none more so than me, it was an excellent set up and the music was immense, living up to its rock 'n' roll theme. We should've stayed and experienced the club, 'Vanity', but something was lurking for us at XS, something that would push me over the edge.

CHAPTER 20

The driveway within Encore's compound was awash with palm trees and pretty flowers, making the surroundings picturesque. Even as we entered there was a golden feel to the venue. Visions of grandeur and expensive décor signified the hotel's upmarket status.

We were stopped by a rep as we strolled to the bar. His name was Jay and he asked if we were going to XS, telling us he had queue jump tickets for $20 each rather than pay at the door for $30. Because of how smoothly things ran with Tony at the strip club, we took advantage and went for it, but wanted a quick drink in the quieter bar first.

Jay joined us and we quizzed him about XS. He was a small guy with a stocky frame and skinhead. He was clearly a gym goer, and potential steroid abuser, as the muscles that unearthed themselves from under his white polo shirt looked disproportionate to his pea head. Jay told us that tonight's theme in XS was a pool party, so beach attire was preferred. He mocked us for dressing smart, saying we should've got into the spirit of things by wearing flip-flops and swimming shorts. Even if we had known that beforehand I don't think we would've gone for it. We were far too cool for school, us northern lads! Most guys that passed us weren't dressed accordingly either, but the women were more into the spirit of things as they flaunted their pristine bodies. Several who passed by us wore bikinis and sarongs, causing jaws to drop from the eagle-eyed boozers at the bar. It was in those moments of concentrated perversion that we decided to drink up quickly and see what the rest of the women inside looked like.

We signalled to Jay that we were ready for XS: ironic really as I felt like I'd already experienced extreme excess since arriving in Vegas. He was trying to make a sale to another group of lads, and once he closed the deal he led us all towards the venue, reaching the long queue that snaked around the corner. Running into Jay proved to be a masterstroke because he ushered us ahead of everyone else to the front. The people in the queue stared with curiosity and jealousy as if we were VIPs. I suppose it would be easy to spin a story that we were famous icons from England. The Americans would never know, especially if we claimed to be professional 'soccer' players. We had been asked by a fellow blackjack player at one point if we knew the Queen just because we were English, so it shouldn't have been too difficult to conjure up a story that we were famous.

On first look, XS seemed like it was dead. The lights were off, the music was loud, but there were no people inside. We didn't have a clue what was going on so we just followed the crowd in front that headed around the edge of the walkway.

We came to a set of double doors where bouncers controlled the real entrance to the club outside. We didn't know what to expect, but with it being a pool party, everyone had amassed in the gardens. I was expecting the pool to be within the club itself or outside on a small terrace in a VIP section, where only a limited number of people could enjoy it. Oh how wrong I was! Once the bouncer let us through we were presented with this dreamlike, heavenly realm resembling something from the Playboy Mansion. This really was something special that lay in front of us. It looked like the kind of place where A-list celebrities come to party all the time. I'd never been to a club as unique and full of the most unattainable women known to man, who pranced about in swimwear. This was a haven for beauties and people with status. The place was vast, flooded with palm trees, neatly trimmed hedges and exotic flowerbeds. The smell of freshly cut grass on a humid summer's night dominated the air. Paths led like a maze to all sorts of destinations, separated by luscious grass verges. The swimming pool was in the shape of a huge ring, acting as a moat to the central bar, which had a few roulette and blackjack stations inside and a higher minimum bet than we were used to. The pool looked a tranquil blue, sparkling in the night from the lights under the shallow surface.

On any other occasion, I would've been tempted to jump in, join in the pool antics and make an arse of myself, but I was more likely to throw up in it than swim. I was still feeling relentlessly tired and run down, and my condition had worsened since leaving the Hard Rock. I staggered about like a freak, struggling in my own mixed up world, half regretting partying so late as I started to realise my own limits as age was perhaps catching up with me after days of alcohol abuse. My head started pounding and cramps developed in my stomach. Why was this happening now in a club of this magnitude? It was sod's fuckin' law playing an evil bastard prank and there was nothing I could do about it to gear myself up. I just had to try and ride it out!

Although the club was unbelievable on first sight, probably the swankiest in actual appearance I'd ever seen, I couldn't help but think this wasn't really our sort of place. It was great to have the initial experience of seeing it, but it was a poser's paradise and the place reeked of pretentiousness and arrogance, making the air turn sour. The more I people watched and ear wigged, the more I saw how fickleness and shallowness gathered in great abundance. These people were incapable of a conversation that didn't revolve around materialism, money or appearance. It was incredible.

It was crazy how easily humanity can lose its basic sense and instincts when huge quantities of money are involved. It was embarrassingly obvious that most women were only after one thing, yet it didn't seem to faze the old, soulless business clowns, who were probably only successful because of the number of people they'd screwed over, or the dodgy deals they'd conducted to get to the top. Both were just as bad as each other, typifying narcissistic tendencies.

Mandy would probably feel right at home here, and it was pathetic that she clearly wanted something from this world. It was seeing these people that gave me an image of what the elusive 'Mr Amazing' might look like, and how he was as a person given his profession, wealth and where he lived. I had a strong sense that he was part of this false elite back home, a completely characterless and insecure control freak. I bet he dressed in an expensive tailor-made suit, had wispy hair that was thinning from years of business stress, held a smug look on his face thinking how 'amazing' he really is, and carried a charmless sneer that made people from the real world feel sick.

We couldn't really be shocked by this attitude in XS. After all, we were in Vegas, a world built upon this money driven state of mind. It wasn't that I felt uncomfortable being in this environment, and I certainly didn't feel out of my depth as a person. I knew we could survive in this world, but could these people survive in ours? They wouldn't last five minutes in our local pub at home! Arrogance alone would see them banished straight away.

I always felt that if I suddenly became rich, more likely out of a lottery win than work, then I wouldn't change or lose the values I grew up with. I wouldn't change my dress sense, where I shopped, or where I ate or drank just because I had a bit of money. I wasn't interested in buying a big house and spending money on the interior design, or even buying a better car. You can only occupy one room at a time, cook in one kitchen, watch one TV, sit on one chair, and sleep in one bed, no matter how big your house is, and you'll still get stuck in the same traffic jam as everyone else in the morning no matter what car you're driving. That's the way I saw things anyway. I was a grounded inner-city Mancunian kid through and through, and possessed all the values that came with such an upbringing. I was more interested in using money for real experiences like travelling and experiencing the unknown in the world. That's what life was all about for me - see as much of the world as possible before you depart it. Taking one of the many famous drives through America, armed with nothing but my music, and tearing up the open road in a state of complete freedom was something I constantly fantasised about. For me that was true living, a feeling of complete liberty, free from the pressures and manipulation of 21st Century living. That was the paradisiacal setting and ultimate goal I held.

I broke from my fantasy when another wave of fatigue rushed over me, making me feel shaky and dizzy. It was playing a huge factor in hampering my ability to enjoy myself and was severely ruining the evening. I was struggling to stand up straight, and I desperately needed to sit down before I fell down. We were stood at the centre bar by the swimming pool and I thankfully found sanctuary by perching on the surrounding wall. I was keeled over with my head in my hands, rubbing my eyes to awake me from this god forsaken pain. I debated whether to go back to the hotel I was that fucked. My body was screaming to do so, but my mind wanted to persevere and not miss out on a single thing, however useless I'd become. Maybe this was one of the tests I had to endure to progress further, much like the films I watched on the plane coming over that encompassed madness and despair. Perhaps this was my time to experience such pain and misery, Vegas' way of testing me to see if I would pull through and not be labelled with the tag of 'someone who couldn't handle Vegas.'

Turner, Johnny and Ian stood a few metres away and had been talking to three Polish girls, two brunettes and one blonde, all quite good looking, which wasn't surprising. The three girls were all very tall and worryingly slim, giving me a sense that they were either models or were striving to be. I don't know if the lads had spun a story, but they appeared quite engaged in conversation. The girls were probably just feeling them out to see how much money they had, or if they could have some influence in furthering their careers. I just couldn't bring myself to get drawn in because of my inability to stand up straight or even talk sense. Also, after the previous night's breakdown in front of Lucy, I was adamant that meeting women wasn't the answer to all the riddles in my head.

I remained glued to the wall, pathetically feeling sorry for myself as I fought to overcome the fatigue and stomach cramps that'd incapacitated me. I heard a murmur from the others as my name was mentioned. I tentatively looked up to see them pointing at me with the three girls waving delicately and smiling animatedly. I was forced to lift my hand up awkwardly to acknowledge them, but I wanted to flick the Vs at them instead. The attractive blonde noticed that I looked miserable and made the effort to talk to me, calling out to me in a strong Eastern European accent. 'Hey, are you ok down there? You can smile you know.'

I didn't care for the patronising comment. I nodded unconvincingly and remained polite. 'Not too bad.

I'm just a little offside.' I made the effort to galvanise myself and rose inelegantly to my feet using the rail for support. I refused to let this beat me so I thought a little conversation might take my mind off it. I kept it short and basic, asking where she was from, where she'd been tonight, how long she'd been here, the sort of pleasantries we're accustomed to in general chit chat… or chat shite. The answers she gave didn't really register, but she asked the same questions in return.

She was called Irena, which meant 'peace'. If only I could find some fuckin' 'Irena' in my mind! She had lived in Los Angeles for six months in the hope of becoming a model, along with her friend, Yetta, who was the more attractive brunette. I smiled when she revealed her profession, which she took to be because of her glamorous career choice, but really it was in appreciation of my own perceptions that they were model wannabees. I could tell she was a bit of an airhead who didn't have a clue about anything, but I entertained her and went with the flow, knowing that she was probably waiting to see if I had modelling contacts or a huge wedge of cash. She typically steered the conversation to finding that sort of stuff out about me, asking me about my job and whether it pays well, and whether I had any interest in the modelling or entertainment world, all the while subtly shaking her empty champagne glass in my face as a hint for me to buy her another. You've come to the wrong guy, sweetheart!

I did begin to feel a bit more human and maybe that was a necessity for what was about to happen. Out of nowhere, from my blind side, an older guy rudely interrupted my flow and bombed into our conversation like I was a mirage. The conceit oozed out of him as he talked over me.

'Well hello pretty lady, what might your name be then?'

He was about late 40s with irritating, twatty black hair, half slicked back in a feeble attempt to hide his receding lines. He was about the same height as me but larger, more due to fat than any prolonged stint in the gym. He wore a crisp black shirt with a silver tie that knotted perfectly between his collar points, and pin stripe black suit trousers with polished shoes like he was about to go ballroom dancing. He was clearly a bit tipsy from the way he had ambled over, but not drunk enough for me to forgive his attitude.

Irena entertained him, smiling as she stated her name. He took her gently by the hand and kissed it softly. You've got to be kidding me, I thought. What a creepy fuck.

'Bradley! Bradley Jefferson,' he affirmed with arrogance shining through. I couldn't believe this prick full named himself, speaking in a slightly posh and over pronounced American accent that sounded fake. He'd still not even acknowledged that I was there. I could've been Irena's boyfriend for all he knew, but that wasn't going to stop this egotistical twat.

'Oi, Donald Trump!' I said with authority. 'What do you think you're playing at?'

He turned around slowly, cockily looking me up and down in a patronising way as if my casual attire of jeans and a short-sleeved shirt didn't quite match up to the expectations of his own world.

'Oh, I'm sorry, do forgive me. Are you two together?' he asked.

'No, but I was talking to her before you barged over.' The brief moment of feeling normal had now been wiped as I felt rage starting to build.

'I apologise! I just thought I'd introduce myself to the lovely lady here. I hope you don't mind?' His tone continued to drip arrogance.

'Not at all,' Irena butted in, clearly entranced by his apparent wealth. He cupped a near full bottle of champagne in his right hand. I wasn't at all bothered about Irena, I didn't want any part of her and they probably deserved each other, but I was fuming at the complete lack of respect and bad attitude shown.

'See, the lady doesn't mind.' He grinned, which wound me up further. He turned back to Irena adding, 'Would you like a top up of champagne my darling?' Unsurprisingly, Irena accepted with a glint that suggested she'd hit the jackpot. He didn't offer me any as I clutched at a full bottle of Budweiser.

He carried on schmoozing up to her in a lecherous way. His slimy hand glided around her shoulder, and he turned to show the smuggest of grins at me. That wound me up further.

'I was just wondering, Bentley?' The sarcasm seeped like acid.

'It's Bradley actually.'

'Whatever.' My voice remained icy cool. 'I was just

wondering! Are you always a prick to people or only when you're trying to impress women?' He removed his hand from Irena's shoulder and spun to fully face me.

'What did you say?'

'Oh sorry! I said, do you flaunt money and champagne as a cover up for having a small dick?' I remained unfazed in my reactions. He looked at me blankly for a moment as a few onlookers sniggered at what I'd said.

'Listen boy! I suggest you turn around and walk away. You don't know *who* you're dealing with. Accept that the best man will win.' His tone was smooth, but he was inwardly seething.

I nodded slowly, but the comment about 'the best man will win' was not the ideal thing to say to me at the moment. I went up like a bottle of pop as visions of Mandy's 'Mr Amazing' swept to the surface, and I perceived him to be exactly the same as this prick. That thought escalated the anger within me to an unprecedented level, and as his words sank in, it tipped over to a point where it took control of my cool. He turned to shrug me off, but the smirk was wiped off his face when my clenched fist swung and crashed into the side of his cheek, sending him hurtling onto the floor. The champagne bottle skimmed across the ground in the other direction, splashing into the pool. The crowd gasped in shock. I had completely lost control and all I saw was a concrete representation of 'Mr Amazing' in a sea of red mist. Without thinking, or hesitation, I was on top of him firing a few right jabs into his conceited face, and spots of blood formed on his top lip. I felt hands try to grab me off him, but I was too possessed and wouldn't let up on this rain of punches, shouting, 'You fuckin' prick, you fuckin' arrogant cock sucker! Who am I dealing with eh? You don't know who *you're* fuckin' dealing with!' Every punch landed on its target as I brought the upmarket XS down to the level of a Mancunian street brawl. My rage was gargantuan, The Rolling Stones' twisted track, 'Paint it Black', echoed through the nearby speakers, and the words and song's tone mirrored my current state as my punches were perfectly conducted in time to the pulsing, sharp rhythm.

Someone managed to haul me off, but I refused to turn around as I wanted to get back on him. He was helped to his feet, dazed and confused, and when I broke free from the clutches of the unknown onlooker, I rushed at him again, planting another right hook sweetly on his jaw that sent him crumbling into the swimming pool a couple of metres away, to add insult to injury. I was ready to jump in after him and drown the bastard.

A much stronger set of arms grabbed me and I became powerless to move within the clutches of three bouncers. I tried to wriggle for freedom, but I was immobilised underneath their collective grip. The crowd fell quiet as they watched this snarling Manc lunatic being hauled away, continuing to hail a barrage of abuse and insults directed at Jefferson.

The bouncers led me to a back door away from the pool area and tossed me about six feet in the air before I slammed onto the concrete outside. They laughed, then told me that I was barred. One remained at the door to monitor me to make sure I didn't try to get back in. Blood was on my hands and I felt a pain in the knuckle of my middle finger, but I didn't care, I was too overwhelmed with adrenaline.

I shouted, 'Fuckin' shithole anyway,' and lit up a well-earned victory cigarette against the forces of evil, and for some reason thought the best thing to do was a kind of Stone Roses/Mancunian swaggering dance a few feet from the bouncer who had laughed at me. He didn't have a clue what I was doing.

Ian, Johnny and Turner pushed passed him, and Ian went ballistic at me. 'Ricky, what the fuck?!'

Rage continued to consume me and I started to shake. 'Fuck him, that fuckin' prick. I'll fuckin' kill him!'

Johnny interrupted, 'Were you just dancing like Ian Brown?'

I didn't want to smile but couldn't help myself as his comment served to momentarily break the cycle of fury I was under.

The crackling from the bouncer's radio, and subsequent chat, led us to believe that he was talking to the police through his headset about a disturbance.

'We've got to get the fuck out of here guys!' Turner yelled.

We all bolted and followed the path at the back towards Las Vegas Boulevard, avoiding the main entrance in our escape.

Mid-sprint Johnny turned to me. 'Why were you dancing like Ian Brown?'

I had no answer for him.

CHAPTER 21

We found ourselves in O'Shea's next to Imperial Palace on the Strip. I'd calmed down in the half hour or so that had passed since being forcibly ejected from XS. I was shocked at what I'd just done now that the adrenaline had subsided. It was so uncharacteristic of me and totally not in my nature to act so thuggishly, but part of me knew that Bradley Jeffer-fuck deserved it. It usually wasn't me who dished out the comeuppance though. It was a further sign that issues from the past were still not resolved and now it had driven me to attack someone, however justified it might have been.

I think Ian sensed that something had finally snapped in me and I probably surprised him more than myself. He threw me over to an empty booth, ordering me to sit down and barked instructions at Turner and Johnny to get us a drink and leave us to it.

Johnny was supportive of my actions. 'Ian, go easy on him. I heard what that dickhead said. He proper deserved it.' He nodded approvingly at me.

'That's not the point Johnny,' Ian said.

He turned his attentions to me. 'Ricky, what the fuck is going on? Did you not listen to a word I said today in the diner?'

'I don't know what's going on! I know I shouldn't have done that but he was an arrogant prick.' My head was buried in my hands while my elbows rested on the table.

'And it reminded you of Mandy's new fella I presume? Look, you've got to let this go. You can't go around punching people because they might remind you of someone you've never met.' He paused for a second before continuing, 'Maybe this was a good thing though. Maybe that's what you needed to get it out of your system.'

'I don't know Ian. It might make it worse. I hadn't fully realised what this is doing to me. I've not been in a fight since I was about eleven.'

'I must admit, I've never seen you in one, let alone act like Mike Tyson. You've got to get a hold of yourself kid.'

Johnny handed us our bottles and couldn't resist a joke, 'Eh. Don't go launching that at someone, Begbie.' He was referring to the psychotic character in Trainspotting.

I sniggered, 'Just give me a minute. I'll be over in a bit.'

Ian got up, advising that I wash the blood from my hands before walking about in my current state. He left to join the others. I watched as they all disappeared from the casino into a room around the corner out of my view. Ian signalled over letting me know where they were. I sat alone trying to compose myself and come to terms with my disappointing actions.

I took the opportunity to scout the surroundings of O'Shea's. The difference was stark between this bar and the super resort we'd just run from. It looked dirty in comparison, but in a way that entrapped me due to its charismatic appeal. The smell was dominated by the odour of fried food, cigarettes and alcohol. The patrons appeared to be a bit rougher than other resorts, dressed casually with a laid-back attitude, giving the place plenty of personality. It was like Bill's, the place we'd eaten on our first full day, holding a similar appeal to those unmoved by the classiness of other complexes along the Strip. This was a much more grounded and suitable place to drink copious amounts of hard liquor in. It felt more like home than anywhere else we'd been in so far, possibly the Vegas equivalent of a working man's pub.

I'd calmed down and was finally able to stop my hands shaking, which made the pain in my knuckle more prominent. I kept it moving by stretching my fingers out, and because I had mobility, I didn't think it was broken, more likely just bruised.

I should've moved with the others because being sat on my own meant I was vulnerable to the clutches of a deviant spectator who set her sights on me. An extremely rough-looking, large woman caked in makeup continued to make eyes at me. She wore a sky-blue dress that looked filthy and revealed far too much of her blotchy, cellulite ridden body than I cared to witness. She smiled, only to reveal about five teeth that looked like they needed shaving, resembling someone who should've been starring in the film, 'Deliverance', with overtures of banjo music playing as she waddled over to me. My plan of averting my eyes had not deterred her one bit. She took it upon herself to join me, sitting on the seat opposite. I had my suspicions about what her main role of employment was, and thought how is it that we were approached by the foul hookers, but not the gorgeous ones? Maybe I shouldn't think too much about the answer to that.

She confidently introduced herself in a broad southern accent, 'Hey sugar. Now what's a lovely looking piece of pecan pie like you doing sat here all alone?'

Jesus, I was in trouble. I could hear the distress rise in my voice, 'I'm not alone. I'm just about to join my mates in there.' I pointed awkwardly to the other side of the floor.

'I've got a better idea. How about partying with me back in my condo? I've got some white stuff back at my place. It'll be fun,' she boasted.

My words blundered and spluttered trying to formulate the right reply. I politely declined through fear that she might wrestle me to the floor and sit on me, imprisoning me underneath her thunderous thighs if I was anything other than respectful. I made my excuses to leave and quickly shifted up from the booth. As I headed towards the bathroom to wash my hands, I caught her desperate words on my departure. 'Maybe next time sugar?'

'Maybe fuckin' not,' I muttered under my breath.

I found where the others had disappeared to, a much brighter room adjoined to the casino, which looked more like a large McDonalds than an actual bar with its fluorescent lights and plastic chairs attached to stanchions and tables. In the ten minutes I'd been rooted to the booth fighting off crazy hookers and washing my hands of blood, the others had wasted no time whatsoever in making moves, already clustered amongst a group of four girls and several guys, playing drinking games. Turner told me they'd been invited over minutes earlier, showing the sort of welcoming committee attributed to the North of England. He went on to tell me that the girls were Canadian and the six guys were American.

The beers were $1 for about ¾ of a pint, making the tip to the barman match the value of the drink, effectively doubling the price, but compared to what we'd experienced throughout Vegas so far, $2 was a massive bargain and even cheaper than Manchester prices. Drinking at these prices meant that the fun and games became quite excessive.

The forfeit for the loser in our onslaught of various drinking games was a shot of tequila, but not just any shot of tequila, probably the most disgusting tequila known to man, so disgusting that it triggered the gag reflex. What made it worse was the sucking of the lime afterwards. It tasted like it'd already been in someone else's drink, taken out, left to dry, and then served up again.

With the sudden snip in prices and being with our new-found friends, the night had veered back on track. The games, drinks and laughter flowed. My earlier blip was all but forgotten and the night moved swiftly on at an alarmingly fast pace. The highlight was a friendly drinking contest involving a boat race against the Americans, which we marginally, but proudly, won.

The Canadian girls were a huge part of the night's entertainment because of how crazy they were. Once the drinking games petered out we seemed to gravitate towards them...or perhaps it was vice versa...either way the banter was prolific. It quickly became apparent that they had no boundaries and were spontaneously wild. Flashing their breasts and drinking just as heavily as we were, showed the kind of provocative attitude that was a massive contrast to the intentions of the girls in XS. The Canadians weren't particularly glamorous, or attractive for that matter, but they all had humongous breasts that proved difficult to avert your eyes from when the flashing occurred. Their humour and conversation was full of smut and filth, matching us in terms of shock factor in some of the things they were saying, which was completely different from the prim and proper revelations of the Phoenix girls we'd met in the MGM. Turner clearly welcomed this and I waited for the inevitable proposal from him to play, 'Never Have I Ever', at some point, but the forthright Canadian girls didn't need a game to encourage them to reveal information about themselves. The night was in danger of becoming 'Carry on Vegas' at this rate. We were just waiting for Vegas' answer to Barbara Windsor to appear.

The entertainment continued when three of the girls started 'motor boating' each other as the alcohol flowed. I couldn't believe my eyes as the night turned into one of ruthless debauchery, a huge contrast to the earlier seriousness that had now become a distant memory. The 'motor boating' was taken to new levels when Johnny took it upon himself to get involved. One girl, Mary, was up for being the receiver when he boasted about how great he was at it. She taunted him, saying one of her friends could do it far better than he could. After much faffing, deliberating and awful trash talk, they conjured a way to determine a winner. Basically, whoever could keep their head nestled in between a pair of tits for longest without coming up for air, was the winner. Monika, one of the other girls, who was also guilty of being a serial flasher, stepped up and gave quite an impressive effort, savagely embedding and shaking her head into Mary's chest. When she finished, Johnny lunged in like a man possessed, head nuzzled in the middle of those huge melons. The funniest thing was Turner's face. He was oblivious to all that was going on as he was trying it on with the other friend, Anna. He turned around at this precise moment, unaware of what Johnny was doing. He did a double take, looking startled and exclaimed, 'What the fuck, Johnny?' Then burst into laughter as he tried to wrap his head around how this warped scenario had come about.

Johnny finally surfaced and gasped for air, feeling a little dizzy and blurry on his return to the waking world. Mary complemented him on his efforts but decided that Monika was the winner. How she determined that I don't know, but it didn't matter who won or lost, it was the taking part that counted...at least that was Johnny's conclusion.

I lit up another cig, and whilst puffing away to fire

it up, Mary decided to set another challenge involving me. She asked Ian to film it on his camera phone for posterity purposes. How fortunate she did as the image that was captured in the background was priceless. Mary's challenge was for me to put a cigarette in between her boobs, and using only my mouth or teeth, pull it out within ten seconds. This may have seemed simple, but the size of Mary's tits was a big obstacle to overcome, especially as there was some weight holding down and wedging in the cigarette.

'What do I get if I win?' I asked.

'I'll buy you a shot of tequila, honey.'

I shuddered. 'Don't bother! I'll do it for pride.'

I discarded my current cigarette and plucked a fresh one from the crinkled pack, placing it in between her cleavage. I waited for Ian to be ready with the filming and buried my head in the middle of her heaving bosoms, attempting to extract my piece of meat like a rabid dog. It proved more difficult than I anticipated, but with perseverance and determination I managed to yank the cig out with my teeth at the ten second mark, before proudly turning to the camera and lighting it, albeit it was slightly bent. The original purpose of this video lost all meaning when we watched it back straight after. Turner pointed out the random piece of footage caught unbeknown to us at the time of filming.

In the background of Ian's film, we noticed Johnny talking to the fourth Canadian, Julia, but you couldn't tell what was being said. We could make out her apprehensiveness and the clear mouthing of 'No, no, no' whilst putting her arm across her chest, as if the conversation was something to do with boobs. Perhaps the excitement of the 'motor boat' game had led Johnny to try another game. He then goes one way out of the picture, and Julia goes the other way, and you don't see him again until the very end point. In the split-second pause at the end of the video, the camera captures and freezes on Johnny stood with knees slightly bent and his head forcefully buried deep in the breasts of Monika, who has a very casual, nonchalant look about her. Where she appeared from I do not know, but she had somehow in only a few seconds become topless. Johnny's hands are by his side and his head is ridiculously slumped into the centre of Monika's breasts, as if he'd just collapsed into them. God knows how this happened or what was said to enable him to do it, but between us we thought of many desperate and dirty excuses. The video got better on every re-run and there were a lot of re-runs! We could imagine him pestering all the Canadian girls just to 'motor boat' them at all costs, frisky to emulate what he'd just done with Mary not five minutes earlier. Even the rejection from Julia in the first part of the film wasn't enough to dampen his spirits. Persistence was the key to his mission and he was eventually rewarded in the best way possible for all of us to cherish. Could this happen at home? Or was it only in Vegas? Such antics rarely happened back in Manchester, but the ease with which this all came about made it feel like an everyday occurrence here. You just had to go with the flow and follow the line as the boundaries got pushed further and further.

Meanwhile, Ian had secured the jukebox and was hammering the great rock 'n' roll songs. I was really in the swing of things, especially when The Rolling Stones anthem, '(I Can't Get No) Satisfaction', came on. My Mick Jagger impersonation came into effect and I pranced about the bar strutting my moves, dancing on my own makeshift stage.

One of the American lads, Robbie, was proving to be a good laugh too. He had already pulled Monika shortly after the 'motor boat' debacle, and was constantly groping and kissing her. He was a marine, and in his military discipline he kept calling all of us 'Sir'. His best line was when the girls convinced me and Ian to take our shirts off. That they managed to persuade us to do this in the middle of a Vegas bar was obviously due to the amount of alcohol we'd consumed, and the relaxing of our own boundaries. They were clearly used to the femininity of waxed, clean chested men and were mesmerised by our chest hair. Even the marine was astounded and in his Texan accent, drawled, 'Damn, you Manchester boys are a bunch of hairy fuckers ain't ya? You look like god damn Chewie from Star Wars!'

Time really does fly when you're having fun, and it had surpassed seven o'clock in the morning. Turner had made a backdoor exit with Anna to the girls' hotel at Mandalay Bay. Later, he confirmed his second lay of the holiday, but told us that he got caught in the act when the rest of the girls returned to the hotel. They were disturbing images indeed as I imagined the scene as those poor Canadian girls walked in on Turner's buck naked bare arse going ten to the dozen, a vision that'd mentally scar the toughest of men.

Monika brought Robbie back to the room too, and Turner went on to tell us that one of the rooms was separated by a curtain that didn't fully touch the ground, so it was easy to see underneath. When Turner went to the bathroom after everyone had returned, he noticed a pair of women's feet stood parallel, red knickers around her ankles and someone's knees planted on the floor between them. One can only imagine the depravity that was going on.

It was a strange night for so many reasons, frustratingly starting off with the lost money, terrible gambling luck and the feeling that I could pass out or throw up at any given moment, to fighting in and getting kicked out and barred from XS, to making a miraculous recovery, downing several beers and shots till stupid o'clock in the morning, and meeting exceptional groups of people along the way, who we shared one hell of a hysterical night with. Also, it was bizarre that we had started the night in one of the world's most exclusive and outrageous clubs, but ended up in something much more like the local pub of Vegas, creating our very own spontaneous and outrageous fun. Vegas was certainly throwing up some weird scenarios.

What was clear from the night's Royal Rumble was that my demons had not been exorcised. My reason for being here and my moment of clarity had yet to come to fruition and, with only two days remaining, time was running out and I was getting worried! After everything we'd done during the night, coupled with our outings during the day, the night should've drawn to a close at this ungodly time of the morning, but we were fortunate it didn't.

CHAPTER 22

Back at Planet Hollywood, Ian stumbled lethargically back up to the room after an onslaught of vodka had left his speech slurred. With Turner tucked up at Mandalay Bay, Johnny and I again failed to see sense, deciding to have a nightcap whilst playing on the slot machines. We threw in the loose, wrinkled bills that remained from the night. Johnny toyed with the idea of pranking Ian again, but we both dismissed the idea knowing how much effort it would take.

We started off by recapping the night in O'Shea's, still bemused by how the night had ended up considering the seriousness of the events preceding it. I guess that's what Vegas has the ability of doing, unexpectedly shifting the pattern of the night to whatever scenario you wanted to be in.

We then began talking about more sombre topics, and how we both envisaged things changing when we returned home, agreeing that this may be the final chapter in a life we'd grown accustomed too. The discussion changed course and took on a graver tone.

'I know we've not really talked a lot about Mandy, but obviously it's still on your mind or else you wouldn't have planted one on that guy. Is everything ok?'

I looked down, still a bit shamed by the incident. 'Not too good judging from tonight.'

'Yeah I could see that.'

'It's like this rage boils up every now and then, and I feel like I'm losing control and I can't stop thinking about it. I'm not proud of what I did but it was purely from this inner anger I've got about everything. I just wish it would go,' I sighed.

'It was a bit of a surprise to see you react that way, but don't worry about it, these things happen. He did deserve it though.' He let out a laugh. 'I overheard what he was saying. If you hadn't have hit him then I might've done on general fuckin' principle.' He was trying to reassure me.

We sat quietly for a second or so before he spoke again, 'It was a proper shitty thing what Mandy did and I don't think I ever told you that. I left it to Ian to talk to you about this shit, but for what it's worth I'm sorry it happened. To be honest though Ricky, I don't believe a word of the shit she's come out with. Even if it is happening that she's engaged to some prick, I don't think it's genuine…it feels more like a business deal.'

'You might have a point. But you know what? I don't know what the main issue is anymore. There's so much shit to take in that I don't know which part hurts the most.'

'Right now, this second, what is it that hurts the most?' he asked sharply.

'My hand,' I quipped, which was absolutely killing me.

He laughed.

I continued, 'I want to know why she did it. Why she left in the way she did? And what I did to deserve it?'

'That's a lot you need to find out and you might not ever get to find out.'

'Yeah I know that. The thought of not knowing kills me.'

'Maybe you don't really know a person until you break up with them. That's when you see them for what they really are, when the fog clears. Maybe you knew what was always there, but because you were too close to it you just couldn't see it. I think you were manipulated into not seeing it. It's a clever trick, but one you're better to be well away from.'

I looked at him, impressed by his wisdom, 'You might be right.'

'I know I am. She couldn't do something so ridiculous and so impulsive unless there was an element of her that was always like that. Think about it. Nothing happened in her life to set her off the rails that may explain this. She was always that person and it became more noticeable towards the end. True colours were showing.'

'You saw it in her?'

'We *all* saw that she tried to control you a bit and used money against you.'

'Did you think I was controlled?'

'No, I don't. But she did try. The way I see it, the fact she earns a lot more than you was her ace in the hole and why she thought she had the power in the relationship. And the more she earned, and the higher she rose in the solicitor ranks, the more it went to her head in the last few months. But that was always going to happen with her. When you started going out she didn't have the praise or the seniority she had at the end. And you...well you stayed at the same level and you never should've done. You settled for what you had rather than what you wanted.'

'You mean sticking to the boring office job.'

'Yeah I do mean that.'

'I'm trying to sort that out.'

'Yeah you are. And I'm glad you've got your interest back in music because that's where you should be. Just make sure you're doing it for the right reasons.'

'What do you mean?'

'Don't do it to prove a point to Mandy. Do it because that's who you are, and I believe that *is* who you are.'

A silence ensued as we both sunk into our own thoughts, still monotonously pressing the spin buttons on our respective slot machines. I thought about what Johnny said and how my closest friends seemed to think I should've been on a different path that I couldn't see all this time. I wish they'd told me earlier. Maybe I wasn't meant to be on that road until now. I thought about whether it was for the right reasons or just because the renewed interest stemmed from my break up, but I knew I wanted to be involved in music for myself and for no one else, I just didn't know in what capacity.

Johnny broke the silence, 'I'll tell you the truth though mate, and we all agree on this. There are two things: the first is that you give yourself too much of a hard time sometimes and you need to move past that. You are not to blame for someone leaving in those circumstances.'

'Fair point, I know I need to stop blaming myself. Go on then, what's the second thing?'

'The second thing, and most importantly.'

'Sounds worrying.'

'When you get back home from Vegas you need to...'

CHA CHING CHA CHING CHA CHING CHA CHING......

Suddenly, the rattle of falling coins rang like a storm battering on a window. A red light on top of the machine Johnny was playing on flashed violently like we were in the middle of an air raid. We stared at each other; mouths parted, eyes wide, looking around in dismay. What the fuck was going on? Had we set off the alarm to the slot machine? I expected security to surround us and whisk us away to some back room in the casino and beat us to a pulp for cheating, but we were innocent! Johnny pointed at his screen, slowly lifting a heavy, limp finger. I saw that he was pointing at the number of credits sparkling on his screen that were shooting up at a rapid velocity, hitting the hundreds of thousands, which in actual money was in the thousands of dollars. A few people gathered behind us as we waited for it to stop. It was a good job this wasn't prime time as the area would've been swarming with bystanders. At eight in the morning there weren't that many people around.

We didn't know whether to laugh or completely

shit ourselves, but I felt a sense of bewilderment. The alarms and noises of coins splashing came to a halt and the credit reading was 212,520!! Meaning he had won $2,125. The jammy bastard! I was so happy though! It was what we all hoped for: just one of us to win a significant amount and finally we had it. I knew the only way we could win would be from slot machines because we were nowhere near bold enough to take games of blackjack or roulette to this level of money, as we'd proved in the MGM!

Whatever we were talking about before the sound of rattling coins was lost in the rapture that followed. Johnny didn't know what to do with himself, but I calmly advised that he had to repeat the bet in case he won again. He hit the 'Repeat Bet' button authoritatively, which came to nothing. Without taking any further advice, he firmly slapped 'Print Ticket', and we scurried off towards the cage to cash in the winnings, not wanting to hang around in case of a mugging from the blind side.

Johnny's hands were shaking when he handed over the ticket. The cashier congratulated him. She knew we weren't a couple of high rollers judging by our giddiness and agitation. In the grand scheme of things, many people all over Vegas would probably be betting $2,000 a hand at least, and would see a $2,000 win as a bad return on their investment.

The cashier counted the money into $100 piles and then folded it into a band to keep it nice and tight, making it look like the kind of roll a gangster carries for spare change. Johnny pocketed the wedge with the biggest grin on his face, 'Fancy a beer? It's on me!' We sat and toasted his win in the Heart Bar with a bottle of Budweiser each, going over what had just happened like it wasn't real, laughing wildly in shock and disbelief.

We never did get back to the serious tone of the conversation, but in that moment, it didn't matter. We'd become submerged in a sensational feeling, and even though it wasn't me who won directly, it felt like I had.

Once Johnny finished his last drop of beer he turned to me, 'I've got a great idea. I'm gonna surprise everyone tomorrow, or later today as it were, so I'm gonna get some kip for a few hours. I'll text you when I'm up, so make sure you and Ian are ready.'

What surprise could he possibly be planning? He wouldn't tell me even if I asked so I humoured him, but in Las Vegas, the surprise could be anything!

CHAPTER 23

The last twelve hours or so had been crazy. Vegas was really throwing up some situations that couldn't be experienced back home. Johnny had promised to treat us all, and what he'd planned was taking our adventures to another level.

We were walking across the sweltering tarmac at Las Vegas airport, kitted up with flight jackets and headgear, about to embark an ECO-Star helicopter for a tour of Grand Canyon!

Johnny had sorted this out online when he got back to his room the previous night, which was a grand gesture that held true to the gentleman's promise we had made, that any significant win would result in some sort of sharing of the spoils. I didn't anticipate a gambling win of this magnitude, and even if I did, a few drinks at night was the height of expectation, not a trip into the mysterious Grand Canyon by helicopter. I couldn't complain, or could I? It hadn't occurred to me beforehand the courage it would take to board one of these bloody death traps. If Ian and I thought the roller coasters were scary enough, then this would surely rival or surpass that fear. It seemed like a great idea to add it to the bucket list at the time, caught up in the hype and far-fetched dreams pre-departure, but to actually go up for the first time ever in a helicopter was an idea that scared the life out of me. I tried to untangle the knots in my stomach, ridding my mind of devastating and depraved thoughts of plunging helicopters and huge fireball explosions.

Johnny was obviously up for it, and the news didn't seem to faze Turner, but Ian had the same reservations as I had. Maybe this was one of those things that had to be done. Perhaps the exhilaration of a trip into one of the world's finest landmarks, experiencing natural beauty in such daredevil like circumstances was just part of guiding me out of this cauldron of darkness I seemed to be swirling around in. The guilt and disappointment of being lowered into a fistfight hadn't helped matters, especially with the throbbing pain I felt in my battered and bruised knuckles now that I was free from alcohol and adrenaline.

I was learning that this whole trip was about facing the unknown and saying yes to new propositions. Whether that would eventually aid me in my quest to push through to the other side of this constant turmoil remained to be seen. This excursion was just another of those experiences that exemplified doing things I wouldn't normally do. When we were waiting in the hanger I'd caught a glimpse of the brochure which stated, *'Abandon your world and worries as you experience the exhilaration and splendour of the miraculous Grand Canyon.'* Perhaps the slogan was a sign that a helicopter ride through Grand Canyon would go some way to hauling me out of my current plight.

We approached the doors to the helicopter, and

Marvin, our pilot and guide for the day, went through the last of the health and safety checks before we boarded. He was a tall, stocky fellow, wearing a flight jacket and military hat with shades of grey infiltrating from the sides. He was ex-military and his wrinkled, ridged complexion and wafer-thin lips showed his years. His eyes were shaded by some sort of horror seen in his life, but I couldn't think of a better way of enjoying retirement from service than to work in such awe-inspiring surroundings.

The four of us eased ourselves onto the chopper and into our seats. We all put on our headsets complete with microphones so we could speak to and hear each other throughout the journey.

The blades began to rotate quickly, the noise progressively grew louder as the chopper began to shake, causing me to tightly grab the sides and push my body downwards in a hysterical panic of gut splitting nerves. I felt like screaming, but I remained quiet, eyes virtually shut until a voice pounded through my helmet. 'Open your eyes you wet wipe. You too Ian!' Turner yelled.

I felt the helicopter rise and shake from side to side in an abnormal motion. Was it a natural movement or were we in trouble? Paranoid, deluded thoughts clouded my logic. I plucked up the courage to open one eye to see we were a good twenty metres off the ground, but I was looking at this through a glass floor I hadn't noticed when I got in. I was looking down at the runway from this ever-increasing height, seeing everything becoming smaller under my feet, which made me feel a bit queasy.

The chopper pushed forwards in a perfectly straight line and the blade gathered momentum. We continued to rise at a tangent further away from civilisation, roaring our way into the unfamiliar wave of an orange horizon in the far distance towards the might of Grand Canyon.

Once the trembling fear subsided and my breathing relaxed, I was able to compose myself and enjoy the ride much more than I first thought I would. We cruised at a fairly low altitude so we could look out across the golden, barren sea of sand and rock in the clear, unpolluted visibility of Nevada. It was truly something spectacular! The sun bounced off the small jagged mountain ranges that moulded the captivating sight. Despite the noise of the helicopter it seemed so peaceful - nature was drowning out man's inventions. We all remained still and quiet, independently absorbing this truly remarkable vision. The magic of the desert was completely wrapping its power around my soul. I couldn't help but sense some sort of destiny and feeling of homecoming about the place, as if I'd been here before and this was where I belonged. The words in the brochure came back to me again, 'Abandon your world and worries...' For the time being I had completely lost my troubles.

Marvin broke the silence that we shared by updating us that Lake Mead was ahead. He educated us with a few facts, telling us it was the largest reservoir in the United States and was fashioned from impounded water from the Hoover Dam that ran for 112 miles beyond. He went on to tell us of a B-29 Superfortress aircraft that crashed into the lake in 1948, and still remained at the bottom today as well as two other smaller planes that had crashed throughout history.

We approached rockier cliffs and climbed higher to hurdle the highest tip. Once we were clear the Lake loomed in its full motionless glory. It was untarnished, pure and serenely blue, holding a neat reflection of the unspoilt sky. It was immense and dispersed through the cliffs, running for miles upon miles fading into the desert sunshine. Marvin continued his barrage of knowledge, providing more interesting facts about how a few old communities were still submerged underneath, and that sometimes you could see the ruins of St. Thomas when the water level dropped below average. We flew further along and came to a marina with several boats clustered together. Many sailed in the open water and some participated in the various activities the lake offered, such as fishing and water skiing. There were five marinas on the lake: Forever Resorts at Callville Bay, Echo Bay, Temple Bar Marina, Las Vegas Boat Harbor, and Lake Mead Marina in Hemenway Harbor. In addition, there were several small islands, and we were currently flying past a couple as we glided around the shore and ridges.

We banked left. Marvin notified us that the Hoover Dam was up ahead, and once again he revealed insights into the history of this landmark. It appeared to us immediately after rounding the shoreline, and we cockily hovered, confronting this gargantuan world-famous presence in a David vs. Goliath stance, sandwiched between two huge mountains. Several tourists congregated around the area, but none were seeing it in the same astounding way we were.

We didn't hang around for long, shooting off to the right in search of the main attraction that was Grand Canyon itself. Even the journey there was breathtaking as the red rocks and mountains glistened in the sun.

Twenty minutes or so whizzed by, spent admiring the view and soaking up this scenic encounter with nature in wistful silence. Marvin's voice broke the trance, speaking to us through the headphones, 'Only a few minutes away boys.' He went on to tell us a couple of enlightening facts that emphasised its vastness, telling us that the Canyon was 277 miles long and 18 miles wide with depths of up to 1800 metres. Phenomenal! Yet not the largest in the world! I never really knew how the Canyon was formed and even scientists debated it today. Marvin gave us the most logical explanation, that it was formed by the erosive activity of Colorado River chipping away at the mountain ranges that once stood in its place, as well as the forces of the continental drift over a significant amount of time.

An air of excitement punctured my stomach when we were moments away from it being in full view. From the angle of approach we couldn't see anything, but once the helicopter banked right, the majestic formation of one of, if not the world's most impressive natural landmarks came into full view, continuing for miles and miles as far as the eye could see. It was a momentous sight to lay our eyes on for the very first time.

We passed sacred lands held close to local tribes over the beautiful Kaibab National Forest. Upon reaching the edge of the Canyon, the South Rim dropped away, and the North Rim and Eastern End came into view. This was an unbelievable scene and there was no wonder why it was regarded as one of the most magical views in the entire Canyon. We all froze gobsmacked. Marvin reiterated its impact, 'Quite something isn't it boys?' It certainly was a stunning piece of scenery that couldn't be equalled by any man-made beauty, even Las Vegas itself. In that moment of tranquillity, all anxieties were lost and I was left completely calm and with a renewed appreciation and respect for nature, life and the world. The sheer size of the whole Canyon dwarfed our own existence. The browns and oranges bounced off the clear blue sky, making the mountains and cliffs carry a strange tint of blue and purple. It was such a psychedelic image to behold.

We then flew directly over the drops, and the calmness washed away as fear caused the blood to rush on seeing such depths, as if all of a sudden, we'd leapt a mile into the air. Frightening! We carried on meandering our way through the cliffs, unable to take our eyes off all the various mountains and ridges, completely captivated and locked into our own world. None of us could say anything to each other. Just a series of 'Wow's' and gasps were all we could muster!

We continued to track Colorado River throughout the Canyon where it weaved and dissected the mountains with a blue enchantment of spiritual worth. After a magical visit to Marble Canyon and Point

Imperial, we ventured to a daunting dive through the famous Dragon Corridor, the deepest and widest part of the Canyon. My nerves twanged yet again at the abrupt plunge in depth.

We exited the Corridor and ventured back towards Colorado River where Marvin was ready to set us down some 300ft above the water, a depth far enough down to make us feel totally belittled and swallowed up by the mountain. Included as part of the tour was a thirty minute stop on a private helipad away from tourists where we could just marvel at this power that was consuming us.

We stretched our legs and scoped the immediate area where we'd landed, which had a fabulous view whichever way we turned. The heat was still blistering and any wind was blocked by the cliffs. It was so calm and peaceful that I could fully understand and feel why the Native Americans regarded Grand Canyon as being key to their existence and spiritual empowerment.

No one else was around so we sat down on one of the free benches as a few nibbles and water bottles were passed around. We were chilled out, absorbing the moment, chatting amongst ourselves about the experience. We relayed the events of our trip to Marvin after he asked what we'd been up to so far in Vegas. Recapping the events after only four nights and three days made us realise just how much had happened; individually and collectively. It's in these moments of clear reflection when you comprehend just how much had been accomplished. We laughed as we went over what had happened so far with the strip club, the

Canadian girls, the girls from Phoenix in New York New York, the nerve-wracking raised stakes betting on blackjack in the MGM, pranking Ian with a condom down his boxers, the roller coaster rides, the drunken antics and so on. Not only that, revisiting all the hotels we'd been to and the contrasting emotions always felt playing at the tables were now forming integral memories that we'd cherish forever.

For me though, Eva had been the biggest thrill. I'd told her of Johnny's win and our subsequent trip to Grand Canyon, something she revealed that she'd never experienced. I found out snippets about their road trip and where they were staying and all the quirky things they were encountering on the way. We also relived our night together on several occasions in a cheesy, uncontrolled barrage of soppy messages. I would never tell the others about that.

We'd been talking for fifteen minutes or so when the most bizarre incident occurred. Marvin was in the middle of telling us the plan for the journey back, stating that we'd be able to fly over Las Vegas before returning to the airport. As he neared the end of his briefing, Turner dropped his water bottle and his face turned to complete stone, almost grey with fear. He looked through us into the distance, and whatever it was he saw clearly spooked him. That look transferred to our faces despite us not knowing what was going on. Marvin was sat next to Turner and his face dropped too. The pit of my stomach crumbled and I debated whether to look, preferring the route of ignorance is bliss.

'Whatever you do boys, don't make any sharp movements.' Marvin sounded genuinely concerned.

'Why? What the fuck is it?' Johnny cried.

'Just fuckin' do as he says,' Turner enforced.

The suspense was killing me and I ever so carefully turned my head around to see a fuckin' cougar stood proudly, yet menacingly on a large boulder about fifty metres away looking in our direction. Now this was the sort of situation not to be expected in such circumstances, and instantly I froze with dread. If the idea of a helicopter ride scared the life out of me, then this was close to what a near death experience must feel like.

'What the fuck do we do?' Ian exclaimed!

'All of you stand up very slowly and make your way over to the chopper, but I cannot stress enough to go slowly and quietly,' Marvin firmly advised.

'Does this type of shit happen often on these tours?' Ian asked nervously.

'It's never happened on one of my outings but there have been sightings in the past, never any incidents. They don't usually come out in the daytime. Don't worry they won't attack unless provoked,' Marvin answered.

'Well don't you do your Ian Brown dance Ricky, that'll be enough to provoke it!' Somehow, Johnny found the courage to joke, and we all couldn't help but laugh hysterically, trying to keep the noise levels down for fear of attack.

The cougar hadn't moved but carried on staring, weighing us up to see if we were worth the hassle. Slowly but surely, we all clambered back into the chopper as the cougar sauntered forward towards us. The sound of the chopper firing up seemed to startle it as it took a few defensive back steps. We breathed a sigh of relief, feeling cheated that our time in the Canyon was cut short, but it didn't matter, we'd experienced enough – more than we bargained for. It was just another incident amongst everything else that had happened so far that highlighted just how crazy this part of the world was – natural or man-made.

The ride back had a far more relaxed atmosphere to it than the serious quietness endured on the way over. I couldn't help but marvel at completing such a mind-blowing experience, something that was on many people's bucket list. There was a huge sense of achievement about it. I'd never even have thought to board a helicopter before, but after the initial fear subsided, it was a massive rush and something I'd certainly do again.

We neared Las Vegas, approaching from the south to circle the city. It's quite amazing to have two such extremes within one area; one man made, the other natural, but both offering very different attractions and pleasures. Circling Vegas wasn't that special really, not compared to seeing Grand Canyon. I think it was one of those rides that would've been more appealing at night. With the sun still beaming, the magic of the lights igniting the late afternoon didn't have the same effect as the quintessential image of the Vegas Strip at night.

CHAPTER 24

Once we returned from the helicopter ride there was a bit of time to kill before the night. It had occurred to us that we hadn't yet set foot inside the Bellagio, one of the more famous Vegas hotels. Before we could do that, it was a must to witness the famous Bellagio Fountain Show.

We found a central spot in one of the standing areas off the sidewalk and waited a few minutes for the show to begin. Suddenly, the music got louder and it was Gene Kelly's famous, 'Singing in the Rain', that came bellowing through the speakers hidden in the trees. The Fountains began to move and sway in different directions in time to the rhythm and melody. I found myself completely locked into the movement. The Fountains rose highest when the song peaked or hit a crescendo. The sound of the falling water from these high peaks was stifling, like the force of the ocean smashing into rocks. The money and vision that went into this unique show must've been astronomical. Everything was timed perfectly and captured the mood of the songs played, moving in sweet harmony to the songs essence. I'd seen clips of the show on TV, but until you see it for yourself you can't possibly appreciate how stunning they are. I could've sat there all day and absorbed the different variations each song would bring.

Once the song ended we entered the building that acted as a link between the Bellagio Hotel and Caesars Palace. We took the turn that led us to the Bellagio's shopping mall that eventually led to the casino. The mall was much like that of the Wynn with the top brands having shops scattered throughout the main walkway within pristine architecture and design. We also passed Jasmine Restaurant, which Ian pointed out was meant to be one of the world's finest places to dine due to it overlooking the spectacular Bellagio Fountains amongst other attractions it possessed.

We came to the casino that was separated by a change in flooring from tiles to carpet, like that of Planet Hollywood. I tried to remember if I recognised anything from 'Ocean's Eleven', but nothing sprang to mind. The casino was very much like the one in the Wynn, being a slight step up in class and edge from all the other mega resorts, if that was possible.

I surrendered to the temptation of gambling, taking up a pew at a blackjack table. There was only one other player and he remained quiet, possibly not having the best of runs, but I still threw down my $50. The others didn't fancy a gamble so instead looked on as the cards were dealt. The game started well as I won the first couple of hands, putting me in a position of safety. I must've only been on for four games before finding myself $120 in profit. I decided to have one more hand before pocketing the winnings. I bet $40, but unfortunately, the cards turned against me and I lost. Still, I walked away from my first gambling experience in the Bellagio $80 up. Hardly the exploits of the millions taken in the heist in 'Ocean's Eleven', but still a boost all the same, and a nice little earner in what was only ten minutes of playing time.

On Ian's recommendation, from research conducted beforehand, Voodoo Lounge at the Brazilian themed, Rio Hotel, was where we settled on checking out that night. We were drawn to the fact that it sat on the 51st floor of the building, recognising the buoyant atmosphere that could be created by this unique location. The hotel is situated on W Flamingo Road, off Las Vegas Boulevard, and was of a similar standard to that of the Hard Rock and New York New York. It had got to the stage where things didn't impress us as much as the first couple of days, so despite it's obvious magnificence, we had become impervious to being left in awe. The same could be said for the women. It got to the point where we couldn't comment on them anymore. It was just standard practice to see gorgeous women everywhere, and it was more of a shock to see someone unattractive now.

After a long walk across the whole of the ground floor, we paid our way in at the kiosk to Voodoo Lounge and were greeted by two lifts that took you up to the club. The back of the lifts looked onto a brick wall, but as we bolted upwards, they now looked out on the whole of Las Vegas. I took in the awesome view - despite it initially causing me to experience a little vertigo. The view was better than the helicopter ride over Vegas earlier, supporting my claims that the night being lit up by thousands of lights was a much more appealing spectacle than the daytime view. All the big hotels were in focus and, as we rose higher, the lights formed patterns that seemed to submerge the resorts and roads, almost drowning them out of sight. From this distance, at this time of night, we could clearly see where the city ended and the desert began. The desert looked like a constant black hole of nothingness, making Vegas seem like an island in its own entity, a lost world of some sort. It really did hit home that we were literally in the middle of nowhere.

The view made me appreciate the dazzling vision that the pioneers of this new Las Vegas have built, but it made me think about whether the original innovators of the past, who created a more outlaw like settlement, would have embraced this change or hated what it'd become, and which version I would've preferred if I was fortunate enough to see both. I suppose pre-1980s it really was a glorious place in a very different way to today, full of the original sinners who gave it the 'Sin City' name. I see Vegas these days as a fantastic and fabulous dream like world. Sometimes I've been completely lost for words out of sheer admiration for it. However, the Vegas I was experiencing is built upon the past, and the myths and legends that went with that. Its controversial reputation is now immersed in history, and the danger and excitement from that period of time is probably what creates so much curiosity and appeal today.

We got out of the lift and were greeted by a huge chalk drawing on the wall depicting a skeleton figure dressed in rags, very symbolic of voodoo. It reminded me of the character Baron Samedi in the James Bond film, 'Live and Let Die'.

It was very quiet inside and I wondered whether the fact that it was a Monday had something to do with the emptiness. But this was Vegas in June, party capital of the world, famous for 24/7/365 partying, so surely there can't be any quiet nights? The people at the bar proved me wrong by heading in one direction. It then became obvious that everyone was outside, and that's precisely where we headed as soon as we each grabbed a beer. The area outside was a circular base that wasn't very big considering its reputation. The bar was pushed up near the entrance, and as always there was a VIP area to the east side where you could go down another level and be separated from those not privileged enough to associate with you.

The view of Vegas at night was mesmerising from this vantage point. It really was something special, especially with the lights projecting the city's energy from this distance and the cool desert breeze wrapping itself around us. This was nothing like the Cloud 23 club at the Hilton in my beloved Manchester. The lights on the Strip were like a burning tidal wave cutting through the heart of Las Vegas, and all the other beacons of light that shone around it seemed like shavings that had splintered from the fiery stream on Las Vegas Boulevard. There was something magical about a Vegas night. It was insatiable with so much going on within its confines. Little did you know from this altitude what lay absorbed in each shining light, the spectrum of emotion that was packed from end to end: joy to despair, euphoria to depression. I'd only been here a few days and even I had felt both extremes, being bounced about from one end to the next. The term 'stability' seemed to be a concept lost under the Vegas night. That was not what it was built for!

As I stood on top of this huge hotel, I remembered a passage from 'Fear and Loathing in Las Vegas' that had been imprinted on me, a passage that indicated the end of an era. Hunter S. Thompson talks in detail about the 60s movement in San Francisco, describing the time as '*riding the crest of a high and beautiful wave*'. But when the movement ended he finds himself in Vegas five years later and describes what can be seen in the aftermath from his own unique view:

'…you can go up on a steep hill in Las Vegas and look west, and with the right kind of eyes you can almost see the high-water mark - that place where the wave finally broke and rolled back.'

I couldn't help but stand at the top of this monument away from the noise and try to look west to see what Hunter saw, perhaps even the remnants of a broken wave. Sadly, I saw nothing. I guess not being under hallucinogenic substances meant that my eyes weren't quite the right kind to see something so magical and enigmatic.

Not a lot was happening in Voodoo Lounge. We all seemed very subdued and I think the rush of the Grand

Canyon trip had taken a bit of drive from us. Despite the perception that Vegas never sleeps, you could certainly tell that it wasn't as energetic as other nights. Maybe it was taking a rest before the hoards gathered for the next six nights. Even in Vegas Mondays can appear quiet. It will always be a shit day to drink on!

We suggested moving on from Voodoo Lounge as it would've been hard to stay there till the early hours, and it was a good opportunity to try somewhere else. I suggested New York New York, but after talking to the bar staff in Voodoo Lounge, it became apparent that Monday's are in fact quiet in Vegas, and New York New York would be a wasted effort. With one eye on a monumental finish to the trip tomorrow, we thought it best to chill back in Planet Hollywood and have what would be an uncannily early night for Vegas, but still late in the grand scheme of things.

CHAPTER 25

It was surprisingly quite lively back in our hotel. I think we'd struck gold with Planet Hollywood because it always appeared to be the more energetic place at stupid o'clock in the morning, seemingly appealing to the masses who desired to indulge in excess till the early hours. We chose to hang around the Pleasure Pit and have a bit of a gamble then sit in the Heart Bar with a few beers. We weren't in the mood to search for craziness or force the issue to have another mental night. It was in the back of our minds that we only had one full day and night left, and I think taking it easy was a good strategy so we'd be fresher, ready to bow out in spectacular and appropriate style on our final outing.

Despite still not finding the answers to all the riddles, the past hadn't been on my mind as much throughout the day. Maybe the adventure to Grand Canyon had exorcised me in some mysterious way and had imposed a calming effect that was still lingering. Perhaps the slogan of 'Abandoning worries...' really had worked and I was naturally pushing through to the other side. I spoke too soon.

In the middle of Turner telling a joke, I broke concentration to address the buzzing coming from my mobile phone that caused the table to vibrate. I'd heard the joke before so was already laughing before the punchline came, but the laughter promptly stopped when I looked down at the screen. Startled and shocked, I tried to subdue treacherous feelings as the name, 'Mandy', flashed before my very eyes. I swiftly deteriorated into a whirlwind of sickening confusion and anger, and I was back to where I started once again. Why was she ringing now at what would've been mid-morning back in the UK? The name continued to flash, but I wasn't going to answer, I couldn't. It would probably be made out to be accidental anyway, just like the calls received back home. I think an element of fear stopped me from answering too, just in case she spoke this time. Whatever she had to say couldn't have any benefit and would likely create more mess in my head! I let it ring out and waited a couple of minutes for the potential voicemail, but no message came through. The damage had been done yet again and I uncontrollably slipped back into the past, trying to analyse why she persisted in ringing, accidental or not.

One thing was certain. The exhilarating helicopter ride over Grand Canyon was just another thing that was masking over the cracks of my wavering emotional state. I had learnt during this trip that no amount of women, money, alcohol, laughs with friends or the general experience of Vegas was going to solve anything. The trip so far had been memorable, one to treasure forever. I was grateful and fortunate to be here, but I was always searching for answers and revelations. The fact that the past would be waiting for me upon my return, forcing me to deal with it further on a much more depressing level, coupled with post-holiday blues, was a troubling idea. I was getting sick of torturing myself as well as letting someone else do it. Something drastic needed to be done! With only one full day and one full night remaining, my quest for the truth, and the reason for being here, was getting more urgent.

'Don't slip Ricky. Don't go off on one like yesterday,' Ian warned.

'I won't. I'm just sick of it. Why call now?'

'She's even pissing *me* right off. It's encroaching onto *our* holiday now as well as yours.' Johnny surprised me with his forceful tone.

'What're you gonna do? You gonna ring her back?' Turner asked.

'He better fuckin' not do,' Johnny butted in.

'Am I bollocks! I'm not that daft!'

Ian offered his thoughts, 'This needs sorting Ricky. You can't go on living like this. It's been a couple of months now and if you can't get through it here of all places I don't know where you can. We go home in about thirty-six hours. You said you knew Vegas would give answers, but you're running out of time. There's not much more we can do that's gonna solve it.'

'He's right. You've said that money, girls, booze, gambling, and Grand Canyon haven't worked. What else is there?' Turner added.

We paused for a moment whilst I closed my eyes to think. There was hope in one option that had been left unexplored, one that carried danger and a potential risk to mentality. Up until now I'd been kind of adopting the attitude of The Beatles song, 'Let It Be'. I had let it be, but still hadn't found any answers and Mother Mary hadn't come to me. The Beatles were most likely surfing on a higher plain when they came out with such wisdom. It then dawned on me what I had to do. I had to take that trip to the desert and take a daring step, which was a huge and potentially stupid leap of faith! Could the earth's natural hallucinogens help me find the answers in the same way many before me had found peace and understanding throughout the decades?

'I do have one idea. It's a long shot and a last-ditch attempt,' I broke the silence.

'What's that?' Ian sounded wary.

'Riders on the Storrrrrrm!' I sang in my best Jim Morrison voice.

'What do you mean?' Turner asked.

'I know what you mean!' Ian exclaimed. 'And how do you think we're gonna do that?'

'Do what?' Johnny excitedly asked.

'Come on Ian. We've talked about doing something like that for years. Now's our chance and we have a genuine reason to do it.'

'Oi! You two! Explain!' Johnny was getting agitated.

'Alright! It's risky, but it's your head. I'm not gonna do it with you, but I'll go along if we can find a way to do it.'

'This ain't funny now. What is it?' Johnny shouted, perched on the edge of his chair.

'Take that trip to the desert, and...simply put... get a little high!' I answered.

Johnny asked, 'On What? Weed?'

'Hmm…something a little trippier than that. Something more psychedelic I'm thinking.'

'I like it. I like it a lot!' Johnny replied giddily.

'So do I. Sounds like another adventure,' Turner agreed. 'And Ian, if you don't want to drop anything you can look after us instead. We could do with a spotter to make sure no freaky shit happens…well nothing too freaky anyway!'

'Fair enough, but where do you propose we get something like that from now, smart arse?'

'This is Vegas. It can't be too hard to find someone who deals with drugs. What about the guys who send girls to your room? Maybe they know?' Turner suggested.

'I'm not sure whether to trust them.' Ian was apprehensive.

'Do you know a drug dealer who you can trust, Ian?'

'That's a good point.' Ian was still wary. 'Well we can't just ask about to anyone who looks a bit dodgy. We might end up getting thrown out of the hotel or something worse. I don't think they take drugs lightly in Nevada.'

'That's not to say the place isn't rife with it,' I responded.

'Well as a last resort we could sound out those guys who advertise women, but for now let's just have a think and see what happens. I'm definitely up for it. You've got me all excited now,' Johnny proclaimed.

It was my round for drinks so I stood up and made my way over to the bar, arms folded resting on the top, engaged in thought as to whether this was a good idea or not...even if we could do it. There was a group of girls ordering a large round of cocktails, so I perceived it would be a while before I'd be served considering the various spirits being thrown into each one. I went over the risks of a trip to the desert, convinced that this was the only option left. I'd seen programmes and read about what the hippie generations advocated in the 60s, and how they connected with the universe when they took certain substances. A flutter of dangerous excitement consumed me at the very prospect of emulating those seekers before me. Maybe it was time to see what they saw!

A guy approached and sat on the stool next me. He was quite tall and stocky, with medium length brown hair that curled at the ends. He was older than me, probably in his early forties. His face had character with wrinkle lines embedded underneath his dark stubble, hinting at a misspent youth of smoking, drink, and drugs. He wore a black t-shirt with a rock 'n' roll emblem in the middle, casual light blue jeans and blue converse trainers that looked brand new. I turned to acknowledge him and he nodded to me and began to talk, 'Hey friend, s'up?' He had a strong American accent.

'Not bad pal. How's it going yourself?' I replied, thinking just how friendly the Americans had been over the last few days.

'I'm good dude. You have a strange accent. Where're you from, man? Australia or something?'

'Ha! No, Manchester, in England, the UK.'

'Ah Manchester, I love Manchester, great city and culture, man. Manchester United yeah, I love them.'

I perked up. 'I'm a United fan. The greatest football team in the world!'

'Yeah, they are a great soccer team. I saw them play a couple of years ago on tour in Philadelphia. They rock.'

'Football,' I corrected with a smile.

'What?'

'Football. We call it football, not soccer. Never mind.'

'Yeah, football, sorry.'

'You Americans always change our words,' I joked, to which he chuckled.

'Yeah we do, that's what we're about.'

We both paused for a second and he continued, 'The music in Manchester is awesome too, like Joy Division and Oasis.'

'You like them? That's pretty good music taste considering you're from...where are you from?' I asked, rather impressed that he obviously knew his stuff.

'San Francisco, California.'

'No way! I'm a huge fan of the 60s scene that came out of San Francisco, and LA. Big Brother & The Holding Company, Jefferson Airplane, The Doors, I love all the psychedelic stuff,' I enthused.

'I love The Doors. Jim Morrison man, an absolute rock god, but my favourites are The Byrds and Bob Dylan, I love that shit, man.'

'Yeah, they're ok. Not my personal favourites but

I appreciate their talents. Who else do you like in Manchester?'

'I probably don't know as many bands as you but New Order and Happy Mondays are great too. I love their female vocalist. She has a lot of soul.' I was astounded by his knowledge of our music culture.

'I'll tell you something... sorry I didn't catch your name?' I asked.

'Clint!'

'Ricky, great to meet you.' I shook his hand and went on, 'Manchester at that time ruled the world. We were the centre of everything in the music and youth movement, a bit like how San Francisco was one of the main places in the 60s.'

'I know what you mean, Ricky. San Francisco has changed a hell of a lot. Has Manchester changed?'

'Yes and no. Yes, because times change and maybe more people place an emphasis on the so called "trendier", commercialised parts of the city these days, which has a lot of pretentiousness about it. But there's still an undercurrent of cool places representing the true Manchester spirit, and lots of people working to keep our unique culture, music and arts scene alive.'

'I think San Francisco can be said to have gone down a similar route.'

'Musically it's not the same anymore. People in general are more interested in the commercial scene, and what used to be commercial is now underground. I think I'm born way after my time. I would've loved to have been around back in the day, but I feel that era has long gone and will never be repeated on a large scale.'

'Maybe you're right. Even I missed out on the hippie vibe in San Fran at the time, and I wish I would've been there for that. My soul belongs to that time.'

'It saddens me to see how the current pop scene has claimed the souls of the youth today. There aren't any characters in the mainstream that have such a depth that it strikes a chord. It's too much about making a quick buck now, and you really have to search the underground scene to find anything of any substance. You could probably say the same. I don't see much psychedelic material coming across the Atlantic anymore? I'm sure it exists somewhere though. We just ride the coat-tails of the shite that you keep throwing over to us.'

'Haha. You're right man, but you throw some shit back at us. Who's that Ed guy people keep raving about? He's no Dylan that's for sure. Now there's a genius.'

'Exactly, where are the geniuses?' I questioned.

He shrugged his shoulders and offered me one of his Lucky Strikes, taking one for himself too. I accepted and he lit both with a silver Zippo that had the famous 'lick' symbol of The Rolling Stones plastered across the front.

As he took a couple of puffs he asked, 'So what brings you all the way to Las Vegas then Ricky? You're a long way from home! Is it a bachelor party?'

'No, nothing like that, but everyone we speak to seems to think that's why we're here. I'm with my friends sat over there. We're just on the holiday, sorry, vacation that we always wanted to go on,' I explained.

'Cool, seems a long way to come though.'

'Well it's Vegas. You have to make the effort and not necessarily have a special agenda for coming. To tell you the truth, I'm here because I'm searching for something,' I revealed.

'What? The American dream?' Clint guessed.

'Ha. Not exactly, well maybe. I'm searching for answers - I'm at a crossroads in life.'

Clint became more interested, asking inquisitively, 'Oh yeah, like what?'

'Love, life, career, purpose, direction!'

'That fucked up eh?'

'Just a bit.'

'You know what you gotta do don't you? Clint looked me dead in the eye.

'I have an idea but go on?'

'You gotta get yourself into that desert man. It has answers only a true believer can understand. It's magical out there. That's what I did many years ago when I was about your age.'

A rush of excitement enveloped me. 'It's funny you should say that. We've just been talking about going tomorrow, but we're missing a certain ingredient for the trip.'

'Do you know about the special cactus, Peyote?'

'I've heard of it, but I don't know the ins and outs.'

'It's Mescaline.'

'Ah! Mescaline. Isn't that what Aldous Huxley took in the "Doors of Perception" book?'

'You know your literature.'

'Well its Doors related. I've not actually read it. I just know the reference.'

'It's fantastic. You should read it. It's a shame you haven't already to give you a heads up.'

'That good then?'

'For what you say you need, this is the thing for you.'

'What does it do? I'm not going to go mental, am I?'

He laughed at my naivety. 'No. Nothing like that! The Native Americans used it thousands of years ago. That's where it originates from, but let me tell you man, this shit gives you deep introspection that can only be described as spiritual. You'll see and hear things that will completely blow your mind. Trust me! You'll find the answers you're looking for with this shit.'

'That sounds a bit crazy...I don't know if I'm ready for it. Maybe I'm all talk and no balls.'

'Trust me Ricky. You're into your rock 'n' roll and the 60s vibe, right?'

'Yeah!'

'You need to experience this. You'll dig it.'

'Let's say I did want to take it. Could you hook us up?'

'I got a guy in Vegas who hooks me and my guys up with whatever we need. One phone call and it's done.'

I thought for a second and the idea of 'buying the ticket, taking the ride' came into my mind. Options were narrowing with regards to what I was going to do to free myself from the past. I still thought it was a dangerous proposition, and I wondered how I had come to be thrust to the brink of such extremity and desperation. Things could easily go wrong, but this *had* to be done! If the others were up for it then I would take that leap of faith with them and find out for myself. There was no better place than Vegas and the desert to try something so daring that could expand my mind and release me from this pain.

'Fuck it! Let's go for it!' I firmly said.

'I'll tell you what. You get me a beer and I'll give him a call shortly.'

'You're on. So, tell me more about peyote. What can I expect? Will I throw up?'

Clint carried on talking about the effects of this potent drug, which led him to talk of his solitary visit to the desert many years ago. He didn't go into detail, but he emphasised that his experiences were hard to explain and perhaps the only way to fully understand was to go through it myself. He went on to say that his mind was clearer afterwards, stating that it was one colossal way of exploring your inner self that no one else could really grasp.

He explained that his contact hooks him up with weed from time to time when they get to Vegas, but he'd had no need for anything harder these days. He was telling me about the history of Vegas and how he used to come in the 80s, just at the time it started to change and take shape into the Vegas we knew today. He educated me on how it all started back in the day and the changes it had undertaken over the last decades.

Clint drifted off outside the Heart Bar to make the phone call that would bring this trip to its hazardous finale. I brought the drinks over to our table and began telling the others about the conversation we just had. Obviously, there were immediate concerns as to whether we could trust Clint, but I had a good vibe from him.

'Are we really going to be able to trust anyone one hundred per cent in this situation?' I pointed out.

For me, it was a necessary risk to take and I had faith. The others were a bit more sceptical, especially Ian, who didn't want to see us having a bad trip whilst he was sober. He brought up the situation in the film 'The Hangover', where one of the characters is falsely sold 'roofies', the date rape drug, when he meant to purchase Ecstasy. I could imagine that story on our last night. No recollection and fear of having been sodomised. The ultimate biffle! Then, the notion of 'what happened in Vegas stays in Vegas' would certainly have to be enforced. Luckily, Ian's decision not to partake would enable him to protect us and remind us what happened if anything did go tits up.

To ease the others' anxiety, I suggested bringing Clint over once he returned so they could weigh him up. I told them a bit about his background, knowing that his music taste and choice of football team would have them sold in seconds.

Clint returned and looked around for us. I gestured to him as his eyes caught our table. I introduced him to everyone and he took a seat.

I nodded my head towards him and asked, 'Any luck?'

'No problem. He's on the Strip as we speak and he's heading over here shortly. Don't worry, I've told him to sort you boys out with some mild stuff as this is your first time,' he explained.

'I suppose that's something, I don't want to overdo it on a first trip, just enough for answers.'

'Answers you'll get my friend,' he assured me.

We sat drinking and sharing stories, and the others began warming to him. Clint was here with two other guys, who were currently playing blackjack, but he had bombed out for the night. His two friends, Kyle and Luke, eventually came over after they'd finished gambling. Clint told them both of our mission and they re-emphasised his original point about the powers of the desert. It made me feel excited, yet there was also a nervousness that something could turn bad.

We all spoke about music, sharing ideas and similar views about the greatness of bands throughout history. The evening was proving to be quite stimulating, and it made me realise that we weren't that much different from people who lived in a city also famous for its music and unique cultural traditions.

Clint's phone rang and he went to meet his guy outside, returning ten minutes later. He secretly handed me a few small plastic bags with peyote buttons inside.

'Right here you go. Be careful. You need to make sure you eat well in the morning, take plenty of water with you and make sure Ian looks out for you if he's not dropping,' he instructed.

I felt like a drug mule with these bags shoved into

my jeans pocket, which made me a little paranoid that I was going to be searched somewhere between the bar and my room, even though it was only a few minutes away. The panic of the infamous sign about Marijuana as one enters Nevada filled me with dread, 'Possession: 20 years.' I wanted to end the conversations quickly and get to my room where I knew I'd be safe. In my deluded state, eyes seemed to be locking on me from everywhere and I'd not even taken anything to induce such paranoia yet.

If we were going to experience the desert properly we would need sufficient rest. I recommended calling it a night given our wild plans. We all shook hands with Clint and his two buddies and they wished us luck, letting us know they'd be in New York New York Hotel tomorrow evening if we were about. They were eager to find out about what was going to happen and how this endeavour would end... and so was I.

CHAPTER 26

Ian and I stood waiting at the pick-up point outside Planet Hollywood. I was anxious, persistently stepping in circles and obsessively altering the position of my arms. Ian was quite the opposite, unenthused about what was about to happen despite Turner promising him that he would change his mind when they arrived. Turner had called us forty-five minutes earlier, telling us to meet him and Johnny at the entrance and to bring a few bottles of water. Before I could ask what was going on, he hung up.

There was a strange aura gliding through the air, like the world was changing around us with a new age looming upon us, which was totally beyond our control. For me, it was a vaguely unnerving realisation that life was boiling down to an epic showdown of man versus himself.

This daunting, risky trip into the Nevada Desert was all I had left to cling onto in a world where the issues of the past hadn't been dealt with, and that was the life waiting for me back home. So far, I had experienced Vegas to the best of my ability and that would never be taken away from me, but the rude awakening I yearned for hadn't occurred. In this desperate attempt to salvage something from the wreckage, I trusted for the first time in a long time in my own instincts and the unpredictable hand of destiny, fate and of course the several buttons of peyote stuffed inside my shorts pocket. I went over Clint's wise words from the previous evening and had to start believing in the peculiar powers of the universe, the desert...and the drugs that'd help me surf on a higher plain to reach a level I'd never experienced before. I didn't advocate drugs like cocaine, heroin or any form of pill. I didn't see the point in them and I always had a good time on a night out without them. But the lessons from the 60s movement made me think that the more natural drugs were the ones I could understand - those that could be used for purposes such as these – a need for self discovery and personal growth. I'd never needed to discover myself to such an extent before and hadn't gone beyond the giddy realms of a cannabis rampage. This was a big jump!

Even from the underground foyer we could tell it was a glorious day as the sun's strength made both entrances hazy with what seemed like blinding white rays shining from the heavens. I lit a cigarette whilst waiting, knowing that as soon as I sparked up, Turner and Johnny would arrive, much like waiting for a bus in the cold drizzly rain back home.

Ian and I didn't say much – we were both preoccupied with our own agendas. There were just the random mutterings of, 'Where are they?' and 'What are they up to?' As I neared three quarters of the way through my cig, a horn blasted from behind, causing us both to shriek and sharply turn to see a perfectly polished, gleaming white Hummer coast through the lot. Johnny's head peered out like a stupidly grinning meerkat with his arm resting on the side like a trucker.

'What the fuck have you done, Johnny?' I shouted, flicking the cigarette butt to the side.

'Well how else did you think we were going to get to the desert?' he answered. It hadn't even occurred to me how we were going to get there. I was too concerned with what was going to happen out there to give it any serious thought.

'Ian, you're going to be the sober one, so you get the pleasure of handling this bad boy. Be careful with her, it's under my name,' Johnny warned.

'I get to drive this?' he said, still stunned.

'Yep. You sure you'll be able to handle her? This isn't like your Clio you know.'

'If you've managed to drive it this far, considering that piece of shit passion wagon you drive back home, then I'm sure I can,' he responded.

Ian's mood had changed. I think the thought of driving down the Strip in this ridiculously oversized bastard of a Hummer was one that had him sold, and it did give the prospect of our journey a bit more edge and prestige.

'How much was this?' I asked.

'Don't worry about it. My treat out of the winnings, and we've only hired it for the day so it's not that much,' Johnny said.

'What's the sound system like?' Ian added.

'The bollocks! We've only got the radio because no one's brought any CD's.'

'Hold that thought. Wait here, I'll be down in a second,' I cried.

I hurriedly ran back inside the hotel, hearing the others shouting in the distance trying to find out what I was up to. I quickly rushed through the reception to the lifts, eventually ending up back in my room. I searched my untidy suitcase, now full of dirty laundry, and eventually pulled out three CDs packed at the bottom that I'd made in advance, very originally titled 'Las Vegas 1,2&3'. I'd pre-prepared these CDs for the slim possibility of hiring a car to make the drive more befitting of an American road trip.

The Hummer was parked slightly askew taking up two spaces, and the others looked blankly at me for answers upon my return. I tossed the CD's into Johnny's midriff, and he caught them before they struck him. 'Nice!' he exclaimed, on closer inspection. Ian was already in the driving seat working out all the gadgets the front panel displayed. Turner had sneakily called 'shotgun' and was already sat in the front passenger seat. Johnny opened the door for me and I clambered in and sat on the pristine, cream coloured, leather seats. Despite the air conditioning being on full blast, I was already beginning to stick to the seat, whether from the violent heat or my own anxiety, I wasn't sure!

We quickly realised that on this all important, perilous trip, we had no idea where the fuck we were going. Obviously to the desert, but whereabouts? It was a big place! Without any real guidance as to the safest or most dangerous spots we were like blind mice. We knew the direction to the airport was southbound on the Strip, so we thought we might as well drive straight on and keep our eyes peeled for a suitable spot once we got far enough away from civilisation to be at one with nature.

Ian was a bit nervous about having to drive on the right-hand side of the road, and we didn't help his confidence by constantly making him aware of potential threats that caused him to panic. It would be just our luck to crash before we'd even turned onto the busy Las Vegas Boulevard. Slowly, but surely, he managed to negotiate his way onto the hectic road, and now that he'd calmed down, the rock 'n' roll music thunderously poured out of all open windows as we cruised through the heart of Vegas. It was like nothing any of the tourists had heard before, probably expecting an OTT white Hummer to be filled with wannabe bad boys playing the latest rap craze. What they got instead were four lads from Manchester playing, 'Rock 'n' Roll Star', by Oasis. It instantly elevated our mood, and with songs by AC/DC, Led Zeppelin, Pink Floyd, and Jimi Hendrix following, we bolted like men possessed by the rock 'n' roll devil down the highway in search of our final destination.

We'd been driving south for an hour or so, well away from the hectic madness of Vegas and into a different kind of quiet madness. The number of cars had slowly decreased from the nose to tail traffic coming out of Vegas, to the clear, almost deserted roads. The pumped-up atmosphere of the car had hushed. Maybe Johnny and Turner didn't have that much to find out about themselves, more than likely excited for the experience rather than any meaningful soul searching. My trip was certainly going to be different. That lingering cloud that hovered over me forced me to recollect the past again, as if the cloud, knowing it was in danger of being parted by the sunshine, was having one final thunderstorm to discourage me from breaking through to the other side. Johnny Cash's cover of 'Hurt' started playing and somehow seemed to sum up the past few months in one emotive, poignant passage.

The meaning of the hardships imposed on me, the reasons for silly little missed phone calls and pathetic messages ran through my mind, making my stomach twist at every misdemeanour that had attacked me in the past months. The answers and clues to the way forward were approaching. Alternatively, there was the insufferable prospect of a bad trip, but hopefully I'd suffered enough and fate would be kind. I knew Turner and Johnny would be fine as their moods in recent times had been rich and trouble free. There was no need for them to be put on a downer, but I could go either way, 50/50 at best. My luck on 50/50 roulette had not panned out well so far, but now I was betting a whole lot more on the same odds. Jim Morrison once said, '*Drugs are a bet with your mind.*' Well, I was about to throw down the ultimate stake.

The terrain on the side of the smooth road started to become jagged and uneven. We'd taken a couple of turnings down even remoter roads. The golden desert was turning into an orange cauldron filled with gigantic rocks, ridges and valleys, a similar vision to that on the approach to Grand Canyon.

We felt lost in some sort of parallel empire where we were the keepers of our own kingdom. I hadn't been paying attention and had no clue as to where the hell we were! We had no map and I wasn't keeping a tab on signs to welcome us to wherever we were. Were we somewhere between Baker, Barstow and Berdoo? Who knew? If we were to meet some unforeseen horrible demise it would be months, even years before anyone would find us out here. Only Clint and his buddies knew we were going to the desert, but it's a pretty big place to find four tree trippers from Manchester.

I remained quiet as the conversation turned to whereabouts we should stop. I sensed we were close as we'd been driving far enough not to be noticed by anyone. We came upon a huge toothed rock by the side of the road that towered over us to create a large shadow on the tarmac. Something caused me to uncontrollably cry out the words, 'Here! Stop here! Park the car behind that rock over there out of sight. Well about as out of sight as a huge white Hummer can be in the bright sunshine,' I added.

Ian backed up the car into a small gap on stony ground and we exited, stretching our legs as we stood. I grabbed my Mizuno rucksack before emerging from behind the rock onto the side of the road. I stood for a second to admire the scenery. The sun was directly overhead, the sky as clear and blue as the Caribbean Sea, and the psychedelic dusty orange enveloped us for miles on end, piercing the horizon at different serrated points. I felt very much at home as a wave of tranquillity blessed my soul. That same strange sense of belonging that I'd felt near Grand Canyon reared up again as if I was standing at the gates of my own destiny. It just needed some Ennio Morricone western style Spanish guitar music to complete the atmosphere. 'The Sundown', from, 'The Good, the Bad, and the Ugly', sprang to mind.

None of us dared to speak first as we stood side-by-side admiring the views. It was a moment to relish, soaking in the last remnants of reality – or was it illusion? Reality may come shortly and what we'd been subjected to all this time might be like, 'The Matrix'. I slung my bag off my shoulder and gulped several mouthfuls of water before digging deep into my pocket to retrieve clear plastic food bags with cactus nestled within. The rest all turned to me.

'So?' Turner asked. 'We doing this or what?'

'No time like the present,' I answered.

'I'm ready!' Johnny said.

'Me too! Let's fuckin' do this!' I urged.

Ian let out a sly laugh, 'See you boys on the flip side.'

'You just make sure nothing bad happens. Watch the car, and knock us out if you have to if things get too crazy,' I told him.

'Don't worry I'll look out for you,' he reassured. 'Just don't go fannying about too far so you get yourself lost.' He sounded like a schoolteacher on a day trip.

I pulled out a handful of peyote buttons, handing

a few each to Turner and Johnny before taking a few for myself. We all looked at each other, nerves evident from our expressions. This was it! I was expecting some sort of speech to toast the event, but Johnny impatiently lifted his hand and quietly said, 'Cheers mofos!' That was motivation enough to start biting, chewing and swallowing this stuff. Oh god, the taste!! Our faces screwed up, but we persevered, adding a couple more buttons into our mouths, knowing that it wasn't going to taste like a prime double decker hamburger. After I'd finished shovelling them into my mouth I keeled over and gagged, reaching for my water in a desperate attempt to keep the peyote down for fear that I would lose the effects. Turner and Johnny made similar motions, and Ian could hardly contain his laughter, taking out his phone to film us all retching. It was the most rotten thing I'd ever put in my mouth. Luckily, nothing regurgitated and we regained composure, choosing to sit quietly on a rock just down the dip off the side of the road.

The water was nearly depleted as we gulped most of it just to get rid of the taste. Clint had told us the effects would take around forty minutes to kick in, so we played the waiting game, silently listening to our minds for any wayward thoughts that proved too weird for reality. What would happen? How would we know if we were tripping? I had heard that my body would tingle and I may start with giggles, which was nothing new from my experiences with cannabis. However, the euphoric feelings, elaborate colours, heightened appreciation of music as well as a heightening of the five senses, and a possible meeting with the sixth sense, was a trip I'd not experienced before. The nausea subsided and I felt settled, but in this instance, normality was to be the calm before the storm.

We'd been sat down for ten minutes or so and still nothing came to suggest I was tripping. I took out my iPod from my shorts pocket in preparation for the wave that was hopefully about to submerge me into another world. I searched for my 'best of the best' playlist, a guaranteed onslaught of a few hundred or so of the best songs known to man, which were fit for such a defining occasion. Peyote was meant to heighten the emotion and connection felt with music, and being such an obsessive lover of music, I wasn't going to go on this trip without my trusty 'bible' to count on. I lay back against the huge rock with my eyes closed. I didn't want to talk to anyone. I just wanted to soak in the sounds and mentally prepare. Duran Duran's, 'Ordinary World', began, and I smirked to myself at the irony of the coincidental lyrics that seemed to be speaking to me at this important time. Johnny Cash showed the sadness of the past, and now this song provided hope for the future.

CHAPTER 27

Half an hour passed rapidly and still I felt nothing, but the second I heard Johnny's first titter for no apparent reason was the first sign that the end of normality was lurking around the corner. He sat with his head stooped, pulling at some lonely bit of decayed vegetation lodged underneath a rock. How could that be funny? Turner watched with glaring eyes and began giggling, but my trip had yet to blossom. I tried not to force it, remaining composed, centred, and chilled, and still lying back against a boulder.

After a minute or so I turned my head slowly, transforming into a completely different character that I'd never met before.

'When this hits me, I'm gone. I don't want to speak to you. I *will* not speak to you till it's over. I will go forth into the wilderness and find what I'm looking for. I will not return until I find it or until death parts me from this surreal world. I must go and retrieve my life. I must go and find my soul. I must find my being. I need answers, but you cannot aid me on this trip. This is my own selfish journey. I love you all. Thank you for being here to share this moment with me. I hope to see you all very soon, but I must go, I don't know where... out there! I must go...I must go!' I spoke authoritatively, in a slow epic voice like I was going to my honourable death in battle. Perhaps I was.

'You go where you have to. May your guides be by your side and steer you in your quest for knowledge.' Johnny had stopped giggling, turning serious and just as weird as I had become.

Turner piped up, 'We know you've had a bad time. We know what this means to you. We've been with you all this time but you need to open the door and see what's on the other side for yourself now. There's no more we can do for you kid.'

'I respect your kind words. You are my friends, but they are calling me, they keep calling me. I will return a different man. I promise and swear on the souls of your grandchildren,' I announced, unaware of who or what was calling me or who had grandchildren for that matter. Did I really just say that?

'We don't have any grandchildren,' Johnny pointed out.

'I know. I hope one day you will. Maybe I've seen the future already?' I answered.

Meanwhile, Ian had a puzzled look on his face, remaining perfectly still in a state of confusion. I didn't know whether he was about to laugh or walk away from this freak show.

'Do not fear Ian. You cannot come with me either. I will be safe. Don't worry,' I reassured him.

'I'm not worried! You just carry on being weird,' he replied.

'I love your fearless attitude,' I mumbled, pointing

at him with what had suddenly become an extremely inflated and throbbing hand. The bruising on my knuckle from when I'd punched Bradley Jefferson was a glowing shade of deep red too.

At that point, I realised that I should've left the moment I opened my mouth as it had become painfully obvious that the drugs had begun to take hold. I saluted my friends in military style for some inexplicable reason and disappeared into the valley behind the rocks, gliding over the dunes like some predator in search of a kill. I distanced myself from the others, and patterns and colours emerged like a kaleidoscope in the corners of my sight. They grew wilder, working in tangent with mystical stars in broad daylight that looked like they weren't far from my own grasp, twinkling and sparkling with every step I took.

I looked on bemused, skipping through tracks on my iPod until I hit one that connected with the situation. I landed on one that spoke from beyond the grave, eerily haunting me as the sound propelled outside the ear phones into the surrounding air, like God himself was making his presence known.

'Is Everybody In? Is Everybody In? Is Everybody In? The ceremony is about to begin. WAKE UP!!!!' I ducked for cover in a terrified frenzy as if under attack by some aircraft fighter. The words echoed across the State of Nevada. I was certainly awake! I was too frightened not to be, but I looked to my inner strength to regain composure and ride it out. The voice was a familiar one, but under the spell of peyote I momentarily feared it. The monologues from Jim Morrison's, 'American

Prayer', began - a passage well worth taking heed of, imposing such deep wisdom that it was a fitting way to start the trip!

The weirdness of the words was almost unbearable – telling me that I've seen my birth, life and death, asking whether I had a good world when I did die, and if a movie could be made of it. I struggled to see sense and could only ask myself, 'When who dies? I've not died, have I? No Ricky, you haven't! Get a grip and listen to the verses. Think of the words.' I persevered through paranoia, and the speech began to connect on a deeper level than I ever could imagine in typical consciousness. I empathised with the verses that spoke of cosmic movies and living a life that was great enough to be broadcast to the world. However, I feared that I would be taken on a twisted journey by ghosts of my past, present and future like a Dickens novel. Perhaps the ghosts of my past were the ones calling me? Paranoia struck again. 'Fuck these thoughts,' I said to myself. 'Cut through illusion and abandon all that isn't true. Use the subconscious to find the reality.' It was important to remain strong and to not let anxiety control my actions.

I continued through the desert track, speculating deeper into nowhere. I started to shake from an improper coolness in the air, yet the heat was blistering, wrapping around my body to fluctuate my temperature at an abnormal rate. Every sound caused me to turn abruptly and investigate with paranoid and tentative eyes. I struggled to make sense of the wild effect. I started to see the blurred perceptions of what reality and delusion really were. Maybe I was drifting into the realness of reality and all that had been witnessed and experienced in life was fictitious, and only now was I beginning to see the way the world worked. The colours merged and entwined throughout my vision. All the rainbow colours mixed, twisted and turned like psychedelic realms of an unknown entity, forming into shapes that were beyond this world that no logical words could describe. I reached out to touch, pulling back when I felt my hand inches away. Heat shed from the colours, appearing to give off a gas that made the solid waves evaporate and swirl, latching onto my fingers and spinning around my hands like a purple haze. It was beautiful, yet terrifying! What were they? Was I meant to follow? Were they angels or spirit guides? I didn't know.

Select monologues of Morrison's poetry had ended and I felt dazed and emotional at hearing his teachings, trying to interpret the wise words. 'Oh Fuck!' I thought as 'White Rabbit' by Jefferson Airplane sneaked on next, a song about hallucinations whilst tripping. The colours became stronger and wavier, like the sea had been dyed and washed over into the desert. All I kept thinking about was seeing things that aren't there, hence, 'White Rabbit', a term derived from Alice in Wonderland. This could be a tricky bit to handle, but for some reason I felt that I needed to go through it to see what was on the other side. My mind couldn't shunt the words, 'White Rabbit', and before I knew it, white fluffy bunnies hopped about in front of me. Their eyes were a deep devil red, filling me with horror. 'Please don't attack me,' I whispered with dread. Fortunately, they didn't look like they were in assault position, and for the time being I avoided the evil side of the trip that could've scarred me forever. I had to clear my head and remember that this was definitely a hallucination. Without doubt an army of rabbits with violent red eyes would not be out here in the desert, hopping about all around me, or could they? Perhaps they were a guide, so I followed to wherever it was this trance was whisking me away to.

As the song ended, the rabbits softly vanished into thin air and the amplified squeaking halted in a heartbeat. Still I wandered, waiting to be found, or was I meant to find *it*? I took a breather standing at the top of a ridge looking up at the strangely purple and orange sun in the sky, which forced me to squint even with sunglasses on as its unchallenged rays beamed across the desert. Looking up was a mistake as it acted as a catalyst for the hallucinations to flurry again. Somehow, in my twisted mind, I'd invoked the perception of lava slowly dripping off the sun and landing in my vicinity, splashing in front of my very eyes. The droplets that bounced back hit my leg and were scorching hot, burning deeply into my skin through drugged up eyes. Puddles of golden yellow encircled me, and the desert transformed into a terrain of wet sand and lava. I turned away and crouched, eyes tightly closed, remaining still for a few minutes waiting for this wave to pass, searching for what the meaning of witnessing this madness could be, if there was any meaning at all.

Eventually, I felt the turmoil subside and rose to my feet, opening my eyes with caution to the relief that the lava had stopped dripping and the desert had returned to its normal glorious state. The sinister atmosphere I felt had relinquished its hold for now, and all that was left was a temporary feeling of peaceful happiness and heavenly emotion.

I came to feel at one with the music that I felt pierce my soul. It was like the songs were trying to tell me something if I chose to listen and not just hear. I walked, almost floating, listening to classic, dark tracks from Pink Floyd, Velvet Underground, Jimi Hendrix, Thirteenth Floor Elevators and sounds from 1960s San Francisco, skipping through them quickly to cram as much psychedelia in as possible to enhance the experience.

In the distance, I could see three familiar figures on top of another ridge to the east of me, two of them dancing, possessed like wild creatures of the night. I could make out clothes being swung around by two of them, and the other figure stood still, refusing to get involved. All the figures had outlines of yellow that glowed and effervesced majestically. I was seeing the auras of my friends. I became overwhelmed with a deep connection and love for them, which made me tearful, afraid to lose them, privileged to know them. I held my arms aloft and shouted, 'I love you guys!' Two of the figures halted their dancing and turned to face me, recognising me in the distance, shouting back, 'We love you too.' I nearly burst into tears and quickly had a word with myself to get a grip.

The music continued to make me highly emotional and I was hearing the sounds, melodies and lyrics differently. Maybe the answers were in the lyrics? Icy tremors suddenly rippled down my spine when the opening to Jefferson Airplane's, 'Somebody to Love', came firing through the earphones. The opening line, speaking about truths that are actually lies, hammered into my brain like a telepathic thunderbolt from beyond this fucked up world. For some reason, I couldn't let that statement go! The colours and patterns continued to dance in front of me. I wondered whether I should ask questions out loud to retrieve answers.

'What truth is a lie?' I growled, and by vocalising the words I felt a jolt like I'd broken free from a shackle, telling me that somewhere between the conscious and unconscious mind, what I'd been told about the recent past was turning into a lie. How did I not see this earlier? Of course, it was! It was crystal clear that the exaggerated text was sent to rip me apart and cover-up what was really going on. It was as if I could now visualise reading between the lines whilst in this euphoric trance, and I could see how Mandy over-elaborated her and 'Mr Amazing's' relationship. The embellished words: 'amazing man', 'really happy', and 'plan our future', from the message she sent were part of her blind shallowness and were an overstatement of how it was going to play out. It was clear to me now that the feelings, foundations and reasons for this new relationship were built on a superficial false hope. Every time I went over the message all I saw were the actions of a desperate woman, who had made a real error in judgement. I felt no pity that she was going to become the victim of her own wicked game. It continued to play over and over like a broken record and it now started to make me laugh as I found truth. The illusion had been dissected with this first incision.

I danced and jigged like a tribal dancer befitting of the lands I was roaming. I was like a man possessed by some demon from the hippie movement. I swanned effortlessly, waving my arms around in complete freedom like I was back in that monumental time in history. I began to laugh uproariously and before I knew it I fell helplessly to the floor, finding myself in fits of howling giggles that seemed to hauntingly ring around the desert. I had found my first answer and was completely sure of its revelation. I jumped up, continuing to dance and sing aloud, a solitary joyous tear broke through the duct to run down my cheek. It was a tear of happiness, signifying so much under this spell I was currently bound to.

I wiped the tear and eventually knelt with my hands dug deep into the sand. I grabbed it by the handful, feeling the grains flow through my fingers like an egg timer that scattered in several directions as it fell to the ground. After a few seconds, I was back on my feet, continuing the trek deeper into the unknown desert longing for more!

Some hallucinations remained constant. Everything seemed to be in exaggerated 3D, and the sharpness of the jagged rocks was emphasised, distorted and some even moved and moaned, but I was impervious to these effects. The sun carried on dripping, silver glows appeared on rocks, the clear blue sky turned a spiritual purple, and paranoia worked in conjunction with feelings of extreme highs as I skated precariously on the border between both emotions.

It was time to probe into an entirely different zone and listen to a track that could send my head into a dangerous and disturbing trance, even without the influence of any sort of hallucinogens. The ghostly guitar strummed at the beginning of one of the most psychedelic and controversial rock songs of the 1960s, 'The End', by The Doors. I instantly fell under its lucid spell as my soul connected and locked into a plain above any natural known high. Morrison's voice kept guiding me, and the lyrics echoed my presence in the desert. I felt that something was about to be born from this song, almost a preparation for a showdown of some sort. The time was nigh, whatever I'd come to search for was about to make itself known. The heightening of the sixth sense that I'd heard about was becoming finely tuned. With that potent awareness engulfing me, the mellowness I currently felt abruptly halted when a figure strolled across my path about fifty yards in front of me, sending a freezing cold shiver down my spine that had me rooted to the spot.

The face was covered by long, dark, wavy hair, and it was dressed in ancient looking white garments. It seemed to float rather than walk, but it moved ever so slowly, snail's pace even. My mind, which had been calm for a while, had now gone into a hysteric panic. I was unable to decipher the reality or illusion of what appeared in the distance. Was it a real figure or was this who or what I'd been searching for? I gathered strength again, letting my mind clear of any misinterpretations. I tried to meditate with my eyes shut whilst sweat poured profusely from my forehead. I carefully re-opened them and the figure was still present, appearing to look straight at me. It was too far to make out any sort of facial features, but I dared to approach, believing this was all part of the plan. I began to tread slowly, not wanting to scare it or appear confrontational. As I drew nearer, the figure turned to carry on walking into the shadows where the ridges overhung. I was still fearful but I followed as 'The End' still rang out through my earphones.

Whatever it was had disappeared around the corner, back into the open sun and flat, desolate land of dusty sand and fragmented rock. I walked a little faster, jumping over the rocks until I reached the corner out of the shade and into the open light, finding the figure facing me about thirty yards away. An abundance of white feathers fell from the sky like snow congregating in a magnetic pull towards this mysterious apparition. Thousands fell, and when merged with the sun's rays, the golden sand, and tinged orange rocks as a backdrop, the sight was exquisite. I had heard about the significance of feathers from a spiritual point of view, being symbols of one's personal situation. They can come to you in times of sorrow and joy, symbolising that everything happens for a reason and that you are well protected by some higher force. They can also be construed as seeing truth, higher plane thinking and spiritual enlightenment. All these interpretations were related to my troubles, and whether this was a hallucination or not, there was certainly some deep subconscious meaning to the feathers fluttering in my path.

I stood still for a second before cautiously walking forward. It was hard not to be afraid despite what I kept telling myself. I mean, this was some seriously trippy shit I was seeing - a figure that had no bearing on actuality whatsoever. Had I just conjured this figment up in my mind, or was this really happening? My heart was beating faster, causing more sweat to run down my cheeks and drip onto my t-shirt. The colours had become less fluent, but the white feathers continued to gently fall, and a ring of silver stars showered the figure. I was still afraid, but still I progressed until I courageously stood only a few yards away. The head faced to the ground. I took a step back as it began to lift, a bit freaked out that there appeared to be no face. I was also bewildered when I noticed there was no shadow on the ground coming from this spirit despite the sun burning intensely, whereas mine was a beautiful, fine black outline. The open bit of flesh where the face should have been was aged and weathered. The flowing locks of dark brown hair blew in a wind that I couldn't feel as it swept across the face. The white garments gleamed as the sun seemed to shine directly on them, giving off a glow that made me think this entity was from a different world, whether that world be in my imagination, or from the other side, I didn't know.

I stood in silence, too fearful to say anything, and part of me didn't want the figure to say anything. Without a mouth, I wouldn't have been able to grasp where the communication was coming from, if it could communicate at all. An element of terror struck when a thought came to me that this could be a symbol of death, but then I reminded myself of Blue Oyster Cult's classic,

'Don't Fear the Reaper'. On the other hand, perhaps this was some sort of guide waiting to take me by the hand to make me feel normal again, as Joy Division alluded to in 'Disorder'. I carried on gazing, going down the same road as earlier. Ask a question, I thought, before quietly letting out the trembled words, 'Why am I here? Why did things get so fucked up back home? What is my destiny?' After I asked, the stars flashed like a beacon, the wind grew stronger and this time I could feel it as the sand kicked up, showering parts of my legs. Then, for some reason my own thought process was changing. I started to think and feel things that I'd never known, and before I knew it I was realising so much. I became hounded with images from the past.

The revelations from earlier were stronger than ever, but now other thoughts rushed to the forefront and their impact hit hard. Firstly, when I thought about why the harsh text message from Mandy had been sent, I was overcome with a feeling of despair in the pit of my stomach. A deep rage rose like a gargantuan wave of red mist and I briefly fell back on my arse. At first, I thought the trip had sent me in the wrong direction and coming here was one big mistake, but suddenly it thumped me. The feelings I felt were that of Mandy's, anger brought on through a need to assert control. The missed phone calls were all part of that need to continue to control me and try to stay in my mind. I uncontrollably drifted through the memories of our relationship and was beginning to put the pieces of the jigsaw together. The way she was as a person was something I'd become blind to over the years through her subtle manipulation. She had become, or probably always had been, drawn to money and status. Her life had become surrounded by the notion of more and more material wealth. Nothing was ever good enough anymore, it was all about moving into a big house with flash cars and expensive clothes, totally seduced by money. Her actions spoke volumes and even the way she was when we went out had changed. She'd become arrogant and rude to staff in restaurants and bars over the most miniscule of incidents, all because she felt she had risen above her station and become consumed by her own arrogance. I remembered the discouragement she portrayed towards any sort of interesting idea I had away from the norm, as if she couldn't let me go above her plateau. She was like a true narcissist and needed to be in control, smugly putting me down with statements such as, 'You'd be nothing without me', 'I'm the best thing to happen to you' and, 'I wouldn't get out of bed for what you earn.' But more fool me for putting up with such shameful comments and demoralising actions. Maybe deep down she knew that if I were set free then life could take me to places she couldn't handle or accept, and the only way to keep me from trying something new was to emphasise her own self-worth and undermine mine in the process. I think our relationship was always doomed from the start, and she was patiently biding her time until she met someone else who had the wealth and the connections to raise her own profile, and give her all the materialism she coveted. The calculating manipulation ran deep, and I learnt that I was a victim of psychological warfare.

Once I realised this, the pain that had lingered for so long now miraculously diminished, like the message had been received loud and clear. I now knew we had to split so that I could become the person I was meant to be. It was all so obvious and I couldn't believe it had taken this long and this extreme scenario to finally understand what everyone else probably already knew.

With regards to 'Mr Amazing', revelations from earlier expanded, and all I felt was emptiness and a feeling of materialistic satisfaction based on greed, as if the whole relationship revolved around money and superficial status. It was a complete sham that would inevitably lead to profound unhappiness, if it hadn't already. Whether or not the nuptials would take place didn't matter, the perception in that instance suggested it wouldn't last long. When you base love on money, then your loving days are over. That's why she bolted without an explanation because she knew I'd see right through her if we had a face-to-face showdown.

I focused on my own position in life, and felt that I could start a new journey that was about to fully explode in a fascinating way now that restraints weren't holding me back. Even my working life would improve in this fresh, positive outlook, and I wouldn't be imprisoned and stifled by the tedious rituals of a nine to five position that contributed to decaying any motivation to change. 'Do Anything You Wanna Do' by Eddie & The Hot Rods, sprang to mind, a song I held close to my heart, speaking of breaking out of the city in search of adventure, being sick of thankless day jobs with a burning desire to discover who I was and knowing that I was someone better than I had been for the last five years.

What I'd been doing in music felt right. Strong images of gigs and bands started to scatter in my mind and I knew I had to get involved in some way. I thought about travelling, liberated from typical working life and being able to travel to parts unknown and do what I wanted to do. I didn't know if this part was just my mind being euphoric or whether it was a sign of things to come, but I didn't care. The very image was enough of a motivation to persevere and enter a new chapter in life.

Visions moved on and ones that I hadn't counted on seeing suddenly became known to me. From behind the angelic figure, another presence strode slowly into view. As it neared I recognised the familiar and beautiful face of Eva, dressed exactly how I remembered her. What the fuck was going on? I couldn't comprehend whether this was part of the trip or whether she'd just randomly appeared to me, but whichever way I looked at it, it made my heart sink. I walked towards her as she neared, now unafraid of teetering nearer to the figure that had shown me so much. I was yards away from her when I reached out to take her up in my arms, but as I did she vanished into thin air and I ended up wrapping my arms around my own shoulders, knocking myself off balance, which caused me to stumble forward much closer to this ethereal being than I would've liked.

Images and feelings swept through my mind and body like those experienced earlier, and interpreting its logic proved more difficult than deciphering the past. That first night with Eva played over, and the feelings I felt rushed back again. There was a happiness that I'd not felt in years when I thought of that night, but it was coupled with a profound sadness at the truthful fact of our world's being poles apart. Why was I being shown this? Maybe it was to show me that I was capable of feeling something for someone else and not to let the past ruin any future relationship. That's all I could retrieve from the vision, but something wouldn't let me delve any further. There was emptiness in my mind when I asked, 'Why are you showing me this?'

Everything felt peaceful: the atmosphere, the desert, but most importantly the turmoil in my mind and stomach. I was certainly still high and hallucinating, and had probably peaked, but I was certain I'd seen some form of distorted reality. Through listening to The Doors, I had experienced their whole philosophy. *'When the doors of perception are cleansed, things appear to man as they truly are, infinite.'* This was originally William Blake's quote, but another direct Jim Morrison quote leapt to my attention. *'There are things known, there are things unknown, and in between are the doors.'* The relief at finally being able to open the door to the unknown having stood waiting at the entrance for so long was a high, even without peyote.

The wind died down and the sun began to dim. The figure that had appeared to me began to diminish slowly into thin air along with the halting of falling feathers. I guess whatever it was had shown me all I needed to know and now it was up to me to put it into practice.

As the last remnants disintegrated into thin air I became saddened. I believed that I had just seen some sort of guardian angel and wondered whether I would see it again. Part of me hoped not as that would mean I'd be in trouble again at some point in the future.

The last bit of the figure's garment vanished and I noticed a small lizard near where it once stood, which scampered away further into the desert. *Now* I was a little freaked! Had the lizard been there the whole time? Had I initially followed the lizard and my mind had conjured it up into being an angelic figure, or had the angel morphed back to being at one with nature? It wasn't worth trying to work out, not in my hallucinogenic state. I had untangled enough of the puzzle without starting on something beyond my reckoning, so I started off back towards the others. My work here was done!

Time simply had no meaning under this mystical spell and I had no idea how long I'd been away for. I took a slow walk back embracing all I'd learnt, churning the past over and over in my mind, finding that all the negativity had gone, extracted from me like I'd just been part of some deranged exorcism ritual. Now that felt truly 'amazing'!

I returned to find the others sat where we'd noticed the first waves stirring. Turner was lay back on the rock and from over his sunglasses he asked, 'So, how was it?' I couldn't describe or explain it to him, the trip was too bizarre, but I told them the outcome.

'Clint was right! There's something a bit magical out there, and in this stuff. Incredible!' I shook my head in disbelief pointing to the empty bag of peyote buttons. 'Don't worry about me anymore, everything's sorted.'

'You sure?' Ian showed his concern.

'Oh, I'm quite sure.'

'What happened out there?' Turner was intrigued.

'I can't explain! Let's just get back and enjoy this last night properly. As it should be!' The three of them laughed and stood simultaneously. We all embraced, recognising the importance of having come through one hell of an experience unscathed.

Turner and Johnny were more animated about their experiences on the journey back. Ian pitched in taking the piss out of them as they'd apparently felt the love of the drug and tried to hug and kiss Ian in a daze of flower power hippiness. Turner and Johnny had attempted to get naked and dance free as birds in the desert sunshine, while Ian didn't want to see such horrific scenes and managed to stop them, but not without videoing them first. He threatened to hold them to ransom over it. There were no revelations to be had with Johnny and Turner. It just seemed their trip was a mixture of being at one with the universe, made up of a bit of love, with a pinch of despair, but not quite as meaningful as the way mine had panned out. Johnny described his trippiest moments, consisting of a conversation with a goat, seeing an army of lemmings fall to their death from a nearby ridge, and seeing a ship dock on the sand, that he was sure was the 'Titanic'. Turner's own debauched mindset seemed to form a large proportion of his trip, including visions of naked Native American women dancing in front of him trying to entice him into some sort of sordid orgy, which then manifested into a vision of seeing every girl he'd ever slept with, who wanted to make a Turner sandwich out of him. He said he was walking about with a massive erection for most of the trip, which under the influence of peyote, was freakishly huge.

CHAPTER 28

We had one more night left and with my new-found positivity I was going to go out in one hell of a blaze of glory with a celebration of epic proportions, beginning with a toast to my desert angel. This time, the past wouldn't influence the night. Tonight was all about what a free man could do on his last night in Las Vegas with a clear head and conscience!

The effects of the peyote had quietened and we were slowly returning to normality, whatever that meant after today's trip. The lines had become a bit blurred in that department. I kept seeing the odd flash of dazzling colour in the corner of my eye, but the hallucinations had stopped...I think. The revelations from my trip remained as strong as ever, and the past had become just that... the past, a point in my life that I could look upon as a catalyst for what was about to happen to shape my own personal crusade.

The plan was to end up at Coyote Ugly within New York New York having heard many glowing reviews from various people who'd already visited, including Clint and his buddies, who presented it as an option. Before that, it was essential to visit Fremont Street, the 'Old Town' of Las Vegas where much of the legendary stories up until the 1980s took place, in terms of renowned shows and performances on one hand, and the brutal mafia influence on the other. It was a place of history and, despite putting it off for five days, we knew it was an area that had to be explored, even if only for a brief period of time.

We arrived just in time for the famous 'Light Show', the main attraction of the famed 'Fremont Street Experience'. This mesmeric show consists of an overhead canopy running the length of five football fields through the Fremont Strip, which is lit up by flashing lights, high resolution images and high definition sound for the selected show. We were in time to see 'The Queen Tribute Show' that played the classic, 'We Will Rock You', followed by 'We Are the Champions'. It was quite the spectacle, especially when all the visitors sang along. It was a shame that we didn't have time to hang around to witness the other shows available, such as 'Bad to the Bone' about the bad boys of rock, and 'KISS Over Vegas', a tribute to…well, KISS!

Once the show ended I was gasping for a drink and to feel the blast of an air con unit again. It was the first time the night had started to reflect the raw, dry, desert heat that we'd felt during the days when we were exposed to the sun, but at least we had shorts on then. It was more agitating with jeans and a shirt on, so to escape the furnace, we went into one of the nearby casinos. There were plenty to choose from in this part of town as they were bunched together, making Fremont Street a much more intimate place than the Strip.

We opted for Binion's, a casino now cemented in Vegas folklore, as it was where the World Poker Series was born. It was also the place where you could have no betting limit on any game you played, not like that would matter to any of us! Another feature was that they had a 'million bucks' in cash on display in a secure, see through cubic container. I wondered how many villains had been tempted to dare a chance smash and grab with it?

The betting minimum was lower here than on the Strip, so it was comforting to know that, in theory, we could play for longer than we could at the higher minimum games within the mega resorts. In the end this didn't make one bit of difference to the outcome as I still lost $70 just as quickly as if I'd been betting on the Strip. A series of failed double downs was my downfall.

Turner and Johnny got some food from the restaurant within Binion's, and while they were eating, Ian and I took a walk to soak in the vibe of the Old Town. We had a brief stint in the famous Golden Nugget, which to be honest looked very similar to Binion's, and then we watched a guy dressed in a lizard costume pack himself into a see-through box about a cubic foot in size. The best bit about this was that he managed to get a small hoop all the way from the top of his head down to his feet, but the only struggle seemed to come when he was trying to get it over his cock! There were street entertainers everywhere, from one man shows on street corners, to bands playing on stages. People roamed the street spoilt for choice in what to see or do next, and you couldn't walk a few paces without being drawn into some bizarre daredevil act going on. It was like a circus with weirdness stemming from every corner. 'People are Strange', by The Doors sprang to mind.

I got the impression that Fremont Street was why several people stereotyped Las Vegas as being a glorified Blackpool. Apart from the heat there were several similarities. It was a shame we couldn't fully discover the world of the Old Town, but we didn't have enough time after setting off later than usual. With this being our final night, we were itching to get back onto the Strip, and to Coyote Ugly, for one final blow out of Las Vegas imposed booze-fuelled madness.

Our taxi back to the Strip served as a reminder of the impressions Mancunians make on the world. When the taxi driver realised where we were from, he brought up the fact that 'people from Manchester are crazy.' He was referring to a few years earlier when much of our city descended onto Vegas to support local Boxing hero, Ricky Hatton, for the few fights he had in these parts. Judging by what the driver was telling us, it seemed that Manchester had truly left its mark on one of the world's most iconic cities.

Coyote Ugly was a lot smaller than anticipated. It was so packed to the rafters that the air con struggled to break through the heat that seeped off everyone on this scorching night. There was an electric, laid-back atmosphere that encouraged people to let themselves go, ridding themselves of their inhibitions and egos at the entrance.

Just as the film, 'Coyote Ugly', portrays, girls danced away on the bar to emulate the on screen action. Cheers and whistling rang out from several guys congregated below them. They had a perfect view, catching a cheeky glimpse up the short skirts on show. Professional dancers were on the bar tops adjacent, but not pole dancers, more like club dancers. Bras hung from the ceiling rafters too, which I presumed were from previous punters throwing them up there rather than some sort of design idea. It looked cool though, and gave some indication to the sort of shenanigans that could potentially go on in the joint, making the urge to get involved amongst the cluster of people overpowering.

A vibration from my back pocket prompted me to check a message that came through, just before I started my first illustrious dance move.

It was from Eva. *'Hey gorgeous! Hope you're ok? Where have you gone tonight?'*

I replied, *'Hi. We're in Coyote Ugly in New York New York. I'm feeling fantastic, having a great night. What are you up to?'*

'We're just on our travels again heading somewhere else now. Glad you're ok. You appear very positive. Has something happened?'

'It's been an incredible day. I'll have to tell you about it sometime. It's too much to explain in text.'

The mood between the four of us had turned somewhat excitable as alcohol fuelled the final night's determination to go out in style. We danced like idiots to a series of cheesy power ballads that filled the room, making us 'air grab' and 'air guitar' at every opportunity. Individuals nearby looked at us and laughed. Somehow, our taking-the-piss idiocy influenced them and they began to join in the merriment. A few more people gathered, and before we knew it we had inadvertently started our very own circle with about twelve other people, all air guitaring and air grabbing at every opportunity. Some were girls, quite attractive too, which acted as a catalyst for Turner to engage in 'operation grindfest' yet again. He approached every girl he could from behind and started grinding with no questions asked, raising his fist and punching the air towards the roof every time the girl entertained the idea. Johnny obviously had to join in through sheer competitiveness, but Ian and I were fine to leave them to it and immerse ourselves in the circle we'd helped create.

We started to take it one step further and get people to dance in the centre for a few seconds before exiting, and then we would nominate someone else to do another dance move and so on. More and more people became interested and it was like a scene from an 80s high school dance by the end of it. Those who moved well took advantage and began dancing to a professional standard, meaning there was very little chance that any of us four would try and follow suit.

It wasn't long before the nomination process was lost. People just kept going into the middle and throwing out their moves and shapes at will. Bloody impatient Yanks! Half the venue eventually became involved and it elevated the harmonious atmosphere inside, actually having a 'Coyote Ugly' feel about it. It was crazy that this all started because of us rocking the air guitar.

The circle was proving to be great fun, and even the DJ was getting involved. The fact that we helped create it had been well and truly lost now and no one knew who the fuck we were. It had fast become a glorified dance off...I was just waiting for it to turn into the inevitable 'grind off'.

The circle began fizzling out and normality on the dance floor was slowly returning as the tunes switched to the 90s. There had been a delay in girls dancing on the bar tops while this was going on, but it slowly resumed. I sensed the DJ was getting bored of the dance offs and wanted to see some tits and arses wiggle directly in his eye line under the spotlights.

I felt buzzing in my back pocket, reminding me that my conversation with Eva had not finished from earlier. It was a mystifying message from her that read, *'Why don't you tell me about your day, now?'*

I frowned and stared at the screen, baffled. Did she want me to ring her or attempt to put a full day's drug induced antics into one text?

I replied, *'What do you mean hun?'*

Almost immediately a response rang through.

'Turn around!'

I paused for a moment thinking what the hell was going on. Had she sent the message to the wrong person? At that juncture, Ian tapped me on the shoulder.

'Is that Eva over there?' He pointed behind me.

I turned, and thought my eyes must be deceiving me - or I was still tripping. Eva stood by the bar, shining like a ray of light beaming down from the sky. She saw my reaction as I turned and she smiled graciously. I was completely gob-smacked and darted towards her, trying my best not to clatter into people on my surge, firmly wrapping my arms around her as soon as I was within range. She giggled into my ear, sending a tingling sensation down the right-hand side of my body that nearly made me faint. Her arms gripped tightly around me, and I held her there for a few seconds just so I could come to terms with what I was seeing, but more importantly, come to terms with the importance of seeing her in the desert under estranged, drug fuelled eyes. Her smell spiralled through my senses, that same scent that locked me into a trance of submission on our first night. I moved to look deep in her eyes and kissed her softly. The taste of her brought back nostalgic memories. I pulled away and fixated again on those beautiful hypnotic eyes. She wore a plain black dress, tightly cut to reveal every inch of her stunning body. Her dark features bloomed under the light and, just as I had been on our first night, I was absorbed once again under her powerful spell.

'What are you doing here?' I managed to ask.

Her head gravitated to the side, searching the depths of me as she held me in her warm gaze. She seemed embarrassed, struggling to say what she wanted, letting out a couple of 'um's', before a voice by the side of me spoke.

'Hey Ricky! She's been talking about you all damn trip! So much so that this was my idea to surprise you just so I could get some damn peace!' It was Annalise, who once again revealed the privacy of their conversations, making Eva blush, much like our first encounter.

'Are you surprised?' Annalise continued.

'Of course I am. I'm more than surprised! I'm overwhelmed!' I spluttered.

'Well I knew it was your last night and wanted to see you again to make it just as special as the first,' Eva answered. I was ecstatic and in complete shock that she drove all the way back here just for me.

'Listen. I know we come from different worlds, but let's forget about that tonight and enjoy it properly for what it is,' she declared.

I nodded in agreement and turned to the bar to buy her and Annalise a much-deserved drink.

'This is so crazy. You're actually here? Where are you staying?' I asked.

'Here at New York New York. We'd just got into Vegas when I messaged you and thought we'd stay wherever you were. Planet Hollywood was too expensive at such short notice. Luckily the rooms here were cheaper.'

'Oh, and we got separate rooms before you ask!' Annalise interrupted, to which I laughed, and Eva blushed again.

I turned to Eva, 'I can't believe it. You've just given this trip the perfect end and I thought the day had been the perfect send off,' I revealed.

'You have to tell me what happened. What did you get up to?'

I took a moment to look at the dance floor and see that the party was continuing in its full, unadulterated glory. This wasn't the time to reveal the story so I grabbed her hand, whispering, 'I'll tell you later. Come on!' I led her over to where Turner and Johnny were. Their faces were mystified and shocked to say the least when they saw me with Eva, forcing me to explain what had just happened. Annalise was linked with Ian and we all huddled in a confined space at the edge of the dance floor. The circle had fully dispersed now, and Turner and Johnny were in full 'last night lay' mode. I explained to both Eva and Annalise the competitive nature of them both as they competed for the attentions of about six girls they purposely danced near.

Eva and I couldn't keep our hands and eyes off each other as I clutched her around her waist from behind. Her fingers interlocked into mine as we gently swayed along to the music. The emotions I felt were strange. Was I caught up in the elevated hype of a holiday romance? Was I hypnotised by the attractiveness of someone so different to my own culture? Was this a reaction to being free? Or, was this in fact very real? If so, how would I handle the prospect of having to leave her behind a second time knowing that our lives were thousands of miles apart? She'd already said let tonight just be tonight. Although that was a great attitude to have, I couldn't escape that lump in my throat at the question, 'What next?'

She turned to Annalise for a few brief words, both chuckling at whatever was said. Eva turned to me and told me to wait there as she and Annalise made their way off the dance floor.

A few minutes had passed and the girls who currently danced on the bar tops were ushered off for the next bunch to go up and strut their stuff. To my complete surprise, making their way up the few steps were Eva and Annalise with two other girls. They took their positions on the bar as the music lowered for the DJ to introduce the next group. Eva winked at me as she approached the end spot, and when the music began, she started moving erotically to the 90s R&B jam that had a heavy groove and a funky bass. She looked spectacular and danced at a standard high enough to give some of the earlier circle dancers a run for their money. Annalise was no slouch either and they both bounced off each other's energy as if the whole thing had been choreographed since childhood. I clapped and cheered along with the rest of the crowd, feeling proud of the wolf whistles that rang out in front of me directed at Eva's stunningly sexy looks. I think at that moment, even Johnny, Ian and Turner could say they were envious as they stared, tongue-tied like many of the other onlookers.

Turner turned to me and said, 'I should've gone over to Eva while you were trying to pluck up the courage to do so that night.'

I responded cockily, 'No shot Turner, no shot!'

We both laughed and he turned back to me, 'Seriously mate, I'm so fuckin' glad you did go over.'

One of the barmen took up a siphon and showered the girls with a barrage of water, soaking them to the very core. They all gasped as the coldness shocked them, which momentarily made the dancing stop, but Eva took it upon herself to retrieve another siphon from next to where she stood and returned the favour. The crowd laughed, but our smiles were soon wiped off our faces when she turned to us, looking at me before aiming the siphon straight towards the four of us, marinating us in cool water, which was rather refreshing considering the blistering heat that sweltered around us. I looked up at her once she stopped, flashing her a joke-like glance that suggested she'd pay for that later.

A saturated Eva and Annalise returned only to be bombarded by playful concerns over their hosepipe actions. Eva remained cool, 'It looked like you boys could do with cooling off!' Her dress was wet through, and her usually straight hair had developed curls with beads of water dripping onto her shoulders. She was a picture of sexuality, looking like a model that had just appeared in a suggestive perfume advert.

As for us, all the time that had gone into dressing up for the last night was now a wasted effort. Hairstyles had been well and truly ruined. But in the environment and surroundings of Vegas, these minor burdens were all part and parcel of what was expected. In Manchester, it may have been a different reaction, especially if the customary cold wind was howling through the streets as it so frequently does.

Last orders in Coyote Ugly fast approached, and the night had rapidly withered away. Unwilling to let the pace of time beat us, we left the bar in favour of the casino, where we settled around a table near the central bar.

It occurred to me that I was yet to engage in my big gamble for the evening, something I'd promised myself before I left Vegas. I wanted one final large stake flutter in a last chance saloon bid to chase the 'American Dream'. With the way the day had gone so far with the desert and Eva's sudden appearance, I felt lady luck was planted firmly in my corner, so why not try and complete a trio of good fortune in one day?

I reminded Turner of the big bets I'd promised, which galvanised him into joining me so he could watch for the final time as I took centre stage on the blackjack table. This time he wouldn't be alone. Eva was also curious to see the outcome, although I had to explain the rules to her. Was this my time to shine? Was all the spiel spouted prior to the departure going to boil down to this last game? Would the newly found revelations lead to a huge win now I had a new-found positivity? Surely, I wouldn't be lucky enough to achieve such heights with only hours left in Vegas?

By this time, I was quite drunk, probably not in the best frame of mind to be playing high stakes. I found the first table I could that had spare seats. The minimum bet was $25 and I was ready to take the final step in my gambling love affair with Vegas by unfolding $300 neatly on the table. I just hoped and prayed that this would pay off like it had done in the MGM on the third night, and I would walk away with a big win, or at least put a dent into the overall expenditure that Vegas had demanded off me. I laid down a $50 marker, nervously waiting for the cards to be dealt. My hands began to shake and the tension got the better of me. Being dealt sixteen twice in a row and being beaten by the dealer both times was not a good start at all. A ray of sunshine did glimmer when I won the next two, but the losses came frequently, and I found myself down to my last $50 very quickly, which vanished within seconds when the dealer boasted blackjack with a King and an Ace. It stung deeply!

There was a sense of relief that my gambling in Vegas was now over. No more of the thrills and exhilaration of gambling at this level. No more moments of joy or being completely pissed off convinced that the cards were fixed. No more lucky escapes or that 'get out of jail free' feeling by winning on crap cards when the dealer busts. However, the greatest feeling of all was no more big losses! My gambling time in six days had cost me approximately $800 in total, quite a lot of money when thinking it over, and that included winning a fair few times. If I had the option to do it over again, would I do the same? Of course I would! Maybe next time I'd have better luck having learnt from this year's novice experience. Yep, I think I was one step away from joining Gamblers Anonymous when I returned home!

The others were chastising me for my stupid bets, and even Eva had latched onto taking the piss out of me as we sat drinking beers.

I noticed a familiar character hovering behind one of the tables in the distance so excused myself from the others. Clint, the guy who'd played such a huge part in making all today's events possible, was observing a game of poker. I made my way towards him. The concentration he portrayed in watching the cards changed to a friendlier expression when he saw me. He reached out to shake my hand, using the other to pat me on the back in a show of solidarity.

'Ricky! How are you man?'

'I'm great! How's the gambling going?'

'Fucked. How about you?' he laughed.

'Equally as fucked. Just blown $300 very quickly. That's it for me now. No more gambling on this trip.'

'And how about your other gamble earlier today? Did you go?' he quizzed.

'I did!'

'And did you see?'

'I saw!'

'Wow! And how do you feel?'

'Free! Liberated! Reinvented!'

'Yeah. It gets to you like that. Tell me. What exactly did you see?'

I'd not really divulged too much to my friends about what I saw, thinking they'd not understand what I'd experienced as it differed entirely from theirs, but there was a difference with Clint. I felt that he'd seen something similar in his time in the desert from snippets of information he told me the previous day. I didn't feel embarrassed telling him all the details, from the heightened sensitivity and connection with music, to the crazy psychedelic turns of weather, to the mysterious shadow that may or may not have been a guardian angel of some form. I went on with the story, more confident in describing the detail and its hidden meanings. He nodded along in tune to my words, fully accepting what I described. He had heard others have similar experiences and he included himself in that bracket.

'I waded into the desert many years ago. My mom had just passed and I was in a dark place man. I was truly fucked. Just like you I felt this to be the only option left. I swear she appeared to me as an angelic paranormal light, and she liberated me from my fear and grief. I swear I heard her voice say, *"Everything will be ok, sweetheart. I'm with your father now. You carry on living your life the way you know how to. You needn't worry anymore!"'*

His voice broke off towards the end, and I felt myself well up at the sorrow of his story. It was sad to hear the lengths that people go to in order to find answers. I was now firmly part of that club: a desert tripper, a twisted seeker, willing to sacrifice sanity to find a connection with a part of the universe unheard of in abstinence.

We turned to more light-hearted topics when I mentioned the bizarre images of Eva, and that she'd returned from her trip up the West Coast to see me one last time. He noticed her in the distance and praised me for my efforts, asking vehemently, 'Now do you see Ricky? Do you see what power the desert has? Are you now a firm believer?'

I beamed a smile that didn't require my answer to be vocalised.

'Ricky, you did it man, you're one of us. Vegas and the desert are powerful places and that should be respected. You came here looking for something and you went out there and you found it. Never belittle that experience man. You're lucky enough to have had it. Go back over there with the guys and your girl and enjoy the last night and be well my friend.'

I said my goodbyes to him as he made one final declaration, 'Reasons! Seasons! Lifetime! You think about that Ricky.' I watched as he returned to the tables and pondered that statement for a second. I knew exactly what he meant and he was right. They were inspirational words I'd heard before, and Clint's timely arrival on this trip was just another event that cemented the true testimony of that statement.

I returned full of smiles, taking my place back next to Eva, resting my hand on the top of her leg.

'And what are you so smiley about?' she jokingly asked, running her fingers through my damp hair.

'Oh…Nothing.'

'It doesn't look like nothing.' She rested the palm of her hand on the side of my face, planting a soft kiss on my lips. 'Who was that?' she asked, after pulling away.

'*That* is the reason why you don't sense any sadness in me anymore,' I replied.

Now was the right time to retell the madness of my trip. She listened intently and revealed her thoughts on the matter, being someone who believed in the powers of the universe. She was pleased to see me truly happy without the sadness and woe in my eyes that she detected so easily on our first night. Tonight, she saw a different side of me, the real me.

She whispered, 'So, you wanna come back to my room?'

'I don't know about that. I'm a good boy you see,' I mimicked her answer on our first night.

'You weren't so good a few nights ago Mr Englishman,' she returned.

'Not so good? I thought I was dynamite,' I quipped.

'You know what I mean.' She playfully hit me on the head.

I told the others that I was staying with Eva, even if it was only for a few hours till the sun came up. They were going to persevere into the early hours by all accounts. Turner and Johnny had planted seeds with a few girls and were keen to see how they blossomed throughout the night. Annalise said she'd stay with them for a bit too. It was a good job she had Ian for company.

Turner called to me as I began to walk off. 'Ricky! Where do you think you're going?'

'What do you mean?' I asked.

'We started this trip with a toast and one of my epic speeches. Don't you think we should finish it in the same way? After all, this is the last time we'll all be together on a night out in Vegas.'

I hadn't thought of it like that before. It saddened me.

'Ha! You're right. Go on then. What have you got in mind?'

After ordering a round of tequilas for all of us, except the teetotal Annalise, we stood with our shots outstretched, and Turner began to speak. 'Guys…. and gals of course. Well what can I say? It's been epic. Remember this moment. This is important. Last night in Vegas. It's been one hell of an experience and I'm gonna miss this. Thanks to all of you for making this trip what it is. To Vegas!!' he shouted.

We all shouted, 'To Vegas,' downing our shots.

I then left them in the bar and Eva turned to me and said, '"To fucking Vegas" would be more appropriate.'

CHAPTER 29

The only sounds that could be heard in Eva's room were the rhythmic heavy breathing of its two occupants. I lay naked in bed next to her. Our bodies oozed with sweat after a sexual encounter so intense it left me drained of life. She reached for my hand, interlocked her fingers in mine and then broke the pattern of panting.

'Well Mr Englishman. I guess it wasn't a one off a few days ago.'

'You're telling me. I think we upped our game that time.'

'Well this chica is satisfied.'

'Glad to be of service.'

'I could just kidnap you and take you home and have you do that at my beck and call. Imagine!' she remarked, before moving onto her side to drape her arm over my chest.

'Feel free to enslave me in whatever way you desire.' My tone was submissive and I reached for a cigarette.

Eva turned a little more solemn and sincere. 'I just don't know how I'm going to handle this when you leave. It was bad enough the first time and I thought about you constantly. At least we had an opportunity to come back, but you're leaving in a few hours and that'll be it. I know I said let tonight be tonight, but it's damn hard.'

'Don't talk like that. We'll keep in touch and we'll just see what happens.'

She was right though! Even though the first time was difficult to say goodbye, this time it would be much harder to simply walk away.

'I've still got a bit of time so let's not be morbid. You said we'll enjoy the night and worry about it after so let's just do that, shall we?'

'Ok, what shall we talk about then?'

'I'll let the lady choose.'

'I know! Now you've been liberated in the desert. What now?'

'Oooh! Now you ask? What now indeed? I have no idea!'

'Come on. You must have some idea. You said your visions showed something about music.'

'It did.'

'Well you need to do something in that then. Didn't you say your friends always thought you should be in music?'

I nodded.

'Then go for it. What's stopping you?'

'I don't know. Confidence maybe? I don't know what to do within music. I have no experience.'

'You'll learn as you go along I'm sure. You should consider writing. I think you'll be good at that.'

'Writing?'

'Yeah, writing! You know, creative writing!'

'It's funny you say that. I wanted to do a creative writing course a few years ago. But I always thought short stories, novels, you know, that kind of thing.'

'Well why not relate it to music. Start off blogging and writing reviews for fanzines to get your confidence up and see how it goes. Come on it's a start and you have nothing to lose. Look, I've listened to you and read texts from you for nearly six days now and I think if you put on paper the sort of insight you say to me then you can do yourself a massive favour. Just go for it.'

'It does sound interesting. I've never thought about blogging or reviewing. But you know what, it sounds appealing. My photographer friend at home will point me in the right direction. Writing? I like the idea! Ricky Lever, "Rock Journalist to the Future Stars".'

And just like that, my immediate goal when I returned home was set, and it created a flurry of excitement inside of me that felt natural as if that was where I belonged. Maybe the vision of Eva in the desert was to do with this conversation, and she was the one to point me in the right direction. Maybe she *was* the guardian angel on some level. After all, she did appear behind the mysterious figure.

'Thanks Eva! How do you know things about me before I even know them?'

'I guess we're just connected that way.'

'Scary, isn't it?'

She put on her music through her iPhone, and a selection of fantastic bands/artists such as Stevie

Nicks, Janis Joplin, and Mamas and Papas formed the soundtrack to our final hours together. We carried on talking about music and the prospect of me being involved in a professional capacity. The more we talked, the more enthusiastic I became. I even started to make mental notes of bands I'd like to review and possibly interview, if I got that far.

The whole evening with Eva had rapidly passed by, and within the blink of an eye it was time to make a move back to Planet Hollywood, knowing that there were only six hours or so until I had to leave the hotel for the airport. I didn't want to leave and I wished I could've stayed a few more days.

I reluctantly brought up the subject of parting and Eva grudgingly accepted the inevitable, but not without stopping me from standing up a couple of times first by pulling me back onto the bed and pinning me down. Finally, we both got up and I retrieved my slightly damp clothes that were scattered around the floor. Once I was fully dressed I looked at her and a feeling I didn't care for ripped through my insides when I saw her immaculate face and gorgeous, dark wide eyes staring back at me full of emotion.

Eva raised a hand to my cheek, 'I'm glad I came back.'

'So am I. You really did make Vegas complete.'

'Listen, I know it was hard the first time so I'm not going to make it difficult again. I'm so glad I met you Ricky and I've had a wonderful time!' She carried a glint in her eye. 'I'm not going to say goodbye here. I don't know why, but I have strong feelings for you and I know that sounds ridiculous considering it's only been a few days,' she bravely revealed.

'Yeah but....'

'No, let me finish,' she interrupted. 'I have to say this. This isn't the end you know. I know it's silly but I just feel that this isn't the end at all. I don't know how or why, but something inside tells me different. All I'm going to say is have a safe flight home and keep believing in yourself to do something special.'

I may have been caught up in the moment or reeling from the disappointment of ending a holiday romance of sorts, but I felt similar, so I respected her wishes without making a big deal of it, replying, 'I feel the same you know. I'm so happy I met you too, and you're right, this isn't the end. All I'll say is have a safe *drive* home.'

I moved to hug her, ending with one final soft and expressive kiss. After that I turned towards the door and smiled at her, winking before letting myself out, but before the door fully closed, I heard Eva shout, 'Fucking Vegas, remember!'

I poked my head back inside and smirked. 'Fucking Vegas indeed!' I shut the door and strolled towards the lift, feeling the fuzzy sensations in my head that meant I was still drunk. Being lay down with Eva had disguised that. I drifted off into quiet reflection, thinking of the beauty I'd just left. Waves of sadness rippled over me, but I knew this wouldn't be the end of my adventure with her, especially with the way the world was with social media. I could see and speak to her every day on Skype if I wanted to. It wasn't like pre-2000 where I'd be restricted to being a pen pal. There was comfort in the knowledge that she'd remain part of my life in one way or another when I got back to Manchester. But still, it didn't stop yet another feeling of loss hitting me in that instant.

I exited the lift and walked nonchalantly through the casino of New York New York as the chilled classic, 'Rocket Man', by Elton John, aptly played on my departure. I marvelled at the grandeur as the sounds of the slot machines and the smell of pinewood flowed around me. The others had left so I was setting myself up for one final trek up the Strip, bypassing the toilets on my way to the exit... no danger of falling asleep in there this time, I thought.

I'd not seen daylight for what seemed like an eternity, and the famed lack of clocks inside Vegas hotels meant that time had escaped my subconscious thinking. I dragged myself outside and back into the waking world. It was only with the arrival of the evocative desert dawn towering above the concrete jungle that I got some indication of the time. Having been submerged in darkness and false lighting all night, I was not used to the sun's penetrative glare. It forced me to squint and raise a hand up to my lethargic eyes to shield them from this stinging light.

I looked up Las Vegas Boulevard, contemplating the gruelling walk back to Planet Hollywood, which I could see in the distance like a honing beacon to my sanctuary. A taxi would've been welcomed, but was out of the question due to my cash being liquidated over the course of the night. I stood for a matter of seconds, distant and lost in my own movie as a montage raced through my mind that depicted the entire trip in just a couple of moments, layered to the tune of Led Zeppelin's, 'Good Times Bad Times', or something equally as raucous and bluesy. I savoured the events of the last few hours a little longer as they were so instrumental to my fresh outlook on life. Perhaps I was trying to put off the inevitable by being absent in this trance, wishing for a halt in time itself to enjoy this desert settlement a little longer. But sooner rather than later, I had to make my move up the Strip.

Exhaustion began to take hold and I practically crawled on hands and knees through the brutal heart of Las Vegas, just trying to keep it together long enough until I reached the hotel where I could give in to weariness and pass out. The dryness inside my mouth mixed with stale Jack Daniels left a bitter taste that felt strenuous to swallow. I was still deeply under the influence of alcohol. The combination of brightness, drunkenness and being deprived of sleep had left me feeling unsteady, and I was running on fumes. The adrenaline that had acted as fuel for six nights solid was now subsiding, and the abnormal stamina built upon an obsessive need to experience Vegas to its excessive limits had been depleted.

I recollected once again on the trip to pass the time. The experience had gone above and beyond expectation, bouncing from both ends of a spectrum that had darkness at one side, and euphoria on the other. However, it was those roller coaster moments that made me somehow believe I was embedded in Vegas folklore. Not that I would be remembered for anything specific or that would gain global recognition, but in my own world I'd accomplished what I set out to do, perhaps even finding the enigma of the 'American Dream', or at least an altered version aligned with my own perceptions.

I carried on my lacklustre excursion down the Strip, noticing that the sea of taxis seen in the prime of the night had vanished in the quiet morning, like vampires taking a rest in their coffins before the sins of the night occurred again. A few people walked the streets in shorts and vests ready for the day, staring at my obviously drunken and dishevelled state as I passed them. Being seen this way would be embarrassing back home, but in Vegas, the 'walk of shame' didn't exist. In fact, this type of behaviour was encouraged and it'd become a regular occurrence over the course of the past few nights.

I'd been walking for half an hour or so and I finally reached Planet Hollywood. I staggered up the steps with considerable effort before taking one last look along the Strip, drawing a fond farewell smile. It looked different somehow now it was robbed of its flashing lights, not quite having the same magical effect unless it was supported by the backdrop of the insatiable night and clear black sky, illuminated by the twinkling piercings of silver continuing above and beyond the strength of the human eye. The aura was quiet and empty, making me feel ill at ease. Vegas wasn't supposed to be like this, certainly not the way I'd been experiencing it. Perhaps the mirage had faded now the end was nigh, and the real Vegas was what I could see through hazy eyes!

I turned towards the hotel entrance, not wanting to see the image of normality anymore, and dragged the handle towards me, struggling as I tugged and pulled to enter through the huge, dark tinted doors. The heavy nights and cigarettes took their toll now as I'd taken advantage of the relaxed indoor smoking laws, a luxury no longer allowed back home, yet being slightly breathless still didn't stop me sparking one up for the short walk back to the room.

Once I was in and my foot hit the soft, psychedelic patterned carpet, I tried to focus, but it suddenly became tricky. The abrupt darkness sent all light spiralling out from my view and peripherals, creating a blurred perception of my surroundings that consisted of pink and purple waves embedded in streams of neon lights that dispersed from the walls, ceiling and floor. As my sight was temporarily incapacitated my hearing heightened! I could make out the music that filled the room amongst the chatter of gamblers and the ringing of slot machines, which sustained the old rock 'n' roll classics of a celebrated age. I was pretty sure it was, 'Hotel California', by The Eagles, or was I imagining it? Maybe in the midst of my heavy journey the line about checking out, but never leaving, had been left lingering and imprinted on my mentality, as if Vegas was imprisoning me in a similar way.

My vision began to sharpen after the brief lapse and I assessed my environment. Typically, people still searched for a life changing win at the gambling tables so early in the morning, hoping to completely change their life with one game. I already felt fortuitous having found my own emotional version of that statement earlier on, so I easily resisted temptation, choosing to head directly back to my room, extinguishing my cigarette at a conveniently placed ashtray next to the lift on my way.

Once I found my room, it appeared as six numbers rather than the three digits I knew it was. Double vision drunkenness had set in. I fumbled for the key card and buzzed myself in, searching for the light as I stumbled through the door. Ian was nowhere to be seen, and I presumed he'd gone for a nightcap with the others and crashed in their room, or had got lucky himself.

I awkwardly wrestled off my clothes before dropping onto the bed, knowing that I only had a few hours sleep before I had to get up and say my goodbyes to Vegas. The calming feeling of lying down and being off my feet was a sensation better than any gambling win at that moment. The room was cool from the air con blasting from the ceiling, so I scrambled underneath the thick white duvet of the soft double bed and settled into a fortress of comfort.

My final thoughts before slumber were about the trip and how it had defined my very existence. The way I felt in that moment confirmed that I'd collided head first into the proverbial wall. Sure, I was liberated, but I was fatigued beyond reckoning from the palpable intensity the past few days had brought.

I grabbed hold of sleep, which didn't take long after slumping down face first into a feathered pillow.

At first, I thought the knocking of a door was planted firmly in the middle of a hazy dream, but as it continued to get louder I realised that the sound was coming from the conscious world, just a few feet away to be precise.

I muttered, 'It must be Ian locked out. The bastard forgetting his key card and making me get up at this time to let him in, I'll kill him!' I yanked myself up with an almighty force, pissed off as I floundered towards the door as the knocking persistently pecked at my head. I was ready to unleash a tirade of abuse.

I jerked open the door, and just as I was about to hurl the first offensive word in his direction, I stopped short. The misty eyed, tired look on my face relinquished in a flash, the pit of my stomach dropped like an anchor, and any feelings of fatigue were swiftly turned into adrenaline as if a potent drug had manifested its way into my bloodstream. I was pretty sure that what happened only hours earlier would be the final surprise on this trip that had thrown up so many, but in this unnatural part of the world that never ceased to shock, I never expected this final bombshell with only a few hours to spare. I stared at the figure that stood in front of me. Finally, I managed to find the words that were momentarily lost, seemingly absorbed by my racing heartbeat. 'What the fuck are you doing here?!'

CHAPTER 30

The astonishment in my tone was clear. I was half thinking the hallucinations had returned. I rubbed my eyes to check I really was awake.

'Mandy?' The puzzled tone continued.

'Hello Ricky.' She was cool and calm.

I really didn't know what to say.

'Aren't you gonna invite me in? I've come a long way you know.'

'Yeah...how come you're... why are you... what the hell is going on Mandy?' I opened the door wider to allow her to enter, but I don't know why. I guess my mind was trying to comprehend the turn of events, making it a struggle to think clearly.

'Nice room!' She slowly strutted in. Her wavy blonde hair had been freshly highlighted with a brown that interweaved throughout its thickness, making the blonde less profound. She was pristinely dressed in a tight fitted black blouse that accentuated her large breasts. Her sky-blue jeans were fashionable, reaching down to the top of her ankles before they tapered, which allowed her flash Gucci black heels to sparkle. In all honesty, she looked great, and that unmistakeable scent enveloped me when she strolled in, the familiar smell of 'Eternity' by Calvin Klein, instantly thrusting me into a cage of nostalgia.

She made her way over to my bed, perching herself on the end, folding one leg over the other and putting her brown Louis Vuitton bag on the floor.

'You haven't answered me Mandy. What are you doing here?'

'Well I tried calling you yesterday to let you know I was coming over, but you wouldn't answer.' Her tone was almost arrogant, as if nothing had happened in the past two months.

'So you *meant* to talk to me on that occasion as opposed to hanging up?' She didn't respond. 'Would a text or a voicemail not have been enough?' I quizzed.

'I wanted to tell you properly.'

'You mean like when you left? Properly like that?' I felt irritated.

She turned away embarrassed.

'Yeah. You better look away!'

After a moment's pause it dawned on me. 'How did you know which room I was in?'

'Well you can get most things with a tip in Vegas I hear.' She was correct on that.

'Please Ricky. I know I've hurt you but I was a mess. I was confused. Come and sit down and I'll explain.'

I was reluctant, but I slowly made my way over, grabbing a t-shirt off the back of the chair to try and look semi-respectable, but not before a cocky remark made its way to me. 'You're not very brown, are you?'

'I didn't come here for a tan.' I was equally as snotty.

I sat a good distance away from her for fear of entrapment and being sucked back into what was once my familiar world. But the more I looked at her, the more I saw a difference. There was an ugliness residing within her, and that's what I could see through the false portrayal of her glamorous look, especially with the recent removal of my rose-tinted glasses. I sensed a deflated and dejected aura about her despite the initial confidence she had portrayed when I opened the door. She forced an awkward smile, so awkward that it was like the pressure had finally caught up with her.

'Your face has caught the sun though, even if the rest of you hasn't! I always liked it when you were tanned.' She tried to be light-hearted and create some sort of memory, but I remained quiet, not really knowing how to respond. A silence began to grow.

'Again, Mandy! Why are you here?' I started to get a bit angry at the thought of having my holiday gate crashed and violated by the ex.

'Well me and Jill fancied coming out for a break and I knew you were here so I thought it was as good a place as any.'

'To crash my holiday? In what fucked up world have you arrived at the conclusion that coming to Vegas on my last night would be a good idea?'

She shrugged.

'Well?' My voice remained hard.

'To talk,' she mumbled.

'Talk about what? Things are pretty clear to me!'

'What do you mean?'

'Oh come on Mandy! You fuckin' walk out on me without a word and you don't want to speak for months, and now you show up here expecting everything to be ok? You must think I'm a right dickhead.'

'I know I could've handled things differently!' she exclaimed.

'You really are deluded aren't you, after what you put me through you twisted bitch!'

Even she was shocked at my outburst, but I was growing fond of these newly formed balls and spine. 'Aren't you supposed to be getting married to your "amazing man" and "planning your future together"? What the fuck is going on with that?'

'Look I'm sorry for all that, I made a mistake.' She looked down at the floor.

'What do you mean?'

'I was wrong about everything. I don't know what was wrong with me but I realise what's important now and it's you.'

'YOU WHAT??!!' I shouted, shocked beyond belief. I stood up. 'Are you kidding me?' I continued to rant.

'Things haven't worked out. I was wrong.' She looked uncomfortable.

'With "Mr Amazing" you mean? Ha! Like I didn't see that one coming.' The sarcasm was cutting as I thought about the earlier desert revelations.

'We've finished and it's over.'

'Oh! So he's dumped you because you were no longer

any use anymore. He just used you while you were with me, did he? Seems like it was all a bit of fun for him to be with someone in a relationship. He probably got off on all that sneaking about and danger at my expense. I suppose that's karma for you, isn't it?'

'I'm sorry! I never should've left you for him, but it was me that finished with him. I want you back Ricky. I realise that it was a mistake to let you go,' she pleaded.

'Oh Jesus!'

I sat back down and put my head in my hands and thought for a second. It wasn't so long ago that I yearned to hear those words come from Mandy, serving as an instant remedy to the pain I felt. Hearing those words now after the day I'd had caused a moments confusion that triggered pandemonium in my mind. I thought back to the desert and to all those revelations and feelings that felt so strong and made so much sense at the time. In this instant, it was like it never happened. Until, over Mandy's shoulder, I caught the slightest glimpse of a lizard on the window sill outside. It disappeared just as quickly as I saw it. Surely it wasn't real, but the image was enough to spark a renewed revolution in my mind. Perhaps the effects of the peyote hadn't quite worn off, but the vision was enough to bring me back from drowning in a sea of shit. Suddenly, everything I learnt hours earlier reaffirmed its importance. This was the manipulative work of a narcissist. It wouldn't work this time. I would *not* play into her hands. She couldn't make me feel like shit again.

'I'm sorry Mandy. I can't do that. I can't go back. Ever!' I stood firm.

'You what?' Her face turned to stone. She clearly wasn't expecting that reply. How dare I reject her!

'I'm better off without you. Truthfully? You're a disturbed woman. Maybe you always were, but I'd like to think you weren't always like this because what does that say about me, to not recognise it after five years? Maybe you've slowly turned into this person over time, but the things you did can never be forgiven or forgotten. You put me in a right mess. You left without an explanation and jumped into bed with the first person who had a bit of money, a flash car and showed an interest, even when you were with me. You even got fuckin' engaged and moved in with the fucker, and you told me by text in the cruellest most uncalled-for way. You're a selfish bitch and the fact that you flew all the way out here and thought I'd get back with you is laughable and shows just how up your own arse you really must be.' It was liberating to give it to her with both barrels.

'I only sent you that message because I wanted to hurt you. I was confused. I thought you didn't care anymore.' That pleading tone appeared once more. I took pleasure in knowing that another of those revelations in the desert had just proved to be true, that the text was meant to hurt me!

'Fuck off! You thought I didn't care? In what world did I not care? I dedicated everything to you. How deluded are you Mandy? How far do you want someone to go for you?'

'It seemed like your mind was elsewhere.' Her words had no shred of truth in them and appeared desperate.

'How? You started with the mood swings and because your job can be stressful I put it down to that. I left you to it but supported you. I think you're trying to justify your own actions here. Don't even *dare* blame me. You shacked up with some lawyer dickhead for status purposes and it backfired! Don't even try to wriggle out of it!'

She couldn't answer. I moved towards the window and a silence fell upon us for a minute. She looked vulnerable after I'd torn into her, but she now recognised that I was onto her ways and had worked her out.

Eventually she broke. 'So that's it then? You're just gonna throw away five years like that?'

'Are you kidding me? How can *you* of all people say that? That is bang out of order! You're the one who fucked everything up, not me. You cheated me out of five years of good memories with what you did. Do you even realise the shit I've been through these past couple of months, not knowing where you were or why you walked out? And then to find out about *him* from Wendy as well!'

'I'm so sorry Ricky. Really, I am.' She began crying.

'I think you should find yourself another "Mr Amazing" because that's where you obviously belong. You're just a gold-digger at heart. That's who you are now! What happened to you? You've come to the right place if you want to try your luck. Hang about near the VIP areas and see where that gets you.'

She wasn't impressed with my wounding advice, but she continued to apologise through what I concluded were crocodile tears. I was impervious to her pleas for forgiveness.

She eventually came to the million-dollar question and asked, 'Have you slept with anyone since you've been here?'

And there it was. The question of all questions. After all I'd suffered because of her selfish actions, I now had the opportunity of a lifetime to drive the knife in further and take revenge in its full, merciless glory. I thought for a second, smiling deviously inside at the prospect of giving her the truth. But you know what? I wasn't her! There was absolutely no need to twist the knife and add insult to injury. I'd already told her what I thought of her for her own benefit, and to let her know that she can't treat people the way she does, and that there was no chance of having me back. The idea of gaining petty revenge no longer appealed to me. I didn't have a thirst for it anymore. I just wanted to move on and not needlessly hurt her. Perhaps telling her the truth would give me some sort of satisfaction, if only for a few minutes, but ultimately it would be a hollow victory and what would I achieve? I guess I'd finally gone past caring now! The cliché that when you no longer care, the other person wants you back was proved to be correct again.

'Not that it's any of your business....... but no, I haven't!'

Not telling her about Eva made me realise that I had finally moved on and had grown up a bit more. I just couldn't be that spiteful, and that showed the difference between us both. I had every given right in the world to respond with the truth, but it didn't matter. The relationship was over!

'I think you need to go. There's nothing more to say. You can say sorry a million times but it's not going to work. I'm a different person now! Much stronger! I don't see any kind of future with you whatsoever. I realised how much you put me down and held me back from doing what I wanted to do because it didn't fit in with your life. Well it won't happen again, ever!'

She looked shocked at the strength I'd gathered, which was a side of me she'd never seen before and probably never imagined encountering when she had the ridiculous idea of trawling over to Vegas for me. She'd underestimated me, and I don't think she anticipated that I'd be driven so far by pain and undergo such a transformation, and perhaps she had good reason to feel that. If I hadn't had my monumental revelation earlier on, would I have succumbed to her charm and fallen back into her arms for all the wrong reasons? It seemed like a lucky escape and I could only put it down to an act of fate that I got my head straight only hours earlier.

I think she took my manner and adamant words seriously because she didn't plead any further, and she saw that there was no coming back to me.

It ended with her saying, 'Well I guess this really is goodbye then?' The tears had caused her eyes to look puffy and red. I actually felt pity for her now…nothing more, nothing less.

'I suppose it is,' I replied. She rose from the corner of

my bed and stormed towards the door, looking back as she pulled it open.

'Mandy! You take care of yourself. I hope you find what you're looking for. I really do mean that.' She didn't acknowledge me and proceeded to slam the door. As it closed behind her I added quietly, 'I know I did.' I was finally at peace.

CHAPTER 31

We sat exhausted, sapped of life inside Las Vegas Airport. My head felt muzzy and weary after possibly one of the most eventful days and nights of my life. The others looked just as tired and downhearted as we tried to come to terms with leaving. Ian had passed out in Johnny and Turner's room the night before as predicted, but their night was quite eventful too after Turner and Johnny both managed to pull inside New York New York. Neither of them went further than a few snogs at the bar, despite Ian saying they were trying their hardest to go further. Both Turner and Johnny denied such accusations in a feeble attempt to save face. I believed Ian's assessment of the night. He had looked after Annalise till she was ready for bed. Given how quickly Eva and I shunted back to her room, I was grateful that Annalise wouldn't be left alone, and had remained with the best person possible to enjoy the night with.

I'd told them earlier on about what happened the night before with Mandy. Ian was still stunned. 'I still can't believe she turned up just like that. I mean the fuckin' balls on her.'

'You're telling me. Shocked? I nearly shit when I opened the door and saw her there! I thought the peyote was still playing games with me,' I admitted.

'I bet she nearly shit when you told her to fuck off,' Johnny added.

'She wasn't best pleased. Oh well,' I casually added.

'Finally! Halle-fucking-lujah!' Turner was happy, confident that my turnaround was going to last the distance now.

'What do you think she'll do?' Ian asked

'God knows. I didn't even ask where she was staying or how long she was here for. I didn't care.'

'Well whatever she does out here I doubt it'll beat our experience,' Turner bragged, adding, 'And what about you? What are you gonna do now?'

'You'll find out when we're home I'm sure.' I kept my intentions a mystery.

The gruelling fifteen-hour journey back to home life began when we unenthusiastically boarded the plane to Philadelphia and plonked ourselves down in our seats. The Captain spoke as the aircraft began to slowly back away from the stand, warning us that the early stages of the flight might be a little bumpy due to the strong winds sweeping across the desert. The plane taxied for take-off, shaking as the engines fired up, suddenly bursting into life before firing down the runway with a tremendous roar and lightning pace.

My eyes were dropping from overtiredness and I thought that maybe I could sleep for the first time ever on a plane. But, could I doze at a time like this? Absolutely no chance! 'A little bumpy?' as the Captain put it. More like 8.9 on the Richter scale. I had never known a take-off so frightening in my life. The plane shook furiously and violently. The pull in my stomach from the climb was insufferable, and the noise the plane made was horrendous, sounding like a washing machine that was struggling to climb and was about to drop from the sky at any given second. I really did think this was it and that the end of the road had arrived. My head had shifted to madness with crazy images rushing to the forefront of consciousness. All I could think about was the fact that I had built Vegas up so much in terms of a life changing experience, that it was literally going to be a life ending experience, and all the revelations I had about the past were presented to me so that I could go to my grave in peace. Absolute panic bombarded my mind, leading to all these false illusions, far more delusional than taking peyote. All sorts of terribly graphic images raced through my mind. I longed for the Captain to announce, 'Cabin Crew released!' That was always the signal for safety.

I looked across at Turner for reassurance because he was usually so relaxed during flights, but he was sat in the brace position looking incredibly nervous too. I don't think he'd experienced anything like this before either. The noise continued to deafen me, the wind howled and it felt like it was trying with all its might to bring the plane down. There was nothing I could do but attempt to ride out the panic and wait for the soothing words from the Captain...if they were ever uttered.

Seconds felt like minutes and then hours, butterflies swarmed my stomach, but then the heavenly sound of the Captain's voice spoke like an angel as he echoed the words that brought calmness to the aircraft. 'Cabin crew released.' Thank fuck for that. Composure prevailed and we levelled out and moved away from the bastard crosswind.

I settled down somewhat, but the rest of the flight remained uncomfortably bumpy. I attempted to sleep, but it was pointless, like trying to sleep on a roller coaster. I was sat in the middle of Johnny and some random American, who seemed fascinated that I could watch a film on my iPod, and that I was from Manchester, England, and not Manchester, New Hampshire. He was a farmer travelling to a conference in Philadelphia, and clearly he had been locked away for years if iPod technology was giving him a boner.

We touched down in Philly much to my relief. The flight was just too rough and uncomfortable. I was overcome with a strange sensation as I staggered off the plane into the airport. I felt extremely dizzy and the room was slanting. It was as if my alignment was all off, probably brought about from the constant jarring of my body for the last five hours solid. It became difficult to walk and I had to use the walls for guidance, stopping for a breather after every few steps to try and compose myself again. It was one of the oddest feelings of my life, like being pissed without having a drink!

Evening time and darkness fell very quickly in Philadelphia because of the jump in time we'd experienced flying from west to east over America where we lost hours.

We boarded the plane to Manchester, and this time I was lucky enough to be sat next to the window. I rested my head against the side in what proved to be another failed attempt to claw back some sleep.

It was dark outside for most of the journey, and the Captain asked us not to lift the shutters when the sun appeared because it would disturb those passengers sleeping. I couldn't help but have a sneaky peak when I knew the sun was rising. I carefully lifted the shutter to allow a glimmer of light in. The bright rays of the sunrise came from above the horizon in the distance. The huge orange ball of the sun gradually became bigger and bigger, rising at a steady pace, starting from below the plane, eventually rising above it. It was such a colossal sight to behold, probably one of the most spiritual feelings of the whole trip in many respects, being somewhere along the lines of Grand Canyon. It was as if I was witnessing the dawn of time, brought about by the work of some higher power beyond my understanding, which could control our destiny and fate through the metaphysics of its force. It was peaceful, and I related the vision to the whole Vegas trip and my whole change in attitude. I'd stated beforehand that a new age and a new dawn was looming upon us. Witnessing the sunrise in such inspiring circumstances from this part of the world made me realise that the change was finally coming around. It had caught up with us in time for returning home, and the wealth of possibilities that lay ahead were exciting.

CHAPTER 32

Surprisingly, the typical Manchester weather of rain, wind and drab greyness had not greeted us on our return. Instead, it was a pleasant Manchester morning with warmth and a clear blue sky filling the air.

We all jumped in the same black cab at Manchester Airport that would drop us off individually. I was first to be let out. I said my goodbyes to the lads, shaking their hands as I departed the taxi. I didn't know when I'd see them next, but I think I needed at least a month to recuperate before another night out. Alcohol was definitely off the table for now!

I walked through the front door and struggled to lift my suitcase up the narrow staircase. I was completely robbed of energy. I left it in the living room, and then went to the kitchen to put the kettle on. I stopped at the kitchen door, holding my gaze on the table where the letter from Mandy once sat. Little did I know at that point how the next couple of months would pan out, and how life would completely turn on its head.

In true British fashion I made a cup of tea, but sadly I had no biscuits in. I went up to the bedroom and lay on my bed, letting out a relaxing sigh as my head sunk into the soft pillow. The comfort promptly hit me and within seconds I'd scrambled underneath the duvet. There's no better feeling than getting wrapped up in your own bed after a period of time away. I shut my eyes, listening to the instilled quiet surrounding me in the house and from the peace in my mind.

I began to recollect the past six days, half expecting casinos and grandness to appear in front of me as soon as I opened my eyes. Visions of Vegas raced through my mind, and I tried to decipher its meaning and image. It was an adult playground that showcased the extremes of what one could experience, certainly living up to its remarkable reputation of being the 'entertainment capital of the world'. It had been a fitting benchmark and advert in how to live life to its full potential, however unrealistic the opportunities may seem on a day to day basis. It's ironic how mirages are seen in the desert, and Vegas emulated that concept by being as far removed from reality as you could get. It somehow struck at the heart of man's inner-most desires and fantasies. Whereas one mirage is for survival, the other is for over indulgence with affiliations to anarchy. The whole flamboyant atmosphere of the city, the extravagance of guilty pleasures, and the overall vastness culminated into Vegas being the eighth wonder of the world as far as I was concerned.

There was an overpowering temptation and intrigue about the place. People instantly recognised its madness and yearned to connect with it themselves. The very word, 'Vegas', tugs at the psychology of fantasy, and whets the appetite to the point where you can almost taste its golden aura!

Everything about Sin City had lit up my soul. It was

an intense place full of life and emotion, where both ends of the extreme could be felt in every aspect: alive, tired, despair, elation, sinful, soulful, pretentious, and grounded. Basically, you could do what the fuck you wanted, especially if you had money to back it up. It was where dreams and fantasies could be realised!

I began to think of my own journey and I smiled, sniggered and laughed aloud when I thought of various points of the holiday. I was already yearning to be back there and throw myself into the hedonism of a Vegas way of life. Even the lows I'd experienced were met with smiles now, and that was a good place to be in. I recognised that it was the pain of the past that was shaping the transformed mentality of the present and future.

I then thought of Eva, who had been pivotal over the past six days. The very image of her made me weak inside. I'd not contemplated a holiday romance whatsoever, but there was something special about her. I pictured her and held that perfect image close to my heart, holding onto the memories with a great deal of hope that this wasn't the end, and our adventure would be continued in some form in the future.

I had planned for Vegas to be a soul-searching experience, built it up to be life changing, 'The Englishman in search of the American Dream' so to speak! It certainly was life changing on so many levels. I could finally see what I truly wanted out of life now that I was free from anyone or anything holding me back. At last I had a great connection with my mind, body and soul, and I realised that I finally had the freedom and impetus to explore and absorb every experience available on my chosen path of destiny. Would I have become the person I am now without going to Vegas? Who knows? That was a hypothetical question. I was in a dire place beforehand and it could've taken months, or even years, for me to get sorted. Considering Mandy wanted to get back together, it was conceivable that I would've gone back as a quick fix to the pain, but it wouldn't have been right, and somewhere down the line it would've backfired. I was grateful that I managed to see sense just in time, and couldn't believe I had to go to the depths of a peyote binge to see clearly. I'm not saying I would recommend peyote to just anyone. I think that would be an irresponsible statement to make, but for some people it just may be the answer if all other options appear to be exhausted. It certainly worked for me.

Fundamentally, I guess what I gained in Vegas was inner strength, courage and a new vision. My preconceptions around a typical working life had been stripped away, and with this mentality came a real drive to succeed in something different. I had to take that determination and liberation with me now and never let go of its importance. This was my time to shine, and I was eager to get the ball rolling on what would be a new and exciting quest that had the possibility to take me anywhere my heart desired. After months, even years of being lost in Manchester, I had been found in Vegas.

EPILOGUE

In the days that followed my return from Vegas, I slowly began to settle back into some degree of routine, but secretly I began my preparations for the next step in life's journey. The revelations from the desert were stronger than ever. I'd not heard from Mandy in any way and I didn't expect to either. Whenever I looked back at the past with her, all I saw was just that, the past! There wasn't any ill feeling and my memories with her had become a wavy blur where some sort of emotion used to live.

I knew what I had to do even before I left Vegas, and what I was going to put into practice as soon as I returned home. I'd decided life was too short to go back to a job I despised for the rest of my life. Short-term, I needed to work in the same job to set me up for something more meaningful in the long term. I was too young to worry about any kind of safety and security regarding finances, and I was also young enough to turn my life around, so it was time to head in a completely new and illuminating direction.

Within a month of returning from Vegas I left the home that Mandy and I once resided in. I moved into Ian's spare room on a short-term basis, purely for financial reasons and part of the bigger plan.

I took Eva's advice about the writing and got in touch with Matt, my photographer friend, who had some good contacts in the music industry. He gave me the name of the editor of an online music fanzine called, Sonic Bandwagon, that he had done some shoots for. The fanzine was developing a great reputation as being at the forefront of endorsing the best new music. They had recently started a radio show too, such was their growing success, so I made it a priority to contact Jamie Stacks, the chief editor of the mag.

I was asked to submit a review for Jamie to look over and decide whether I had any flair to be a regular contributor for them. I wrote a short review on a local Manchester band called, The Rubys, who I'd seen a couple of times and became quite friendly with. It was well received and became my first published online review. Jamie gave me some pointers on how to develop my writing, but it was an encouraging first effort. I sent it to Eva as soon as it went live, secretly dedicating it to her. She was proud of my accomplishment.

I was entering the wonderful world of music blogging and began reviewing on a more regular basis now I had the hunger to keep submitting. I began writing more live and album reviews, and the feedback continued to be promising. I felt proud and could feel my confidence growing as I started to develop my own style. The more I delved into the industry, the further removed from normal working life I became. I felt right at home and I started to meet some fascinating people who became friends rather than contacts. It felt like I was finally getting my shit together, but I still had another itch to scratch in this new-found freedom, something I didn't want to put off any longer.

I'd always been a seeker, a naturally curious soul who questioned purposes and meanings to life. I had a burning desire to travel and see the world, but there was always an excuse as to why I never just upped and left. I thought about how Lucy, the girl from Phoenix, had travelled so extensively at such a young age, and that got me thinking. Aside from fulfilling the dream of visiting Las Vegas, what else had I truly accomplished? That brought to the forefront travel urges suppressed from years earlier. I needed to grasp this second chance with both hands while I was young enough to fully embrace it.

I'd read books that inspired me and empathised with the lead characters or narrators of the adventures. I put myself in their shoes time and time again, and yearned to see what they saw and experience what they had. I wanted my life to have more meaning. I didn't want to just exist to pay bills and work for an insurance company for the rest of my life. I needed adventure, stimulation and experience! It was a lot of fun writing in music and I'd got my foot in the door and made that first step. My affiliation with music wouldn't end regardless of where I was in the world. I could carry on reviewing for Sonic Bandwagon if bands sent me albums digitally and I had my trusty laptop with me. I didn't necessarily have to be in Manchester. With the seeds planted, what next for this new-found spirit? What next?

I'd been back at work six months before handing in

my three-month notice. It was liberating to finally take that step. There was now a goal, a glimmer of light that sat at the end of the tunnel. I guessed that nine months after Vegas would buy me enough time to scrimp and save to have enough money to enjoy a sizeable trip. It didn't come without its sacrifices though. I lived like a recluse for long periods and you could only catch me at gigs, where more often than not I was put on the guest list in a reviewing capacity. It was a small price to pay for the ultimate reward I kept my eye on. I also had some savings put aside for emergencies only, and I considered this was one of those times to justify the use of that fund. I even gave up smoking such was my dedication to save money for the cause. Now that did surprise me and became the biggest indication yet of how strong willed I'd become.

The day I handed in my notice was the day I went on the internet and booked the flight for my next trip, and one that had been high on my bucket list. America again! But this time properly, and not sugar coated with Las Vegas, which really wasn't America at all. Vegas was simply Vegas, a mirage in the desert! This time I had to go alone and without my friends. I also left the trip open ended. I didn't book a return date to make sure I wouldn't be governed by a specific date or place I had to be in. It was up to me how long I stayed for, providing it was within the visa regulations. It felt amazing to overcome the fear of finances and security and do something so impulsive for once.

I wanted to drive it too, none of this internal flight or rail bullshit. I wanted to really feel the freedom of nothing but me and the open road whilst listening to the most awe-inspiring music as I sped through the land of America, seeing all the wonderful sights the country has to offer with my own soundtrack in the background adding to the essence.

A real life experience awaited, and an opportunity to explore and find out more about myself, building upon the revelations and strength Vegas had given me was an appetising prospect. The possibilities of what could happen out there were exciting and endless. I was full of optimism and carried a swashbuckling, fearless spirit!

• • •

'Ladies and gentlemen! Welcome to San Francisco. The time here is 13.05! We hope you enjoyed your flight with us today and we hope to see you again soon.' The gentle voice of the stewardess was like music to my ears after another exhausting slog over the Atlantic and beyond to finally land in San Francisco.

I disembarked the plane and made my way through the terminal, becoming disheartened when I saw the queue I had to wait in at Passport Control. I was anxious to get out of the airport and begin my adventure. With a travel guide in my hand and my iPod connected to my ears, the time passed by a little quicker. I made mental notes of places I wanted to visit whilst listening to some chilled 60s tunes born from this part of the world. One had to be Scott McKenzie's generation defining tune, 'San Francisco'.

Eventually I was through, and was thrilled to

find that the bags were already circling around the carousel. I picked up my large backpack in no time and advanced towards the outside world to step out into the Californian sun to begin my journey.

My initial plan was to spend four nights in a motel in San Francisco and experience all I could in the time I had, but I wasn't against staying longer if I was enjoying the experience. I wanted to soak in the hippie vibe left over from the 60s in the abundance of quirky and cool bars at my disposal. Who knows? Perhaps I'd run into Clint somewhere along the way.

The plan after that was open. I'd hire a car when I was ready to leave, and that would be the tool to take me wherever the wind blew me. My first thoughts were to take the scenic drive down the Pacific Coastline, stopping at various points of interest before reaching Los Angeles, but there was the option of going North towards Napa and possibly making my way inland towards Oregon, or North Nevada and eventually Utah. Who knew? That was the beauty of this trip, there was no plan. It was to be an exercise in complete freewill and venturing into the unknown.

Of course, further south along the same coastline I was currently on was San Diego, where Eva lived, and I'd promised her that at some point on this trip I'd find my way down there. Eva and I had remained in close contact, and when I told her my plans she was instrumental in advising and encouraging me to come over to live the dream I hungered for. The only stipulation was that I had to come and see her at some point. Not exactly a hardship, it was probably the bit

I was looking forward to the most, but for now, I had to be on my own and learn more about myself. I did want to spend some quality time with Eva eventually, and I wasn't averse to her joining me later if she wanted. That would be an open invitation she could think about when I met her, but it was an intriguing image I had of us driving on the desert roads together. I could live with that!

For now, my immediate mission was to get to the motel in San Francisco, dump my backpack, and then seek out a bar that had some quality tunes blazing out so I could really immerse myself into the culture. At least that's what the plan was - until I turned my phone on and saw several missed calls from Jamie Stacks, my editor at Sonic Bandwagon. He'd also sent two text messages imploring me to call him as soon as I landed as a matter of urgency. I wondered what the hell was going on as I promptly called him back.

He answered almost immediately. *'Ricky?'*

'Hi Jamie. Have you been trying to ring me?'

'Yes. For the last few hours, but I presumed you were still on your flight.'

'Yeah I've just switched my phone on now. What's up?'

'Ricky, we need your help. We need a huge favour.'

'What is it?'

'Well do you remember that we had something big lined up that we were working on a few weeks ago, but we couldn't say what?'

'Yeah!'

'Well it came off, but we're now struggling to fulfil the promise.'

'Go on.'

'Have you heard of the band, Cutthroat Shambles?'

'Yeah, they're meant to be one of the next big things, aren't they? I can't say I've had a chance to listen to their music though.'

'They're gonna be huge, that's for sure. Their EP, 'Halfway to Heaven', and lead track, 'Oblivion', is the talk of the scene. It's an absolutely fantastic rock song! We were given the go ahead to write about them on tour, a real inside look into their world on the road. They had interest from some big players but they wanted us to do it because of the relationship we've had with them since they started out.'

'That's great but what does this have to do with me.'

'Well we had it all planned out and Tommy Ashcroft was gonna cover the whole thing. He's written about them several times and they dig his work, which in truth is why they came to us!'

'Wow. That sounds brilliant. He's a good writer too.'

'The thing is, all this has been booked and paid for but Tommy can't make it now. He's having some major issues with his wife. I think he's on the verge of a divorce to be honest so there's no way he's in the correct frame of mind to do this. Given its importance, I don't trust him at the moment. He's an absolute mess and has taken to the bottle in a big way. I can't send him like this. It'd be an embarrassment for everyone.'

'Ok, but you do know I'm in San Francisco! How is

this related to me? I can't cover any dates in the UK if that's what you're thinking.'

'It's not in the UK Ricky... the tour is in America.'

I fell silent.

'Ricky?' Jamie asked.

'Yeah?' I managed to utter.

'You're the only one who can do this because you're already there. I'll admit, I asked a couple of others with more experience but they can't get there at such short notice.'

'You're kidding, right? You're really asking me to do this?'

'I know you're new to this game but you do have a talent, even if you're still a bit green. I'm counting on you to do this... no... we're all counting on you to do this, everyone at Sonic Bandwagon. This is an exclusive inside access to life on the road with Britain's next big band, possibly bigger than that given the interest from America. They've been harking on about bringing the band over for six months now. This could really put us on the map in a global sense. People will want to read this all over the world.'

'So, let me get this straight. What you're asking me to do is to go on tour with a rock 'n' roll band in America? Write about it? For the whole world to read?' I nearly passed out just saying the words.

'Yes. Is that cool?'

I felt sick from excitement and from the sudden pressure exerted on my nerves. 'Erm... yep... that's very cool.' I sounded anything but cool.

'But Ricky, I have to warn you of two things. They know Tommy very well and when they heard he couldn't make it they nearly pulled the plug on the whole thing. I spoke to their tour manager and convinced her to let us send a substitute journalist, so you coming in last minute might not go down too well with the band. I doubt they'll trust you enough to open up at first. You're gonna have to strike up a relationship with them quickly. And they don't know your experience level so don't mention you've only been in this game six months or so.'

'Ok I can do that. I don't know anything about them though! Do you have any pointers?'

'Well that leads me to the second thing! Be warned Ricky, this lot are crazy. You're gonna have to be on the ball to keep up with them and report accurately what's going on. It's their unpredictability that makes this such an interesting story. People want to know what it's like to be in their company and they want to hear about what they do. The time is nigh to bring rock 'n' roll back to the forefront of people's imaginations. You are in a position to shape that. It's time to make the myths!'

The excitement of being in a position to help shape culture was a bit overwhelming.

'I'll do my best Jamie.'

'Do more than your best.'

'I'll be like an original Rolling Stone reporter,' I replied, cockily.

'I like the fire. That's more like it. You know the lead singer is female, right?'

'Yeah!'

'Dee Darrell her name is. She's gonna be huge, but do your best to stay on her good side. She's a fiery one and she likes to push the boundaries. It took Tommy two years to build up this relationship. You're gonna get two weeks to make an impression. The other three members are guys, but I'll send you all this info in an email later so you have it all to hand.'

'Ok – shit! I'm still shocked. Thank you for trusting me. What do I have to do now then?'

'I'll email you the full itinerary details shortly. Accommodation is all paid for and you have a car waiting for you too.'

'Whereabouts?'

'Sorry, I forgot to say. You need to be in Tucson, Arizona tomorrow but we can't get you on a direct flight at such short notice. I don't expect you to drive direct from San Francisco so we've done a bit of research and found the best way for you to get there is to get back on a flight at San Fran to Las Vegas and spend the night there. Tomorrow you need to pick the car up from the airport and drive down to Tucson. It's about seven hours from Vegas. If you're ok with this I can book you on the flight from San Francisco now. What do you say?'

'Back to Vegas?'

'Yep!'

'On my own? For one night only?'

'Yes. Ricky? Are you in?'

'I'm very much in!'

'Fantastic. I knew you would be!'

'How long is the tour by the way?'

'Three weeks, but it may grow yet. The manager is working on potential other dates. I take it three weeks is ok?'

'Three weeks with a rock 'n' roll band that might get a bit crazy? Sure, that sounds ok to me!'

'You're the man! Right, just sit tight for now and I'll call you back shortly with more details. And Ricky, like I said, this is a big deal, not just for us, but for you too. This is your time kid so do us proud. Talk later. Bye!'

Holy fucking shit! I couldn't believe the conversation that just transpired. The turn of events was unbelievable. I was going to go on tour with a rock 'n' roll band for a few weeks in the US? This was one of those dreams that never in a million years do you think would be possible. This was my 'Almost Famous' moment. I was absolutely fuckin' shitting myself and the adrenaline rushing through my body was causing me to shudder. Fuck, I had to calm down. Why did I give up smoking? I sat on a bench outside the airport and tried to compose myself. Then I thought about Vegas. Fucking Vegas! I'm going back to Vegas. Oh god I think I need to lie down. This was bordering on the ridiculous. How had I managed to land this gig? I was going to burst with orgasmic excitement! I had to tell someone... who? I dug my phone out and searched for Eva's name! She was the perfect person to tell this too. After all the conversations we'd had about music she would be exhilarated at the news. As I dialled, out of the corner of my eye, I caught the slightest glimpse of a lizard staring at me. I looked back at it and smiled.

Eva answered on the third ring, *'Hi honey. I didn't expect to hear from you so soon. Have you landed?'*

'Hey! Yes. I'm finally back over here.'

'Good! What do you think of San Francisco then?'

'I've not quite seen the place yet. I'm still at the airport.'

'Oh. Well get down there, get some flowers in your hair, blaze up a doobie and soak it up. Make sure you mingle with the locals and get a feel for the music scene.'

'I might be getting a bit more of a feel for the music scene than I initially intended.'

'What do you mean?'

'You're not gonna believe this, Eva. I've just had the most amazing phone call...'

A MESSAGE FROM N.J. CARTNER

Thank you for reading *Lost in Manchester, Found in Vegas*. I truly hope you enjoyed it. Reviews are incredibly important to self-published authors, and I would be extremely grateful if you took the time to post a short review on Amazon or Goodreads etc. to help spread the word.

Your review can help the book get noticed.

ABOUT THE AUTHOR

 Born and raised in Manchester and heavily influenced by music, film and literature, I've aspired to work in and around the creative arts since my teenage years. It was only when I hit my late twenties that life took a fortunate turn and gave me the opportunity to fulfil those dreams. I was invited to write for a local online music fanzine, naturally jumping at the chance to review and interview underground bands on the rock music scene. It quickly became apparent from feedback that I had a natural flair for creative writing within the industry, and I continue to be a writer and reviewer on the scene to this day.

There has always been a connection with the Manchester music scene down the years, whether that's from the great bands that helped create the status Manchester currently sits upon, or the work I've done in helping little known local bands push a bit further towards achieving their own dreams. My main passion has always been for music from the 60s and 70s, and the rock icons that made that time so great. The wisdom and attitude shown by those legends played into my own mindset, and none more so than The Doors. It's the chord striking lyrics of my favourite band, and of the many great songs of the times, that have always acted as a mantra to how I've tried to approach life.

Over the years, my involvement with music continued to progress and I now co-host and co-run the Sonic Bandwagon radio show on Stockport radio station, Pure 107.8FM. This enthusiasm for music has become an integral part of my writing, very evident in my first novel, 'Lost in Manchester, Found in Vegas'.

I've always been drawn to novels that explore coming of age as part of the theme. The likes of Rex Pickett and Nick Hornby are personal favourites as they capture this idea of ordinary people thrust into dark times, who eventually manage to come through adversity improved by the experience. But it's the extremities and intrigue of writers such as Hunter S Thompson and Charles Bukowski, and their use of brutal honesty, pushing boundaries into the darker side of life that really attracts me. It is their ingenuity, coupled with their depravity and rebelliousness which has me completely hooked.

The fascination and passion I hold for music and literature had to eventually come to a head. Sure enough, a holiday to Las Vegas with my friends acted as a catalyst for me to throw all these influences and ideas together. 'Lost in Manchester, Found in Vegas' is a story born out of the fires of such artistic inspiration, overlaid with my own voice and approach.

Acknowledgements

Completing my debut novel has been a long, but thoroughly enjoyable journey, and there are several people I'd like to thank for helping make this dream possible.

I'd like to thank my family first of all, for always supporting me and indirectly influencing the soundtrack to the book through their own tastes in music that have inspired me over the years.

To Sheridana, who I love to bits! Thanks for being so instrumental in providing a lot of inspiration around the spiritual nature of the book and influencing some of the characters within it, as well as providing parts of the dialogue and some of our in-jokes. Throughout this whole writing process you've encouraged patience and level headedness, which I've certainly needed over the years. You were an inspiration from the start and the true embodiment of 'Reasons, Seasons, Lifetime'.

Thank you to my close friends. If it wasn't for the shared, obsessive need to go to Las Vegas at the time then none of this would've been possible. Thank you for the advice given after reading early drafts of the book too.

Huge thanks to friends at Brammer, who helped me in the early years when this experience began. It was those early steps that inspired the confidence to take the book further and to what it is today.

I'd like to thank all the people involved in helping get the book released – that includes the team at Spiderwize (Helen, Haylee and Camilla) for making the decision easy to self-publish through them. Their support and advice has been invaluable throughout this process. Big thanks to Jeanette Howe for proof reading in the final stages and helping make the book ready to be published. Thank you to Stacey Knowles for designing the artwork for the front and back cover, and subsequently the tickets and posters. I'm overwhelmed by the time and effort you've put into it and the quality of the work is nothing short of genius. To Matt Johnston, a huge thanks to you for being my photographer at gigs over all these years and providing the photo in the *About the Author* section.

Thank you to Michael Knaggs for the advice around publishing – who knew that a chance meeting in Bury would lead to a friendship. Special thanks to Mia Page, who after reading the book in its final stages gave me the final push to go ahead and launch it. Thank you to Manchester 235 Casino for providing the perfect venue to mirror the book's theme for the launch. I'd like to thank all the bands who played at the book launch: Mohawk Radio, Jess Kemp and Matt Fryers. An extended thanks goes to Matt Fryers for writing and recording, 'Searching for Answers', the official song to go with the book. To have an actual recorded song to go with the book's journey is simply the coolest thing imaginable. And an extended thanks to Mohawk

Radio for allowing me to attribute their music to that of Cutthroat Shambles.

To Judy Marsh, I cannot express my gratitude in words for the help, advice, encouragement and support you've given me over the past couple of years. Your huge contribution to helping me achieve my lifelong dream will never be forgotten. It was your belief that drove me and I'm forever in your debt. Knowing that I'll have you with me from the start for the sequel fills me with the motivation and confidence to do all of this again.

Also, a huge thank you to those people I met in Vegas, however small or large a role our meeting played in the overall story, it served as inspiration one way or another.

Finally, just a huge thank you in general to everyone involved - I'm overwhelmed by people's support in helping me achieve a lifelong ambition.

LOST IN MANCHESTER
FOUND IN VEGAS
SOUNDTRACK

Elvis Presley – *Viva Las Vegas*
Bruce Springsteen – *Streets of Philadelphia.*
Big Brother & The Holding Company – *Combination of the Two*
The Cult – *She Sells Sanctuary*
Motorhead – *Ace of Spades*
Dean Martin – *Drink to Me Only*
Kenny Rogers – *The Gambler*
AC/DC – *Highway to Hell*
Creedence Clearwater Revival – *Run Through the Jungle*
Vangelis – *Chariots of Fire*
Prince – *Cream*
Massive Attack – *Unfinished Sympathy*
ZZ Top – *Gimme All Your Lovin*
Rolling Stones – *It's Only Rock 'n' Roll*
The Doors – *Break on Through (To the Other Side)*
Joaquín Rodrigo – *Concierto de Aranjuez*
Peter Gabriel – *Solsbury Hill*
Oasis – *Talk Tonight*
Roxette – *It Must Have Been Love*
Fleetwood Mac – *Dreams*
Robert Tepper – *No Easy Way Out*

Fleetwood Mac – *Go Your Own Way*
The Eagles – *Life in the Fast Lane*
Led Zeppelin – *When the Levee Breaks*
Guns N' Roses – *Welcome to the Jungle*
AC/DC – *You Shook Me All Night Long*
Alice Cooper – *Poison*
Def Leppard – *Pour Some Sugar on Me*
Mötley Crüe – *Girls Girls Girls*
Dean Martin – *Volare*
Tom Petty – *Free Fallin'*
Bob Dylan – *Like a Rolling Stone*
U2 – *Vertigo*
The Who – *Won't Get Fooled Again*
The Beatles – *Lucy in the Sky with Diamonds*
The Killers – *Mr Brightside*
Johnny Cash – *Folsom Prison Blues*
Iggy Pop – *Lust For Life*
Rolling Stones – *Paint It Black*
Rolling Stones – *(I Can't Get No) Satisfaction*
Gene Kelly – *Singing in the Rain*
The Beatles – *Let It Be*
The Doors – *Riders on the Storm*
Oasis – *Rock 'n' Roll Star*
Johnny Cash – *Hurt*
Ennio Morricone – *The Sundown*
Duran Duran – *Ordinary World*
The Doors – *An American Prayer*
Jefferson Airplane – *White Rabbit*
Jefferson Airplane – *Somebody to Love*

The Doors – *The End*
Blue Oyster Cult – *Don't Fear the Reaper*
Joy Division – *Disorder*
Eddie & The Hot Rods – *Do Anything you Wanna Do*
Queen – *We Will Rock You*
Queen – *We Are the Champions*
The Doors – *People are Strange*
Elton John – *Rocket Man*
Led Zeppelin – *Good Times Bad Times*
The Eagles – *Hotel California*
Scott McKenzie – *San Francisco*
Mohawk Radio – *Oblivion*

Official Song written for Lost in Manchester, Found in Vegas

Matt Fryers – Searching for Answers